THEIRS TO DEFY

A Marriage Raffle Novel

STASIA BLACK

For Lee Savino, whose tireless encouragement and cheerleading made finishing strong possible <3

In the not too distant future, a genetically engineered virus is released by an eco-terrorist in major metropolitan areas all over the globe. Within five years, almost 90% of the world's female population is decimated.

In an attempt to stop the spread of the virus and quarantine those left, a nuclear war was triggered. It's still unclear who began attacking who, but bombs were dropped on all major US cities, coordinated with massive EMP attacks.

These catastrophes and the end of life as people knew it was collectively known as *The Fall*.

MAP OF THE NEW REPUBLIC OF TEXAS

CHAPTER ONE

DREA

Compared to all the other places Drea had been imprisoned, President Goddard's personal detention center was pretty nice, all things considered.

It was in the basement of Fort Worth's Omni Hotel. He had to have had it built special—a series of ten cells, bars and all. Smaller than you'd find in say a local county jail, but then, these were obviously just meant to hold one person apiece.

Because that wasn't creepy. That the president of the Republic kept his own little jail-slash-torture chamber in the bottom of what was essentially the capitol building.

"Ya know, like you do," Drea whispered under her breath, working her way down the bars, testing each one for weaknesses again. "Not abnormal at all."

She rolled her eyes at herself. It had been a real *genius* move joining the delegation from Jacob's Well coming to the capitol yesterday. She'd been so sure she could convince the President to give her some troops to go back down to the Gulf Texas island, Nomansland, to rescue the women she'd been forced to leave behind three months ago.

Her women. The women she'd promised to keep safe. *Come to this island*, she'd said. *We'll fortify it against the outside world*, she'd said. She'd been so good at making speeches. *Enough of men ruling over us! We'll band tzogether and protect ourselves!*

She swallowed against the bitter taste in her mouth.

Too bad she hadn't been as good at fulfilling all those grandiose promises. Their greatest asset—secrecy—had lasted all of six months. She'd grasped too far, reached for too much. Elena told her not to keep accepting refugees. Elena said they should close their borders, ignore the outside world, become an island unto themselves.

But had Drea listened?

No.

Drea had not listened. Drea said they could still take in women if they were careful. They'd use computer messages and neutral meeting places.

Nothing is safe enough, Elena said. *There's one of us to every ten of them.* Them being men. The Xterminate virus had wiped out 90% of the earth's female population. *It's made them all animals. They'll never stop hunting us.*

Elena was right.

Two months after they opened up the island to refugees, one of their supposed 'rescues' turned out to be bait. The woman had a GPS implant so those watching could see where she was taken. It wasn't the Black Skulls MC's men who first besieged the island, but they took over pretty soon after.

Drea and the women had weapons stockpiled, but they were no match for the all-out assault that lasted for days on end.

In the end, surrender was the only choice if they were to survive.

Though the months of abuse that followed hadn't much felt like survival. More like hell on earth.

The Black Skulls were one of the biggest players in the female slave trade. And they set out immediately 'training' the women who'd first come to Nomansland for shelter and safety.

And *then*, when salvation *did* come? Did it come for the whole island? Oh no, of course not! A group of men came to rescue their wife who happened to be locked in a closet with Drea and they decided, oh look, we'll save this one too.

Her. Drea.

Out of all the women there who actually *deserved* rescuing, they plucked *her* out, the one who'd led all the rest there like lambs to the slaughter.

It had been her hubris and foolish pride to ever think that she could ever—

She growled in furious frustration at herself as she continued feeling along every bar of her cell.

She'd spent every waking moment of the last three months since her 'rescue' trying to get back to them. Trying to undo her wrongs, atone for her sins.

Hence this ill-thought out trip to the capitol.

If the President could have just given her something. Maybe not a battalion of troops, but what about a strike team. A helicopter. *Something.*

But noooooooooo, apparently President Douchie McDouchebag was a misogynistic pig who had a problem with women doing anything with their mouths other than sucking—

Well, suffice it to say, the second she questioned His Almightiness, she'd ended up in this cell.

She shook her head. Hadn't she learned by now that if she wanted something done, she had to do it herself? No more trusting in the inherent goodness of her fellow man. That was a crock of shit. Maybe her fellow *woman*, but definitely not her fellow fucking man.

If she was gonna free her women, she was gonna have to do it herself.

"And hopefully not fuck it up this time," she muttered under her breath. But *no*. She couldn't afford to think that way. She go and get them free or die trying.

She tugged again at the bars. They were steel, she was pretty sure. So bending them and trying to slip through wasn't an option. And the joints and pegs were on the opposite side of the door so she couldn't jimmy those loose. But maybe if she—

"You sure are pretty."

Oh goody, the guard had decided to do rounds again. He sure did them an awful lot considering she was the only prisoner.

She didn't give him the satisfaction of a reaction to his words. He was middle-aged, had hair that was more gray than brown, and a potbelly that hung so far over his belt she imagined it had been half a decade since he'd been able to see his toes.

But he thought she was pretty. Of course he did.

Drea stilled.

"And with all that pretty blonde hair. I bet you could make a fella feel reaaaaaaal good."

Drea breathed out a sharp breath.

Don't lose your temper. Don't lose your temper.

Do use *all* the tools at your disposal. Even if it makes you want to gag on your own dreadlocks.

She slowly crossed her arms over her stomach in a way that propped her boobs up and out. She rubbed her arms.

"Say, it sure is chilly in here," she said, face slightly downturned so that she was only looking at the guard through her eyelashes. "Do you think I could borrow your jacket?" She bit her lip and continued blinking up at him. "I promise I'll be good."

Shit, she was laying it on too thick, wasn't she? He'd see right through her act and—

"Well, I could always warm you up."

Or not.

She smiled and dipped her head. "If it wouldn't be too much trouble, I mean. I know all you men here at the capitol have such important jobs. Working for the *President* and all."

"Aw he wouldn't mind me seeing to the comfort of a prisoner. The New Republic is all about treating folks humane."

"Oh my gosh," Drea said, jumping up and down and clapping her hands —she was just purely channeling Sophia, the Commander's daughter, now.

Jesus, never thought she'd see the day. She might only be eight years older than the nineteen-year-old Sophia, but it felt like five decades separated them.

The guard was just eating this shit up, though.

Men were so fucking easy.

She'd shake her head if she weren't so busy keeping to her act.

That's right, buddy. Reach for those keys.

She fought to keep her eyes on his face while his hand went to the keyring at his belt.

He lifted a warning finger. "Step back now. Don't give me any trouble or you'll regret it." He touched the retractable billy club on his belt.

"Oh no, sir," Drea simpered. "I would never. If I could just have a friend in this cold place, it would mean everything. I'll do anything just to have someone on my side helping me. I'll pay you back however you want."

He grinned lasciviously. "However I want, huh?"

Drea nodded over and over, feeling like a bobblehead. She backed up against the far wall right beside the twin bed, hands up where he could see them.

He reached down and readjusted himself right before sliding the door open.

Patience.

Not yet.

He stepped inside the cell.

Not yet.

Smile. Look innocent and harmless.

She giggled and ducked her head as he shrugged out of his guard's jacket halfway across the room.

NOW.

She struck while his arms were still half-caught in the jacket, yanking and twisting it to trap his arms at the same time she swept his legs with a low kick.

Dad would be so proud.

Right as the guard hit the floor she was on him, yanking the billy club off his belt. Because the other thing Dad taught her?

Hit first and ask questions later.

It was something of a family mantra.

In one swift downward motion, Drea had the billy club extended and she got to work.

The guard was a screamer, so she went for the throat first. One swift hit to his larynx had him grasping his throat and choking.

She *tut tut tutted* at him for being dumb enough to expose himself like that. Because obviously her next hit was going to be to his scrotum.

That was just female self-defense 101.

She struck a few other of the best impact points to make sure he was disabled. One hard blow to the solar plexus, then, when he curled in on himself, a couple of strikes to the kidneys from the back.

He gasped for air and—was he crying?

She shook her head at him. Pathetic.

Let it never be said that she ever behaved like one of those clichéd blondes from old horror movies who always celebrated too early without double checking that the monster was really dead. Drea always made sure that her enemy was *down*.

She raised the club one last time and put all her weight behind a hit to his knee. He howled like a banshee

She reached and grabbed his keys off the floor from where the guard had dropped them, then she hurried out of the cell and locked it behind her.

Only to find the door to the stairs was being pushed open.

Shit.

Of course there were probably cameras on the cells. Someone had seen. *Or heard.* The question was how many they'd sent down to subdue her.

Screw it. She'd come this far.

She raised the billy club and ran at the door, knowing surprise was her best weapon.

"Drea?"

Wait, what?

"*Eric?*"

She was running so fast she couldn't stop herself in time and she collided with Eric. He wrapped his arms around her and together they rammed into the door, knocking it shut.

For a second it was just the two of them, breathing hard, him looking down at her. Wow, his eyes were a really nice gray, weren't they?

Wait, wait, wait.

Record scratch. Back the fuck up.

She hated Eric, *The Commander*, Wolford. He'd founded the new community at Jacob's Well after The Fall and ran the larger territory of Central Texas South.

Okay, maybe *hate* was a strong word. But she strongly disliked him. He was a chauvinist pig who'd come up with the most ridiculous, degrading system of treating the women in his territory. Giving them out as fucking raffle prizes, for Christ's sake. She'd had to lie and say she was a lesbian or else he was gonna try to force that shit on her.

And he too had refused to help her go back to Nomansland even though it had been men from his community who'd taken her from there in the first place.

Drea jerked away from Eric. "What are you doing here?"

He raised his arms in an *isn't it obvious?* motion. "Rescuing you."

Drea huffed out a laugh and then waved behind her at the guard on the floor of her cell. "Thanks but I can rescue myself just fine." She pushed the billy club back into its retracted position and shoved as much of it as she could in her pocket.

Eric crossed his arms and leaned against the wall. "You got out of your cell, but how exactly were you planning to get out of the city in the middle of a coup?"

Wait, what? She couldn't have heard that right.

"A what?"

"A coup. You know, when someone comes in and tries to take over—"

"I know what a goddamned coup is." Drea narrowed her eyes. "What makes you say one is happening here?"

"Oh you didn't hear? President Goddard was just assassinated. About..." He looked down at his watch. "Twenty-eight minutes ago."

Drea felt her eyebrows all but hit her hairline. Shit.

"Even better, they think it was someone from our group. I'm surprised your pretty head is still attached to your neck."

Despite herself, Drea's hand lifted to her throat. As soon as she realized what she was doing, she dropped her hand and glared at Eric.

"And why do they think that?"

He waved a hand to brush her off. "Shay's sculpture *may* have exploded and either someone in her clan or Vanessa's is most likely working for Arnold. Colonel Travis I mean."

Travis.

The governor of Travis Territory who, according to which rumors you listened to, was either a benevolent leader or a power-hungry slave trader. Drea had seen enough in her life to know the second was more likely the truth.

And now he'd assassinated the President.

Fuck. Her. Life.

Drea blinked, thoughts racing a million miles a minute.

Because if her instincts were right and he was a slave trader, he'd have dealings with the Black Skulls. Who were holding her women captive.

And Travis had just become the most powerful man in the country.

Drea's head snapped toward Eric. "And you're so calm about this... *why?*

"Well, it's all finally happening now, isn't it? I've been waiting for the shit to hit the fan for a long time and," he held out his arms. "Shit, meet fan. Now come on. I know where the President keeps his private helicopter."

"Why didn't you fucking open with that?" Drea growled, pushing past Eric.

"You're a very difficult girl to rescue."

Drea pulled the billy club out of her pocket. "Call me a girl one more time."

Eric lifted his hands in a surrender gesture. "I apologize. You're a very difficult... er, *complex* woman."

"And I rescued myself, remember?"

"Ah, but I'm the one with the helicopter, remember?"

———

"You were saying?" Drea put a hand on her hip as they looked out the window of the door that led out to the President's private helicopter pad.

The helicopter pad currently swarmed by soldiers wearing black and gray fatigues.

"Shit," Eric swore. "Those are Travis's soldiers. I thought they were at Jacob's W—" Then he shook his head. "It doesn't matter."

He took Drea's elbow and started pulling her back toward the stairs of the four-story parking garage that was a block away from the Omni.

Drea jerked out of his grasp. "Okay, we tried it your way. Now it's my turn." She strode in front of Eric and started down the stairs.

As she did, she realized this had been her problem all along.

She wasn't the kind of woman who waited for other people to help her get shit done. No, she blazed ahead and did it herself.

Why the hell had she even come to Fort Worth pandering to that asshole of a President in the first place? She should know—you wanted shit done, you did it *yourself*.

Well, lesson learned. How much time had she already wasted? She was going back to Nomansland to rescue her people. Today. Fuck everyone else.

"What are you— You don't even know this city. Have you even been to Fort Worth before?"

She didn't answer him until they got to the first floor of the garage before turning to face him. "No. But I know how to hot wire one of those." She pointed to the Harley she'd seen on the way in. In fact, there was a whole bunch of them lined up. She smiled sweetly and tilted her head at Eric. "Now, you don't mind riding bitch, do you?"

Eric's face darkened as he glowered at her. "I hate motorcycles," he muttered. But he did start walking in the direction of one of the Harleys.

She had the thing hot wired in three minutes flat and she handed a helmet to Eric. "Safety first."

He took the helmet but stared down at the growling motorcycle as she slung her leg over it. "You realize this is most likely a Black Skulls motorcycle."

Drea just grinned. "Where do you think I learned how to hot wire a hog? 4H?"

Seeing how Eric's eyes went saucer-wide almost made the whole shitty day worth it. Drea patted the seat behind her.

"Climb on."

Eric shook his head like he was rethinking his decision to ever come back for her in the first place. But he put the helmet on and climbed on behind her.

And if she noticed how good it felt having his strong arms around her waist? Well, that was just her damn hormones talking.

She turned her head to the side, not looking all the way back at him. "Hold on tight. I'm not gonna take it slow, and if you fall off, it's your own damn fault."

Eric's only response was anxious swearing.

Drea laughed and closed the face visor on her helmet before pulling out of the garage. Having the purr of a big twin engine between her legs felt far better than she'd like to admit. Eric would be in for a surprise when he realized they weren't heading for Jacob's Well.

And as she rode south, the morning sun to her left, she thought, *aw, this might even be fun.*

CHAPTER TWO

ERIC

Eric hated motorcycles. Hated them. He had ever since he was a teenager and his new best friend Arnie had double-dog dared him to steal his dad's motorbike and take it for a joyride around town.

He hadn't even made it to the end of the street before the bike tipped over and skidded sideways. He was lucky he hadn't been going any faster or he would have broken his leg for sure. Still, his leg was ripped up all to hell, almost down to the bone in a couple places. He was out the entire junior season of football.

He hadn't so much as looked at a damn murder-cycle since then.

And here he was stuck on the back of one clinging to a crazy woman with her hand on the throttle.

"Slow down!" he shouted but with the wind screaming around their ears, she couldn't hear him. Or maybe she could and she was just ignoring him. Drea was good at that. Damn stubborn woman.

He glanced over her shoulder and saw another curve in the street coming up. "Jesus," he swore, tightening his arms around her tiny waist. He frowned. She was so small. Was she not getting a large enough share of rations?

She was living at the single female dormitory in Jacob's Well.

Eric hadn't wanted her staying there. Only thirteen women lived there, but the truth was it was the closest thing to a brothel Jacob's Well had.

If a woman was past child-bearing age or decided she'd prefer not to be limited to five men such as the marriage raffle system confined them to—at least in theory, they hadn't had much problem with infidelity under the new system—she had the option to live in the dorm.

Such women generally shared their favors freely and were thus understandably popular and treated like queens wherever they went, no matter their age or looks. But a woman like Drea?

Eric's guts twisted just at the thought of the animals that would be mobbing her door if she indicated interest.

But she wouldn't.

She's a lesbian, remember?

Thank God for small favors—just because she was so against the whole Marriage Raffle thing—that was all he meant. And her being a lesbian exempted her from the lottery, he'd decided.

He'd never been in the business of forcing things on anyone. The Marriage Raffle system had been devised as the way to make the best out of a bad situation and to keep the peace. How else was he supposed to keep a town, much less a territory, of men in line with such limited access to female companionship? Lord knew it had made savages of the rest of the country. The rest of the *world*, whatever there was left of it.

But then, he'd never counted on coming across the likes of Drea Valentine, had he?

If only she weren't so damn stubborn, and opinionated, and—

"Jesus Christ!" he shouted as she took a turn with barely the slightest slow in speed. She leaned and he leaned with her. He didn't care if squeezing his eyes shut made him a chicken. If he didn't, he was afraid he'd upchuck his breakfast bagel all over the inside of his helmet.

"Shit!"

He barely heard Drea's shout above the wind. It was a panicked shout. What could have the badass woman who stood up to world leaders and took out prison guards twice her size sounding so panicked?

Eric's eyes popped open right as the tires locked and the brakes squealed.

Momentum shoved him forward even tighter against Drea's body and she held her own, he'd give her that. She kept the bike upright and they were slowing down.

But not fast enough to avoid the line of spikes that had been laid across the road.

"Fuuuuuuuuuuuuuck!" Eric yelped as the motorcycle skidded straight into two menacing looking spikes.

Then the world was fuck upside down and— He was airborne and—

Holy—

Jesus, he couldn't—

SLAM.

Owwwwww was the only thought he managed before the world went black.

———

"Shit, you think his head got cracked? Y'all both sure went flying. I've never seen anything like it."

"Eric? Eric."

That voice. Eric knew that voice.

"Eric, goddamn you, open your eyes right fucking now, or I swear I'll fucking—"

Drea.

Eric forced his eyes open.

Drea's face was right in front of him. Close. Really close.

Wow, her eyes were blue. Really, really blue. She probably hated that. She was such a badass, he bet being blonde with blue eyes totally pissed her off.

The thought made him smile.

"Eric? Are you fucking smiling? Shit, do you think he has brain damage?"

"Hey dude, can you track my finger?"

Who was she talking to? It was a man's voice. Eric moved his head slightly to the right, following Drea's line of sight and saw a skinny guy dressed in a worn t-shirt and ripped jeans with a bandana on his head.

He was waving his hand in front of Eric's face but Eric was too busy looking at the beat-up truck idling behind him and Drea. Looked like the guy had managed to stop before hitting the spikes.

Shit, the spikes.

"What happened?" Eric asked, trying to sit up and look around. "FUCK!" he yelled as pain screamed down his left arm.

"Shit, what?" Drea yelled. She put her hands on his stomach, feeling up and down his torso. Jesus that wasn't helping.

"His arm's broke," the guy said. "And I haven't seen road rash that bad since my Aunt Patty Mae went ass over ankles on her scooter when she was racing my cousin Grady and me. She—"

"It's definitely broken." Drea's voice was cool and matter of fact.

Billy was nodding. "We should set and splint it as soon as we can. But first we've got to get the hell out of here."

Eric glanced down at his arm and dammit, it was bent at an angle that was *not* natural. Not to mention shifting it even slightly send a blinding pain shooting through his whole damn body. "Mother fucking piece of—" he swore before gritting his teeth.

"Does anything else hurt?" Drea interrupted. "Eric?" She snapped her fingers in front of his face when he apparently didn't respond quickly enough for her. "I said, *does anything else hurt?*"

He wanted to roll his eyes at her, but every little shift of his body— *Ow!* Son of a—

"No," he bit out. Hadn't she fallen off the bike too? Who'd made her inquisitor in chief. "What about you?"

She just stared at him a moment, a look he couldn't decipher on her face. "I'm fine. You broke my fall."

Then she moved back and stood up. "Come on. We need to go. We're just sitting ducks out in the middle of the road like this. Billy, help me get these damn spikes off the tarmac."

Eric struggled again to sit up and Drea shot a short, "Don't move," at him before joining Billy at the edge of the road to drag the strip of spikes off to the shoulder.

Eric ignored Drea's snapped command, gritting his teeth against the pain in his left arm as he forced himself up to a sitting position.

"Little busy over here."

That was when he saw the bodies.

Two of them, blood pooling on the ground beside each.

They were wearing Travis's colors—black camo that was completely impractical in the Texas landscape and heat. It wasn't meant to blend in, only to intimidate. That was Travis's M.O.—make your enemies cower and whimper at your feet. And anyone who didn't play by Travis's rules? He just swept them off the board. Total destruction. The post-Fall world was the perfect playground for such an egomaniacal sociopath.

Eric shook his head as he looked from the two dead soldiers back to Drea and the guy—Billy.

Which one of them had taken the soldiers out? Drea couldn't have had a gun on her. He'd rescued her from prison. She was good but not even she could manufacture a gun from thin air.

That only left Billy. Sure he looked like a happy-go-lucky guy, but anyone who managed to survive The Fall this long and still have access to a truck and a weapon was someone to take seriously.

Eric locked his jaw and forced himself to his feet. Fucking hell, his arm hurt. It was the worst time imaginable to break his damn arm. He briefly glanced skyward. *Really? I can't catch one damn break?*

Then he huffed out, walking closer to the truck. He had to clutch his broken arm to his chest like he was an injured bird but you gotta do what you gotta do.

He climbed up into the cab of the truck. The keys were still in the ignition. Okay, so maybe the guy wasn't the brightest crayon in the box. Whatever, all the better for Eric and Drea.

Eric turned the key and the truck's engine roared to life. Eric didn't waste any time. Drea and Billy both looked up at the noise but Eric had already jammed the car into gear and was speeding toward them.

Billy jumped backwards to get out of the way but Drea stood motionless. Good girl.

Eric stomped the brakes and jerked the wheel, turning with a screech of tires and bringing the truck to a stop so that the passenger door was right in front of Drea. She didn't even flinch as the cloud of rocks and dust was kicked up all around her. She just grabbed the door and hopped up on the benchseat beside Eric.

"Drive," she ordered and Eric was only too happy to oblige.

Problem was, they hadn't gone more than fifty feet before Drea dropped a hand on his uninjured forearm, shouting, "Stop."

Eric squinted at the road. Were there more spikes ahead he wasn't seeing?

"I said, *STOP*."

Fine, fine. He put his foot to the brake pedal again, slowing their speed. He wasn't willing to stop all the way, though. She hadn't been wrong about the sitting ducks comment. And when those two sentries back there failed to check in? They'd be having company reaaaaaaaal soon.

"We have to go back for him."

Eric stared at her, not bothering to hide the fact he thoughts she was nuts. "Are you crazy? We don't know who the hell he is. He could be working for those bastards back there for all we know. A lookout in plain clothes and when you shot—"

"I didn't shoot them," Drea said. "He did. To protect me after he saw the spikes take us out. We were in the middle of the road after crashing. You were unconscious and I was freaking out thinking you were dead when those assholes must have come out from the ditch where they were hiding."

She'd been freaking out thinking he was dead?

"I didn't even see them. They were almost on top of me when Billy shot them. I only turned around at the gun shots and they were right there. Maybe four feet away."

Eric blinked, trying to focus in on what she was saying. Wait. She couldn't mean—

"We have to go back for him," she said. "He saved my life."

"Oh come on," Eric scoffed, shaking his head at her. "I never took you for a bleeding heart. We don't know anything about him."

"I don't leave my debts unpaid." Her face went hard. "Now turn the damn truck around and go back for him."

Eric glared out the front windshield, finally bringing the truck to a stop. Was that why she'd been worried he was dead? Because she considered trying to 'rescue' her a debt she owed him?

"I barely trust half the men in my own camp and you're willing to trust this stranger you just met how many minutes ago? For all we know he put the damn spikes there in the first place."

"Just shut up and—"

"Fine." Eric slammed the truck in reverse and then hit the gas pedal. She wouldn't change her mind. She never did, once she got set on something.

The truck jerked into action. Eric locked his eyes on the rearview mirror and navigated around debris and shit in the road that had been much easier to avoid when going forwards.

"Jesus Christ," Drea swore, her head swinging around to look out the back window. "I don't mean you have to get us fucking killed."

Eric ignored her and kept going, only slowing down when he saw Billy standing in the middle of the road where they'd left him. Billy jumped to the side when he saw the truck heading his direction in reverse.

Eric gritted his teeth against a fresh round of pain shooting up his broken arm as he stepped on the brakes yet again and brought the truck to a stop. He reached over with his good arm to roll down the manual window.

"Get in the back of the truck if you're coming," he yelled.

"Hey, you stole my truck!" Billy said, walking toward them and pointing at Eric. Then his focus shifted to Drea. "And *you* never gave me my gun back."

"Of course I didn't give you back your gun, do you think I'm an idiot?" Drea leaned across Eric to talk to Billy out the window and Eric blinked. Jesus, didn't she realize— Her breasts were almost skimming his—

"Now get in the damn truck bed if you don't want to be left out here to be picked off like road kill."

Eric was too busy trying to remember how to breathe with Drea so close but when she pulled back and he heard a thunk in the truck bed, he figured Billy had gotten on board with her plan.

She was persuasive like that. And hot. Her body he meant. Not like — He just meant that when she'd leaned over like that, the heat of her body had— Jesus, did he have a fever or something? He wiped at the sweat on his forehead with his arm.

"Now you." Drea glared at him when he looked her direction. "Switch seats. The last thing I need is you passing out in the middle of the highway."

Eric punched the gas before she could unhook her seatbelt. "I got it, thanks." He held his broken arm against his chest. Fuck it hurt. He'd need to splint it soon. But he was not giving up this little bit of control.

Drea let out a small, exasperated noise. "You're hurt. What the hell am I supposed to do if you black out while you're driving?"

Eric rolled his eyes. "I broke my arm. I'm not bleeding out. And let's not forget what happened the last time you were in charge of the moving vehicle."

If he thought she'd been exasperated before it was nothing to the offended noise she made at that. "There were *spikes* in the road. It had nothing to do with my damn driving."

"Well maybe if you'd been going slower, we would have been able to stop in time."

"Is that why you're only going fifty-five miles an hour, Grandpa? There is a war just starting. Might be nice to make it out of the area before reinforcements arrive."

"Jesus," he swore, shaking his head as he looked over at her. "I'm trying to conserve gas. Everybody knows you conserve up to twenty percent more gas by going fifty-five rather than seventy-five."

"Yeah well we won't be around to enjoy all that gas we're saving if the bad guys catch up to us because you're driving like you've got a stick up your ass, will we?"

"Fine," he growled, "you want faster, you'll get faster." He pressed harder on the pedal, shaking his head as he looked at the fuel gage that was only slightly above half full.

———

"Are you happy?" Eric threw his good hand up as he looked around the empty road and barren landscape around them. His left arm screamed in pain at the movement. "Ow, fuck," he swore under his breath.

Drea looked up from the map she was scouring, her mouth dropped open. "Oh my God, are you still going on about the damn gas? Jesus Christ, I've never met anyone so whiny in my whole damn life."

Eric clenched his jaw. The pain in his arm had only gotten progressively worse over the last two hours, though he wouldn't have thought that was possible. And between the increase in speed and Drea directing them down back roads that seemed to lead all over the damn place except in the direction they needed to go, yeah, he was not in the best mood.

Drea must have noticed how he was favoring his arm because her glare intensified as she handed the map to Billy and stalked toward Eric.

"That arm needs to be set. We shouldn't have even waited this long."

"What?" Eric took a step and twisted his body with his broken arm away from Drea. "No, it'll be fine."

She shook her head like he was being an idiot. "Do you know how broken bones work? The longer you wait to set it, the worse it gets. Bones start healing almost immediately and it'll start healing wrong. We need to set it so—"

"What the hell do you know about broken bones or setting them?"

"I know that your forearm isn't supposed to be bent at that angle, for one."

Eric cringed, the pain in his arm seeming to pulse even harder at her description. Driving had been a distraction and he'd been living in a little land called denial that had really been doing great things for him. He'd like to stay there awhile longer, thank you very much.

"I know a little bit about it."

Both Drea and Eric spun to look at Billy in surprise. Eric didn't know about Drea, but he'd forgotten for a moment the other man was there.

"What?" Drea and Eric asked almost at the same time. Then they glared at each other.

"I know about what to do for broken arms. I was a resident at Harris Methodist Medical before— well, *before*."

Drea narrowed her eyes. "You're a doctor and a sharpshooter? I don't buy it."

Billy looked down, his hand going to the back of his neck like he was embarrassed or even ashamed. "I grew up hunting with my dad and well," he looked up and met Drea's eyes. "I guess we've all done whatever it takes these last few years, to survive, you know?"

Drea tilted her head back and forth in a maybe so gesture then she nodded Eric's direction. "You're up, Doc."

"Wait a second," Eric said, lifting his good hand. "You're just gonna take his word for it? We stole his truck. What if he tries something? To take me out?"

Drea's eyes rolled so hard Eric was surprised she didn't tip over. She pulled a gun out of the back of her jeans. Presumably Billy's. "Hey Billy, promise not to hurt my friend worse than he already is and I won't have to fuck you up. Sound like a plan?"

Billy nodded, eyes wide. "Works for me."

"Jesus," Eric swore, tilting his head back.

"All right, come on over to the truck. I've got some cardboard stuffed behind the seat that will work great as a splint. Duct tape too."

Cardboard and duct tape? Oh yeah, this guy sounded like the doctor of the frickin' year.

Drea just continued searching the map, unfolding it and refolding it several times.

"Do you even know where the hell we are?" Eric leaned back against the truck while Billy tossed through stuff in the truck bed tool box.

Eric looked around. It was flat, flat, and more flat. All there was to see was sky.

And Jesus was he tired. He hadn't slept last night and between that and everything that had happened this morning, well, it was all hitting him at once. If his arm didn't hurt so damn bad and he hadn't needed to focus on driving, he'd have passed out ages ago.

Drea lowered the map and narrowed her eyes at him. "Of course I know where we are."

"Doesn't look like it," he yawned.

"And you don't look like you belong anywhere except the set of a horror movie with your arm all bloody and fucked up like that but you don't see me saying anything about it, do you? I even let you drive."

Eric hissed out through his teeth, fighting both the pain and the desire to snap back a response that wouldn't do either of them any good.

"All right, come on over," Billy called out from where he'd set up shop in the bed of the truck.

When Eric climbed up and sat where Billy told him to, Billy peered sideways at him, then over at Drea. "You two sure do carry on. Reminds me of these neighbors I had when I was in med school. Dan and Shirley. I'd be up studying and they'd be carrying on the same way, all hours of the night. Shirley nagging Dan about the dishes or the bills and Dan yelling back about the casserole being burnt or her shopping too much."

"Can we get on with this please?" Eric asked impatiently.

"So, you two married?" Billy asked.

"No!" Eric's head snapped to look up at him. "But don't you go getting any ideas. She's a..." Eric looked to the side. "That's not her— She likes women, all right?"

"I don't know about that," Billy said.

"What the fuck does that mean?" Eric glared at him again. "You just met her and I've known her for... awhile now."

Billy shrugged. "I'm just saying. When Dan and Shirley weren't fighting like cats and dogs, they were—" He raised his eyebrows significantly. "—*you know*."

Eric felt the back of his neck heat and he looked down to the bed of the truck. "Just set my damn arm," he growled through gritted teeth.

Which Billy did in short order.

And all right, Eric *may* have screeched like a woman in childbirth when Billy set the bone, but at least the skinny bastard did seem to know what he was doing. Billy moved with practiced ease as he wrapped the cardboard frame he'd made around and around with duct tape.

There was nothing much to do about the bloody ripped up skin of the rest of his arm and upper shoulder though. Billy offered to take off his shirt to lay it over the wound, but Eric declined. He'd just let it scab up and it would be fine.

"Yeouch, there's a nasty gash here, though," Billy said, leaning in closer to Eric's bicep. "I'd say it needs stitches. I left in such a hurry after I heard about the President though, I forgot my kit."

Eric's teeth had been gritted for so long, he had a tension headache.

"I said it's fine," Eric ground out, jumping down from the bed of the truck. Enough with being babied. "We need to find a place to set up camp. You said we're close to the Colorado river?"

Drea had stopped obsessively checking the map but she peeked down at it one last time. "Yes. It should be about a mile and a half in that direction."

Eric breathed out a long exhale. Okay. They just had to get to the river. Billy had a gallon of water in the truck but they'd all but emptied it.

And Eric was sweating buckets and already thirsty enough to down what was left in the jug. Not a great combination, especially considering his injury. Not to mention that the sun was starting to dip in the sky. They had maybe a couple hours at most before sundown. They needed to set up camp before then.

"You got any other supplies you're hiding in there, Doc?" Eric asked Billy.

"Just what you see on me," Billy said quickly. A little too quickly, if you asked Eric. But if he was hoarding food it must have been a tiny protein bar or something because Eric didn't see anything on him. He was rail thin and nothing was bulging in his pockets.

And Drea had already looked through the backpack of supplies he'd brought along. There were a few practical items—a stainless steel pot that would be good for boiling water to purify it, a couple peanut butter sandwiches, one of which they'd already split, one spare change of clothes—in Billy's size, so no help to Eric—a thin picnic blanket, a switchblade which Drea promptly pocketed, a small foldable grill to set out over a fire, a box of matches, several candles, one small oil lamp, and a couple water bottles.

Then there were the impractical items which Eric had only seen because Drea tossed them to the side. A nudie magazine. A small stuffed bear. A picture frame that she'd taken the picture out of, handed to Billy, and then tossed the frame.

Billy didn't say anything, he just put the picture in his pocket, picked up the bear, and walked off on his own for a little before heading back their way several long minutes, no bear in sight.

"Jesus, it's obvious the bear was sentimental," Eric said under his breath to Drea but she just shrugged. "Hitting the river is just the first leg. After that, it's another thirty miles or so to town and I'll be trading off carrying that pack. I'm not taking anything we don't strictly have to."

"What town exactly is that?"

Drea swiped at the sweat gathered on her forehead and looked toward the dropping sun. "Llano."

Eric felt his brows rise and he looked around them. "We're that close to Llano? That means we're already in Central Texas North." He frowned. Shouldn't there be more hills if they were in the Hill Country? He took a step forward, meaning to take a better look around, but he stumbled, a wave of dizziness hitting him.

"Whoa, cowboy," Drea said, lurching forward to steady his arm. "Are you feeling okay?"

He blinked hard and the spinning world settled back the shape it was supposed to be. "Yeah. Fine. Just lost my footing there."

Drea looked at him skeptically but he started walking, trying to effuse confidence. Fake it till you make it, right? That had been his motto the past eight years. He hadn't known shit about being the leader of a community but he hadn't done too bad with Jacob's Well. Not too bad for a dishonorably discharged First Lieutenant, anyway.

"There a reason you're heading back toward Fort Worth, cowboy? Cause the river's this way."

Eric stopped in his tracks, closed his eyes briefly, then turned around. He would not be goaded into a response. Not even by the most infuriating woman on God's green earth.

She'd shouldered the backpack and was already heading into the open field off to the left of the road. Billy was following eagerly on her heels. Eric rolled his eyes, prayed for patience, and went after them.

CHAPTER THREE

DREA

Drea didn't like Eric's coloring. He was too pale for as hot as it was. He was certainly sweating a lot and every now and then he'd let out little pathetic, pained grunts. Each time he did, Drea's stomach twisted tighter.

She looked across the fire to where she'd laid him out on the picnic blanket. The mile and a half had taken much longer than it should have because she kept having to slow down for him. He'd collapsed almost as soon as they'd arrived at the river and she'd laid out the blanket. The ground was uneven and rocky, but Eric was out and snoring to wake the dead within minutes.

"Seems like he was tuckered," Billy said as Drea set a pot of river water to boil on the grill they'd arranged over the fire. "You think he's gonna make it wherever you're headed tomorrow?"

Where *you're* headed. Not where *we're* headed. Drea's eyes moved to Billy. Measuring. Assessing. There was more than met the eye to the man, that was for sure.

"So, Billy, tell me, what were your plans? Where were you heading before we hijacked your ride?"

He shrugged, his eyes dropping to the fire.

"Aw, well, you know," he shrugged, tugging on his ear. "Nothing really set in stone. It's just been my policy that when I hear shooting, I get gone. Mama always told me to steer clear of trouble. And ever since I pulled Janie Tucker's pigtails in third grade and got a black eye for it, I started listening." He offered a nervous smile.

Well he was a shit liar, that was obvious. Which meant he probably wasn't a smuggler. There was generally a modicum of deception skills needed for that. Either that, or the ability to use brute force, along with a killer instinct and Billy didn't have either. After he'd shot those border guards at the spike trap, she'd been able to disarm him with barely any effort. Same with the knife in the backpack. If it had been her, she would have gotten her hands on her weapons first chance she had, especially if someone had just stolen her wheels and firepower. But not Billy. So what was his deal?

Drea nodded slowly. "Fair enough." She let the crackle of the fire fill the silence between them for several moments.

"Still, a man like you, with your skills. A doctor is a handy thing to be. And you're good with a gun? You're useful. You must be welcome everywhere you go."

He shrugged, eyes fixed on the fire. "I've been able to take care of myself over the years."

"Oh yeah? That's all a man or woman can ask for these days."

Another silence fell. Drea tilted her head, watching Billy as his eyes shifted nervously between the flames, up to her, and off into the woods. Twitchy motherfucker, wasn't he?

"I gotta go take a piss," he announced suddenly, standing up and swiping his hands on his jeans like they were sweaty.

Drea nodded. "Hey, go for it. We aren't headed anywhere any time soon."

He hurried off into the woods. The second he was out of the light of the fire, Drea hopped to her feet and ran as swiftly and quietly after him as she could. She'd always been more of a city girl than a country mouse, but she knew how to be quiet and sneaking had always been something of a specialty of hers.

Billy hadn't gone far either.

She didn't know what she'd find. Him talking on a sat phone? Eating some food he'd been hoarding?

What she didn't expect?

The telltale noise of pills rattling in a bottle.

Son of a *bitch*.

"So William," she said, stepping out from behind the trees. There was just enough light filtering down through the branches from the full moon to see him.

Billy yelped, clutching the bottle to his chest and taking several big steps back from her.

"I don't suppose you'd restore my faith in humanity and tell me you have a heart condition and those are your blood pressure pills?"

"Uh, um," Billy stuttered, "Yeah, I um, I'm sick and these are, uh— I need these for—"

Drea rolled her eyes and stomped forward, reaching and grabbing for the pills. Billy wasn't about to let them go, though.

"No! You can't have them!" He wrapped his arms around them, jerking back so roughly that both he and Drea went to the ground.

"Get off me!" he yelled when she landed on top of him. "You can't have my fucking pills! I need them!"

He was stronger than he looked and he almost bucked her off a couple of times. Not surprising. This wasn't her first run in with a junkie.

Good thing her daddy had taught her to fight dirty.

She punched him in the balls and when he gasped in pain, clutching for his junk, she grabbed the pill bottle out of his hands. Then she rolled him till his face was in the dirt, put her knee in his back and wrenched both his arms until he was properly pinned.

"The truth now," she spat. "Where were you headed?" She shook the pill bottle. "There's only, what? Six or seven pills left in here? You wouldn't have left town unless you were sure you could score more."

For a second he didn't say anything and she yanked his arm behind him even harder, to the point of threatening to break it, and shoved his face into the dirt even more.

"Fine, fine," he finally shouted. "I'll talk! But you're wrong. I wasn't heading anywhere. I don't have another score. Those were the end of my stash from my last job but I don't have another one lined up."

"Why not go back to where you used to work?"

Silence.

As soon as she applied the slightest pressure to his arm he started talking again, words spilling over one another. "I can't go back. Ever. I stole the shit and ran. If I ever show back up there, they'll kill me. I was just happy you were headed the opposite direction. Cause I know we aren't right outside Llano. And this isn't the Colorado River. We went east, not west. I'm betting it's the Brazos. So why are you lying to the other guy?"

"Shit," Drea swore, climbing off Billy and getting to her feet. So he was just a junky with no connections. Well that didn't fucking help her. He was a liability if anything. Eric had been right this morning. They should have just left him behind.

She lifted a hand to her forehead. Think, Drea. *Think.*

"Whatever, ya know," Billy said, sitting up and lifting his hands in surrender. "Not my business. But you should know. That gash in his arm? It needs stitches. Not to mention, these conditions..." he waved around them. "You need me in case he gets sick."

"Oh so you're one of those?" Drea propped a hand on her hip, pulling out the switchblade and flicking the blade out. "No loyalty. Anything to survive. Anything to support your habit, no matter who it hurts?"

"Whoa, whoa, whoa," Billy lifted his hands, "look, I have a problem, okay? But that's all. And I'm trying to say that I can help you. Both of you. And like you said, I'm welcome wherever I go. Everyone needs a doctor. And I won't say a thing to what's his name—"

"Eric."

"I won't say a thing to Eric about where we really are. That's your jam, hey, whatever. I'm cool. But if you could really just give me those pills back, then we can—"

"Oh, these pills?" Drea raised them above her head like she was going to chuck them into the woods and Billy's entire body went on alert, eyes locked on the pills. For a second, she thought he might charge her, the glint in his eye was so wild.

She lifted the knife higher.

Fuck. You could never trust a junkie. Except... you could always trust them to be a junkie. And that was something she could just maybe work with.

"I tell you what, Billy boy. Let's make a deal. I've got a plan where we can both get what we want."

"You'll give me back my pills?"

She smiled. "Even better. I'll get you all the heroin and pills you could dream of. All you have to do is help me with one little thing."

CHAPTER FOUR

BILLY

Billy needed another fix. Bad.

That Drea chick, she was gorgeous. Gorgeous and ballsy and not a little scary. He liked her. A lot. He'd definitely like to fuck her.

But more than all of that, he wanted another pill.

No, he *needed* it.

She just didn't understand. He had pain. A lot of pain. The little white pills took it away.

If she'd just let him have *one* more.

"So, don't you think it's about time we took a rest?" Billy said, looking over at Drea significantly. "I don't think Eric's doing so great."

"I'm fine," Eric mumbled. Honestly, it came out so garbled it was more like, "Iiii fiiii."

That dude was so beyond *not* fine.

Yesterday Eric had been okay. Sort of. They'd spent eight hours on and off walking south, making it about twenty of the thirty-five miles they had to go before they hit College Station.

But today Eric had woken up feverish and weak. It didn't take a doctor to tell his arm was infected.

Drea pretended not to notice, shoving the last bite of peanut butter sandwich down his throat and dragging him to his feet. After only a couple miles, he was stumbling so bad Drea had to put her shoulder under his good arm. She'd been all but dragging him for the last three miles.

Billy would have offered to help. He really would have.

As soon as she gave Billy another pill.

He hadn't had one since last night and that was bullshit. Yeah, fine, he'd agreed it was probably the decent thing to do to give some of the oxy pills to the guy with a broken, busted up arm.

Okay.

But he'd sacrificed two of his pills already. That meant, between the two Eric got and the *one* Drea had 'allowed' Billy, there were only four left.

Four.

He could burn through four in a day and a half if he was under a lot of stress.

And wandering around the middle of fuckall nowhere with two relative strangers, one of whom was a pill-Nazi and the other who looked almost literally dead on his feet?

Not Billy's idea of a calm summer afternoon.

Anxiety—that was a clinical condition too. He needed the pills.

Should he slow down on how many he took? Sure. He thought about it sometimes.

He always meant to wean himself off them. But then all the shit had gone down at the clinic and he was on the run, and fuck but that was stressful. He'd just been settling in at the little place he'd found in Fort Worth. Then he heard over the shortwave that the damn capitol was under attack. Jesus, he just couldn't catch a break.

So he'd quit one day. For sure. But he'd wait until everything had settled. Once the Republic was running smooth and he had a stable situation again. It was just crazy to expect him to lose his support system while everything was haywire. He wouldn't even be able to cope with waking up in the morning without it.

He'd tried once. And stayed in bed for a day and a half, shaking, sweating, barfing his guts up and feeling sure he was about to die.

Nope. No thank you.

One day, sure. Just not right now.

Billy hiked his backpack up higher and continued forward, looking all around them. Damn, they sure were in the middle of fuck-all nowhere. There was nothing around except fields. Fields, fields, and you guessed it, more fields.

Eric stumbled and Drea only barely managed to keep him on his feet.

"Can't," Eric gasped, his legs giving out.

He was a big guy and all Drea could do was help him sink somewhat gracefully to the ground.

"A little help here?" She glared up at Billy.

Billy threw his hands up. What did he do? He hadn't laid the spikes out on that damn road. And he sure as hell hadn't forced her to drag this Eric dude all over the country.

But when he made the logical suggestion that they leave Eric by the riverbank this morning and then come back for him when they had wheels, she'd freaked the fuck out on him.

"I am *not* leaving him behind," she'd all but bitten his head off.

Billy took a step toward where she was now bowed over Eric and she held up a hand, not looking at him. "Don't. Just don't."

Billy threw his hands up again. Well what the hell did she want from him? *Help. Don't help.* Which was it?

Damn, he'd forgotten how difficult chicks were. Not that he'd been especially good with them before The Fall, either.

He'd been a skinny resident working seventy-hour weeks and while he could always make his patients laugh, he never had much luck with the ladies. Chicks didn't want a guy that could make them laugh. They wanted muscles. Or money. Maybe one day he'd have the money, but as a resident he was still up to his eyeballs in med school debt.

So he'd lost his virginity far later than most people—when he was twenty-two—in a hasty closet fuck with a fellow resident, Sheila, who'd just brought a patient back from coding for the first time. Sheila always liked to fuck when she was on adrenaline highs and he was the lucky guy who happened to be around at the time.

Then, when Xterminate hit, the hospitals were flooded with dying women. There was so much death. Billy had gotten into medicine because he liked helping people. People were sick and he could make them better.

Except Xterminate was a problem no one could solve.

Billy had never felt so helpless in his whole life.

But more and more women kept in coming every day.

Plenty of doctors just stopped showing up. But not Billy. Even when his dad brought in his mom and two sisters. Hoping that he'd have some sort of connections to a cure because he worked there.

Billy still remembered the hope in Dad's eyes when he asked about the rumors that the CDC was testing a cure on small groups of women.

"You can get them on the list, right, Billy? You can pull some strings and get them on the list for the trial medication?"

Billy had nodded mutely.

The next day he told his dad the CDC had come through. His mom and sisters were in the last, most agonizing stages of the disease, and he gave each of them two pills from the bottle he'd stolen, at morning and bedtime.

Their crying and screaming calmed almost immediately. Dad was ecstatic. He fell down on his knees and thanked God.

And Billy? He slipped away to the restroom and took one of the pills himself. It was just your garden variety opioid but suddenly the impossible became *slightly* more bearable. Enough to keep putting one foot in front of the other, anyway.

His mom and sisters died two weeks later. But they died peacefully, without pain, which was more than he could say for so many others around them.

Dad didn't see it that way.

The last Billy ever saw of his father was watching him joining the angry mob of men setting fire to the east wing of the hospital.

Billy had run then. First to the pharmacy, where he grabbed ten bottles of pills. Then he got in his car and drove and drove until his battery charge ran out. He joined some looters pilfering a liquor store and then he broke into an abandoned house in a pill and alcohol haze for he didn't know how long. Weeks. Maybe even months.

The family of the abandoned house he'd chosen to squat in must have shopped at bulk stores because he found boxes and boxes of food in the garage.

He lived off cereal, Pop-Tarts, canned food, and alcohol. He'd really hit the jackpot because they even had a wine cellar. He didn't know why these people had bugged out, probably Xterminate, but he was happy to take their leavings.

He didn't even know about the bombs dropping, he stayed so fucked up all the time. When the electricity went off in the house where he was squatting and the water stopped coming out of the spouts, he figured it had just been cut off because the bills weren't being paid.

The Texas tapwater was shitty and instead of just living with it like most folks, Fancy Family as he'd come to call whoever'd lived there before him had those huge jugs of water like at an office water cooler.

Billy only stumbled out of the house after he'd emptied the last cooler of water, all the alcohol was drunk, and he was down to his last bottle of pills.

And found out he'd missed the damn Apocalypse.

Drea sat up suddenly, her back going stiff. Billy couldn't see her face since she was angled away from him, but when she swiped an arm across her face, he blinked in surprise. Was she... crying?

When she swung around to look at him, though, there was no trace of tears on her face. She just looked stoic and determined. Shit, Billy had never met anyone more determined in his life, and he'd spent time with some seriously scary, ambitious people.

"This is what we're going to do," she said, putting a hand over her eyes and scanning the countryside around them.

"Over there." She nodded toward a farmhouse in the distance. "We'll take him up there and set him up so he's comfortable. My cache of supplies is only about another ten miles, and the compound another two after that."

She looked up at the sun. "If we keep a steady pace, we should get there right after sundown. We'll wait for full dark anyway."

She looked back toward Billy, leveling him with her gaze in a way that sent a chill down his spine in spite of the Texas heat. "Then we strike."

CHAPTER FIVE

DREA

"Mama?" Drea asked, leaning over Mama.

Mama was sleeping on the couch. But she'd been asleep so long. And she didn't look right. Mamas weren't supposed to be that color. So pasty pale.

It wasn't like Sleeping Beauty sleep either. Mama used to be so pretty. Plump with nice, flushed cheeks. Not anymore, though. She looked more like the old hag lady with the apple than Sleeping Beauty.

Drea looked at the pokey stick and the spoon with leftovers of the ugly yellow liquid on the coffee table.

Mama'd been real talky right after she stuck it in her arm. How long ago was that? Two days, maybe?

Real talky. Wanting to dance around the house. Talking wild talk. Saying Drea was her princess and they should go on the road singing and dancing. Two dancing princesses. She kept saying that. Two dancing princesses.

Drea said she was tired of dancing and Mama yelled that Drea was a bore, why was she always such a bore?

Mama danced by herself after that, clumsy with a scary smile on her face.

Drea tried to remind her she needed to eat. Drea scraped the mold off the bread and put some peanut butter on a piece but Mama wouldn't eat it.

"You tryin' to make me fat?" Mama yelled before throwing it at the wall.

Finally she musta got tired cause she fell on the couch and fell asleep.

But she'd been sleeping so long, Drea was getting worried. Especially when she went potty on herself and the couch about an hour ago.

"Mama." Drea shook her shoulder. What if Mama never woke up? Who'd be there to tuck her in or tell her stories or go to the grocery store and get food? Okay, so Mama didn't always do those things, but sometimes she did.

And a little bit of a Mama was better than no Mama at all.

Drea had a Daddy somewhere, but Mama always said he didn't want them. That he didn't like little kids, especially little girl kids. Mama said Mama was the only one who would ever love Drea.

"Mama," Drea whispered again. She climbed up on the couch and laid down in the crease between Mama and the back of the couch. Mama was so skinny that Drea fit no problem.

The tiny rise and fall of Mama's back was the only thing that kept Drea from completely panicking. Mama was breathing. As long as Mama was still breathing, it was gonna be okay.

But her skin was chilly. Big time chilly.

Drea breathed through her mouth so she wouldn't get sick at the way Mama smelled and pulled the old blanket from the back of the couch. She covered both of them with it.

Drea thought about closing her eyes and trying to sleep along with Mama.

But Mama had been asleep so long. Drea didn't know when Mama had last eaten. Drea finished the rest of the moldy bread last night and then felt bad about it cause she hadn't saved any for Mama.

But if Mama woke up, she could go to the store and get them some more. Maybe some milk too. And Cheerios. Drea's stomach cramped up at the thought. Milk and Cheerios would taste so good right now.

"Mama?" she tried again. "Mama, if you still wanna dance, I'll dance with you. I promise. I'll dance as long as you want. I won't get tired this time. I promise."

Drea started crying then. She couldn't help it. She was so tired. Not sleepy tired. The other kind of tired. Where you just want to lay down and stop tryin' *so hard. She just wanted her Mama. "I won't be a bore. Please Mama. Can you just please wake up? Mama. Mama. MAMA!"*

Mama jerked awake, twisting and half falling off the couch. "Wha's goin' on?" Then Mama's bloodshot eyes went wide as saucers. "You," she hissed out.

"Mama?" Drea asked, tears still wet on her cheeks.

But Mama just looked around like she didn't know where she was. Her nose wrinkled in disgust and then her eyes came back to Drea. "You," she said again. "I always knew you was sent from hell to torment me."

"Mama." Drea reached out, just wanting to be held, for Mama to go back to sleep now that she knew she was alright. Drea would let her sleep and when she woke up, everything would be all right.

"Get away from me!" Mama shrieked, shoving Drea back so hard that Drea knocked into the coffee table and fell on her backside.

Mama stumbled to her feet. "You're Satan's spawn. A child of the devil. Satan came and raped me one night. Domino knew. That's why he never wanted me anymore. Because of you. You took away everything I ever wanted. You little demon cunt! You poison everything you touch. I should send you back to where you came from!"

Then Mama was on top of her and Drea couldn't breathe.

She couldn't breathe! Mama was—

"Mama!" she tried to gasp but nothing came out.

Mama was choking her. Why was Mama—

Mama!

Drea jerked awake, sitting up, hand to her throat.

"You okay?" Billy asked.

She scrambled back from him, stumbling to her feet.

"Fine," she coughed out. "I'm fine."

He lifted an eyebrow at her like, *you don't look fine.* "Bad dream?"

"I said I'm fine," Drea snapped and turned her back to him.

"So you finally gonna let me know what's in that box?"

The box. Right. She looked down at the box that was in her arms. In sleep she'd still clutched on to it.

Even her unconscious knew better than to trust an addict when it came to the important things. Small wonder.

They'd gotten into the outskirts of College Station a little after noon and dug up her cashe that she'd buried here a long time ago. She'd taken one look to make sure everything was still there and then she'd laid down to get some much needed rest. She'd barely slept last night because she kept waking up to check on Eric.

Now she stretched and checked the sky. The sun was setting. Okay, that was good. They were still on track.

"So if you won't tell me about the box, tell me about this place. Unpack a little bit of the mystery that is Drea... Let's start with an easy one. What's your last name?" Billy came up beside her. When she didn't volunteer anything he rolled his eyes. "*Okaaaaay*. Was this the house you grew up in when you were a kid?" He gestured to the big white house whose back yard they were in.

Drea scoffed. "Never lived in a house in my whole life."

She'd lived with her mother in that shithole apartment until she was five and then Child and Family services gave her to Dad.

Cause yeah. A neighbor came to the door to yell at her mother for screaming her head off. The door was unlocked, apparently, and when the neighbor came in, they found her mom on top of Drea. Strangling her own kid and calling her a demon.

Goodbye homicidal Mom and shitty apartment in south Houston. Hello Daddy dearest and the Black Skulls MC clubhouse in College Station.

Out of the frying pan and into the... yeah. So it goes.

"Drove by this house a lot," was all she said to Billy. "Always had the prettiest gardens out front."

The garden was long gone now.

But the box she'd buried in the back yard the night she'd skipped town a decade ago, heart shattered and swearing she'd atone for her sins one way or another?

It was exactly where she'd left it.

Nice to know some things in life never changed.

She squeezed her eyes shut, breathing in deep as she held the metal box closer to her stomach. There was still dirt caked on the sides but holding it was, she didn't know, such a tangible link to the past. Sure, it was a horrific, bloody past, but it was hers.

"So what's inside?" Billy asked again. "Come on, you've left me hanging for hours now. Just lemme take a peek."

Drea's eyes flew open and then she narrowed them, looking back at him. Foolish to let her guard down for even a second with that one. She knew better when it came to addicts.

She was standing between him and his next fix—a dangerous place to be. It was probably only the promise of a longer-term hookup that was keeping him from wrestling her right here and trying to get the little pill bottle in her front pocket back.

He'd been getting more and more fidgety all day. They couldn't have that if they were gonna pull off her plan.

"Back up," she ordered.

His eyebrows furrowed in confusion and she repeated her demand, overenunciating each word. "*Back. Up.*"

He lifted his hands and did as she asked, scooting backwards on the dry grass. His eyes zeroed in on her hands as she reached down for the bottle in her pocket. Jesus, he looked like a salivating dog. Down boy.

She uncapped the top and shook one of the small pill pieces into her hand. "Here." She held it out to him and he took it eagerly. But the happiness on his face was quickly overtaken by a frown.

"What the fuck?" He popped the half in his mouth, swallowing without water. "Where's the rest of it?"

She'd cut the pills into halves with the switchblade while Billy was sleeping this morning.

"You just need enough to curb the craving. I need you sharp for what we're about to do."

He narrowed his eyes at her. She could see the arguments on his tongue and she didn't fucking have time for them.

She clicked the button to release the switchblade and flipped it expertly in her hands to show off her familiarity with handling blades. "Remember, after tonight, you can have all the pills and shit you want. Just a little longer. But if you cross me..." She expertly slashed the knife toward his throat, stopping just short of hitting flesh. Didn't stop him from screeching and tumbling backwards, grabbing for his neck and then looking at his hand to see if she'd drawn blood.

"You have *got* to work on your bedside manner," he muttered under his breath.

"What was that?"

"Nothing," he grumbled. He sat back up, but several feet further away from her than earlier.

She threw one of the smaller water bottles his direction. He barely managed to catch it in time as she pulled the box up and out of the hole.

She spun the three small dials into the correct combination. 531. For May 31st. Her mother's birthday.

"Got any food in there?" Billy asked.

She threw a can of peaches in his direction.

"Fuck, can't you ever just hand something over nicely?"

She just threw a can opener his way next.

"Goddammit!"

She smirked, continuing to pull items out of the box.

Her back up Glock. She lifted the cool metal to her lips and kissed the side of the barrel. "Mama's missed you, baby."

She set it beside her, on the side opposite Billy. It wasn't loaded, but better not to even tempt him. She needed him for what she had planned and it would be so awkward if she had to teach him a lesson first.

She ruffled through several stacks of gold and silver coins and finally her hand closed around the object she'd primarily come for. She pulled it out triumphantly.

"I don't get it. You have a sat phone? So why don't you just call for help?"

She turned and leveled him with a glare. "And who exactly am I supposed to call? The police? The Army? Ghostbusters? Even the Capitol is gone to shit now. We have to do this ourselves."

Billy tugged at the collar of his T-shirt. "But do you really think this will work? I mean, it's just you and me, walking into that big compound full of bikers with guns..."

She smiled and tilted her head at him. "Don't you remember, Billy? We're going to take care of that before we ever get there. Now give me the can opener back. We need to eat some peaches and then get our asses on the move."

She pulled out a few more gadgets from the box and Billy's eyes went wide.

"Holy shit, is that a—"

"Less talking, more eating." She glanced up at the sunset. "It's almost lights out. Game time."

CHAPTER SIX

BILLY

This Drea chick was fucking crazy. He was going along with a crazy person's plan.

Billy hadn't survived this long by being stupid. Head down. Never stick your neck out. Turtles were his fucking spirit animal.

So there was no way he should be walking beside Drea, heading straight into the city that was the nest of one of the most notorious MCs. The Black Skulls had crushed all their other competition in a brutal gang war that coincided with the Texas War for Independence. Except that while New Republic troops were fighting off the Southern Alliance, the Black Skulls were systematically crushing and absorbing every other MC in the greater Texas area.

President Goddard might have thought he kept them contained to their South Texas coastal territory, but that was a crock. They moved product all throughout the Texas territories. *Beyond* even, if you believed the rumors. Guns, pre-Fall luxury items, drugs, women—if it was illegal and expensive as shit, they trafficked it.

And yes, Billy knew way more about it all than he'd prefer to.

So, knowing exactly how dangerous the situation they were walking into was, why didn't he just try to smash Drea across the back of the head when she wasn't looking—assuming such a thing was possible with Commando Barbie—grab the three and a half pills left and make a run for it?

The sane side of him hoped it was just because he knew that it was for exactly that reason. Three and a half pills was nothing. And as crazy as Drea's plan was, if they succeeded, he would have all the shit he wanted for the foreseeable future.

So that was why he crept down the darkened streets after her, shadowing her like... well, a shadow.

It certainly wasn't because he liked or respected her or anything.

So, okay, it was sort of moving how she'd taken care of Eric when he'd helped her drag him up to the farmhouse and they'd gotten him settled in bed. Billy had already asked Eric but he decided to ask her if she and Eric were like, *together* because they definitely had some sort of thing going on between them. But she'd just done the bite-his-head off thing again. No, she'd snapped, they were just friends and Billy should stop being such a goddamned idiot.

But then he remembered how much she and Eric had bickered before he'd gotten so sick and well, it made him feel kinda warm inside.

Because he'd seen a lot in the years since The Fall. And someone genuinely looking out for another person when they weren't getting anything in return for it? He'd like to say he'd only seen it a handful of times, but yeah, he hadn't seen it *at all*. Ever.

The only people he'd dealt with were the strictly I-scratch-your-back-you-scratch-mine kind.

Drea grabbed his arm and pulled him into an alley so dark he could barely see his own hand in front of his face. Thunder had been rumbling all night and clouds blocked most of the moonlight.

"Okay." She shoved the satellite phone at him. "As soon as they answer, you say what I told you to say. Just like we practiced. Don't fucking ad lib. Just stick exactly to the script."

Shit. His hand shook as she handed him the sat phone. He could still back out. Hand her the phone and just fucking run.

But his fingers closed around the phone and when she dialed the numbers, he only gulped and nodded when her eyes met his again.

She pushed the last number and it began ringing. She moved close, holding the phone up to both of their ears.

His heart started racing. Not only from the danger of what they were doing, either. When was the last time he'd been so close to a woman? He'd slept with a city whore once but the whole thing had struck him as terribly depressing so he hadn't done it again.

Having his dick strain against his jeans wasn't exactly helpful when he needed to be concentrating.

"Who the fuck is this?" a deep, pissed off man answered the phone.

Drea bumped him with her arm when he didn't answer right away. "Um," then he swallowed and shut his eyes, focusing and pitching his own voice a shade lower, "Fuck man, this is Grinder. Up at Bryan Station. Fucking Army's up here, man. Goddard must have sent them before he got iced. We need back-up. Right the hell now."

"Grinder? What the fuck you sayin', man?"

"The fuckin' Army's here—"

"Shovel," Drea moved around to whisper in Billy's other ear. "His name is Shovel."

"Shovel," Billy said, eyes on Drea. "We're fucking dying up here."

How the hell did she know these guys well enough to recognize them by *voice*? Looked like he wasn't the only one with secrets.

"Fuck," Shovel swore. "Why aren't you calling on the shortwave?"

"They got some kind of signal jammer. Nothing was going through. Try it on your end. You'll see."

Drea held up a black device with a flashing red light and the clouds shifted just enough for Billy to see the wicked smile on her face. Damn, the more time he spent around this woman, the more terrifying she got.

"Goddamn, you're right. All we get is static. Okay, fuck. Hold tight man. I'll tell the boss. We'll let you know—"

"Fuck man, you're cutting in and out. Almost— of batt— Battery's low. Might lose y—"

Drea grabbed the phone from him and punched the disconnect button.

Then she spun and crouched low to the ground, peeking out from around the corner at the building on the opposite side of the street. It was four stories tall and looked like it might have been an apartment building before The Fall.

Another thing—it was lit up like a pre-Fall Christmas tree. The whole building had electricity.

It didn't take long to see that their tactic was getting results. A big garage door opened and then, like the rising chorus of a symphony, motorcycle engines roared to life one after the other. They poured out of the garage like a line of picnic ants.

Shit. Billy couldn't believe that actually worked.

"Now for part two," Drea whispered, standing up and smoothing down the tiny scrap of black cloth that was supposed to pass for a dress. The dress had been among the last items in the box, but it looked far different when she first pulled it out of the plastic. It was longer, for one, by about eight inches before Drea had done surgery with the switchblade. Then she'd cut a long slash down the front almost to her belly button so that her fucking amazing cleavage was all but spilling out.

When she'd first turned around, Billy's jaw had dropped open. She'd literally put a finger underneath his chin and shut his open mouth. "Drooling isn't a good look on anyone, darling."

She was definitely a woman willing to use any and all assets at her disposal, that was clear.

Billy couldn't decide if he admired her for it or if yeah, it was just terrifying.

She switched out her boots for a pair of heels she'd found in the farmhouse and then she slipped on the black hat with a little veil that covered most of her upper face—another farmhouse find.

"Come on," she whispered, waving at him. "Before it closes again."

They hurried across the dark street right as the first raindrops fell. Billy only took a second to blink up at the well-lit building.

Damn. This was so above his pay grade.

Then again, he was getting paid in the only currency he gave a shit about, so fuck it. He was neck deep in it now. Might as well see it through. What else did he have going on in his life anyway?

He and Drea barely got across the street in time to duck under the garage door before it slid shut again.

Shit. That was close. Billy rubbed his neck and looked at the door before glancing around them.

The garage was huge, basically a parking garage turned into a space to work and store bikes and trucks. It was lit up and cars and motorcycles were in various states of disrepair, up on blocks all around the space.

"Hey, who are you?"

Drea's eyes widened and she waved at Billy. He jumped to his feet and saw a huge, muscled guy standing at the other end of the shop glaring their direction. Fuck his muscles were big. "Oh. Um. We're here— I mean, this is— Um. We're here because— She's a—"

"Jesus Christ," Drea swore, swinging her Glock around and shooting the muscled guy in the knee.

"Holy shit!" Billy jumped back from her. It had barely made a noise because of course in addition to having a shiny gun in that little box of horrors of hers they'd dug up, she had a silencer too.

The man cried out and reached for something on the counter. A gun. Double shit!

But Drea was already on top of it. As soon as she'd taken the shot she covered the distance between them and dug the pointy heel of her shoe into his back to keep him down. "Don't even think about it, Tweeker."

"Holy shit, that you, Bella?"

Bella?

"Don't fucking move, you piece of shit."

Drea shoved her heel in deeper but the man—Tweeker?—just started laughing. Billy came closer, feeling like he should be doing something. He had no idea what, but... something.

"Suicide always said you'd be back. Heard you and him had a real nice reunion in Galveston recently."

"*Thomas* and I have unfinished business, it's true. But that's not why I'm here. Where's Bulge? He's Pres here now, right? Since Thomas's moved on to bigger and better?"

Tweeker turned his head and spit Drea's direction. "You can shoot my other knee out, I'm not telling you shit. You're just a dumb bitch who never knew her place and I hope—"

Before Billy even registered what was happening, Drea shifted the gun so that it was aimed at his back and then pulled the trigger. Twice. He heard two dull *thump, thumps*.

Then she climbed up off of Tweeker's lifeless corpse and Billy just stood, mouth agape, staring at her. "You just killed him!" he whispered, completely fucking freaking out on the inside.

Holy shit. Okay, this wasn't fun and games anymore. Not that it had ever been, but still. Dead body. Right there. On the ground not three feet away from him.

So yes, he'd shot those guys who'd set out the road spikes and it wasn't like he hadn't seen dead bodies before, but he was trying to get *away* from all this shit. He promised himself he'd left it behind for once and for all and now here he was neck deep in it again.

"What?" Drea looked at him like nothing was the matter. "He was a raping, murderous asshole. Trust me, the world's better off."

She looked around the garage, then walked over and opened a panel on the wall, swinging the small bag she'd been carrying across her back. Billy didn't go over to see what she was doing. No, when you hung with a chick who went around killing people without a blink of the eye—while you were trying to infiltrate a murderous MC just so you could re-up your stash of narcotics to feed your habit—maybe it was time to start rethinking your life choices.

Billy ran both his hands through his hair, staring down at Tweeker's lifeless face and the pool of blood growing on the concrete floor all around him.

Shit, did he have to be named Tweeker?

Not that Billy did meth—he was a strictly opiates kind of guy—but still. Fuck. Was this some kind of cosmic sign? Get your shit in order or else?

"Let's go."

Drea strode in front of him, features cold as ice.

Maybe it was just a sign that he should cut ties as soon as possible with deadly assassin chick.

"After you," he muttered.

She opened the bag she'd brought in, pulled out a length of rope, and then opened the door off the garage, holding it open with her hip while she put her arms behind her back. "Tie me like I showed you."

He obliged, eyes flicking up and down the empty hallway.

He tied the loose double infinity knot quick enough though, and then he started 'marching' her down the hallway, following her whispered directions of left, left, right, left through the surprisingly empty building.

Damn, when bikers went out on a run, they really went out.

But then they opened a door to voices. A lot of voices. All the hallways they'd gone down so far seemed like service hallways. They'd gone through a kitchen. Passed by a room that might have once been a conference room or a gym.

Now they'd apparently made it to the front of the building. It looked like a lobby. So this place had been a hotel, or like he'd first thought, some sort of fancy, expensive apartment building?

The lobby was a huge open space with a bar on one end. About fifteen or so bikers were scattered all around on couches and chairs, women in various states of nakedness draped across them.

The women didn't look good. Almost all of them were bruised or had some sort of lacerations on their bodies.

Billy had seen the sort before.

He wondered how long they'd lived in captivity here and if this was their first stop on the trafficking trail or if this was where they'd ended up after making the rounds around Texas or up through Mexico.

He felt Drea stiffen in front of him, obviously seeing the women too. But she kept her head down.

Billy felt fucking terrified but he clung to the peptalk Drea had given him before they'd entered the city.

"Let's face it. You're a shit liar, Billy."

"Great. Glad we had this talk."

He'd been about to turn away when she reached out and put her hand on his arm. It was a touch that made him feel warm down to his bones.

"But you have a superpower."

He looked up at her, feeling lost and entranced at the same time by her beautiful blue eyes. "I do?"

"Yes." She smiled then. "You're an addict. And I've never met an addict who couldn't stare me in the eye and convince me their grandma was dying and needed drugs with absolute sincerity. So just remember. You need the shit they have locked up somewhere inside that building. And the only thing standing between you and your next fix are a few teeny tiny lies. Got it?"

So Billy cleared his throat and then spoke up. "Tweeker said this is where I could bring the new whore for Bulge?"

"Who the fuck are you?" A man sitting on a plush chair that was on a raised area like a stage at the back center of the room stood up.

He shoved a chick who'd been sucking his dick off to the side, standing naked except for his pants that were shoved down to his ankles and his motorcycle boots. He was huge, big as a tank, and tattoos covered his entire body. From his exposed legs to his junk, all the way up to his shaved head.

The only space that was clear of ink were a few spots on his face. Billy had only seen a more intimidating motherfucker once in his life and he'd barely lived to tell the damn tale.

He's the only thing standing between you and your beautiful, beautiful reward, he reminded himself. A pile of pills. A plethora of Percocet. An ocean of Oxy.

He could fucking do this.

"Hey man," Billy said, shrugging like he didn't give a shit. "Suicide sent me with this whore for Bulge. Said she was some kinda present. That she'd been trained up special. That's all I fuckin' know."

Bulge stood for a long, silent moment, assessing the two of them. Billy's balls were sweating so much in a second it was gonna look like he'd fucking pissed his pants.

But then Bulge grinned and opened his arms wide. "Fucking shit timing, man, but bring her to Papa! All these fucking whores are boring and lifeless as shit."

He pulled off one boot and pant leg, then kicked the woman who'd previously been giving him a blow job in the side until she skittered off the platform. He pulled off his other boot, kicked off his jeans the rest of the way, and sat back on his throne-like chair, legs spread wide, hard cock jutting up against his stomach. He gave it a tug as Drea and Billy walked forward.

Just as they'd planned, Billy untied her when they were just halfway across the room. Drea had merely glossed over this part of the plan, so Billy wasn't prepared when she started to swing her hips and rub her hands sensuously down her body.

Now that he saw her moving along to the beat, he realized there was music playing, low grinding rock with a hard base.

And fuck could Drea dance.

She kept her head bowed as if submissive, but the way she ran her hands up and down her own body—Jesus fuck. Billy shifted uncomfortably as he made his way over to the wall like she'd told him to.

When she dipped low, legs spread and then teased her hands up along her inner thighs before slowly standing back up again, apparently Billy wasn't the only one reaching the breaking point.

"Get the fuck over here and ride my cock," Bulge demanded, "Right fucking now." He grabbed himself and pumped his shaft up and down as Drea approached. And damn, but the guy lived up to his name. His cock was a good ten inches and thick as a damn anaconda.

In spite of his orders, Drea still moved with a practiced ease that had Billy's blood ringing in his ears. Holy shit, she was pushing this too far. Was she actually gonna fuck the dude? She was so crazy intense, he wouldn't put it past her.

At first he'd thought coming here was all about getting help for Eric, but he was quickly realizing there was a hell of a lot more going on here. She obviously had a past with the MC and he didn't think it was just as a woman they'd trafficked at some point.

Whatever had gone down, she was here for comeuppance.

For revenge.

For blood.

Billy watched in horrified fascination as she stepped up onto the platform area. And then—holy shit, what was she—?

Billy almost swallowed his own tongue. In one motion, she slipped the straps of the dress down her shoulders and then, before he'd even blinked, the slinky material was pooled around her waist.

Billy was at just the perfect angle to see her gorgeous, perfect tits in all their perfect titty glory before she hiked one leg up on the tattoo'd bastard's plush recliner.

There wasn't an eye in the entire fucking room that wasn't zeroed in on her as she climbed on top of Bulge.

So no one missed a single splatter of the blood that sprayed up his chest or the look of horror on his face as Drea—

Cut.

Off.

His.

Dick.

With the switchblade she had hidden the only place she could—up her damn pussy.

CHAPTER SEVEN

DREA

She didn't waste a second of the shocked surprise that momentarily froze the room.

The switchblade was sharp, but Bulge's dick was thick. She couldn't get through the whole damn thing without sawing at it and that was time she didn't have. She'd sliced a little more than halfway, though, and he'd bleed out soon.

It was a more dignified death than the bastard deserved anyway.

No time to dwell. In about two seconds, it was gonna sink in that she'd just killed their Pres and then shit was really gonna hit the fan.

Time to do some damage.

She leapt off Bulge's chair and landed right beside his jeans. In the same motion, she grabbed for the two guns he kept strapped to his belt. SIG-Sauer P228s. A little too much gun for her taste but Daddy had taught her how to shoot anything that had a barrel and a trigger.

And she knew exactly which targets to hit first.

She'd clocked the room while Billy and Bulge did their back and forth. First she lined up on Handlebar—just for shits and giggles she lowered her aim from right between his eyes to zero in on that stupid novelty mustache he was so damn proud of.

Bang.

One rapist motherfucker down.

About twenty more to go.

She ducked behind Bulge's chair as she aimed for Smokey. He was old as fuck but the one everyone would be looking to with their other two highest ranking members down.

Bang.

Down he went and she pulled back behind the chair as gunfire exploded all around her. Well. Looked like they could draw even when they were all drunk as shit. Whether they could aim and hit anything, now, that was another matter. At least the damn throne Bulge sat on was thick. None of the rounds got through it.

"Give yourself up, you crazy bitch," someone yelled when the fire died down, "or I kill him."

Drea jerked her head up and her chest cinched when she peeked around the chair and saw Budweiser with his gun against Billy's temple.

Fuck.

She'd told Billy to get to the side of the room and then slip out the back as soon as shit started to go down.

Best laid plans...

She glanced at her watch and then took one more peek at the room.

Screw it. It was now or never.

She stood up, both guns extended, aimed at the next highest-ranking members. With a shake of her head, she jarred the hat she was wearing loose, veil and all. As soon as her face was revealed, she heard several *holy shit*s around the room along with other, more colorful curses.

Others, she knew, were still too busy staring at her tits, in spite of the fact that she'd just murdered three of their own.

"Bella?" asked a man, standing up from a table on the left of the room, not too far from where the bastard had the gun to Billy's head. "Belladonna? Is that really you?"

Drea only allowed her eyes to flick briefly in his direction.

It was Garrett. Road name Peewee. Damn. She hadn't counted on him being here. He was a giant of a man with a biker's beard and a trunk so wide he was the definition of the term barrel-chested.

She thought for sure he'd be with the riders sent out to help defend the northern border. It was usually only the highest-ranking bastards who stayed behind while the lackeys were sent out. And to become a high-ranking Skull, you had to do shit you could never clean off your soul.

She and Garrett had been good friends once, a lifetime ago. He'd grown up in the club, same as her.

But she'd just killed his dad.

Handlebar.

She'd just killed his dad right in front of him. So somehow she didn't think he'd be feeling too friendly toward her at the moment.

But she couldn't let that get her off track. She was on a mission.

"I'm here to reclaim my birthright," she said, looking out on the seventeen men still left standing, including Garrett and Budweiser, the fucker holding the gun to Billy's head.

"My father was the President of this chapter and he was unjustly *murdered*. But I can forgive and forget. I'll deal with his murderer in time, you count on that. All I ask for is my rightful position in my father's place as President of this chapter."

"Ain't no girl can be Pres," scoffed Tex Mex, one of the old-timers. His gray beard was so long it laid over his huge beer gut almost all the way down to his belt.

"Why not?" Drea said, eyes mapping out the room and everyone's positions in it. She'd have to be careful of the women. Internally, she kept up the count that had been going on ever since she'd last glanced at her watch. Thirteen. Twelve. Eleven. Ten.

"Fuck this," Budweiser said, cocking his gun.

"Wait!" Drea cried. She didn't have a clean shot. Billy was in the way. And it wasn't time yet—

But then, as if her thoughts had conjured it, Budwieser's head exploded. Drea's head snapped toward the sound of the gunshot. Only to see Garrett with his gun out, pointed in the direction where Budweiser had just dropped to the floor.

Garrett shot Budweiser.

Garrett's on your side.

She barely had a second to register the thought before the lights cut out and the room went pitch black.

Shit!

She forced herself to breathe and focus. And to *fire*.

She'd had her gun trained on Biscuit and Hat Trick, knowing the lights would go any second. They hadn't had women on them so she took the shots. She and Billy had set a timed charge on the main power feed line, set for six minutes, so she'd known the lights were gonna go.

The girls screamed all around the room at the chaos, but they didn't need to be afraid.

See, Drea had a plan.

She dropped down and felt for her hat. As soon as her hand closed over it, she pulled out the sleek night-vision goggles she'd taped into the top lining, slipping them on and immediately taking aim at two Black Skulls closest to her.

She took kill shots. *Bang. Bang.* And they were down.

They'd lost all rights to compassion when they'd signed up to be part of this murdering, rapist, slave trading MC.

Except Garrett. He never had a choice, did he? Handlebar was a mean bastard. She knew for a fact he used to beat Garrett. Sometimes within an inch of his life. One time when Garrett was a teenager, Handlebar took a bat to him and shattered his shoulder.

Another man stumbled in the darkness, hands out like he was trying to find the wall.

Bang.

Three more, huddled together behind one of the couches. She checked their faces first. None of them were Garrett.

Bang. Bang. Bang.

Drea had begged Garrett to run away. But he said no. He said he didn't have a future apart from the MC. He thought he was nobody without it and wouldn't listen to her arguments to the contrary. When he wouldn't, she'd begged her dad to do something about Garrett's home life.

He was the MC President, wasn't he? How could he look the other way when something like that was happening on his watch? But Dad just said other folks family matters were their own private affairs. She should have known then that Dad wasn't the shining hero she thought he was.

Drea had been prepared to run away *with* Garrett because she knew it might be the only way to get him to go. She wasn't an idiot. She saw the way he looked at her. She didn't know if she felt the same way. Garrett was two years younger than her so she'd always seen him as more of a little brother. But maybe in time...? If it meant getting him away from his monster father?

But then Thomas and his dad showed up and Garrett and his problems fell by the wayside. Everything paled when Thomas Tillerman walked into the room. His dad had a little of the same magnetism. Enough that Dad promoted him to Sergeant at Arms within just a couple years. They'd come from a sister chapter of the Skulls, but still, that was almost unheard of.

Thinking of Thomas made Drea's blood boil so much that when she came across two more bastards who'd actually made it to the door she slipped on her brass knuckles. Especially when she saw them dragging women with them to use as shields.

She aimed and fired at the one furthest away, pausing to be sure of her shot. *Bang.* He dropped and the woman he'd been holding jumped back, arms flailing in fright. But she quickly found the wall and hurried away.

The closer biker, though, he was holding his female shield too tight to get a good shot. So Drea grabbed him by the elbow, swung him around, and slammed his face with her brass-knuckle-covered fist. The crunch of bones was fucking satisfying.

She put the barrel of the gun to his forehead and pulled the trigger. *Click.*

With her goggles, she saw the look of excitement cross the man's face. He thought he'd escaped the executioner. Oh how cute.

He reached for his waist and the piece he kept there. He had to drop hold of the woman to do it. Bonus. She skittered backwards away from him.

"Looking for this?" Drea asked sweetly.

Bang.

She dropped him. "Dead by your own hardware. Damn. That's gotta sting."

She shook her head as she stood up and looked around.

Women crouched down to the floor all over the room. There were still a few bikers scrambling for doors and windows but one man stood in the center of the room, unmoving, hands at his side. He wasn't trying to run or and he wasn't reaching for his gun.

Drea pulled her dress back up her torso and lifted the straps on over her shoulders, then she walked closer with her gun out in front of her.

As she came around his side, she saw his face.

Garrett.

His face was absolutely blank. Drea frowned. Did he have that much trust in her? That she wouldn't shoot him?

"It's okay," he called out loudly. She ducked and took a step back. He must not know how close she was because he continued talking at an almost yell.

"I'm ready, Belladonna."

She cringed at his use of her middle name. *Belladonna.* It was what they all used to call her. Who named their child after a poisonous plant?

You poison everything you touch. I should send you back to where you came from!

"I'm ready to meet my maker and face judgement for my crimes."

Drea shook her head and reached out. Garrett jerked at her touch like she'd just shocked him with electricity.

"Garrett. Garrett, it's me. It's okay."

Right then, the lights came back on, blinding her. She jerked back, scrambling to get her goggles off.

She managed to a moment later and Garrett was exactly where she'd left him. He'd had time to get the upper hand on her if he'd wanted to. His own gun was holstered at his waist, though. He could have easily pulled it and shot her. He hadn't.

"Bells," he whispered, and that one word was so full of sorrow and devastation. "I'm so sorry, Bells."

She shook her head and tried to smile, reaching again for his hand. She realized at the same time how ludicrous the action was. She was still in the slutastic dress, covered in blood from the men she'd just slaughtered. She quickly moved her eyes around the room.

"It's not safe," she said when Garrett went to pull her into a hug.

"Shit." He swiped at his eyes. Was he crying? "You're right. Of course."

He did pull out his gun then, but only to step up side by side with her. They went first to where Billy had crawled underneath the pool table, his entire body shaking, arms over his head.

Then Drea went around to the women while Garrett went to make sure the rest of the clubhouse was clear and there weren't any more bikers hiding out. "You're safe now. I'm not here to hurt you."

They all scrambled back away from her. All except one.

She'd pulled a throw from one of the couches over herself to cover her nakedness but it was still clear she was rail thin. She had brown hair that had a slight wave to it and intelligent, brown eyes.

"There's more of us downstairs. If you're really here to help us, go down and free the rest." She held out a large keyring—the old fashioned kind, little pieces of metal instead of keycards. No doubt she'd picked it up off one of the men Drea had shot.

Drea took the keys. "How do I get downstairs? And what's your name?"

"Gisela," she said as she led them back to the hallway they'd come through from the garage.

There was a door but Drea was confused, because it did have a keycard reader. Gisela held out a keycard and it opened.

She flipped a light switch as she, Billy, and Gisela climbed down the concrete steps. Right away, they were met with soft, feminine cries in response.

Drea ran down the rest of the stairs as fast as possible. And when she got to the bottom—

"No!" she cried, sprinting forward.

Lining the dank, barely lit basement, stuffed in every available crevice, around water heaters, exposed pipes, and other large equipment were... cages.

Cages.

Inside each one huddled a naked, shivering woman. The cages weren't even big enough for the women to stand up in. They could only sit or stand at a crouch.

Drea ran to the closest one and fumbled with the keys on the keyring she'd grabbed from Gisela.

"I'm getting you out of here. I'm sorry. I'm so sorry." It was all she could say. Over and over as she tried key after key.

"Fuck," she cried when none of them worked. She'd been working so fast and frantically, she wasn't sure if she'd missed some, maybe the one fucking key that would open the cage lock. There were about fifty damn keys on the fucking keyring.

Finally she let out a growl and pulled out the Glock she'd picked up off one of the bastards upstairs. "Move back. Can you move back, sweetie?"

The woman inside the cage nodded and cemented her body to the back of the cage. Drea breathed out and aimed with more care and precision than she ever had in her life.

Bang.

But this time, instead of taking life, she was giving it.

The woman inside the cage let out just a small scream but then Drea wrenched the door open and helped her crawl out to freedom.

Joyous cries sounded all throughout the basement, echoing off the concrete walls. The woman Drea had just freed began sobbing and threw her arms around Drea as she helped her to her feet.

"Oh thank you. Thank you, thank you!!"

Drea couldn't tell if her hair was blonde or brown, it was so greasy, and from the way she smelled, it was obvious showers weren't common.

As she moved to the next cage, she saw another reason for the stench. Each girl had a bucket in the corner of their cages. A fucking *bucket*.

This is your father's legacy.

Drea hardened her jaw and raised her gun. The woman had already flattened herself against the back of the cage, ready for Drea.

"Good," Drea heard from behind her. "I'm glad you found them.

Drea spun and glared at Garrett. Why the fuck hadn't he told her about this room right away?

As if anticipating her question, he just stood up straighter. "I had to make sure the clubhouse was secure. I had to know you were safe first."

"Start on the other side of the room," she snapped at him. "But *careful*. Anything happens to any of them, don't forget I've still got my switchblade on me."

Just a short pause before, "Yes, ma'am."

And on they went, freeing woman after woman. As they got deeper into the basement, the cages were stacked two high. Some of the women couldn't stand, their muscles were so cramped.

In the end they pulled thirty-three women out of the cages, in addition to the twelve upstairs.

It would have been thirty-five but two were dead from malnutrition.

"They feed us once a day but those two just lost the will," said Gisela. She'd started organizing the other women as each one was freed. Garrett and Billy had gone upstairs and brought down clothing, blankets, and food. Gisela had immediately begun passing them out, getting the stronger women to help her with the weakest.

Another girl nodded. "Wouldn't eat. Wouldn't do anything but lay in their cages waiting to die."

Drea tried not to let it in as she helped the last girl out of her cage. It was one of the stacked cages. Right underneath one of the dead girls.

She was shaking so bad as Drea helped her to her feet.

Gisela hurried over. "It's okay, Maya. You're free now. No one's ever going to hurt you again."

Drea winced at the assurance. She'd made statements like that. So confident she could protect the women she'd tried to shelter at Nomansland. So sure of herself.

"So what now?" Gisela turned to Drea, bright brown eyes expectant. She was wearing a Black Skulls T-shirt that dwarfed her tiny body, coming down almost to her knees. She had to be just as hungry as everyone else, but she hadn't even touched the food Garrett had brought down in a duffel bag.

"Well," Drea said. "First, let's get upstairs and out of this stinking basement."

Gisela nodded and clapped her hands. "Okay girls. Up the stairs. Let's leave this shithole behind once and for all."

More cheering. It was like they'd been waiting for permission but as soon as it was given, they mobbed the staircase leading up to the first floor.

Gisela had to hurry over and organize them so they didn't hurt each other in their hurry to get upstairs.

Drea looked to Garrett. "You fortified the clubhouse like I said?"

He nodded. "Locked her up tight. Found three more hiding out. The rest fled."

Drea nodded. Though calling this place a 'clubhouse' was somewhat laughable. The clubhouse she'd grown up in had been a retired army barracks. Far from what you'd call a particularly inviting space. But this place must have been an office or apartment building back before The Fall.

While they'd replaced the exterior doors with steel ones and boarded up what were once clearly glass storefronts, it was only moderately defensible. Maybe if they had more time, but they didn't.

Because soon there would be a lot of pissed off bikers coming back when they found out the call that had gotten them out of the clubhouse was a fake.

Drea looked at her watch. They had ten minutes. Fifteen at the most.

"What now?" Gisela asked once Drea made it to the top with Maya and they'd reunited with the other girls who'd been raiding the kitchens.

"First, you eat." Drea grabbed a bagel from the bag Billy brought up. Both Gisela and Maya backed away from him as he passed. Little wonder after all they'd been through at the hands of men.

Drea's eyes flicked to Garrett. The girls seemed no more skittish of him than they did Billy. Did that mean he hadn't had any direct interaction with them?

He still worked for the club that trafficked them, though. For the last eight years. He knew what they did. And still, he'd stayed.

He glanced her way like he could feel her eyes on him and she looked away quickly, back to Gisela.

Then she looked at the women as a whole. Some were huddled together, holding on to one another. A few were off on their own, arms clasped around themselves, rocking back and forth. More still were on the floor, maybe their legs weren't strong enough to stand.

Drea swallowed hard but then forced herself to stand up straight.

"You need to get moving. Half the club will be back any minute."

Her words were met with cries of shock and fear.

"Where will we go?" asked one girl. "We have nowhere. We'll just be picked up again by someone else. Enslaved again."

"Besides," Gisela said, kicking one of the men who lay bloody on the floor where Drea had shot him in the head. "We're tired of running. We want to fight. Like you."

A few others echoed her. The others just looked scared as shit.

Drea put a hand to her forehead.

Shit.

This hadn't been part of the plan.

She looked at the half-starved girls again. Some of them were still shoving food in their mouths so quickly it was sure to make them sick. Others were struggling into clothes many sizes too big.

Drea had never seen a more rag-tag army. She looked down at her watch.

Seven minutes.

No time to stand around with their thumbs up their asses.

"Anyone know how to shoot a gun?"

Eight girls out of the forty-five held up their hands. Gisela took a step forward. "I was the best of all my friends at first person shooter games when I was a kid."

"Jesus," Billy swore behind Drea.

"Shut up," Drea said, turning to address the women. "Okay, anyone who wants to fight can. Garret, Billy, you stockpiled the weapons off the bodies?"

"Did you one better," Garrett smiled. "I took a little trip by the armory." He went over to a second duffel bag and opened it up. It was stuffed to the gills with guns. Machine guns. Shot guns. Pistols.

Drea grinned. "I knew there was a reason I kept you around." She meant it as an offhand comment but Garrett's face went serious.

"I swear to you Drea, I'll do whatever it takes to make it up to you."

But Drea just shook her head. "It's not me you have to make it up to."

Garrett swallowed and looked around at the room of women, nodding.

He held out the bag of guns and Drea ushered the women forward. "Let's go, let's go. There's no time to be shy. Come on, I have a plan."

CHAPTER EIGHT

GARRET

Garrett had been in love with Drea Valentine as long as there'd been air in his lungs, it felt like. He remembered the first time he saw her. It felt like his first memory.

That blonde hair of hers, it was glinting in the sunshine when she first stepped outta her daddy's truck.

She looked tiny standing there next to Domino. Barely come to his hip, seemed like. So thin Garrett was sure her bones must be hollow like a bird's and she'd just fly right off. Right there off the pavement and up into the big old clouds. Like an angel. That's what he thought she was. An angel come down from heaven.

Except Garrett didn't know why a little angel'd be visiting Domino like that. Domino Valentine was a scary motherfucker, even back then.

If Garrett had memories before Drea, it was nightmares of that skull face of her daddy's. It'd be coming for him at night, floating down the hall. It'd open it's mouth and swallow him whole and he'd scream and his mama would come in his room and hush him so he didn't wake his own daddy.

Cause Handlebar was a mean, scary motherfucker, too.

Turned out Mama had about had enough of living with bruises and broken bones, and it wasn't too long before she took off. She left a note for Garrett. It said: Mama loves you.

Garrett slept with the note under his pillow for a year.

Then Handlebar found it and gave him a hiding so bad he walked funny for a month.

Garrett wasn't dumb. Least not as dumb as everybody thought he was. He figured he clamped onto Drea like he did cause everything else in his life was shit.

But then there was her.

Beautiful. Innocent. Good.

And sad.

She looked so sad sometimes.

He'd see her alone in the courtyard of the clubhouse, playing in the dirt with a stick, and her sweet little pink cheeks would have tear tracks running through the dust the Texas wind always seemed to kick up.

They were the only two kids who lived at the clubhouse full time, so he'd sit down beside her and grab a stick, too.

He didn't say anything. He learned real quick she'd run away if he tried talking. So he didn't say a word, just dug around in the dirt.

At first she was still real skittish like, moving away from him to the other side of the courtyard's dirt patch. But she didn't run back inside.

So Garrett considered that progress.

And as that first month went on and he kept on going out each afternoon after school every day, she stopped moving so far away. Every day, closer and closer.

Until finally, one magical day when those blue, blue eyes of hers flipped up his direction.

His breath caught in his tiny little chest.

Was she finally gonna talk to him?

"You're doing it wrong."

Then she went back to digging at the ground like she hadn't just shattered his universe and torn his chest wide open and planted herself inside forever.

She'd spoken to him.

To *him*.

And she'd *looked at him*.

And she was sitting right beside him. And not moving.

He was gonna marry that girl.

He decided then and there.

He stared at the Drea of today. No little angel anymore. Now she was a warrior goddess. Watching her earlier... god*damn*.

She gave a gun to every woman who wanted to fight and then led them into the triple wide garage downstairs and had them all hide behind bikes, cars, drop cloths, everything and anything.

She was fucking crazy, and beautiful, and crazy fucking beautiful.

He hid crouched down behind a big ass shovelhead Harley, as close as he could get to her. She was wound tight as she waited for all the bikers to pull back into the garage.

Garrett had been doing his job a long time. Too fucking long. He'd been in turf wars with the cartels before The Fall ever happened and goddamn, after, it was all-out war for half a decade. But he'd never seen anyone as cool going into battle as Drea fucking Valentine.

He could barely see her chest moving she was breathing so calmly as she glanced between the fender and the fork, only pressing the remote to send the garage door shutting behind the bikes after everyone was in.

It was the signal, and her warriors responded even though she'd only had minutes to sketch out the plan.

Including Garrett.

He stood up with his Thompson M2053 sub-machine gun and let 'er fuckin' *rip*.

Fifteen pissed off women plus fifteen sub-machine guns? In addition to Garrett? Yeah. It was over in minutes. Drea's army had all lined up on one side of the garage so there wouldn't be any friendly fire and even the women who'd never shot more than a video game gun when they were kids caught on pretty quick.

And Garrett didn't miss the mix of tears, smiles, and satisfaction on the women's faces. It might be a gory form of closure but Drea had known it was just what they'd needed. To give the bastards who'd hurt and tortured and traded them like they were cattle *exactly* what they deserved.

Garrett looked out on the bodies of the men who'd called him *brother* and felt... nothing. Fuck that wasn't true. He felt damn relieved, that's what he felt.

Like he'd been underwater in a sinking car and there was just that inch of air left at the top and he could keep gasping at it, making it for one more minute, a few more seconds, sure the end was coming for him.

But right around the corner, there was the reaper. Just waiting for him. Just waiting to take him to hell.

So he just kept trying to suck in air and praying to God even though he knew he had no right to.

Because Garrett knew what the club's main income was. Always had. Handlebar saw to that. He tried to get Garrett to lose his virginity to a girl from 'the docks' that dear old Dad tied to a bed for his sixteenth birthday present.

It was right before everything happened with Drea's dad and just after Garrett's shoulder had finally healed from surgery.

Having your father beat you with a baseball bat so brutally that your shoulder shatters to the point of needing a shoulderblade replacement? Yeah, really makes you think twice before telling your dad to go fuck himself or to outright reject any presents.

No, Garrett didn't fuck her.

Garrett banged the bed into the wall for five minutes while apologizing profusely to the girl but knew it didn't really matter because she'd be going back to 'the docks,' wherever the hell that was. Handlebar had only told him enough to haunt his nightmares without being able to actually do anything about it.

Not that he *did* do anything about it when he finally learned the ins and outs of the whole operation.

Not for a while anyway.

The world had gone tits-up by that point. His whole plan to go to the FBI and take down his dad and the whole MC with all the information he'd been gathering ever since Drea left went down the fucking drain.

What FBI? What police?

The Skulls only got more brutal in the aftermath—but still, one nightmarish trip into Southern Alliance Territory on Skulls business was enough to convince Garrett that as bad as the Skulls were, at least here it was the devil he knew. And the Skulls weren't selling people as slaves to be fucking *eaten*. Maybe that was a low bar but for fuck's sake!

And from inside, it was a system Garrett had a hope in hell of subverting now and again. Still, he knew if any of the girls went missing right after he was made full club member, it would look suspicious. Handlebar always thought he was too soft, even after he became the club's enforcer and spent day in day out using his fists to break people's bodies.

No, Garrett waited a full seven months before he made his first move and saved the first girl. Finding a safe place for her to *go* was tricky too. But he did it, and he did it quiet.

Garrett made it look like she was lost in a car accident on the final leg of her 'delivery' to the client. During the next few years there were several such *accidents*.

He was most proud of the boat full of twelve girls that was 'lost at sea' in the Gulf of Mexico on a trip from Galveston to New Orleans. He took a speedboat out in the middle of the night, offed the captain, got the girls, and sank the bigger boat. Garrett had contacted the family of two of the girls and they agreed to take the rest of the girls in and find safe places for them.

Suicide got suspicious after that and tore the whole fucking club apart looking for the traitor. But Garrett was good at playing big, dumb, and compliant. It was how Handlebar had treated him his whole life, so everybody bought it.

Even bossman himself, and Suicide was usually much more shrewd when it came to reading people. But sometimes if something's so close under your nose, it'll always stay a blind spot. That was Garrett. One big old six-foot five, two-hundred-and-ninety-pound blind spot.

But all in all, he only saved nineteen girls.

Nineteen.

Out of hundreds. Maybe even thousands. It wasn't enough. Not nearly enough.

But it was how he'd justified his continued existence in this world. It was why he didn't just let himself drown. Or put a gun in his mouth and pull the goddamned trigger.

More likely though, deep down, he was terrified it was the justification of a coward. A better man would have found a way to save more.

Or a better woman.

Garrett stared at Drea as she bent over a desk, examining a map.

Fuck but she'd turned out so much more amazing than Garrett ever could have imagined, and he'd thought about her and imagined a *lot*.

"What?" Drea asked, flashing those blue eyes as she glanced his way, "Why are you staring at me like that?"

Garrett grinned. "Just remembering the day you told me I was digging in the dirt wrong."

Drea huffed. "Well you *were*. The whole point was to smooth it all out so you could draw pictures. Then smooth it all out again. You were just jabbing at it."

She demonstrated jabbing, making *oof, oof* sounds.

Garrett shook his head. Like usual when it came to him, she got it all wrong. The whole point was to spend time with her.

"Okay," she said, standing upright after circling a point on the map. "So go to this house here just off the highway. Your first. 483 Sycamore Lane. We left him in the upstairs bedroom. Now he's in rough shape, so be careful when you move him, okay? And take a gallon of water so you can make sure he's hydrated."

Goddamn but she had the most beautiful lips on God's green earth.

"Garrett."

The top one was like a little bow. And so pink even though he knew she'd rather stab her own eye out than ever wear lipstick.

"*Garrett*."

"What?" He blinked. "Sorry. Got it. Water. Third house on the left. Upstairs."

She put her hand on his and the touch of her skin sent electrical current straight to both his heart and his dick.

Fuck. It'd probably piss her off if she noticed his stiffy when she was all concerned about this friend of hers.

This *male* friend of hers.

"So who's this guy, anyway? Boyfriend or something?"

"No! *Jesus*." Then she looked back down at the map and muttered under her breath, "Why does everyone keep asking that?"

The way she looked away so quickly and the color in her cheeks said different, though. *Not that it's any goddamn business of yours*, he told himself. He wasn't a little kid anymore. Life had taught him enough lessons to know he wasn't the sort of guy that got the girl.

"Don't worry, Bells," he reassured her. "I got this."

CHAPTER NINE

DREA

"So what now?" Gisela asked Drea, crowding around her.

Drea took a step back. Whoa, whoa. She wanted to put up a hand and say, *okay kids, let's all just step the fuck back for a second.*

But just a couple of hours ago these women had been— Drea shuddered remembering the cages. And now they were... Drea looked around her at all the hopeful faces.

Well, fuck.

Was this how the Pied Piper felt?

"Okay," she said, hoping her voice sounded firmer than she felt. "We need to fortify. We might have the night or a little longer before Tillerman finds out what's happened here and—"

"Who?" asked more than one girl.

Drea ground her teeth. "Suicide. We have a little while before Suicide finds out what's happened here." She hated feeding that bastard's ego by using his stupid fucking road name, but fine, it would be easier for everyone if she just used the name they knew.

"We've restored main power and should be safe spending the night.

Galveston is only a three hour trip away but I don't think Suicide will attack directly until—"

"Suicide ain't in Galveston anymore."

Wait... *what?*

But several girls around the one that spoke up nodded their heads.

"Where is he?" Drea asked.

"He took over San Antonio," said Gisela. "It's Black Skulls territory now. I overheard Bulge and them talking. They're working with Travis. Real close."

Son of a *bitch.*

"What about the women?" Drea pressed. "All the women he was holding at Nomansland island?"

Gisela shrugged but another girl, a skinny blonde who was more bones than girl stepped forward, her entire body shaking like a leaf. "I heard Tweeker talking about girls. He said Suicide had a whole stable of girls with him when he took San Antonio."

"Motherfucker," Drea swore.

Then she took a deep breath to try to calm herself down. She'd get her women free. It just might take a little longer. And in the meantime, *these* women were depending on her now.

"Okay, well for right now, that's good for us. With the shit Travis is pulling, Suicide will be balls deep in the civil war that's brewing."

Drea looked around at the group of women. Everywhere she looked, she saw cutting clavicles and too-sharp cheekbones and if they lifted their shirts to expose their bellies, she knew she'd be able to count their ribs. A pussy was enough to sell a woman without bothering to put weight on her.

She took a deep breath and focused on the task in front of her. "We'll fortify and stay put for a couple weeks. Get you guys healthy and fed."

She nodded toward Billy. "Billy here is a doctor."

She didn't miss the way several of the women still cringed away from him.

"He won't hurt you. If he so much as lays a hand on you, you let me know and I'll chop his balls off." She thought of Bulge. "You know I'm good for it."

Laughter went through the crowd and Billy shifted behind her, his crossed arms moving lower to cover his family jewels.

"No but seriously. He's a good guy."

She met Billy's gaze as she said it and his eyebrows dropped, like he was confused but also moved that she'd say such a thing.

But it was true. He didn't have to help her. He'd put his life on the line for her, a complete stranger.

No, not for you—just so he could score big.

She frowned and turned back to the girls.

"Okay, so first things first, help yourselves to the kitchens. Try not to eat too much, too quickly. Then we can—"

"Belladonna! Peewee's back with the man you sent him to get."

Drea didn't even try for dignity as she ran out of the room for the front of the lobby where Garrett half-carried half-dragged Eric through the door.

"Eric!" Drea shouted.

Jesus, he looked so much worse than when they'd left him only hours before. His cheeks were flushed but the rest of his skin was an odd waxy color. His eyes were slits and Drea didn't know how much he was comprehending about what was going on around him.

"Come on, let's get him to an elevator." She turned back to the girls. "Gisela, which apartment should we go to?"

Gisela ran toward them, pulling out a keycard. "This is a master key. On the fourth floor, apartment 401 to the left of the elevator. Bulge kept it for visitors. It should be clean."

Drea nodded, eyes going to Billy even though she was still speaking to Gisela. "And the pharmacy? We're going to need antibiotics."

"Anything like that, all..." Gisela leaned in, whispering, "...*product*, it's up on the second floor. They store it in a locked room you need old keys for." Gisela held the same old-fashioned key ring from earlier. It was odd to see antiques like those used in an otherwise modern apartment but Drea grabbed them and then waved Gisela forward.

"Come with us and show me."

"Maya too," Gisela said. "She used to study nursing."

Drea nodded as she helped Garrett get Eric onto the elevator. The other girls joined them, along with Billy. Drea swore she could feel the energy vibrating off him every moment they came closer to him finally getting his fix. Which pissed her the fuck off.

She glared at him. "You help him first. Then I don't care what the fuck you do afterwards. Just that by late tomorrow, you need to be sober enough again to start looking over the girls. Got it?"

Billy looked wounded by her words or her tone or whatever. Tough shit.

He was what he was and she wasn't dumb enough to think that he'd magically become a good guy who cared about anything other than his next fix.

He could stay fucked up for days if she didn't still need him so much.

First they took Eric to the fourth floor apartment and got him settled in one of the three bedrooms there. Then they all headed back down to the second floor and the locked room.

The apartment complex had been very modern, probably built right before The Fall. There were lots of windows and lots of lights. A lot of them were burnt out, but the effect was still almost magical after getting used to a world where, when the sun went down, everything went dark apart from firelight.

They passed a small open sitting areak a game room with several pool tables, and what looked like it might have once been a conference room.

The glass walls between some of the rooms had spider-cracks in it, other panels were shattered completely. And everything else was dirty. The carpets were filthy and there was a sour odor to the air.

"Bikers," Drea muttered with disgust as Gisela put a key in the lock of a door at the end of the hall. It was the one room with solid walls instead of glass, including a hefty metal door complete with biometric scanner.

"We need the keycard, too," Gisela said, peering at the setup more closely. "And it looks like it also requires a hand print and brain scan."

Drea had picked up a keycard off Bulge so she held it up and a lock clicked, but the door didn't open.

"Whose prints?" Billy asked.

"I'll go get Bulge," Garrett volunteered and Drea swallowed bile back down at the thought of dragging that man's dead body around the building so they could open secret doors.

But when Garrett reappeared a few minutes later, he wasn't dragging a body. He only held a bloody towel cradled to his chest.

Drea fought not to turn away in disgust when she realized what it meant. She focused instead on the task at hand, swiping the keycard in front of the censor.

When prompted, Garrett put the stump of Bulge's hand on the hand plate.

"Who knows how to reprogram this shit?" Drea asked. "Cause I'm not hanging on to that bastard's corpse."

"I think Carrie is good with computers," Gisela said. "She was interning in Silicon Valley and had just come home for a few weeks when Xterminate hit."

Drea nodded. "Get her on it." She pushed through the door as soon as it clicked open and paused in her tracks at what she saw. "Holy shit."

"Holy *shit*," Billy echoed from behind her.

Drea swung on him, her finger up in warning but he already had his hands up. "I know, I know. We're just here for Eric."

"Good." Drea turned back to the shelves full of bricks of heroin. "This building was barely fortified." She shook her head. "And they had *this much* product up here?"

There were shelves and shelves *full* of the white bricks. And even more shelves full of all sorts of prescriptions. God, it looked like half the contents raided in south Texas must have ended up here."

"They're the kings in this area," Gisela said. "They kill and terrorize the townspeople. Who was gonna challenge the Black Skulls in their own territory?"

Drea shook her head. "Well look how easy it was to topple the kings. Just one girl and her trusty sidekick." She punched Billy on the shoulder. A little harder than was strictly necessary. But he was doing that weird thing where he looked at her with that befuddled expression. Was he overwhelmed by all the drugs? God, she'd have to watch him so he didn't OD, wouldn't she? It would be all too easy with access to this much H.

"Hey," she snapped in front of his face. "Focus. Find antibiotics and whatever else you'll need for surgery."

"I'll help," Maya said, quietly slipping into the room. Drea had all but forgotten the small woman was there.

Billy blinked and then started looking around the room. It wasn't very big. It was more than a closet but smaller than a conference room. Maybe a storage room. He moved around the various standing shelves.

It was Maya who several moments later called out, "Here. There are antibiotics over here."

Drea hurried around the shelves and saw Billy piling medical supplies in a black duffel bag.

Bandages. A sealed syringe. What looked like a suture kit. A big plastic bottle of hydrogen peroxide. More items Drea thought might be for making a cast. Then he zipped it up and they were ready to go.

Maya came around the corner with several small vials of clear liquid and a pill bottle. Billy examined them and nodded, handing them back. "Hold on to those."

Drea couldn't get back to Eric's side quickly enough.

"Prop the door open," she told Gisela over her shoulder as she rushed to the elevator. "And get Connie on seeing what she can do to reprogram the biometrics."

"Okay, but we might need you to come down to scan your eye and palm print."

Drea just shook her head. "Use yours and give access to anyone else you trust. I'm leaving you in charge of this room."

Drea punched the elevator door button and stepped inside.

She barely heard Gisela's, "Really?"

Drea looked back toward her. "Yes. Of course."

The last thing she saw before the doors closed was Gisela's shocked but pleased face.

———

It took Billy and Maya over an hour to clean out and sterilize Eric's wounds. Drea stayed for every gory moment of it. The deep gash in Eric's upper arm had swollen with infection.

Thankfully morphine had been among the goodies in the Magical Storage Closet O' Drugs. Drea didn't care if it was wasteful to spend it on someone who wasn't having major surgery. Eric was her... her, her friend, he was her *friend*, dammit. And in this one instance she'd forget about the greater good and all that shit.

Finally, *finally*, Billy had all Eric's wounds cleaned, he'd stitched the big gash, and he was just finishing up with the cast on Eric's forearm.

"There we go," Billy said, using the last of the roll he'd been wrapping to create Eric's cast. "In four to six weeks, he'll be good as new."

Drea sucked in a huge breath and held it. Jesus, was she about to cry? Fuck, this day had officially been too long. She nodded and turned away from Billy while she tried to get her shit together.

They'd started out this morning with no food, a plan she hadn't really believed had much chance of success, and Eric dead on his feet.

And now—

She swallowed and blinked hard, over and over. God, she would *not* cry. She'd taken over as leader of this MC compound. She was a badass. She'd chopped off a guy's *dick* for Christ sake.

A woman who did that couldn't afford to have fucking *feelings*. Not if she was going to go ahead with all the things she still had planned. Because this fight wasn't done. It was barely even started.

But Eric was safe now. He was going to be okay. She sat down on the bed beside him, her face still averted from Billy.

She clasped Eric's good hand. It was dirty. All of him was from sleeping on the ground two nights in a row.

She reached over and rifled through the duffle Billy brought up from the pharmacy room, grabbing a packet of moist towelettes. Then carefully, starting at Eric's brow, she washed the grime off his skin. Down his sloping nose and to his cheeks. One and then the other.

He stirred, turning towards her touch and her heart skipped a beat.

But before she could even begin to decipher any of her complicated feelings, Billy spoke up from behind her.

"He's a lucky man."

She ran her hand down her own face, swiping away any tears that may or may not have been there and then turned toward Billy with a glare. "I don't know what you're talking about."

But Billy didn't call her on her bullshit.

No, he had that look on his face he'd had earlier.

"What you did today..." his voice trailed off, his brows scrunched together as he gestured behind him. "Standing up to those guys, fucking owning their asses."

He shook his head. "And then saving all those women." His brows scrunched even deeper. "But not just that. Like, you saved them, but it was more. You, I don't know... you gave them a reason to live, too. You gave them a purpose. When you lose everything..." He looked down. "You don't know how important what you just did was."

Drea just shook her head. "I only did what anyone w—"

"No," Billy cut her off sharply, his eyes coming back to hers. "That's bullshit. No one would do what you just did. No one else in the whole damn world. Believe me," he laughed darkly. "I've fucking seen people. They're selfish assholes." He continued holding her gaze. "I'm a selfish asshole."

Then his eyes went frantic. "But I don't want to be. I want to quit. For you. I swear I was a good guy once. You make me want to be that guy again." Then he reached into his pockets and pulled out a pill bottle. He hurried forward and slammed it on the nightstand. "Here. I took it when we were in the supply closet."

Drea huffed out a breath, shaking her head. "Unbelievable." Once an addict, always an addict.

Billy winced and then he reached in the other pocket and came out with three more pills that he tossed on the nightstand beside the bottle. "And those are the three that I already took out of the bottle."

Drea stood up and got in his face, furious. "Did you take any before you started working on Eric?"

"No, no, I swear I didn't." Billy held up his hands. "I swear on my mother's name."

The way his voice got choked up as he said it, Drea thought he meant it.

Still, he was a fucking addict. It didn't matter how earnest his promises were today. She stared at him.

Dammit, she did *not* need this right now.

So you just throw him away because he's inconvenient?

"Fuck," she shouted, digging her fingers into her scalp and massaging her skull. She'd been an inconvenience once.

And tossed out like yesterday's trash without a thought.

Billy had winced at her outburst, but he still stood there, face open. Waiting for her to break him or save him.

Which wasn't fucking fair. She wasn't anyone's salvation.

"Number one," she pointed her finger in his face, "I'm not fucking perfect. Don't put me on some damn pedestal because I don't want to deal with your shit when I fall off it, got it?"

He nodded rapidly.

"Two. Do you have any more pills on you? Or any other shit?"

"No." He gestured at the nightstand. "That's all of it."

"I don't believe you," she said. "And I'm not going to. For a good long while, so get used to it. Now empty your damn pockets. All of them. Inside fucking out."

He hurried to comply, pulling his pockets inside out.

"Back ones too."

He did.

"Shoes and socks off. You know what? Just strip completely down to your boxers."

His neck colored but he was more than happy to drop his drawers. When she patted him down, she couldn't help but to notice his stiffy and she rolled her eyes. Men. Then again, she had yet to change out of her Boobzilla little black dress, so what did she expect?

"Three," she ticked off on her fingers as she pulled back. "If we do this, you commit to fucking doing it, got it? You get *one* chance with me. All in. No redos. So. Are you in?"

He immediately opened his mouth and she clamped her hand over it.

His whole body shuddered at her touch and Drea almost stepped back, her breath hitching.

What the—

Because she'd felt it too.

Down all the way through her chest, zinging straight to her sex and all the way onwards to her toes.

She kept her hand on his mouth, but suddenly the connection

between them felt electric. She had to swallow before she was able to speak again.

"Really think about it," she said, her voice little more than a whisper. The words that sprang to mind were, *Don't break my heart.* What she said was, "If you break your promise, you're dead to me."

Billy gulped. Hard. His Adam's apple bobbed up and down but he didn't break her gaze. She pulled her hand away from his mouth.

"I promise."

"Okay." She stepped back from him and turned to her own little bag. In addition to her Glock, she'd added a few goodies she'd found in the garage. She had her back to him as she pulled out one item. "I'm going to hold you to that. But right now I need to sleep. Not babysit you while withdrawal starts."

"You won't have to. Drea, I swear, I'll—"

She felt him move closer behind her and she spun, locking one handcuff on his left wrist and the other on her right wrist.

"What—?" he exclaimed in surprise as soon as the metal cuff closed around his arm.

"PeeW—" Drea started to shout before she stopped herself. "Garret," she amended. "Can you come in here?"

Moments later, Garrett appeared in the doorway. He immediately frowned seeing her handcuffed to Billy.

"Bella—"

"Ugh. If I'm calling you Garrett, you gotta cut out with the Bella. It's *Drea.*" She took several steps forward, dragging Billy along with her. She put her free hand on Garrett's upper arm and squeezed. "Thanks for tonight."

He gave her a lopsided grin. "Gotta say *Drea,* you always were a pain in the butt." His grin faded and he nodded at her, his face solemn. "But what you did tonight needed doing. It was a long time coming." His eyes dropped to the floor and he swallowed hard. "You did what I never— I thought that if I saved a girl here or there then it meant—" He stopped abruptly and shook his head at himself. Then he moved like he was going to turn away from Drea but she grabbed his arm to stop him.

He'd saved girls?

One look at him and she knew if she asked him about it he wouldn't tell her any more. But it meant she was right about him. He was a good man. Worth saving tonight.

She hugged him. She meant it just to be a quick embrace but he hugged her back. In a really, really tight hug that was only a tad awkward with her handcuffed to Billy.

But being surrounded in Garrett's warm bear hug felt so good. It made her feel safe... and terrified at the same time.

Because everyone kept talking about how strong she was. About how she'd done the impossible tonight. About how she was some kind of savior.

Did they not realize she was holding on by a thread? That every moment out there when she'd been dancing in front of Bulge she'd been milliseconds away from completely losing her shit, sure she was about to die?

When she'd climbed on top of Bulge and reached down, pretending to pleasure herself as she reached for the switchblade she'd hidden up her own damn cooch, for at least three solid heartbeats, she couldn't find the damn thing.

She was like, shit, shit, where the fuck is it? Did it fall out? Or is it like up near my cervix? *WHAT THE FUCK AM I GONNA DO?*

But then her fingers touched metal and she pulled it out and then she grabbed his dick and started slicing and the blood was—

She buried her face even deeper in Garrett's chest.

And that was when she realized.

She couldn't do this alone.

Fuck.

She couldn't. What was she going to—

But...

What if she didn't have to?

Do it alone?

She pulled back from Garrett, eyes wide as she looked up at him, then to Billy, then over at Eric snoring lightly on the bed.

What if...?

No. That was crazy.

She always thought the Marriage Raffle was insane.

One woman with all those men?

But that wasn't the part she'd objected to, really, was it? Her problem was with the fact that the woman had no choice.

But if Drea did the choosing...

Her eyes flicked around the room, heartbeat racing.

"Drea?" Garrett asked. "You okay? What's going on in that head of yours?"

She swallowed and gave Garrett's arm another squeeze. She offered a weak smile. "I'm not sure, to be honest. I think I need some sleep."

He nodded, stepping back like he was going to leave.

"Wait," she said, following him and again dragging Billy along. "Don't go."

Garrett's eyebrows scrunched like he was confused.

"I need to sleep. But I won't be able to unless I know you're close by. Can you stay in the apartment?"

His features relaxed and if she wasn't wrong, she thought he looked pleased at her request. And when he said, "Anything for you, Drea. Always," was it just her, or did the words seem more significant than just surface niceties?

"That gonna be a problem?" He nodded toward where she was handcuffed to Billy?

"Oh, right," Drea said. "He's the reason I first called you in here. Can you take those pills on the nightstand and promise not to give him any no matter how much he begs, threatens, or whines? The next few days are gonna be rough."

Garrett's eyes narrowed.

"Get some sleep," Garrett said. "Drea." He smiled like he liked the sound of her name on his lips.

She nodded and he closed the door. Yes. Sleep. She was obviously delirious if she was considering what she'd just been considering.

She shook her head at herself then looked down at Eric. It would probably be better to go sleep in one of the other rooms. But while having Garrett in the same apartment was close enough, she couldn't seem to bring herself to leave Eric's room. She'd been so scared as they walked away from the farm house this morning. So sure she'd never see him again.

No, she needed him close. So she and Billy helped scoot his uncon-scious form close up against the wall and then she laid down beside him, on her back. She intertwined her fingers with his good hand as Billy laid down on her other side, sandwiching her in. It was a queen-sized mattress, but still a tight fit.

And yet, with both their warm bodies pressed in on either side of her, it was the first time other than when she'd been in Garrett's arms that she felt like she could *breathe*. That she felt like maybe, just maybe, she'd be okay.

A delusion, obviously.

The odds were stacked impossibly high against her.

But maybe for just tonight, she'd let herself pretend...

CHAPTER TEN

ERIC

Eric wasn't alone in bed.

The thought penetrated through the fog slow. *Not alone.* He frowned, his eyes still closed. The body next to him was warm. And soft. Nothing like the bony angles of guys he'd bunked with during the war.

No, it was a woman in bed with him.

Eric blinked his eyes. Or tried to. Jesus, why were his eyelids so heavy?

Because you're dreaming, dumbass.

Right. That was the only thing that made sense.

Still, he fought against the sandbags weighing down his eyelids and turned his head toward the warm body at his side.

Thick blonde dreadlocks.

His heartbeat sped up.

Drea.

What the hell was Drea doing in bed with him? And why the hell did she feel so damn good exactly where she was?

Most people's faces were completely relaxed in sleep, but not Drea. There was still a small frown furrowing her brow and her lips had a slight purse to them. Was she having a dream... inside his dream?

Eric blinked again and went to lift his arm to wipe at his eyes when—

Jesus, what the—

A thick white cast covered his left arm from the elbow down to his hand. He rotated his arm and yep, it was a cast. And the rest of his arm where the pavement had ripped and torn at his skin—it was all bandaged up, too.

And damn, now that he was looking at it and thinking about it, his arm hurt like a motherfucker. His raw skin stung and the fracture in his forearm ached with a teeth-grinding intensity.

Did that mean...? Eric's head swung back to Drea on his other side.

This wasn't a dream.

At the same time he looked back at Drea, he realized her body was jerking in rhythmic spasm. What on earth?

Eric locked his jaw against the pain as he lifted up a little to look across Drea's body—where he saw Billy who was—

What the fuck? Why was Billy handcuffed to Drea? And why was he tugging at the cuffs like he thought he could get his wrist through the cuff if he just yanked hard enough? Every time he did it, it tugged on Drea's body through the little chain binding their cuffs.

"What are you doing?" Eric asked.

Billy looked up at Eric, face blanching. "Oh— I, I— I just have to go to the bathroom. Didn't want to wake you guys."

"Well we're awake now," Drea grumbled, lifting the hand not attached to Billy's to wipe down her face.

First she turned to Eric. He'd never been so... well, so up close and personal with her before. Theirs had always been more of a stand at a distance and yell angrily at each other sort of relationship. So this— having her pressed up all against one side of his body, not to mention the way she was looking at him—it was something new. Something he didn't even know how to name, much less to deal with.

Still, he couldn't take his eyes away from her face. Had she always had that little sprinkle of freckles across her nose?

"Where are we?" he asked, proud he was managing human language while being lost in the deep cerulean of her eyes. They were like the Caribbean sea he used to see pictures of in magazines.

He didn't like how her eyebrows dropped in concern at his answer. "Do you even remember Garrett bringing you here? We had to leave you behind at a farmhouse this morning. But then we took the compound and I was able to send Garrett to go bring you here."

Took the—? "Compound?" The last thing he remembered they'd just found the Colorado River and were making camp for the night. No, maybe he vaguely remembered waking up the next morning? But everything after that was a blur.

His confusion must have shown on his face but Drea just smiled and reached up, cupping his cheek with her free hand.

Eric's breath went uneven for a moment.

Okay, seriously. What the *hell* was going on here?

Who was this woman and what had she done with the prickly, sarcastic woman who barely seemed to tolerate him most of the time?

"Oh, we had a little run in with some bikers," she said easily.

Bikers? Holy sh—

"But it's all taken care of. How are you feeling?"

Eric sat up a little more, swearing at the spike of pain that shot up his arm.

"He's in pain," Billy said from Drea's other side. "If you just tell me where Garrett put that bottle of pills, I can—"

Drea's head whipped around so fast, her dreadlocks smacked Eric in the face.

"Jesus Christ, it hasn't even been twenty-four hours and you're already trying to bail on your sobriety?" She shook her head.

Sobriety? What the hell was going on?

"No!" Billy said, too loudly. "I wasn't going to. I promise. I was just going to—"

"Fucking addicts," Drea growled, sitting up and swinging her legs over the side of the bed. "Don't think you can get away with fucking lying to me." She stabbed her finger in Billy's face.

For a second it looked like he was going to keep protesting, but then his face fell. "Shit, I'm so sorry, Drea. But it *hurts*. Everywhere. My fucking *muscles* feel like they're being stabbed by a thousand tiny needles from the inside out. I was thinking it'd be smarter to wean me off. Like, smaller and smaller doses every day until—"

"Nope," Drea cut him off. "Cold turkey or I'm done." She slashed her hand through the air. "One chance. This is it. Take it or leave it."

Billy's mouth dropped open like a fish out of water. "But I mean, if you'd just—"

"Take it or leave it," Drea said, even louder. "We're in the middle of a goddamned revolution. Civil war. You think I have time to sit around and babysit a junkie while he detoxes? Fuck no."

Billy winced at her words but it didn't stop her.

"This is the last fucking thing I have time for." Then her voice gentled just the slightest bit. "But we should be safe here for a little while and it would be good for everyone to rest up a few days." She took a deep breath in and then let it out.

Eric didn't miss the way her fingers intertwined with Billy's. What the—! He'd only been out of it for like a day. Had they gone and— In such a short while? That wasn't fucking fair! He'd known her for months and—

What? No. What the fuck was he thinking? He forced his eyes away from their clasped hands, swiveling his head toward the wall. He swallowed hard, a hollow space opening up in his chest. He didn't know why. It wasn't like he had feelings for Drea or anything. They hated each other. They could barely stand to be in the same room without bickering or biting each other's heads off.

"And I think you're worth it, Billy. I'm willing to invest the time in you. To see you through this. So this is your last chance to bow out. You staying or going? Let me know now."

The silence went on so long that Eric ended up looking back over at Billy. And found him staring deeply into Drea's eyes. The pit in his chest fell all the way down through his feet. Shit, there really *was* something between them.

So why the fuck had she slept by Eric like that?

Well, she'd been sleeping beside Billy too, dumbass. They were fucking handcuffed together.

"I'm in, Drea. I'm in, I swear."

But Drea just shook her head. "I don't want your swearing or your promises or any other bullshit. I know in the next few days you'll promise your left nutsack and your goddamned firstborn if it meant you'd get another fix. But Eric here is a witness." She looked his way and he nodded. "We're getting you through this withdrawal. What you do with it after that is up to you."

Billy swallowed hard but then he nodded.

"Eric," she said, turning back to him, blue eyes flashing like she was daring him to disagree with her. "We helped save your life, so now you're gonna help me with Billy through this shit. Got it?"

Ahh, now that was more like the Drea he knew.

He nodded. "Whatever I can do to help."

She gave him a sharp nod, then swung her legs over the side of the bed and stood up.

"Now let's go to the bathroom cause I gotta piss," she said.

"Um...!" Billy exclaimed as Drea dragged him along after her to the ensuite bathroom. Billy shut the door behind them but Eric could still hear her yelling at him to *close his damn eyes, already.*

Half of Eric's mouth tilted up. Okay. Well. This should be... interesting?

Dear God, why had Eric ever agreed to help Drea get Billy through withdrawals? Jesus Christ, of course Eric had heard of the concept but he had no idea...

"Let me have my pills you fucking whore! I didn't mean it. I fucking hate you and just want the shit you promised me when I came into this fucking nightmare."

Eric stomped across the room to where they'd cuffed Billy to the headboard. They'd only been at it for two days and already he was ready to kill the motherfucker.

"Whoa, whoa, big guy," Garrett said, grabbing Eric and averting him to the side before he could get to Billy. "He doesn't know what the fuck he's saying right now."

"Please," Billy cried, hands scratching down his head and up and down his arms. He was covered in sweat and his eyes were puffy and red. He was a disgusting fucking mess. "It hurts." Fat tears ran down hi red cheeks. "It hurts so much." He collapsed to his side on the ground, curling up into a ball, sobbing. "Please," he whimpered, over and over.

Eric turned away in disgust.

Any compassion he'd had for the man had quickly dried up the first time he started screaming that Drea was a mean bitch for doing this to him.

As far as Eric was concerned, Billy was getting exactly what had been coming to him.

So he'd had it rough after the Fall—in some of his fevered mutterings he'd talked about losing his mom and sisters. Well tough shit.

Everyone had lost someone. Everyone had lived through terrible fucking violence. But they didn't get to just check the fuck out by swallowing a little pill, now did they?

So sorry, but the fucker wasn't getting Eric's sympathy.

But he had Drea's.

For whatever fucking reason Eric couldn't fathom. This was the same woman who's single-minded focus ever since he'd met her had been to get back to the women she'd left behind to free them. And now that she actually had some power at her disposal—guns, vehicles, an army of women who would follow her to hell and back she was so revered for freeing them—she was locked in this apartment, ignoring every one and everything helping this asshole through withdrawal. She'd only gone downstairs a few times to get a status update from some women she'd dubbed her 'lieutenants' but other than that, she was up here, locked in with Billy.

Eric shook his head.

Most of the time Drea looked like she shook off whatever taunts or bad names Billy threw at her, but sometimes, he'd see something land. It was subtle. There'd be just the slightest tightening in Drea's jaw. The stiffening of her spine. She wasn't immune to all the verbal digs. The pathetic begging. Eric could see that got to her too. And that was when Eric wanted to rip Billy's fucking head off.

Like right now. Every time Billy whimpered, *please*, Drea flinched.

"All right, that's it," Eric said, exploding off the chair he'd been sitting on. "Drea, you need to take five. Actually, no, screw that. You need to take an hour. Or five. Garrett and I can watch over this piece of shit."

But in response, Drea glared over at Eric like *he* was the problem.

"Actually, I think it's time for you to take a walk. Garrett, go take Eric to get some dinner for us."

Eric scoffed, throwing his hands up. "Drea, be serious, I'm not going to—"

"Oh yes you will." Drea got up from the stool where she'd been perched reading an old book. "You will leave this room right this second and go with Garrett before I lose my shit on you."

What. The. Fuck?

Eric just shook his head. Dammit, she couldn't make anything easy. Not one single goddamned thing.

You know what? Fuck it. Maybe he did need a little bit of space from all this. He grabbed his shoes off the ground and stormed out of the room, trying to hold back the grimace of pain from showing on his face.

Half a day of watching Billy go through withdrawal was enough to have him refusing to take pain meds. Drea said he was being stupid. That taking them for a week wouldn't turn him into an addict. Fuck that. Eric wasn't going near that poison.

Garrett hopped to his feet and followed Eric out of the room, dropping the old pre-Fall magazine he'd been flipping through.

Eric shook his head, jaw locked. He glared back at Garrett. "You don't have to jump to do everything she says like a damn trained dog."

"Hey man," Garrett narrowed his eyes, "maybe you wanna take the asshole down a notch? Or fucking ten?"

"Whatever."

Eric stormed through the apartment and pushed through the double doors to the small balcony off the living room.

He sucked in a long breath of deep air as soon as he braced his good hand on the railing and dropped his head down.

The sun beat down on his head and he closed his eyes.

Only to be yanked backwards the next moment.

"Jesus, are you fucking crazy?"

Garrett pulled him back into the apartment and shut the glass doors behind him, heavy curtains swinging. "You're lucky you didn't just get your head blown off. We don't know who the hell is watching this place. Now let's go get some damn food."

Eric jerked away from Garret's hold on his good shoulder. What the fuck was this guy's problem? Around Drea he was like this over-grown puppy—so eager to please and almost desperate for any scrap of affection she shot his way. But as soon as she was out of earshot he turned back into an intimidating hulk who glared at everyone and barely spoke a word.

So Eric was surprised when, as they stepped onto the elevator, Garrett spoke up again. "Her mom was an addict, you know."

Eric felt his eyebrows all but hit his hairline. "What?" He turned to Garrett. The big guy just stared ahead at the elevator wall as he nodded.

"Yeah. Drea's always been real messed up about it. Her mom OD'd when Drea was like, six. And Drea lived with her most of that time, too. I don't know the whole story, but Child Services took Drea away from her ma after she like, attacked Drea when she was high or some shit. That's when she came to live with her dad here at the MC."

Eric blinked. This was a helluva lot more information than he'd bargained on in one elevator ride.

"Domino always bashed on what a skanked out crack whore Drea's mom was, but if you watched Drea's face, she'd get real defensive. I heard them get into this big fight over it once. Drea shouting that Domino should have done more to try to help her mom. That it was his fault she died. Domino just fucking lost it. He pulled out his gun and emptied an entire round into the wall."

The elevator dinged and opened on the first floor.

Eric was silent as they both stepped out.

Garrett finally looked his way. "Well shit got real quiet after that. So the whole damn club heard Domino when he yelled back that he had tried to get Cathy—that was her mom's name—that he'd tried to get Cathy clean over and over again. Apparently he'd sent her to rehab right after they got married and he realized just how bad her problem was. She started using again a few months after she got back, though.

Then he made her go again as soon as they found out she was pregnant with Drea."

They headed through the lobby toward the kitchens. Gisela was there, leading a group of women through some basic exercises and what looked like self-defense moves.

"I guess it stuck for a little bit that time. At least through the pregnancy. Domino thought maybe she'd kicked it for good. You know, cause they had a family now."

"But she didn't," Eric said.

"Nope." Garrett shook his head. "She made it a couple years that time. But then she started back up. She kept it hidden for longer. But only cause she was boning Domino's VP so he could keep her supplied in drugs."

"Damn," Eric said.

"Domino found out."

"Did he kill her?"

"That's what Drea wanted to know. But no. Apparently he let his club think that he did. But in reality, he sent her off to rehab again. He told her it was her last chance. If she could get clean and stay clean for three years, then he'd let her see her daughter again."

Garrett made eye contact with Eric again. "She asked for a brick of H instead, as payment for disappearing forever. She OD'd three days later."

"Shit." Eric looked back at the elevator right before they pushed through the door that led to the kitchens.

"So yeah, Drea's always been a little sensitive when it comes to addicts."

Chattering voices echoed down the hallway, louder as Garrett pulled open the kitchen door.

"You heard what Belladonna said. We're each supposed to get at least twelve hundred calories worth per day," said a brunette who stood at the big industrial stove, cutting off what sounded like many dissenting voices. "So no, we cannot cook all of the steak to eat at once. The fruit and the vegetables that will go bad and can't be frozen? That we *do* need to eat in the next few days. So if you're on salad duty, get to your station. Now. Where are my bakers?"

Several women held up their hands.

The brunette waved them up to the front of the crowd. "We found where they were keeping the active dry yeast so tonight you can make actual bread instead of just biscuits. Okay, next up is— Oh!" The woman startled at noticing Eric and Garrett, jumping backwards and banging into the stove where several large pots of what looked like stew bubbled. Her eyes darted around like she was looking for some sort of weapon.

Eric's stomach sank. Shit. These women—he couldn't even fathom what they'd lived through. Immediately his thoughts went to his daughter.

Sophia's safe, he reminded himself. He'd called Nix's sat phone as soon as he heard Drea had one and Sophia was safely ensconced with a group in an extensive cave system in northern San Antonio. And for all his many sins, at least he'd kept her from a life like what these women had lived through.

Apparently the cave was getting crowded, though, because in addition to Eric's people from Jacob's Well, there was half an army down there, too. The one the President had sent down to fortify Jacob's Well right before he'd been assassinated.

"I'm sorry, ma'am," Eric said, gentling his voice to a soft baritone. "Drea just sent us down here to get some food for the four of us." He looked around at all the skeletal women and immediately felt ashamed. "If you have any to spare, that is."

Eric wanted to get back to his daughter and his people as soon as possible but Drea was right. They needed this week's respite for more than Billy's withdrawal. The women were half starved and in bad shape.

This was one of the only places anywhere close by with the food, supplies, and amenities they'd needed to regroup. Some of the girls were so weak they might not have a chance immediately going on the run.

Garrett was spending most of his time down in the garage fixing up their transport out of there but it would take a couple more days too. And in the meantime, this place had the basic fortifications they needed to protect themselves. It wasn't like they could hide their group of fifty anywhere else very easily.

The brunette continued watching him distrustfully but finally, she nodded. "Anything for Belladonna."

"Four bowls," she snapped and a woman down the line scurried off to the side of the kitchen, returning moments later with a short stack of bowls.

"Is stew all right? Shit, I forgot to save some of the biscuits from breakfast. But if you give us thirty minutes, we can have a new batch whipped up and—"

"No," Eric held a hand up. "It's not necessary. You know you all are Drea's first priority, not herself."

Eric hadn't said it to get brownie points—it was just a fact—but as a pleased murmur went through the crowd, Eric realized just how much Drea meant to these women. Deservedly so.

When he heard exactly what she'd done to take the compound, Jesus, he'd almost had a heart attack. He'd been too furious at her at the time for taking such *insane* risks to really appreciate it for the amazing accomplishment it was.

She'd risked everything—she'd risked her *life*—for what? For these women who had all been strangers to her before two days ago?

And for you, asshole.

"It's starting to sink in, huh," Garrett said as the brunette handed them each two bowls and spoons.

"What?" Eric asked, still distracted by thoughts of Drea.

"Just how lucky we are to even get to share the same air space as her." He nodded up toward the ceiling and Eric got his meaning.

And he was right. Every day by Drea's side was a fucking privilege.

Neither Eric nor Garrett said a word as they took the elevator back up to the apartment. When they got inside, the first thing they heard was Billy screaming obscenities at Drea.

Eric couldn't help his back going stiff but he told himself to calm his shit as he walked toward the bedroom with the steaming bowl.

As soon as he pushed the door open, his eyes went to Drea. She was as beautiful as ever and— Shit, did he really just admit that to himself? But fuck, there was no denying it. She was a beautiful woman.

Even with dark circles under her eyes and shoulders slumped like she was carrying the entire weight of the world on her shoulders.

She was fucking beautiful. And Lord knew it wasn't just skin deep. She was the complete package. She was more. She was—

Everything.

She was *everything*.

Drea turned her tired eyes to him. "Well are you just gonna stand there in the doorway with your dick in your hand or are you gonna bring me that stew?"

Eric grinned.

"Your wish is my command."

CHAPTER ELEVEN

DREA

Drea laid on her bed and thought about Mama. It was all she did, seemed like. Laid on her bed. Thought about Mama. Cried. Thought about Mama some more. Missed Mama. Cried some more.

She hadn't seen Mama in four whole months.

If only she hadn't tried to wake Mama up that time.

She knew *Mama was always bad after she poked herself with that needle. Drea* knew *better. She shoulda just gone to her room and stayed there and not bothered Mama till she was feeling better. Yeah Mama had been poking herself more and more lately and Drea was hungry more often than not but that wasn't the point.*

Sometimes Mamas needed looking after and Drea hadn't done a good enough job. Then people came and took her away from Mama 'cause of it.

And now she had to live with the big man who said he was her Daddy. Sometimes she thought Mama might be right and he was the Devil because he sure was big and scary looking enough to be him. He had a tattoo of a skull on his face, right over where the bones would be.

He shoved the door open to her room where she'd been playing with her

Barbies. One was Mama Barbie and the other was Drea Barbie and Mama Barbie was hugging Drea Barbie and telling her how much she loved her and they were dancing and they were both happy.

But then Devil Daddy shoved the door open and Drea yanked both Barbies behind her back and held her breath.

"Enough with your mopin' and caterwallin'," Devil Daddy said. "And enough with stayin' cooped up inside this room. You're a little girl. Little girls need sunshine." The shadows of his face tattoo were even more terrifying in the dim light of her bedroom and when he pointed toward her bedroom door, she scurried toward it without arguing.

But when she got to the hallway, it wasn't much better. Devil Daddy lived in what he called an Em-See. She didn't know what that meant. But she did know that everywhere she looked, there were big men with scary tattoos and they all rode loud motorcycles that made so much noise out her window at all hours of the day it hurt her ears.

"Don't worry 'bout them none," he'd said the first day he brought her up to her room. "No one'll touch a hair on your pretty head cause you're the Pres's kid. It's safe as houses for you here."

Drea wouldn't know anything about that 'cause she'd never lived in a house. She and Mama'd had an apartment for as long as she could remember. And now she had a room in this Em-See place.

She stopped in the hallway, frozen in place when she saw two of the other big Devil men staring up at her. The second floor opened up and overlooked the first and all eyes were on them.

"What the hell are y'all lookin' at?" Daddy snapped. "I'm just takin' my daughter here for a walk."

He grabbed Drea's hand and tugged her forward with enough force that she had to stumble to keep up or else she'd fall over and get dragged. She didn't want to draw any more attention from all the men downstairs so she hurried to keep up with Devil Daddy.

"Brenda," he barked once they'd gotten down the stairs. A woman sitting on a man's lap jumped up and hurried toward Daddy. "Did you get those things I asked for?"

Drea backed up and hid behind Daddy as the woman with the painted face came closer. She peeked out around him to watch furtively as the woman grinned wide, bright pink lipstick all over her teeth.

"Sure did, honey. If there's anything else Brenda can ever do for you, you know you only need to ask. I'm really good with kids, too."

She blinked lashes that were black with a lot of caked on goop and started to slide a hand down Daddy's chest. But Daddy caught her wrist almost the second she made contact and yanked it away from him. "Just the things I asked for, thanks."

Brenda's grin fell and she frowned down at Drea. Drea pulled back behind Daddy. She did not like the Brenda lady.

Brenda said something about them being behind the bar and Daddy took Drea's hand again, just long enough to get a brown paper bag from behind the bar that was as tall as Drea was.

Then Daddy led her around to the women's bathroom. He had to kick a man and woman out first, but then he told her to go in and change into the things in the bag.

Drea's mouth fell open. It was clothes? For her? She looked down at what she was wearing and felt her cheeks go pink. Did Daddy not like the purple dress she was wearing? She was careful to keep it clean. She was always real, real careful. She took real good care of her stuff cause Mama hadn't always been the best about remembering to do the laundry or buy her new stuff as she grew bigger.

Thinking about Mama made her want to start crying again, and maybe Devil Daddy could tell because he just shoved the brown paper bag at her and said, "None of that. Go on now git."

She did. But as soon as she got in the bathroom, she was sure she was gonna make Devil Daddy mad. Because she didn't know what half the things in the bag were. She held up long black leather pieces that had a sort of belt buckle on the top in confusion. Was she supposed to... She turned them around this way and that but still had no idea what to do with them.

Some of the other things were less freaky. Jeans. Okay, those she could handle. She slipped them on, one leg and then the other. They were a couple sizes too big but if she held on to them, they'd stay up. Maybe that was what the belt buckle was for? But then there were those long leather flaps that would just get in her way when she tried to walk!

Loud knocking came at the door, then Daddy's booming Devil voice: "How's it going in there?"

"Fine!" she called back, hurrying to pull the black T-shirt on over her head. It *was too big, too, and it had a scary picture of a skull on it, like the one on Daddy's face. Except this one had blood dripping off it.*

"I'm coming in, you decent?" Daddy asked.

He barely waited for her squeaked, "Yes," before he barreled in, frowning down at her. "Fucking Brenda," he swore. Drea was used to Mama saying bad words but so far Devil Daddy hadn't used any around her.

"Sorry kid," he said, running a hand through his hair and then crouching over so he was at her level. "Okay, so let's see what we can do with these. There a little big, huh?"

It was the first time he'd done that—gotten down on her level. And up close... well maybe he wasn't quite so scary. He had blue eyes, like Drea did. If she squinted her eyes a little so that they got blurry, she didn't see the face tattoo so much and his face looked, well, sorta nice, even.

"These are chaps," he explained as he undid the buckle of the leather item that had baffled her. He pulled it around her waist and looped it through the belt loops on her jeans. "You wear these over your jeans and they're kinda like a supple armor. They keep you safe when you're on the road."

Armor.

Drea liked the thought of that.

"Then they just lay over your jeans, like this." He arranged the leather flaps around her jeans, and rolled up her jeans where they bunched at her feet. "We'll get you some jeans that are your size, too. Shoulda thought of that sooner. We'll get you all new clothes. Daughter of mine oughta be dressed like a princess."

Drea bit her lip again because she didn't want to cry in front of Daddy. Why was he being so nice to her? Wasn't he supposed to be the Devil? Or was this all just pretend? He was only being nice to her now like Mama was on her good days, and then he'd turn evil on her when she wasn't expecting it?

"Then you put on the jacket like this." He helped her pull on the leather jacket. It was also too big, but he closed it up for her and grinned. "All right, you're all set. Let's go."

He held out his hand and in spite of how scared she was, she took it.

He took her out back where there was a line of huge motorcycles. Drea was terrified when he said she was gonna ride one.

She froze where she stood but Daddy just picked her up and plopped her down on the closest one. "Well, you're just a lil' bit o' nothin', ain't you? Light as a feather. Get your leg over the other side. That's right, just like that."

Drea thought she might scream in terror until he let her off, but then he did something that had her never, ever wanting to move.

He climbed on right behind her and wrapped one arm around her waist. "That's right, Lil' Bit, you're doing so good."

She immediately sank back against him. She didn't even think about it. It was just like... suddenly it was all okay.

He was her Daddy. He wasn't the Devil. Or if he was, she didn't even care. He was her Daddy. He wanted her. She was his Lil' Bit.

He liked motorcycles so she'd like motorcycles. She'd love them. She'd love everything he loved and would make him so happy he'd never have a reason to send her away.

So, even though she was terrified, when he explained that she could either put her hands on his legs or on his hands as he steered the bike, she nodded with her brow furrowed in concentration. He settled a big, heavy helmet on her head.

When he turned the bike on and the roar of the huge engine made her want to cry and hold her hands over her ears, she forced herself to keep her hands just where Daddy said. She dug her fists into the material of his jeans and held on for dear life. He pulled the bike forward and her stomach swooped.

He put his hand on her waist again as he maneuvered the bike out of the parking lot.

Then the bike took off down the road.

She screamed some. She couldn't help it. Especially on the corners.

But Daddy's big barrel chest behind her back helped steady her through the worst of it. And after maybe five or ten minutes of holding on to Daddy for all she was worth with her eyes squeezed shut, she finally opened her eyes.

Only to find they were flying.

They'd made it out of town and it was just them, the long road stretching ahead of them, pasture on all sides, and the sky, so much blue, blue sky. Blue like Daddy's eyes. Like her eyes too.

Forty-five minutes later when the ride was over, Drea could say she'd almost even enjoyed herself.

But it turned out the best part of the whole day was yet to come. Because after they pulled back into the parking lot of the Em-Cee, Daddy tugged off his helmet, then hers, and he was grinning at her. Like he was proud of her. That alone made her feel like she was still flying down the road, up off into the air into that bright sunny, blue sky.

It was his words, though, that broke her world open and brought back the sunshine. That let her start living again.

He notched his forefinger under her chin, still with that dazzling white-toothed smile of his.

"Sure do love you, Lil' Bit. Always have, always will."

But suddenly Daddy wasn't on the motorcycle looking down at her anymore.

No, she was the one looking down at him.

Cause he was on his knees.

A man stood behind him, gun pointed to the back of his head.

And Daddy, he flashed those baby blues up at Drea for one last time.

"Sure do love you, Lil' Bit. Always have, always will."

BANG.

"No!!!" Drea screamed, jerking up right in bed.

She blinked and choked on a sob, looking around frantically.

"Drea!" Eric rushed into the room, checking all around. When he didn't see anyone, he hurried to sit down on the bed beside her. "Are you okay?"

He pushed a stray dreadlock out of her face and she jumped back from him, wiping at her eyes with her forearm and then getting to her feet.

"Fine," she barked out. "I'm going to go downstairs to check on how the women are doing."

"Okay, but Drea," he stood up. She couldn't bring herself to look his direction. Not with thoughts of Daddy still so vivid in her head. God, what must Eric have thought of her coming in here and finding her like that? There were some things no one ever needed to know about her.

"What?"

"It's okay to need a shoulder to cry on sometimes."

She snapped her head to look over toward him and gave him a skewering glare. "I don't cry."

Then she jogged out of the apartment, ignoring both Garrett and Billy, and lost herself training with the women for several hours.

Gisela was a quick study at hand to hand combat and target practice. Maya was bad at both, but she still shadowed Gisela's every move. A little like Gisela seemed to shadow Drea whenever she was around.

Which she made it a point not to be. It was better that she spent most of her time upstairs. She didn't need any of these women getting attached to her. She'd teach them how to defend themselves but that was it.

She was nobody's leader. She'd learned her lesson and she'd learned it well.

When she came back upstairs several hours later, sweaty and drained from a good workout, she expected to be more relaxed.

But ever since Drea kicked Eric and Garrett out of the Withdrawal Room a few days ago, Eric had been acting... differently.

Like even the way he *looked* at her was different.

Usually when he was talking to her he seemed exasperated and right on the edge of losing his shit.

But the past few days? Like this morning?

He'd been eerily calm. And patient. Even with Billy. Eric had taken turns cuffing himself to Billy—even throughout the fourth night of withdrawal that Billy spent hugging the toilet, losing the small amount of food they'd managed to get down earlier, out one end or the other.

Drea only knew about it because Garrett told her the next morning. She'd slept like a baby in the other room.

She'd assumed she'd have to carry the burden of dealing with Billy's withdrawal entirely on her own shoulders. After all, Eric and Garrett hadn't signed up for this shit. It was her own crusade she'd decided to fight, for some damn crazy reason she still wasn't prepared to examine too closely.

But there they were, every step of the way. Garrett sponging down Billy's face. Eric urging her to go rest in the other room while he fed Billy a bowl of broth.

It had been a week since Billy'd last had any pills and finally, *finally,* he was looking like himself again.

Drea didn't know what she'd expected when she came back upstairs today. More of the same? Billy in bed, back turned towards everyone, face buried in a pillow.

But instead, he was sitting up at the dining room table with Eric and Garrett, playing cards. He looked... showered. His eyes were still bloodshot when he glanced her way but when he offered a tentative smile, it looked genuine.

Drea's chest cinched tight. Had they really done it? Were they through the worst?

After learning everything she had about her mom in that huge fight with Dad when she was eighteen, she'd spent a lot of time volunteering at an outpatient addiction treatment center in town. She knew it took around six days for the worst of the withdrawal symptoms to pass.

Still, in the middle of the worst of it with Billy, it seemed like he'd never get through it, that he'd never get better.

But now here he was, sitting there, sane and in one piece. Whole.

For how long?

Fuck it. She'd worry about that another day.

Today was one to celebrate. It was the day she'd always wished she could have with Mama. The day she'd lived over and over in her head. Mama, clear eyed and of sound mind. Finally able to be the mother Drea had always wished for and known she could be.

Drea walked straight over to Billy and threw her arms around him. For a second he didn't respond. He was just stiff in her arms.

Okay, so maybe he was still mad about the whole handcuffing thing. Fair enough. She wouldn't—

But suddenly his arms slipped around her waist and he squeezed her so tight to him she could barely breath.

"Thank you," he whispered into her hair. And if she wasn't wrong, she thought he might have— Did he just kiss her on the side of her head, right above her ear? Her breath caught and she pulled back.

For a long second, she just stared into the deep brown of his eyes. Yes, the skin around his eyes was puffy and the whites were red, but it was the *way* he was looking at her that held her still.

In the entire time she'd known Billy other than the desperate moment when he told her he wanted to quit, that he really wanted it, he'd been half-gone, his mind always on when and where he could get his next fix.

But now he was looking at her—*really* looking with a clear head for the first time.

She swallowed hard under his intense examination. His eyes dropped to her lips and her breath hiccupped.

No, no, no, she couldn't be—

She let go of him and heaved herself backwards, so violently Billy stumbled a little bit after she yanked away from him.

"Glad to see you finally sober," she said, her voice stiff as she averted her gaze. "Now try to stay that way."

With that, she turned and strode into her bedroom at the end of the hall. As she closed the door behind her, she sank back against it and pressed her palms against her forehead, squeezing her eyes shut.

What the hell was she thinking? She couldn't afford to let herself be distracted right now. The women downstairs needed her. She might not be the one to lead them, but she still needed to equip them to face the world on their own. Not to mention all the girls she'd failed back at Nomansland.

How dare she even play at being boy crazy at a time like this? What the fuck was wrong with her?

And yet, behind her closed eyes, the images that had plagued her ever since her thought experiment a few nights before—three bodies surrounding her—came back with a vengeance. Hands squeezing, mouths sucking, cocks—

She yanked her shirt off over her head as she stomped toward the bathroom. A good cold shower, that's all she really needed.

And maybe a punch in the face so she could get her priorities straight.

She shook her head at herself as she yanked her pants down her legs and kicked them off.

She'd just reached around to unclasp her bra when the door to her bedroom slammed open.

"What the hell was that back there?" Eric's voice boomed. "He's gone through hell this week and then you just—"

"What the fuck!" Drea screeched, arms covering her breasts. She hadn't taken her bra off yet—thank God—but it was so old and the lace worn so thin in spots she might as well have.

Eric's jaw literally dropped open and his eyes scanned up and down her body. Son of a bitch was just gonna stand there and gawk? Really?

Fine.

She dropped her hands to her hips and cocked her head. "Wanna take a picture for your spank bank? Cause I'll wait while you go get your camera."

Eric's eyes jerked back to her face and he took a deep breath. He pointed a finger in her direction. "Put some damn clothes on so we can have a conversation. Billy's hanging on by a thread and you doing that weird drive by didn't help."

Drea threw her hands up. "Oh, so suddenly you care about Billy? You couldn't have given less of a shit about him at the beginning of the week."

"Well I changed, didn't I? Or is your ego so far stuck up your own ass you didn't even notice?"

Drea let out an outraged noise. Son of a *bitch*. "Oh I'm sorry. I guess it was my *ego* that made me storm this damn compound just so I could get some fucking antibiotics because you would have fucking *died* without them."

Eric scoffed. "We both know you did that for *you*, not me. This was your plan all along, right? Come here. Train your army. Go after Suicide or whatever the fuck his name is."

"*Thomas*," Drea corrected with a growl.

"See," Eric held out his hand as if she'd just made his point. "Don't pretend your agenda had any altruistic motivation. You're a cold tactician. And what, you needed a doctor who'd be indebted to you? Is that what this whole week with Billy was about?"

Drea crossed the room in three strides, and with the fourth her hand was swinging. Was it bad taste to slap a man with a broken arm? When he infuriated her as much as Eric fucking Wolford? Hell *no*.

But the slap never landed. Eric grabbed her hand mid-air with his good one before she could land her blow.

And then he spun her around and slammed her back up against the wall, pressing his chest to hers so he could pin her there.

"We aren't all just little puppets in your play," he said through his teeth, getting right up in her face. "Do you have any idea what you've done to that man out there? He fucking worships you. A word from you could make or break him, don't you fucking understand that?" He slammed her wrist against the wall to emphasize his words, and Drea's chest pumped up and down as she searched Eric's eyes.

"Make or break *him?*" she asked, her voice low, eyes dropping to his lips. "Or *you?*"

For a moment, pure fury flashed across his face.

And then he was kissing her.

Oh Jesus, *yes.*

Yes, yes, yes.

She hiked her leg up around his hip and ground herself against him shamelessly. He was already rock hard.

Holy fuck, how long had he been hard? The whole time they'd been arguing?

She dug her fingers into his hair, scratching down his scalp with her nails. He growled against her lips, thrusting his tongue into her mouth.

She thrust right back until they were dueling each other with their kisses. And devouring. Not enough. She needed more. *More,* dammit.

She twirled their bodies again and then shoved Eric back until he was stumbling toward the bed. She ripped her bra the rest of the way off and then launched herself toward him, tackling him down to the mattress. She ignored his grimace of pain—his arm must have gotten jostled. But the bed was soft and he'd get over it.

Her hands went to the button of his jeans and judging by the way his hard cock jumped at her touch, she'd say he was distracted enough by other things not to be too bothered by the pain at the moment.

"Lift your goddamned hips," she ordered.

He glared at her but complied so she could jerk his pants and underwear down his thighs.

And then there he was.

All of him.

And damn but his cock was huge. She always suspected he'd have a big one. Men weren't usually as self-confident as Eric was, with such an effortless ability to lead others if they weren't packing some serious family jewels. Not a theory she'd had much opportunity to put to the test in her life, practically speaking, but damn. Eric did *not disappoint.*

Right when she moved to climb on top of him so she could feel every inch of that glorious cock stretching her to her limits, though,

Eric suddenly grabbed her with his good arm. The next second, he'd flipped her so that she was on her back and he was the one hovering over her.

"What gives you the idea you get to run this show, babe?"

Son of a— He should feel *honored* that she *deigned* to—

But then he dropped down and kissed her so ferociously again that she forgot any and all objections. She wrapped both legs around his hips and grabbed his ass.

"Get," *kiss*, "the fuck," *kiss*, "inside me," she growled.

Eric pulled back and grinned, moving his hips so that the tip of his cock dragged up and down the lips of her drenched pussy. "I don't know, babe. Not sure you're ready yet."

"You son of a—"

Again he kissed her before she could finish her sentence.

Motherfucker. She'd definitely have to shut that shit down. After. After she rode that big dick of his and reached the screaming orgasm she could already feel rising.

He reached down between them to where his cock teased her and dipped his fingers in where she needed his dick to be.

She clenched around the two fingers he slipped inside her, lifting her head off the pillow to bite at his lips. God, she'd never been like this before in bed. She'd never felt so ravenous for another human being.

So when he pulled his fingers out of her and pushed them roughly against her lips, ordering, "Suck," she opened her mouth and did what he said.

Her scent and taste was nothing like she might have expected. It was so dirty. And so goddamned hot, having Eric on top of her, so demanding and dominant.

Which you shouldn't like.

Again, what the hell was wrong with her. She prided herself on being a strong, independent woman. Not the kind who licked at a man's fingers like a dog begging for scraps. No, she needed to put a stop to this right n—

But before she could voice any of her thoughts, Eric began thrusting in with that huge, gloriously thick cock of his.

She hadn't fucked anything other than her own fingers in years. Did sex always feel this—

"Oh!" she cried out. "Right there. Oh God, *right there.*"

He was almost all the way seated when he swiveled and jerked his hips, thrusting the last couple inches until he was sheathed inside, balls snugly against her ass.

Oh God, oh Jesus, yes. This was where he was always meant to be. Their bodies were made for each other like interlocking puzzle pieces. Only when he was inside her like this did any of the chaos of the world slow down and make sense.

Then he started thrusting, and thrusting ruthlessly.

"Come on, Drea. Come. You're going to come all around my cock, and you're going to do it quickly. You know you've been holding out on me all these months. Holding out on *us.* Just admit the truth." He leaned down for a crushing kiss. "You've wanted this as much as I have."

She jerked back from his mouth and glared at him. But she could only keep it up for a moment. Too soon her head was dipping back into the pillow as she arched her back, foot slamming into the mattress so she could thrust her pelvis up toward his with his every stroke.

She bit her lip against the scream building in her throat at the pleasure that rose higher and higher every time his pelvis ground against hers. And then there was how his cock hit that spot so deep up inside her.

Holy shit. She thought the G-spot was a myth. But oh— Was that where—? She'd never felt anything like—

"*Come*, Drea. Come because I'm ordering you to. Do it now!"

"You son of a bitch," she screamed as one of the most intense orgasms of her life ripped through her body.

"Drea, what the fuck is he doing to yo—"

Drea swung her head to the door where, through the haze of her climax, she saw Garrett and Billy standing at the doorway, jaws slack.

Eric gave another pump and then stilled inside her, head bowed to her chest. She felt the tense of his body and the rush of heat inside her as he spilled.

She clenched around him even as she reached out a hand toward the door.

"Wait! Don't go."

Billy had staggered several steps backward but he froze at her words. Garrett was as still as a statue in the doorway.

Eric lifted his head from where he'd buried it in her chest at her words, too.

All three pairs of eyes were on her now.

Three men.

Was she crazy for thinking what she was thinking?

But in the haze of her orgasm that had barely finished peaking, she just blurted it out. "I want you." Selfish, crazy or not, there it was.

She was looking at Eric when she said it, but then she turned to Garrett and Billy. "I want all of you."

Eric's body tensed over hers. God, did it hurt him to hear her say that? She had to make him understand. She cupped his cheeks with both hands and looked deep into his eyes.

And then she did something so rare for her she felt more bare than if she'd stripped completely nude and run down the street in front of her worst enemies.

"The Marriage Raffle ... If it just gave women a choice, I always thought there was a lot of good that came from it. I was even... jealous sometimes."

She dared opening her eyes at this and Eric could not have looked more shocked if she'd said she was a blue-winged fairy come to transport him to an alien planet.

She dropped her hands from his face and tried to push him off her. "Jesus is it so hard to believe that I might want a family of my own? A clan?"

"Stop trying to get away from me, dammit," Eric growled, pinning her as well as he could with his legs and one arm, his cock still hard inside her. "So let me get this straight. You want me—us," he gestured at Billy and Garrett standing silent just inside the doorway, "—to be your clan?"

"What's a clan?" Garrett's usually gravelly voice all but cracked as he asked, it came out so high-pitched. When Drea glanced over at him, she was surprised to find his eyes locked on her face and not her breasts. They'd only ever been friends growing up, but she hadn't missed the way he always checked her out. Pretty much from puberty on, his eyes had been perpetually locked on her chest until her boyfriend beat him up for it once when Garrett was fifteen.

She'd thought it was romantic at the time. More like she should have realized what a fucking psychopath her twenty-year-old boyfriend was to beat up a fifteen-year-old, no matter the reason.

So yes, she knew Garrett had had a crush on her growing up. But it was only this week watching him with both Billy, Eric, and even the women downstairs that she'd realized what she'd been missing in front of her the whole time. Yes, Garrett might not be obvious leading man material, but he was solid. He was the kind of rock steady, good man she'd never spent time with in her entire life.

So she looked him directly in the eyes when she said, "A Clan is a woman and several men who agree to be a family. They live in the same place, support each other, and work together as one unit." She dipped her head and blinked up at him through her lashes, "And they fuck. A lot. So, Garrett, do you want to fuck me?"

CHAPTER TWELVE

GARRETT

Drea 'Belladonna' Valentine had been the subject of Garrett's wet dreams ever since he'd been old enough to start having them.

She was two years older than him, though, and when you were growing up, those two years might as well have been twenty. He told himself that was the only reason she never looked at him as anything more than a little brother, anyway.

Plus she was always too dazzled by Thomas to pay much attention to anyone or anything else around her. The fact that Thomas was a bastard jackhole? Drea didn't see it until it was too late.

If only Garrett had done things differently.

If only he'd stood up to his dad. If only he'd gone to Drea and told her what was *really* going on. He hadn't known everything—but even the little he did know...

If only he could have just convinced her not to confront them directly— If only he'd been able to show her what Thomas was really like.

If only he'd done literally *anything* other than what he did... which was nothing at all.

If only.

But she's back now.

And she wants you.

Finally. *She finally wants you.*

And when she eventually finds out all you've done? Back then he might have been mostly innocent. But in the years since? He'd been neck fucking deep in all of it. Dad made sure of that. The few girls he'd saved here and there could never make up for all the bad he'd done. All the evil he'd been a part of.

A better man would turn around and walk out the door.

But he'd never been the better man.

So he was across the room in three fucking strides and in the next second, had a knee on the bed, dragging Drea up and into his arms.

Shit but she felt like fucking heaven. Her skin. The heat of her. He'd fucked a few whores in his day—never any of the women the club trafficked—but still, he'd swear on the damn Bible he'd never kissed a woman before. Because when his lips touched Drea's, it felt like nothing before had in his whole damn life.

She wasn't timid. She didn't kiss him like she was hoping to please him. Or like she was drunk or high or like she wished she was anywhere else.

She was right there, present with him.

Drea Valentine.

Eric had moved off to the side of the bed and Garrett moved over Drea to take Eric's previous position.

But Drea just shook her head with a devilish grin and shoved him off her.

Wha— Was she just fucking with him? Calling him over just to laugh at him?

But then she spun around on the bed, going up on her knees and looking over her shoulder at Garrett, waving her delectable creamy white ass at him.

Garrett had no words.

Fucking literally because all blood flow had gone south. His dick was so fucking hard he was about to bust the damn seam on his jeans.

He reached down and pulled the buckle free and undid his button if only to loosen the pressure on his aching shaft. But when he saw Drea's eyes zeroed in on what his hands were doing?

Holy fuck, was she trying to kill him? This was so much crazier than any of his fantasies. Even in those she only fucked him because she was bored or high and he was the only one around.

But this, this active wanting?

He yanked his pants down and lifted a trembling hand to her backside. So beautiful. So perfect. Was she really here? Was this reality?

"For fuck's sake, Garrett, I'm not made of glass. Are you gonna fuck me or what?"

Fucking hell. She never swore like a sailor in his fantasies either, but fuck was that hot.

He stretched the last couple inches and grasped a handful of her ass. And she was a handful. Goddamn. She couldn't have been more perfectly designed for him. He was an ass man all the way.

And when he saw her wave Billy over and position him in front of her mouth— No way, was she going to—

Jesus fucking Christ. When she bobbed down and swallowed Billy's cock, Garrett thought he might blow his damn load before he even got his dick inside her.

She was so fucking dirty, and wrong.

And *his*. He was about to make goddamn sure of she was *his*.

Garrett grabbed his shaft and stroked himself hard up and down once. And then he couldn't wait another goddamn second. He lined himself up and shoved himself in. No fanfare. No teasing. He just needed to be buried so deep inside her she never forgot who it was that was fucking her.

Eric might fuck her rough and dominant and Billy looked like he was out of his damn mind with bliss, but Garrett would *worship* her.

He'd make her addicted to him. So she'd never get enough.

Which meant he couldn't come in three minutes like a damn teenager.

He bit down hard on the inside of his cheek and reached around her waist to tease her clit. *Focus on her. Her pleasure is all that matters.*

She bucked back against him as soon as he touched her and the gratification shot through his chest and straight down to his cock.

The way she was bucking against him, she wasn't looking for soft and sweet. That was fine with Garrett. He'd give it to her that way sometime. He wanted to give her everything. But right now she wanted it hard and dirty, goddamn he'd give it to her.

He slapped her luscious ass and fucked her harder. She screeched around Billy's cock and Eric reached over from the side underneath her to tweak her nipples.

God*damn*.

Garrett pinched her clit and he felt the moment she came. She shuddered around his cock and gripped him like a vice.

He'd never felt anything like—

Oh shit—

No, not yet, he wanted to give her another—

"Fuuuuuuuuck!" he roared as he slammed in one last time and shot his load inside her. Inside Drea.

Drea fucking Valentine.

He pulled out and shoved back in again, even more cum spurting out.

In that moment, everything was perfect.

His life was everything it was ever meant to fucking be.

No ugly fucking past. No future.

Just Drea. And his cock buried so far up inside her.

His.

She was his. Like she was always meant to be.

Fucking perfection.

But soon, all too fucking soon, the rest of the world came intruding again. The sound of Billy's heavy breathing. Billy apologizing for getting cum in Drea's hair. Eric saying they should get her to the shower to clean her up.

Shut the fuck up! he wanted to shout at all of them

He slumped over Drea's back and rolled her sideways onto the bed so they were spooning. He still had his arm around her waist and he continued playing with her pussy and clit. Little aftershocks ran down through her legs every so often and he smiled against her back, inhaling her skin.

He never would have moved. Ever.

But an insistent ringing from the other room had Drea tugging away from him and swinging her legs over the side of the bed.

"Is that the Sat phone?" she asked Eric.

He nodded, frowning. "I just talked to Sophia, though. We don't have another call scheduled till next week." He jogged out of the room.

Drea pulled the bed sheet around her and followed him.

Goddammit.

Garrett climbed off the bed too. Shit, he never even pulled his jeans all the way off. He stumbled several steps while he dragged his jeans up his legs. And by the time he got to the living room, it was to see Eric with a tense look on his face and Drea demanding he hand her the phone.

"Where?" Her mouth became a hard line and shit, did her face just go a little pale? "How long ago?" she snapped into the phone.

Then she swore.

"Thanks. We'll evac now."

Fuck. That had to mean—

Drea clicked the phone off. "Scouts watching Black Skulls in San Antonio saw a faction ride out. Maybe thirty bikes headed our way. And some trucks. All heavily armed."

"Shit," Billy said, raking his hands through his hair.

"How long ago did they leave?" Eric asked.

"Last night. They got pinned down and only just got back to the caves to report."

"SHIT."

"It's fine, we knew this would happen sooner or later." Drea said, striding back to her bedroom, dropping the sheet and barking out orders as she went.

"Everyone, get dressed. Then Garrett, go downstairs and tell Gisela what's happening. We don't have much time but she knows what to d—"

Bang bang bang bang.

Fuck!

Gunfire.

They were already here.

"Get down!" Garrett yelled, jumping toward Drea even as his head swung toward the window.

He slammed into Drea right as the window exploded in a shower of glass and bullets.

CHAPTER THIRTEEN

DREA

No! It wasn't supposed to happen like this.

They were supposed to have more time. She had safeguards in place. They were supposed to have a warning so she could get everybody out with time to spare.

You shouldn't have stayed this long.

What if she couldn't get them all out? They'd be sitting ducks. And why? Because she was busy playing house with her fuckboys up in this apartment instead of doing what needed doing and getting everyone to safety.

It was stupid of her to count on the Skulls being distracted by Travis and the raid on the Capitol. *Stupid.* She'd thought for sure Travis would have the Skulls out doing his dirty work, chasing down the Central Texas North and South dissenters.

Another round of rapid gunfire had her hugging the floor while Garrett hunched over her.

Which just pissed her the fuck off.

Because dammit, she wasn't some weak little girl who needed

protecting. She'd taken this compound right out from under their damn noses. *She'd* done that.

So maybe she'd made some miscalculations. But she would *not* fail these women like she had the ones in Nomansland.

And they'd prepared. Mostly. This was not a catastrophe. Just another bump in the road. She repeated it over and over to herself as she took one deep breath in and shoved Garrett off of her.

"Get dressed," she yelled, reaching for her jeans that were crumpled beside the bed.

"What the fuck?" Garrett shouted, trying to shield her but she glared at him and held out her hand.

He must have seen in her face that this was not a moment to fuck with her or try to pull any of his macho bullshit.

She shook the glass off her jeans as best she could and wriggled into them while still laying on the floor. The guys did the same all around her.

And the gunfire kept coming.

She watched the line high above the bed's headboard where the bullets ate up the drywall. Okay, so they were shooting from below. Good. She yanked her shirt on over her head and then army crawled for the door.

At least it was open so even if the attackers could see into the room, they wouldn't see it move. All the guys followed on her heels. The entire apartment was destroyed. Drea stayed low in case the Skulls had snipers higher in the surrounding buildings.

Were Bone or Viking out there? They'd been sharpshooters before The Fall. But no, Suicide usually liked to keep them close.

She grabbed her bug out bag she kept by the front door while Garrett reached up just enough to push the door open.

The gun fire had stopped blasting through the windows. Which meant they weren't necessarily shooting at specific targets but taking a general shoot-the-shit-out-of-everything approach. She couldn't even begin to fathom such a waste of ammunition. They had to know they wouldn't be killing many people that way. More likely it was meant to scare the hell out of everyone inside. Because they thought that women would weep, tremble and surrender at such a show of force.

Motherfuckers.

She kept crawling through the hallway, only standing up after she'd pushed open the door to the stairwell.

"What the fuck are we gonna do?" Billy shouted. His voice echoed around the stairwell as Drea started sprinting down the stairs.

"Calm the fuck down, for starters." That from Eric, and Drea appreciated it. She had enough to freak out about without her own crew adding to her stress level.

Jesus, why did it take so damn long to get down three flights of stairs?

Finally, what felt like ten years later, she threw open the door to the second floor. Maya was at the door to the supply closet, slinging duffel after duffel over her shoulders. She was so tiny, Drea was shocked she was still managing to stay upright.

"Everyone else is headed for the basement," Maya called.

"Enough, Maya." Drea waved her arm toward the stairs. "Come on. There's no time."

"No, I still have to get the anti-virals, they're—"

"Forget them," Drea shouted. "Get your ass over here, now!"

But Maya disappeared back into the supply closet. When she came back, she could barely walk she had so many bags slung over her shoulder and across her body. But she had a big smile on her face.

Maya was still smiling, in fact, when the gunfire started up again and the glass walls that the entire floor was made of began to shatter.

CHAPTER FOURTEEN

ERIC

"Behind the door," Garrett shouted, shoving Drea towards Eric and Billy and then diving the opposite direction.

Eric yanked Drea back with his casted arm and slammed the heavy stairwell door shut right as the glass began flying.

"No!" Drea screamed, fighting against his hold. "Let go of me! Garrett! Maya!"

But Eric only dragged her further away from the door.

"Garrett! Let me the fuck go!"

The door was solid and that was Eric's only comfort as Drea started fighting like a wildcat in his arms. No way was he letting her go. Not even when his broken arm ached and she started screaming obscenities at him and digging her nails into his hands.

"If you don't let me go I swear I'll never fucking speak to you again," she shrieked.

That was fine with him. He was a father. He'd prepared himself a long time ago for the fact that the lengths you had to go to take care of those you loved could mean losing the love of those very same people.

It was only once the gunfire died down and moved on to a different part of the building that he even thought about letting her go.

Even then, he was far more relieved when Billy volunteered to go out and check on them instead of Drea.

Through the doorway as Billy opened it, they could see Garrett crouched over and shielding Maya, but he was covered in glass shards and Eric didn't miss all the blood.

He held on tighter to Drea until she swiveled her head to look at him with the coldest eyes he'd ever seen. "You will let go of me right. The fuck. Now."

A chill went down Eric's spine.

"Drea, they might come back. Let's just w—"

And then Eric's head exploded with pain.

What the—

Had Drea really just *headbutted* him?

He staggered back, stunned, hand going to his head as Drea slipped out of his arms and ran over to Maya and Garrett.

"Drea," he tried to call, blinking hard through the sudden wave of dizziness. He'd always known that woman had a hard head, but Jesus.

The next second, though, he was back in the moment.

Billy was helping Garrett shift over to the side off of Maya and Drea immediately crouched over Maya, fingers to her neck.

"Maya," Drea called. "Honey. Maya. Oh God, Can you hear me? We're here, okay, hon? We're right here."

Please, please let the girl be okay. Eric didn't know who the hell he was asking. He hadn't believed in God for a long time now. But he prayed now, for Drea's sake.

The blood. So much blood, dripping down Maya's temple and her arms.

"She's out cold, but she's breathing," Garrett said as Billy ran his hands down Maya's limp body.

Relief washed through Eric.

"She got shot twice before I got to her from what I can tell," Garrett said, "both on the left side here."

But Billy was already at work, ripping the hem of Maya's shirt and tying a makeshift tourniquet around her upper arm and then another around her thigh.

"Can she be moved?" Eric asked. "We have to go."

Drea glared up at him but obviously she knew he wasn't wrong because she got to her feet.

"I can patch her up in the van," Billy said, scratching at his wrist like he was really wishing this wasn't the week he'd gone cold turkey. Fucker better stay sober, that was all Eric had to say about it. "But we gotta get the hell outta here."

Garrett lifted Maya in one smooth motion, easily hefting her into his arms in front of his body.

The next second, Drea was in motion.

"Carry these," she barked at Eric and Billy, shoving two of the duffel bags Maya had gone back for at them. Then she grabbed the last two herself and stood straight up.

She walked back to the stairwell with a completely blank expression, going past Eric without a word to either him or Billy. When she started running down the stairs again, Eric exchanged a look with the other guys before hurrying to follow her. Goddammit, was she going to shut down on them again?

They'd welded the door to the lobby shut earlier in the week. It was a fire door, made of steel, and the noise of rattling gunshots pinging off the metal shook Eric's nerves.

Shit. They were already in the building?

Drea didn't miss a step. She just jumped over the two motorcycles they'd also driven into the first-floor landing to help block the lobby door in case anyone did manage to get it open.

Eric and the guys followed her but no one could move as fast as Drea when she was on a damn mission.

The bottom of the stairwell didn't just have a door to the lobby. It opened two directions. One door to the lobby and another to a back hallway that took them straight to the garage.

The garage which thankfully, due to the MC's love of their bikes, also had a huge retractable steel door. Which was down and taking heavy fire from the hail of bullets rattling on the other side of it.

"Drea!" Excited and relieved whispers came from the women all huddled behind the armored truck, heads swinging their way as Drea burst out from the hallway.

Drea only glared at them, stomping across the garage. "Why aren't you in the truck?" she snapped. "Move. Now!" She pointed in the back of the truck.

Several of the women looked up at the opened back doors of the armored truck with apprehension. Others were outright shaking and clutching on to each other.

Garrett and Billy went immediately to the back as Garrett loaded Maya. Billy stayed with her but Garrett hopped back down a couple moments later.

Gisela stepped forward from the crowd and took Drea's arm. "I told you this was a bad idea. These are the same vehicles they're trafficked in. You can't expect—"

But Drea only jerked out of Gisela's grasp and turned back to the women. She stabbed a finger toward the wall. "They're going to get through that door. I can promise you they brought more than guns. Do you want to be standing here with your thumbs up your asses when they do? Now get in the fucking truck."

Eric cringed at the way several women flinched and backed away from her. But what Drea lacked in delicacy, she made up for in efficiency, because women did start climbing up into the back of the truck. And as soon as two went, four more followed. Then it was a flood, the girls already in the truck reaching down to help the others up.

There were so many of them. Would they all even fit? They'd practiced loading into the truck only once, and that was without making space for the doctor trying to operate on a woman laid out.

But they stood, side to side, barely a breath between them as the last couple of women stepped up, teetering on the edge because they were packed as tight as sardines.

There were plenty with stark terror on their faces. Jesus, they were forcing them to relive some of the worst memories in their lives, being trafficked all over who knew the hell where. Delivered from one evil fucker to another.

Eric thought Drea was going to slam the back doors closed on them without another word but at the last moment she paused and reached up, clasping the hands of those closest to her. "I'll keep you safe. I swear it on my life."

And the way she said it, the look on her face—Eric's stomach dropped out in fear for her. What did she mean she swore on her *life*? That she'd die if that's what it would take? She'd already taken far too many risks, she couldn't—

"Now back up," she said, her voice gentler than when she'd ordered them in the truck. "And remember, you're locking it from the inside. You have control. No one's locking you in."

She closed the doors as gently as she could and only looked to Eric and Garrett when she heard the click of the inside lock.

And her features were back to being hard as stone. "You two. Up front."

"What about you?" Eric asked.

"She's gonna ride one of the hogs," Garrett said. "I'll jump on mine, too and we can—"

But Drea rolled her eyes. "No way. You'd just slow me down."

For a second Eric thought he almost saw a spark of the old Drea. "I'm gonna take Stella. They still had her in the back, gathering dust. Fucking idiots." She pulled a drop cloth off of a small, bright red motorcycle right by the truck. It was half the size of some of the Harleys scattered around the garage.

Eric read *Ducati* on the side of the bike. And right above that, stenciled along with a fire decal, *Stella*.

Eric would have smiled except for two things. Number one, it was a damn motorcycle and his and Drea's run in with the last one was still far too fresh. And two, all the warmth fled Drea's face the second she glanced back at the armored truck.

She grabbed a small messenger bag from the floor beside the motorcycle and slung it across her chest. She settled the bag in front of her stomach as she climbed on the bike.

Then she glared their way. "Well, what the fuck are you waiting for? A damn invitation? Go get in the truck. Keys are in the ignition."

Eric's jaw tensed and he wanted more than anything to drag her aside and make *sure* she wasn't planning anything that would put herself in danger. But he'd been on enough fronts to know there could only be one commander in a battle. And as much as he'd prefer the control, he knew that leader was Drea right now.

So he gave one sharp nod and kept his thoughts to himself as he marched toward the front of the truck. At least Garrett didn't give him any shit when he took the driver's seat. He was pretty sure he would have flipped out on Garrett if he'd tried to take what little control he was allowed left away.

Garrett had barely pulled his door shut before a huge *BOOM* shook the entire garage. The entire building.

Eric's arm lifted over his eyes instinctively, but then his head swung toward his driver's side window.

Drea.

He was a second away from throwing open the door to go check on her but in his mirror, he caught side of her. She had her bike right up against the armored truck, hidden from view of the garage door, and she was shaking her head fervently. She held up a hand like she meant for him to duck down.

Jesus. Was she serious?

When he didn't move fast enough for her, she started waving even more furiously, so he turned around and growled, "get down."

It was awkward for him and Garrett to duck without getting in each other's way but they managed.

Eric had only gotten a glance at the garage door before he got down, but it was enough to see they'd blasted a man-sized hole in the damn thing.

Because they had fucking explosives. Naturally.

"So fuckin' sloppy," Garrett muttered so low Eric barely heard it. "What'd they fucking use? A goddamn stick of C4? What the hell is Suicide even teaching these new recruits?"

Eric wondered if Drea had somehow signaled the girls to be quiet because they weren't making a peep. Either that or the back of the truck was soundproof as well as bulletproof.

Shit. What was going on out there?

Eric had never liked this contingency plan, not since the first time Drea had come up with it. And he sure liked it a hell of a lot less now that he was sitting here blind with the enemy right on top of them.

Just wait for the signal. Just wait for the signal.

Another several tense moments of silence followed. Okay, that wasn't completely true. He could hear distant voices. One man calling out to another. Then, a minute later, more voices.

It wasn't until he could hear the footsteps that Drea gave the signal: Her revving her motorcycle to life and shattering the quiet was impossible to miss.

Eric sat up, turning the key in the same motion. Then he jammed the old armored truck into gear and pressed the gas with everything he had.

There was only a quick moment when the lights of the truck illuminated the surprised faces of the ten or so bikers spread out all around the garage. Garrett punched the garage door opener at the same time.

The bikers lifted their machine guns and started firing but Eric didn't spare a glance for them. Okay, so he might have felt a *little* satisfaction at smashing into one of the bigger bastards and seeing him bounce off the bumper to the side.

But mostly his eyes were locked on his side mirror, making sure Drea was keeping up with the truck so that she was blocked from the hail of bullets.

The truck bumped roughly as they drove out of the garage and onto the pavement of the street and Eric winced for the women standing up in the back of the truck. There was no time to be gentle about it, though. Drea's bike zoomed out in front of the truck, taking the lead and speeding down the road.

It was late afternoon and not a cloud in the sky. Sunlight blazed down on the road.

Motorcycles roared to life behind them and Eric floored it, knowing there was no time now.

He got maybe another twenty feet down the road before the explosion behind them rocked the car.

"Whooeee!" Garrett whooped, punching the dashboard. "Now that's how you use some fucking explosives!"

"Jesus Christ," Eric swore. "Could you not have waited for us to get a little further away?"

"You nuts? Whole point was to fry as many of those bastards as we could." Garrett leaned toward the window, checking his rearview mirror. "Shit, doesn't look like we got as many as I wanted. We've got about five fuckers on our tail. Three ape hangers who aren't gonna catch us if you keep the pedal to the medal. D's right about those Hogs. They can usually only max out at 110."

Eric glanced down at the speedometer. He was going 85 and he could feel the engine still had plenty more to give.

"But they got a truck that's gaining on us. And shit, another truck just turned a corner and is after us too."

Eric glanced in his own rearview and saw the truck Garrett meant.

Okay. Time for a few evasive maneuvers. Back in the war, hasty getaways were a way of life. The Southern Alliance was infamous for chasing Texas soldiers down after winning a battle. Their motto was a dead New Republic soldier today was one more you didn't have to fight tomorrow.

"Hold on to something," Eric muttered, wishing he could tell the women in the back the same. They had to know this wouldn't be a walk in the park.

He'd have to drive them off the road one at a time. It would be harder if they tried to box him in from both sides. But he'd been in plenty worse spots than this before. Maybe not with such high stakes...

"What is she doing?" Billy asked, sitting up straighter.

"Drea," Eric said in a warning tone as she dropped back from the lead to Garrett's side of the truck. Not that she could hear him. Or that she'd listen even if she could.

The gunfire had slowed down but as soon as Drea became visible on the side of the truck, it started right back up again.

"Goddammit, Drea!" Eric shouted, looking across Garrett and stomping on the brakes to try to get behind her and shield her again.

But right then, she veered off into a side alley.

"Where the fuck is she going?" Eric yelled.

"Don't worry," Garrett said. "D knows what she's doing."

Eric looked at Garrett incredulously. Was he serious?

"Everyone back there has a gun. How is that not supposed to make me worry?"

Garrett just grinned, looking like he was insane. "I got a gun too." He cocked his shotgun. "Plus, most people can't shoot for shit while they're on a motorcycle. Anyone who says different is a damn liar."

If Eric didn't have a truck full of souls, he would have pulled off and gone to find Drea no question. But he did, dammit. And she knew it. How dare she put him in this situation? If they managed to somehow survive this, they were gonna sit down and have a long fucking talk, that was for damn sure.

Garrett rolled down the window and leaned out, lining up his shotgun at his shoulder.

Boom.

He immediately cocked it again and let out another blast.

"What the hell are you doing?" Eric yelled as gunfire immediately started up and Garrett ducked back in the window.

"Drea just pulled out behind 'em. I'm drawing their attention to keep them from noticing her right off."

"WHAT?"

Eric jerked the rearview mirror and rearranged it, glancing back and forth from the road to the mirror.

Fuck. Garrett was right. Drea was behind everyone, leaned low over her motorcycle and creeping up on the truck in the rear.

She pulled so close to the truck that she disappeared from view.

"What the hell are you doing, Drea?" Eric muttered, swinging a wide right onto another road that led vaguely in the direction they meant to go. He'd studied a map, but they'd left in such a hurry, he only had the general idea of where they were.

He was mid-turn when the truck behind him exploded.

He whipped around but again, Garrett was whooping like he was at a prize fight.

"Where the fuck is Drea?" Eric yelled.

But Garrett was apparently not in the mood to be helpful. "Holy shit. I can't believe she actually did it!" He shoved his hands through his hair like he was riding the high of his life. "We always talked about tossing a stick of nitro into an exhaust pipe, but none of us were ever fucking crazy enough to actually *do* it."

"Is she fucking *okay?*" Eric shouted.

"Yeah man, chill out. I saw her drive off down an alleyway before it lit up."

"Jesus Christ." Eric wiped his damp palms on his jeans one at a time. She was going to be the death of him. He'd survived the teenage years with his daughter only now to be done in by a headstrong maniac he'd been dumb enough to start having feelings for and—

"Awwwww, there she goes again," Garrett laughed, leaning out the window and letting off another blast of his shotgun.

Eric glared in the rearview mirror. "Dammit, Drea."

Because obviously they weren't the only ones who'd noticed the first explosions.

Several motorcycles dropped back and the *rat tat tat tat* of bullets flying was all Eric could hear.

"We've got to draw them off her." Eric clenched his teeth against the pain as he steered with his arm in the cast and reached under his seat for one of the sub-machine guns he'd stashed there. He clicked off the safety and shoved his arm out the window, aiming vaguely in the direction of *backwards*.

Then he stomped on the brakes.

The squeal of tires was deafening and the truck began to fishtail. Jesus, Eric hoped Billy wasn't trying to actually sew stitches at the moment.

Eric gripped the wheel as hard as he could with the fingers of his casted hand, controlling the spinout so that Garrett's side ended up toward the oncoming truck and bikes.

"Fire!" he shouted, leaning over and joining Garrett in shooting out his window, firing and not caring about how many bullets the machine gun was wasting. He just needed to get their focus off of Drea.

"Go go go!" Garrett shouted. "She's out!"

Eric felt his eyes widen as he yanked back, tossed the machine gun on Garrett's floorboard and switched pedals again, this time stomping back down on the gas. Motorcycles sped past him on both sides, bullets whizzing around the truck.

The rearview mirror shattered and Eric yelped but kept the pedal to the floor.

He glanced in his side mirror and saw the truck behind them stop and the passengers flee out into the road moments before it blew up in a plume of fire and smoke.

Garrett, predictably, whooped. "That's right, baby! Eat that fuckin' nitro!"

But now that the bikes had gotten ahead of them, they were criss-crossing in front of their armored truck and were firing back in a constant barrage.

Ping, ping, ping, ping as shot after shot hit the windshield. The glass of the windshield was holding just fine against the bullets, though. They were designed for this.

"Oh shit, grenade!" Garrett shouted.

Just in time too, because Eric had been focused on a couple of bikes that had dropped back and were driving on either side of the truck.

He yanked his attention back to the motorcyclist in front of them just in time to see him hurl his arm backwards and a small orb fly through the air.

Eric jerked hard to the left and a *BOOM* sounded behind them as the grenade went off.

The bike on the left barely managed to pull away in time. Eric didn't care if he bashed into the guy.

...Which was actually a great idea, come to think of it. He was just about to readjust to try to take out the bastard on the other side of them—because what if Drea wasn't the only one crazy enough to try that trick with nitro?—when Drea suddenly pulled out of a side street in front of all of them, heading the pack.

"What the hell is she doing *now*?" Eric growled.

He already had the pedal to the floor but he gritted his teeth like he could make the damn truck go faster through sheer force of will alone.

He didn't have to wait long to see what Drea was up to, though. She weaved back and forth across the road, arm dipping into the bag across her chest several times and then arcing outwards.

"What is she throwing?" Eric asked.

"Caltrops," Garrett answered, a grin on his face like he was proud. "Don't feel bad. I didn't know what they were either before Drea told me. Now hold on, this is gonna get a little bumpy." He grabbed the oh-shit-bar and Eric clenched his hands on the steering wheel.

Eric had no idea what a 'caltrop' was but anything that had that crazy motherfucker Garrett reaching for a hold of something was definitely something Eric should brace himself for.

"Oh shit," Eric swore as the truck sped down the road toward what had first just looked like shiny dots against the dark pavement. He'd been confused about what Drea was tossing on the road but as they got closer, the realization of what they were settled in with a horrifying certainty.

"She wouldn't," he whispered hoarsely.

"Oh fuck yeah, she would," Garrett cackled. "Where do you think I been when I disappeared for hours at a time all week? I was welding these babies together."

"Oh fuck, *oh fuck*, OH FUCK!" Eric shouted, not daring to slow down in case it tipped off any of the motorcycles.

There were still a few motorcycles in front of him. Eric made sure to steer clear of them as they came up on the first of the road spikes.

Because that was what Drea had tossed out.

Homemade fucking road spikes.

As if they hadn't had enough fun with the damn things the first time around.

The motorcycles hit the spikes and went flying all fucking directions. Two skidded out and the third flipped end over damn end.

But Eric barely had time to take in the carnage before their own truck was running over the damn things.

Eric cringed in preparation and held the wheel as steady as he could.

Da-dump, da-dump.

And then... nothing.

What the—

Wait. Was that— it?

Eric didn't know. He glanced in his side mirror. Not that he'd really be able to see if the tires were blown out but—

All the other motorcycles were taken out, that was for damn sure. Right as he looked, he saw the last one try to skid to a stop right before hitting the spike.

They *almost* stopped in time, but still ended up skidding out halfway across the road.

Eric whipped his head back around front. His racing heartbeat only calmed down when he saw that Drea was still there, leaning over and speeding along like nothing at all was the matter.

Like she hadn't just risked her damn life a hundred times over pulling all those bullshit gymnastics.

Meanwhile Garrett was laughing so hard he could barely breathe. Eric glared his direction but he only laughed harder. He literally slapped his knees.

"What the fuck is so funny?" Eric snapped.

"Armored trucks," Garrett broke off, dissolving into another fit of laughter before gulping and continuing, "can drive on flat tires." He slapped his knee again. "So Drea just used the spikes on all of us!"

Eric clenched his jaw so hard that his teeth ground together.

Yes, they'd definitely be having a *long* talk when they got to the caves.

CHAPTER FIFTEEN

GENERAL DAVID CRUZ

David had plenty of qualified platoon leaders who could bring back the women who called in with an SOS. But after a brief conversation with their leader, Drea Valentine, he decided to go himself.

"Hello, Alpha Hawk speaking." David paced the circle around the huge stalagmite columns that towered like fat giants in the center of the cavern deep under the outskirts of San Antonio. Other people watched on. It was so packed down here there were few places to go to actually get any privacy. And this was with only about two thousand of his seven thousand troops down here in the more than two miles of caves. The other five thousand were left fending for themselves out in the hill country, more and more being picked off by Travis's forces every day. "Who is—"

"I don't care," she cut him off impatiently. "It's Drea. We need transport across Black Skulls territory and we need it now. We just pissed on the hornet's nest, so the sooner the better."

David narrowed his eyes and turned away from Jonathan's questioning gaze. Jonathan was his top Colonel, right hand man, and best friend for seven years now.

"We have protocols for this sort of thing, ma'am."

"Fuck protocols. I've got some very freaked out women here. They need to get somewhere safe and secure as soon as possible."

"Please identify yourself using your call sign. For all I know, you could be Arnold Travis's agent."

"Jesus fucking Christ, I don't have time for this. Put Sophia Wolford on the damn phone. She knows me and even she could probably get a rescue team out here faster than some pompous stick-up-his ass Army robot."

David stayed cool-headed even though inside his blood was boiling. He'd met so many people like this woman. Did they appreciate the *years* he'd put into defending this great new country of theirs?

No, they could only spit his service back in his face.

That doesn't make your job any less of a calling. His duty went beyond any one person. Including himself or his pride.

"If you're done with the insults," he kept his voice mild, "then we can return to the protocol. Over the past week, you were given a series of rendezvous locations. Would you like to mention one of the phrases that would indicate, in a secure manner," *without name dropping their location or any more of the cave's inhabitants*, he thought in annoyance, "where you are so that we can discuss your extraction?"

"Son of a—" Several moments of unintelligible gibberish over the line that sounded like swearing followed. Then, a female voice calling out, "Billy. Where are the— You *know*, that damn folder with the— No, not the bag of fucking script, the..."

"Protocol locations," David supplied helpfully.

"Yes. The *protocol* locations."

David pulled back from the phone and stared at it for a minute before shouting on the other end had him pulling it back to his ear.

"Charlie Alpha Nine. We're at Charlie Alpha fucking Nine."

David snapped toward Jonathan. "Map."

Jonathan nodded, coming forward with the map he'd already had at the ready.

Jonathan laid it out on the ground and David brought his oil lamp close.

"We'll have to wait for nightfall. The Skulls fly drones during the day to surveil the area. But we have a few trucks coated with anti-infrared paint, so we can move at night just fine."

"Well get your asses out here right after nightfall. Rendezvous point C or whatever the fuck. I got a lot of twitchy survivors out here and waiting around isn't doing them any favors."

With that, she'd hung up.

CHAPTER SIXTEEN

SOPHIA

"Dad?" Sophia asked, pushing through the small group of women that streamed in through the cave entrance. "Hello? Where's the Commander?"

"Whoa, Soph," Finn said, "Back off. Let them breathe. Can't you see they're freaked out?"

Sophia turned on Finn, mouth open. Of course she saw— Did he think she wasn't— "I just need to know Dad's okay, all right?"

Finn was six months older than her and thought he knew everything just because he'd been going out on scrapper runs since he was sixteen.

Several other women from town ushered the women down the long diagonal back and forth staircase that had been cut into the rock more than a hundred and fifty years before, back when these caves had been a tourist attraction. The caves were thirteen stories down, created by underground rivers ages and ages ago, a whole system of them.

Sophia turned back to the mouth of the cave, willing her dad to be the next to step through.

Finn just let out a dismissive puff of breath. "The Commander? Nothing can hurt him."

Sophia ignored him. Why had he even come up here?

"Oh come on, Soph. Are you seriously worried? He fought at Texarkana. That was the ugliest battle of the whole war for Independence. And wasn't he in the army before that? Nothing can kill that tough old bast—"

Sophia turned, long brown hair swirling as she spun to glare at Finn again. "Are you trying to jinx him? God, shut up already."

Finn held his hands up. "Damn, girl. I was just trying to make you feel better and stop worrying."

"Well you're bad at it," Sophia shot back. "So stop."

Seriously, the guy needed to get a clue. How was bringing up times when her dad had been in life-threatening danger in the past supposed to make her feel better about the danger he was in now? If anything, it meant something was more likely to happen to him now. If life was a game of odds, didn't that mean it was more likely for his number to come up now if it hadn't then?

She glared at Finn. "I just need to know he's okay. Besides, what do you even know about it? You've never been in a war."

Finn's eyes flashed. "Just 'cause I was still too young by the time the last one finished. But this is war now and you can bet your biscuits I'm gonna do my duty. I'll be the last one standing if that's what it takes."

It was Sophia's turn to scoff. She let her glare fall on Finn again. He had the shape of a man—broad shoulders, scruff on his face from not shaving for several days, defined facial features—but all she could seem to see when she looked at him was the boy who used to snap her training bra back in the township's equivalent of a junior high.

"You sure talk big, Finn Malone. But don't forget I was there the day you about peed your pants when that bee stung you in seventh grade."

"So you think about me a lot, huh?" Finn sidled up beside her, bumping her shoulder with his. "To be remembering something like that from so long ago?"

Sophia gave him a sugary-sweet smile. "Oh no, it's not that. I'd just never seen a boy so big screaming his head off because a big, bad bee stung him. I wasn't used to seeing boys cry. My dad was military, like you said."

Finn didn't look fazed an inch by her words, he just kept grinning that annoying toothy grin at her. "All I seem to remember about that day was this cute, brown-eyed girl coming to sit beside me and asking if I was hurt, all sweet-like. You remembered what you asked me?"

Sophia paused, caught off-guard by this unexpected little trip down memory lane—especially with Finn of all people.

"I asked if I could take the hurt away," she said, blinking in confusion at the way Finn was suddenly looking at her. Not like a boy—but the way a man does at a woman.

"It was my first kiss," he said, looking at her with more intensity than he had a right to.

Sophia tried to laugh it off. "I pulled out the stinger and then kissed your arm."

"So? Still counts." When he said it, though, his eyes were on her lips. Like he was imagining what it would feel like to kiss her there.

Even the thought had her heart beating erratically in her chest and her breathing going all funny.

She stepped backwards, shaking her head and breaking the spell. Good Lord, what on earth? She really must be upset about Dad if she was letting Finn Malone fluster her.

"Another group's coming," Diego called from the mouth of the cave ten feet behind them.

Dad!

Sophia only just managed to stop herself from running to meet him. She could wait. She knew that lingering too long at the entrance of the cave was dangerous for all of them. The General was bringing the groups back in several vans painted in anti-infrared paint and then the people hurried from the vans to the caves with stiff blankets covered with the same paint over their heads. Still, if anyone in the capitol was looking too closely at this location with the infrared satellites and there was just one slip... Sophia shuddered. It would be bad.

So she kept back as the next group was ushered into the cave.

So only when the boulder was pushed back across the entrance and the blankets were lowered did she run forward and find her dad. It was easy because he was always a head taller than anyone else in the crowd.

He was walking beside Drea and two men Sophia didn't recognize. He looked haggard and tired and *oh*—

"Dad," Sophia cried. "Your arm!" It was in a sling, and gauze was wrapped all the way up to his shoulder. "What happened?"

She wanted to throw her arms around him but didn't want to hurt him anymore than he was so she grabbed his good hand, needing some sort of contact to prove to herself that he was real, that he was safe.

"Soph." He immediately drew her close, pulling her into his chest and wrapping his good arm around her. "It's so good to see you, honey." He squeezed her tight and pressed a kiss to the crown of her head, just like he always did, ever since she was a little girl and he came home from deployments.

Sophia's entire body relaxed against him and when she took her next breath, it felt like the first time her lungs were fully inflating since she'd left his side in Fort Worth a week and a half ago. She hadn't even been fully conscious of it, but she'd been so worried about him, her body had been tense the entire time he'd been gone. She wanted to smack him for being so reckless and making her worry so much.

Of course, he wouldn't have been in danger in the first place if it weren't for... *that woman*. Sophia leveled her gaze on Drea.

Sophia was glad to have her dad back but ugh, couldn't they have left Drea out in the wilderness somewhere?

She felt bad as soon as she had the thought. It was just that Drea always brought out the worst in her. And now that Dad was back, Sophia wanted a little peace and quiet, just him and her. At least Drea wouldn't be haranguing him every other second. There wasn't exactly a township to govern down here in the caves.

"Come on, Dad. I found us a quiet little cubby hole of a cavern and I've already got a bed pallet all laid out for you. Well, okay," she laughed. "I've made it as homey as I could and I think you'll like—"

"Honey," Dad pulled away from her and there was something in the tone of his voice that made the blood freeze in Sophia's veins. "I need to tell you something."

Why was he using his bad-news voice?

Sophia shook her head. "Dad...?"

"I'm sure it's nothing that can't wait for tomorrow," Drea said from several feet away. Sophia swung her head to stare at her. What on earth did *she* have to say about anything? But Drea just kept on talking. "We're all tired, Eric. Let's just get some sleep. We can talk in the morning."

Eric?

ERIC?

What the hell was going on? Sophia swung around to look at her dad. Who was looking at Drea.

She hadn't seen him for over a week, had been out of contact with him for a large portion of that time, terrified he was *dead*, and now he barely had two words for her and was busy staring at... *her*?

Seriously. What the *hell* was going on?

"Fine," Dad said, the word ground out through his teeth.

Sophia knew that voice. It was his I'm-losing-patience-with-you-and-you'd-better-shape-up-and-fly-right voice.

Except when Drea ignored him and turned away, he didn't snap at her for being disrespectful like he would have at Sophia.

Duh. Because she's not his daughter.

Because she's nothing to him.

Nothing.

Sophia took a deep breath in as Drea started down the long staircase with the other two men she and Dad had come in with and turned back to her dad.

She threw her arms around his waist, careful of his hurt arm. Okay. Okay, everything was going to be all right now. She breathed him in. He was warm and solid in her arms.

"Come on," she said when she finally pulled back. "I know you're tired, but I can show you a few things on the way to our cavern. Oh, and we can stop by and get some food, too."

Dad smiled at her but then his eyes flicked toward the stairs. In the direction Drea had gone.

Sophia frowned and then went on, "Now that some of the soldiers are here, we go through food like you wouldn't believe. Sometimes I volunteer down in the kitchens. You thought we stretched rations back in town? Well that was nothing compared to what we do here." She laughed and continued rattling on about life in the caverns.

Once they got to the bottom of the stairs, she briefly introduced him to the people who were staying in every larger cavern they had to pass through as they went deeper and deeper into the caves. But she couldn't help feeling like her Dad was only half-present the whole time. And everywhere they went, his eyes were always searching around the room of each cave.

Like he was looking for her.

Looking for Drea.

CHAPTER SEVENTEEN

ERIC

Eric had needed the sleep.

But apparently it was morning, if the way Sophia was bustling around was any indication. It was dark as ever in the cave, but an oil lamp in the corner was fully lit. He smiled even as he blinked his eyes blearily. Ever since she could crawl out of her crib, Sophia was always up and about in the mornings.

A pang went through his chest as he tried to recall the memories that became more and more slippery every day—him and Consuela in bed on a sleepy Saturday morning, three-year old Sophia climbing up onto the mattress in between them, singing little songs she'd made up as she poked and prodded at them trying to get them to wake up.

"It's the wake-up game, Daddy! Wake up, wake up, *wake UP!*" —the last part invariably shouted right in his ear.

Jesus, it was a million years ago and it was yesterday.

Eric opened his eyes and he looked at his little girl, now all grown up. She was pulling clothing out of a bag—his clothes by the look of it. She must have packed it from their house in Jacob's Well before fleeing the town with the rest of the families. She'd shake out a shirt, examine it, then refold it. Then do the same with the next item she pulled out, until she had a neat little pile beside the duffel bag.

Eric laid in his sleeping bag, quiet, just watching her.

It was going to be a full day. There were so many things to do. So many problems that needed solving. Impossible problems. People would look to him for answers. He'd spent the last eight years of his life building a fortress to protect against exactly the sort of catastrophe that had just happened... and in the end it hadn't mattered.

Here was Sophia, hiding out with a bunch of rebels in an unsustainable situation. He'd seen the so-called 'kitchen' Sophia had so eagerly shown him last night. They were burning through a tragically small quantity of supplies at an alarming rate. The soldiers had brought rations with them when they'd come from Fort Worth but they'd expected to be supplemented by food from Jacob's Well, not be cooped up with no way to renew their supplies.

Eric had also talked briefly with Nix before heading with Sophia to bed last night. There were a little over twenty-two hundred people in the caves. Yes, the larger portion of soldiers were bunked in the other huge cave. Overall, there were two and a half miles of caves and two main cave systems that were not connected and had to be entered via different entrances about twenty feet apart.

But even this more 'civilian' side of the caves was uncomfortably packed tight with people. The fact that Sophia had gotten them this little private cubby hole of a cavern spoke to Eric's rank more than anything.

General Cruz had an additional six *thousand* soldiers hiding in the hills. Fewer and fewer every day from the reports the General received from his scouts, more of his squadrons were being captured all the time.

But mobilizing and moving such a number was an impossibility as long as there were satellites overhead that could track their movement.

Unless they did something, and fast, their sole advantage—actually having an army of their own to oppose Travis's army—would be lost.

No, there was no more time for lounging in bed and reminiscing about days past.

Eric sat up, grimacing at the pain in his arm but forgetting it completely when Sophia turned his way, a huge smile blossoming on her lovely face. Christ she was so beautiful that sometimes it hurt. He wasn't sure if it was a kindness or a cruelty that there was nothing of Connie in her features, except for her eyes.

"Daddy," Sophia cried, hurrying over and flinging her arms around his neck. He couldn't help the little grunt of pain and she immediately pulled back. "Oh no, I'm sorry, did I hurt your arm?"

He shook his head, smiling at her. He lifted a hand and cupped her cheek. "I'm fine. Just fine."

"Are you hungry? Here, I got you some jerky. And some hard tack." She winced as she handed the hard, square biscuits to him. "Not the tastiest, but they do the trick. Oh, and water." She held up a canteen. "At least that's one thing we don't run out of because of the well."

Eric nodded gratefully as he took the food, pausing to give her hand an extra squeeze as he did.

She smiled and for several minutes, they ate in silence.

After Eric had finished half the food, he took a long swallow from the canteen. All right. No more putting it off.

"Honey, we need to have that talk."

Sophia looked at him wide-eyed like she didn't know what he was talking about. She did that sometimes, when she knew there was something difficult to be discussed. It was like if she didn't acknowledge whatever it was, it wasn't real.

But he hadn't raised her to run from difficult things... or had he? Wasn't that what Jacob's Well really was? A place where he could hide her away in an incubator where he controlled all the variables, so he could keep her safe from the violence and evil of the world?

Well, if he had, the bubble had sure burst. There was no pretending Sophia could live her whole life in the picture perfect snow globe he'd tried to capture for her—the perfect town, perfect community, perfect life.

That was all gone now.

And he was far from a perfect father. It was time to admit that once and for all. But Sophia was a reasonable girl. She was as intelligent as she was fanciful. What he had to tell her would mean even more big changes for them, but it was nothing they couldn't weather together.

He took a deep breath. "Honey, you know Drea and I have... well, we've..." Jesus, how was he supposed to explain what he didn't even fully understand himself? "Well, we became close the past week. And Drea decided that she might like to do something like a marriage raffle after all. Except she'd do the choosing instead of having a raffle."

Sophia's brows drew together in confusion.

Okaaaaaaaaay. Looked like he was going to have to spell this out.

"Those two men you saw us come in with? That was Billy and Garrett. They're two of her, er, men, I guess you could call us."

Sophia's eyes shot open wide as saucers at the word *us*.

He nodded. "I'm another."

Her mouth opened like she was going to say something and then it shut again. Then it opened again but still nothing came out.

"Sophia," Eric reached for her hand but she yanked it back. Eric sat up straighter, startled by her reaction. "Soph, it's going to be—"

"But you—" Sophia shook her head, chest moving up and down violently, like if she just breathed hard enough, she wouldn't start crying... or shouting—Eric couldn't tell which.

Sophia scrambled to her feet and started pacing back and forth in the tiny cavern. Three steps one way. Two steps back. Three steps—

Finally she spun back to him again, eyes accusing. "You said you never wanted to get married again! You always said—" She broke off, running her hands through her hair like she couldn't believe what she was hearing. Then she stopped and stared at him in disbelief. "You said Mom was the love of your life! Were you lying all that time?"

"No. Jesus. No."

Eric stood up but she backed away. He wanted to reach for her, to pull her against his chest. Because he didn't know how to explain to a nineteen-year-old that life and love don't always turn out the way you imagine they will when you first look into the eyes of the person you think will be your forever.

"Soph," he said, letting out a long breath. "That's not fair. There are seasons to life. But I swear I loved your mother with everything I was while she was alive."

"Seas—" Sophia started, then shook her head, a sheen of tears in her eyes. "If you loved her so much, then how could you leave her alone as often as you did? Leave us? You think I was too young to remember, but I wasn't."

She pounded her chest with her fist. "I remember Mom crying when you weren't there for our birthdays and for Christmas. She used to show me your picture when I was little so I'd know what my own *father* looked like."

"Soph—" Jesus, she was breaking his heart. "Your mom knew going in to our marriage that I'd be deployed for long—"

"She had to show me your picture so I'd know who you were!" Sophia cried, cutting accusation in every word. "You weren't any more real to me than the princes in the story books she read me. Except that *they* didn't make her cry."

Eric tried to swallow around the lump in his throat but he couldn't. He never knew— Connie never said—

But Sophia wasn't done. "I spent most of my childhood adoring you and *hating* you at the same time." The tears finally crested and spilled down her cheeks.

The sight ripped Eric's insides out. He had no clue she'd ever felt that way. When he *did* come home between deployments, Connie and his little Sophia were always so happy to see him.

And after you left? Did you even give them a second thought?

He had. He swore he had. He just thought the difference he was making in the world was important, too.

The world had been FUBAR long before Xterminate. The terrorist attacks had been coming almost monthly, it felt like. Bombs. Chemical weapons attacks. Jesus, every school kid carried a gas mask in their backpack.

And at the time, Eric had thought, if it weren't for men like him willing to sacrifice everything, even family, to keep the world safe, who would?

But he always just thought it was *him* who was making the sacrifice. Because he was a blind, selfish fucking bastard.

"I never knew..." he whispered, at a loss.

"Of course you never knew," Sophia burst out through what had previously been silent tears. "Mom never wanted you to have the burden of knowing. She said what you were doing was too important."

Sophia looked up at him then. "But what could have been more important than your own family? More than me? More than your *wife?*"

"Nothing," Eric said vehemently, again trying to cross the small space to hug her. "nothing is more important than you."

But again, when he got close to her she just shoved him back, a warning glare in her eye.

"Stop *lying*. For once, just stop it! I forgave you everything back then. After she died and you were finally there, you were all I had. So I told myself it was okay. That you had come for us in the end and it wasn't your fault you'd gotten there too late. That it was okay because you really had loved her."

She shook her head vehemently. "But if you *didn't*... All that time, if she was just a *season* to you—" She broke off, staring at him like he was a stranger.

"Shit, honey. That came out wrong," he pleaded. "That's not what I meant. I loved your mom."

But... had he loved her enough?

Maybe Sophia heard the question in his voice because she just kept shaking her head in disillusionment. Then she turned and yanked the curtain to the cavern aside and fled.

"Sophia!" he called, everything in him wanting to run after her.

But experience had taught him better. When Sophia was really upset, it was always best to give her space to process things on her own before approaching her.

Of course, it had never been *him* that she'd been upset at before.

That you knew of.

He couldn't believe all this time he hadn't known how his deployments had affected her. She always put on such a cheerful face.

But she'd been a kid. He was the parent. He was supposed to be able to see past her facades. To see into the heart of her to know what was going on with his own *child*. Jesus, how fucking blind was he?

He'd ripped his own family apart. And for what?

Ironically, it was Connie getting pregnant with Sophia that had cinched his decision to go into the army in the first place.

He and Consuela met in college. He was studying engineering at Texas A&M and had been in the Corp of Cadets so she knew from the beginning that going into the military was something he was considering.

Their romance was a whirlwind though, he'd admit that. Connie had been a freshman while he was a junior. She was sweet and funny. Jesus, was she funny. He had a habit of taking life too seriously and she was a breath of fresh air.

He'd proposed after only knowing her two months and she was pregnant before they got married a year later.

The pregnancy had come a little earlier than they might have preferred, but Eric had been thrilled as soon as Connie told him. He remembered dropping to his knees and pressing his cheek against her belly, his mind absolutely fucking blown at the thought of a tiny life growing there. Part him and part Connie, *growing, inside her.* How had he never thought about what an absolutely insane miracle that was before?

When he'd looked up at Connie, she'd had tears in her big, beautiful brown eyes. "You're not mad?"

"Mad?" Was she nuts? "You've just made me the happiest man on earth!" He jumped back up to his feet and grabbed her in his arms, swinging her around in a circle until her tears turned to peals of laughter.

Fuck, the memory hurt now, knowing all that would follow. Knowing everything those two bright-eyed naïve innocent kids didn't back then.

He'd thought about abandoning his plans to go into the military. He really did. He and his best friend from high school, Arnie, had talked about it for years and Eric had always assumed it was where he'd end up. Did his dad's memory have a lot to do with it? Sure. Sure it did.

But it was thinking about his baby girl coming into the fucking terrifying world that made the decision seem so clear.

If he went and fought the bad guys then maybe, just *maybe*, she could grow up in a safer world than he had.

Ha.

First of all, the idea that one man could have had any impact on the mess that was the world before The Fall... he shook his head and gave a dark laugh, burying his face in his hand.

He'd been an idealistic fucking idiot.

Maybe at one time, the US Army had been an honorable institution. He liked to believe it had been. But by the time he'd enlisted, the internal corruption and bloat of the organization had made it a mockery of what it once was.

He was a First Lieutenant by that point, stationed at a small outpost in Northern Pakistan. He was in charge of a unit tasked with repairing roads and bridges all over the area. Every few years they all got blown to bits and had to be repaired all over again.

Really doing work that would make the world better for his little girl back home whose childhood he was missing, huh?

Sophia had just turned ten and he'd missed her birthday. Again.

He was done with it. After multiple tours, he was coming up on the ten-year mark of service. It was time. Way past time.

Especially with this latest gig. He and his engineering team moved between units stationed all around the Hindu Kush. He wasn't stationed at his latest posting more than a few days before realizing the commanding officer, Major Waterford, was a real scumbag. He was always hassling the local women when they went past on their way to get water from the central town well.

But fine. There were assholes everywhere. Eric decided to just keep his head down, do his job, then apply for extended leave while he arranged for his exit from the Army as soon as he got back to HQ the following month.

Until one day Major Waterford took it beyond catcalling and lewd comments.

Eric walked into the command tent to give an update on his team's progress. Only to find Major Waterford with his pants at his ankles, huffing and heaving over the body of a crying, struggling woman, hand over her mouth.

Eric ran in and shoved him off of her. The woman immediately yanked her burka down and fled from the room. There was blood on the bed. She'd been a virgin, but just how young was she?

And Eric had the thought: what if that had been his daughter? His little Sophia?

He fucking lost it.

He beat the Major within an inch of his life. If the second in command hadn't come in and pulled Eric off the man, Eric might have killed him.

He was immediately transported back to Headquarters and deposited in the brig. All the while, throughout the process of his trial, more and more information began trickling in about the Xterminate virus spreading.

Not just in Africa and East Asia, either.

In Canada.

Mexico.

And finally and inevitably, America.

All Eric wanted was to get back to Connie and Sophia. He saw all the years he'd wasted, and for what? For a country so corrupt that his guilty verdict had been decided by bribery before he ever stepped foot in court.

The day the gavel dropped and Eric was convicted of both assaulting a superior officer *and* rape, he heard about how widespread cases of Xterminate were in Texas.

Meanwhile, he was heading to Leavenworth.

It was where he would have ended up, too, if not for Arnie.

Eric was strapped in and cuffed to a pole in the back of a military police van when an explosion rocked it. Everything went topsy turvy as the van crashed, tipping sideways and skidding across the road for Eric didn't know how long.

All he knew was that when the van finally stopped moving and he blinked bleary, confused eyes, he saw the back of the van opening to the blinding light of the daytime sun.

And then there was Arnie.

Eric couldn't have been more shocked if the blue fairy herself had shown up and blown fairy dust up his ass. He was sure he'd hit his head harder than he thought and was just hallucinating.

But then there was Arnie, talking just like he was, well, Arnie.

"Shit, man. Sorry about the bumpy ride. That didn't go off quite like I thought." He jumped in the back of the van with a pair of bolt cutters and snapped Eric's cuffs free of the pole.

Eric just sat there, suspended by the straps of his seat belt, still dazed.

"Well come on, old man. You gonna help me out or you want me to cut you out of those damn things, too?" Arnie waved the bolt cutters at the straps, a little too close to Eric's face for comfort.

"No, no," Eric mumbled. "I got it."

He unbuckled the seatbelt and toppled to the ground. Arnie just laughed his ass off. "Damn, you look funny in that banana suit, man."

Eric looked down at himself. He was wearing a yellow prisoner's jumpsuit. Because he was a prisoner.

And Arnie had just blown up a military police van to free him.

Arnie was always doing crazy shit. But this? This was so beyond...

"Arnie." Eric grabbed his arm, finally climbing to his feet and out of the van. "They'll lock you away for this. For fucking ever, man."

But the crazy fucker just laughed. "Who?" Arnie held out his arms, gesturing around him. That was when Eric really took a good look at the country he'd been fighting over a decade to protect.

"What the..." Eric's words trailed off and then he let out a horrified yelp and staggered backwards several steps.

Bodies.

There were dead bodies, just out in the open. Dead, decaying bodies.

Eric ran to the side of the road and threw up.

When he finished and wiped his mouth with his forearm, he gagged again. The smell. Oh fuck, that *smell.*

He shook his head. No. No, this was wrong. This wasn't America.

In the distance was a strip mall. Or rather, what was left of a strip mall. The glass of every single storefront was broken. Looted items were strewn across the parking lot, along with more bodies.

There were burnt cars, some still smoking, and dirt and filth were everywhere.

So maybe this was some Third World country. Eric had seen war zones that looked like this. Trashed cities in Syria. Pakistan. Central Africa.

But not *America*.

"It can't be," he whispered.

"Sorry pal," Arnie came up and slapped him on the back. "They're calling them Death Riots. People go fucking *loco* when all their women get sick and start dying."

Women.

Connie and Sophia. Suddenly it didn't matter what the fuck had happened in this little slice of hell. Eric only cared about what was going on in Kyle, Texas.

He grabbed Arnie's forearm. "Where's your car?"

"Now you're talking." Arnie led him a little ways down the road to his truck.

That ten hour drive down to Central Texas was the longest of Eric's entire life.

If only he'd taken a plane. All flights were grounded by then, but fuck, he and Arnie could have stolen one. A little commuter plane? A helicopter? Anything.

Nowadays it would seem like a no-brainer. Jesus, they would have had their pick! It was before the EMP attacks.

But back then, fuck, none of them had any idea they were only days away from it all coming crashing down. Civilization its fucking self.

There were still rules. At least Eric had thought so. So he'd driven in that goddamned truck. Only driven twenty miles above the speed limit, for Christ's sake. As if any of the police gave a fuck about traffic tickets at that point.

But no. He was an escaped felon, he kept telling Arnie. If they got stopped and anyone looked him up, he'd only be that much later getting to Connie and Sophia. So twenty above it was.

Arnie had already overridden the self-driving truck's safety protocols so he could speed on his way to get Eric. Why hadn't Eric just let him program it to go as fast as it could the whole way back?

Or what if the rioters had decided to break into the house one day later? Or one *hour* later?

One fucking hour could have been the difference between life and death.

If only he'd fucking driven faster.

If only.

But he didn't.

So when he and Arnie stopped in front of his old house on Blueberry Lane, it was to find his front door kicked in, his wife brutalized and left for dead in the center of their living room.

"Connie!" He'd rushed in and crashed to his knees on the floor beside her. He pulled her up into his arms. Her face was barely recognizable because of all the blood.

But she was still breathing. Somehow, some way, she'd lived through it all, something that would haunt Eric forever. She'd felt every single, agonizing moment of all that had been done to her.

"I'll look for Sophia," Arnie said, disappearing down the hallway.

Eric nodded, praying for Travis to find his daughter and at the same time begging, *Oh God, please don't let Sophia be here. Don't let her have seen any of this.*

"So—" Connie croaked, her voice barely audible, blood bubbling out of her mouth along with her spittle.

Eric coughed out a sob and rocked her body. "Shh, it's okay. It'll be okay. I'll get you to the doctor and—"

But Connie shook her head, features crumpling in pain. "Soph— Stair— Stairs."

Eric pulled back, devastated. "Where's Sophia, baby?"

"Stair." Connie choked and coughed, specks of blood flying all over the white undershirt Arnie had bought Eric from a gas station somewhere in Oklahoma.

She whispered something Eric couldn't hear, her eyes falling closed.

"Connie! No! Connie! Stay with me. Stay with me, baby. Where's Sophia? Just tell me where she is and then we'll all get in the car and go to the hospital and—" He cut off as soon as she opened her eyes again, not wanting to miss anything she said.

"Closet," she finally gasped, and then she reached up with what must have taken all of her strength and grasped his forearm. "Promise me. Protect... her." *Gasp.* "Protect."

Eric nodded, tears clogging his eyes so badly he could hardly see her face. "I swear it. Whatever it takes I'll protect our little girl. I'll fight for her. I'll steal for her. I'll kill for her. And I'll die for her. I swear to you that I'll protect her. No matter what. I *swear.*"

With that he pulled Connie to his chest, whispering his promise over and over, kissing her forehead, her hair, just holding her.

When he pulled back, knowing he needed to go get Sophia, he wanted to pretend he'd find his wife still breathing.

She wasn't.

So he laid her gently and reverently on the floor and covered her with a blanket. And then he ran as fast as his legs could carry him upstairs, first to the master bedroom closet. Sophia wasn't there.

Then he went to her bedroom and there, huddled in a ball in the very back of her closet, behind a stack of suitcases, was his little girl.

She'd looked up at him with those big, beautiful brown eyes, the same as her mother's that had closed forever only moments earlier.

"Daddy, I knew you would come and save us from the bad men."

How could the same world hold the cruelty of what had happened downstairs and also the pure beauty of his child's faith?

He swept her up into his arms, squeezed her tight to him, and swore to himself, he'd never *ever* let her go.

You weren't any more real than a prince in a story book. Except they *didn't make her cry.*

Eric dropped his head into his good hand, and then raked his fingers roughly through his hair.

"Fuck!" he shouted as he grabbed the oil lamp and stalked out into the hallways, all of which earned him more than a few looks from the group of people standing in the narrow passage outside.

He needed to go find Drea. Of course, he'd been paying only the faintest attention when Sophia showed him around last night but after asking a few people here and there, he found his way to the main gathering cavern. There were three huge mountainous formations that stood like ancient kings fifty feet high in the center of the cavern and a track had been worn around them. People were gathered all along the worn track, several oil lanterns casting shifting light to illuminate the cavernous hall.

He knew he was in the right place because he heard Drea's voice echoing off the dripping, waxy walls long before he got to the actual room itself.

But she wasn't the only one talking. There were lots of voices. Shouting too.

What the hell had Drea gotten herself into now? He hurried his pace.

"No. How many times do I have to tell you?" It was the low, clipped voice of General Cruz, and as Eric rounded the last corner, he saw he was right.

General Cruz and Drea were in a standoff, a crowd circled all around them. Not just a crowd though. No, behind General Cruz stood a large group of his soldiers, and behind Drea, the women she'd rescued from the compound. More from Jacob's Well and those who'd originally been hiding in the caves when they'd first arrived were gathered too.

This was not good.

"The Black Skulls are allied with Arnold Travis," the General continued. "That alliance was powerful enough to topple the San Antonio territory and murder a president. Now he has the army that was stationed at the joint army and air force bases there, too. All loyal to Travis, who's now proclaimed himself President of the Republic."

"You have an army, too." Drea waved an arm at the men grouped behind General Cruz. "Maybe most of your men are scattered and hiding in the hills, but that's even more reason to strike now before Travis and the Black Skulls can pick them off battalion by battalion."

"And how exactly do you suggest we amass this army of mine without drawing the attention of Travis's soldiers on us? Even if we moved at night during a new moon, you're forgetting, we only have so many anti-infrared trucks. Travis has access to President Goddard's computers so he can watch the infrared satellite feeds. They'll have fixed some of their planes by now, too. I'd be sentencing my soldiers to their immediate deaths if I tried to mobilize them."

But Drea was already shaking her head. "I have a plan. One that doesn't involve us all hiding here like rats until The Black Skulls realize we've been hiding right under their noses. How long do you really think we can keep this a secret?" She asked this not to General Cruz, but to the crowd around them.

"We need to strike *now*. While Travis is still scrambling to get his foothold—not after he's got the whole New Republic by the balls."

The crowd's heads swung back to the General for his response, like they were observers at a tennis match.

Eric got the sense that though none of the soldiers would say it or ever openly disagree with their General outright, a lot of them felt the same way as Drea.

These were men of action. Judging by their ages, Eric would bet many of them had fought in the War for Independence. This kind of go-to-ground, sit-and-wait inaction had to stick in their craw.

The General stayed calm and cool, however, Eric would give him that. Only the twitch of the vein in his neck gave away the fact that Drea was still pushing the limits of his tolerance.

"I will not recklessly endanger my men. So we will *not* be engaging with the Black Skulls or the army left guarding San Antonio until I am confident we have found a plan of action with an acceptable risk quotient."

"Tell that to the women there who are being raped every day," called out one of the women from behind Drea.

Another stepped forward—Gisela. "Drea took down an entire MC compound, just one woman by herself. We all saw her do it." Gisela gestured behind her at the women and they all nodded. "Are you saying that with five thousand, or even five hundred, you can't do what one woman half your size did?"

Cheers rose from behind her and there were murmurs from the General's men, too.

Eric saw the surprise register on the General's face even as he turned to look back at his men. Poor bastard. He had no idea what he was getting into sparring with Drea. So maybe this one time, Eric could throw the guy a bone.

Eric stepped forward. "Nothing can be decided with so many voices or in a public forum like this. Drea says she has a plan but we know Travis has embedded spies before. We need to appoint a council." He thought quick. "Comprised of all represented parties. Then we could discuss next steps in a meaningful way so we can actually form a plan of action."

The General scoffed. "Why would I need a council? I only see one army around here and it's mine."

Drea stepped up so that she was toe to toe with the General. "Oh, so are you saying that you get to be a dictator because you have an army? Isn't that exactly what we're fighting against?"

General Cruz glared at her. "You're twisting my words."

Drea held her hands up. "Just calling it like I see it." Then she looked past him to the men amassed in the cavern. "Don't you think you should have a say in your own future? You respect your General, that's all well and good. He'll be one of the voices on the council. But you should also have a say in your own future."

Murmurs among the soldiers grew louder and Eric could see more than a few heads nodding. Drea's points were landing.

The General's back went stiffer than ever. "Inciting insurrection in my men is not the way to get off on the right foot with me."

"Good thing I don't give a shit about your right foot."

"Excellent!" Eric said, clapping loudly before Drea could say anything else and escalate the situation beyond repair.

"So the Council will be made up of..." He thought fast, "You, General, and another representative your men democratically elect— without any undue influence from you. Does everyone agree?"

Eric looked to the General's men where heads were nodding even more rapidly. He glanced at Drea and she gave a single, decisive nod.

"We should have a Councilperson," said a man stepping forward, glaring at all of them. "We were here long before you came and took over our caves. We've been more than understanding as you crowd us out of our own homes. The least you can do is give us a say in our own futures."

Eric knew from Nix last night that there was unrest among the cave's original inhabitants but that they were a small faction. Most were people who'd originally fled here when the bombs had first dropped but who'd gone back to the surface after a time. They'd only returned when the Black Skulls took San Antonio. So their 'occupation' of the caves only predated the Jacob's Wellians by a few weeks at most.

"Of course," Eric acquiesced graciously. "Choose your representative." Eric turned to the women. "Drea will also be a Councilwoman. And there should also be a representative from those recovered from the Black Skulls compound."

"That will just mean two votes for Miss Valentine," the General objected. "They'll say whatever she does."

"The same could be said of your men," Drea answered icily. "Or do you have so little confidence in your decisions that you don't think you'll be able to convince them you're right?"

The General bristled but Gisela pushed forward again, "Plus, we're sick of our fates being decided without us. Those women under the Black Skull's control are our sisters. There aren't enough women left to waste a single one."

She spoke passionately and as Eric looked around the room gauging everyone's reactions, he saw more than a few of the soldier's eyes lingering on Gisela. They'd have to watch that.

"You should also be on the council," Drea spoke up, surprising Eric. He was going to suggest the Jacob's Wellian's elect who they'd want to represent them—he wasn't sure he still deserved the role of *Commander* after failing the town so badly—

But taking over command of the town had never been something he'd done out of the kindness of his heart or because he cared for the well-being of strangers—even if those strangers were now friends.

And his guiding light was the same as it had ever been.

Sophia.

He needed to be on this Council so he could steer the future in a way that would create the best possibility of a stable and peaceful future for his daughter to live in. If that aligned with the townships' best interests as had long been the case, well then, so much the better for everyone involved.

Eric looked around and saw Nix's clan along with several others. "Do you want me to continue representing you? Give me a show of hands who wants me to continue as your leader and to be your representative on the council."

The number of hands that immediately shot into the air made his throat go tight.

They don't know the real man they're voting for.

Eric managed a tight smile. He knew the townspeople thought of him as a hero. As their savior, even.

Jacob's Well had been like every other town after The Fall. Chaotic with mob violence and looting during the Death Riots. Bodies of dead women lined the streets because the burial squads had abandoned their duties, half of them joining the mobs.

So when Eric had shown up with a battalion of soldiers and two tanks and gone about restoring order, well, it was understandable that the townspeople had begun to put him up on a pedestal.

He'd encouraged it, even.

If they were in awe of him, that meant he had power over them. And power was something he'd desperately needed at the time.

It meant they never stopped to ask how exactly he'd gotten those tanks. It meant they never questioned why he should be their leader and set the rules. It meant they'd be the sheep to his shepherd.

So he took power, and he wielded it, and he wielded it to get more of it until his control of Jacob's Well expanded to control of larger and larger territory.

To secure his hold, he and part of his battalion went to fight for the newly appointed President Goddard.

Eric bribed, begged, borrowed, and stole in order to get into the President's inner circle on the front as they fought back the Southern States' Alliance on the eastern border with what used to be Louisiana. Every word he uttered, joke he spoke, and name he dropped—it was all done with the single purpose of increasing his influence in the young General's esteem.

And he was rewarded. He got to keep Jacob's Well.

Sophia would have her safe place to grow and thrive. She would grow up in an environment he could control. He would keep his promise to Connie. He would keep their daughter safe.

He'd done it for eight and a half years and by God, he'd do it for another eight, and then another eight, and another, until Sophia was a wrinkled old woman in her bed. And even then he'd keep fighting.

He'd give her his last dying breath if it meant she'd live even another second in peace.

It also meant he could never, ever tell anyone the name of the man who'd rescued him that day from the van heading to Leavenworth. The man who'd in effect saved his daughter's life because eventually, Sophia would have climbed out of that closet if he hadn't found her and his nightmares were filled with all that might have happened to her if he hadn't been there.

His best friend had saved her from that fate.

Arnie.

Also known as Arnold Jason Travis.

CHAPTER EIGHTEEN

DREA

Drea knew Eric wanted to talk to her. Or chastise her or some other shit she didn't have time for. He'd tried to get her alone every time the caravan had stopped to let the girls out of the armored truck to walk around. And again while they waited for the General to send his soldiers out to bring them to the cave in small groups.

But every time she saw him walking toward her, she'd busy herself with helping one of the girls or talking to Billy about what treatments they'd need once they got to the cave.

One time she just shoved a protein bar in her mouth so that she could only grunt noncommittally to Eric's barrage of questions: What was she thinking being so reckless? How could she have risked her life like that? Was she *trying* to get herself killed?

Then luckily one of the girls needed her so she was able to escape the judgement in his brooding green eyes.

She avoided him after that, spending her time with the girls who were understandably retraumatized by everything that had gone down getting out of College Station.

The truth was... Drea had been a little worried herself there for a while.

Okay, that was a lie.

She'd been sure she was going to die.

More than once.

The shit she'd pulled?

But nope, she was *not* thinking about that. So when she saw Eric heading her way after David Cruz dismissed them for the voting to begin, Drea turned on her heel and started hightailing it back toward their little cavern. It was a little bigger than a walk-in closet, but technically, it was Eric's walk-in closet, too. Because they were still together.

As much she'd like to pretend that what happened last week between her, Eric, Billy, and Garrett was just the fevered actions of four desperate people who'd just defied death looking for a little comfort... she knew it was more. What that *more* was, well—

Don't be sentimental, she chastised herself. *You're all just using each other. And that's okay. You need them. They need you. That's enough.*

But it did mean she couldn't just keep avoiding Eric forever, so she took a deep breath and planted her feet.

Okay, they'd have it out. He'd shout. That would make him feel like a big man. Then she'd shout because she was nobody's pushover. Then it'd be done with. Maybe they'd have a hot, angry fuck, and then they could move on.

The footsteps on the smooth floor of the cave behind her grew louder.

"Drea."

She closed her eyes at the sound of her name on his lips.

He didn't sound angry like he had yesterday. Still, she didn't open her eyes even when she felt him walk around in front of her.

It was cool down here in the caves. That was what she told herself anyway as chills ran up and down her arms when he reached out and interwove his fingers with hers.

She didn't mean to lean into his body. She really didn't. But it was like there was a magnet attached to her sternum reacting to another magnet inside his chest.

He pulled her in or she sank against him, she wasn't sure which. All she knew was that the next second she was cemented against his body and his arms were wrapped around her like she was a life jacket and he was drowning.

He just held her like that, silent in the dark hallway with nothing but a few candles burning here and there down the walkway, for what felt like minutes.

After the first minute, Drea wanted to pull away. It was awkward. Okay, she got it. He'd missed her or was glad she was okay or whatever.

But when she moved to pull back his arms only tightened. That was when her throat started getting thick.

Because the first question that popped in her head was: when was the last time someone had held her like this? And then came the answer: never. No one had ever held her this close or this long ever in her whole life. Certainly not her mother. She'd be too busy looking for her next fix. And Dad... Drea swallowed and turned her face into Eric's shoulder.

It was several more minutes before Eric said anything, and when he did, it was barely a whisper. "You scared the shit out of me, blue eyes. You're irreplaceable. You know that, right? And I just found you. I can't lose you."

Drea squeezed her eyes shut. Damn him. Goddamn him. He wasn't allowed to slip past all her defenses like this, didn't he know that?

He was supposed to be an arrogant asshole who had his uses, yes, but not so much that he felt as necessary as oxygen to breathe.

It's not him who's the problem. It's you. You'll destroy him. You're poison.

"Hey, we've been looking for you two." Garret's voice was the splash of water Drea needed to finally be able to pull back from Eric.

Even as she turned to look behind her at Garrett and Billy walking their way, Eric still didn't let go of her hand. And the warmth of his fingers intertwined with hers? God, it felt good.

Too good.

This was the worst time in the world to allow herself to be distracted.

Her women being held captive by Black Skulls in San Antonio needed her. They were all that mattered anyway. Jesus Christ, what she'd been through was nothing, *nothing*, compared to their lives being trafficked as *sex slaves* for the highest bidder.

Of the girls she'd just freed—one girl, Lucy, was so shaken she wouldn't talk to anyone. Even now, over a week after Drea had rescued them, Lucy just sat down on the ground and clutched her arms around herself, rocking back and forth. Drea didn't even know how you began to help someone like that.

Those were people who had *real* problems.

It was time for Drea to get her head back in the damn game.

"They voted," Billy said, pale face serious. He still had dark circles under his eyes, but they were clear and focused. "We need to talk."

He nodded his head down the hall, giving a quick glance over his shoulder as more people began to spill out of the main gathering cave.

It was obvious he meant they should talk in private. Drea gave a sharp nod and led the way back to their cavern. They were quiet as they crossed the long steel walkway that bridged an underground creek. Because they were a new clan, they'd been given one of the curtained off cubbyhole caverns instead of being assigned to one of the 'dorm caverns.'

"All right, what is it?" Eric asked, obviously annoyed at his and Drea's moment being interrupted. Every step they'd taken away from the intense embrace, though, felt like walking further and further out of a deep fog.

Clarity returned, and with it, Drea's sense of purpose.

"Who won the vote?" she asked once as soon as Garrett pulled the curtain on their little cavern and lit a small oil lamp.

"Gisela for the women."

"And the soldiers?"

"Jonathan, the General's right-hand man."

"Shit," Drea swore. "That'll deadlock the council if they don't agree with the plan and the original cave settlers vote with them."

"Which they will," Garrett said. "Your plan means this place will be crawling with soldiers. We risk blowing their hiding spot big time. No way that's a risk they take unless they're forced to."

Drea swore again.

"Wait, wait, wait," Eric said. "What the hell plan were you and the

General arguing about in the first place? Just what is it that you want to do?"

Drea looked Eric's way. "It was actually you who gave me the idea."

"Me?"

"Remember you told me about your dad one time? Back in Jacob's Well, during one of our many late night arguments?"

He looked at her sardonically. "You'll have to refresh my memory. There were so many."

She smacked him on the shoulder and he grinned impishly. That smile, gah, it *did* things to her. Which was completely fucking ridiculous! She shook her head and tried to refocus. Her *plan*. The things that needed *doing*.

So she took a couple of steps back from Eric to get away from his pheromones or whatever the hell was clouding her head when she was near him and told him the plan.

He stood open-mouthed afterwards. "But it would have been destroyed by the bomb."

Drea just shook head and explained her plan.

Eric dragged a hand through his hair when she was done. "Jesus. Well. I guess, yeah. If everything's still there. It might just work."

"But to even have a chance, we have to get the General on board," Billy said, pacing and snapping the elastic band he'd taken to wearing around his wrist. "Which is where our idea comes into play."

"Hey man," Garrett scoffed, "there's no *our*. This plan's all on you."

Billy glared Garrett's way. "You said it was a good idea."

"I think my exact words were: it's not the worst fucking plan I've ever heard."

"Just tell us already," Eric said.

Billy stepped closer to Drea.

She had to ask him to repeat himself because at first she was sure there was no way he could have said what she thought he'd said.

But when he cleared his throat and said it again, it came out just the same: "I think you should invite the General and his Lieutenant Colonel, Jonathan, to be the fourth and fifth in our clan."

"Are you out of your fucking mind?" Eric shouted.

"Just hear me out." Billy covered the last bit of distance so he was only inches away from Drea again and he lowered his voice. "We need the alliance. You could go present your plan tonight at the Council meeting and maybe he hears you out and considers what you have to say. Maybe not. Either way, we need them on our side. For more than just this mission. We need this."

"What the hell do you know about anything?" Eric grabbed the front of Billy's shirt and jerked him away from Drea. "You're just a fucking drug-addicted ex-doctor. How dare you fucking—"

"Stop it," Drea shouted, grabbing Eric's arm before he could punch Billy like it looked like he wanted to. "Just shut up for a second!"

Eric spun on her. "Oh come on. You aren't really—"

"I said shut up." Drea threw her hands up, turning away from all of them.

"I've been around power before," Billy said. "And what we have in this clan here is strong." His eyes flicked around from one to the next. "But it could be stronger. For what we're going up against. We need every advantage we can get."

"Family isn't about tactical advantage," Eric snapped.

Out of her periphery, Drea saw Billy shaking his head. "Oh come on, don't be naïve."

"You think she saved your sorry ass because it was tactically advantageous?"

Billy shrugged. "I am a doctor. That's a useful thing to have around in a pinch. So sure, it was a good tactical move to marry me."

Drea felt her mouth drop open. Did Billy really think that was why she'd saved him? And then a more troubling thought followed—*was* it why she'd saved him?

She pushed it all down to worry about another time and took a long, deep breath. This was the focus she'd been missing. It was why she'd formed the clan in the first place. To help her see when she had blind spots. To give her strength when she was weak.

"Billy's right," she said.

Eric spun on her, looking at her like she was crazy. "What?!"

She stood up straighter but Garrett already had her back. "It makes sense," Garrett said. "Whenever there's a rival MC whose assets we wanted, it usually made more sense to absorb them than go to war with them."

Eric threw his hands in the air. "So, what? Any time we stumble on someone you think will help the 'cause', we'll just have to shove more and more beds together? We'll just take them into our clan and you'll let them in between your thighs?"

She would have slapped him but Billy and Garrett flanked her and both advanced on him, fury emanating from them so that in the end she reached forward and had to hold *them* back.

But she did get right up in Eric's face.

"You're a hypocrite," she spat in a low, harsh whisper. "You marry women off to five men like it's *nothing* all the time. But now that the shoe's on the other foot suddenly you're singing a different tune? How convenient."

"I'm not— I—" Eric sputtered.

But Drea was already stepping back. "I will be inviting General David Cruz and Lieutenant Colonel Jonathan Palmer to join our clan. I will have five husbands just like any other clan bride from Jacob's Well. We'll have a marriage just like any other. And our clan name will be Clan fucking *Valentine*." She glared from one man to the next, daring them to nay say her.

Then she stomped out of the room, shoving the curtain aside and letting it whip shut behind her.

CHAPTER NINETEEN

JONATHAN

Jonathan loved David Cruz.

But unlike what half of the Elite Brigade thought, Jonathan did not want to fuck him.

Frankly, it would have been easier if he did. It certainly would have made all the overwhelming feelings Jonathan had for the man easier to understand.

Because ever since the day General David Benito Cruz had stumbled over Jonathan bleeding in that Nacogdoches alleyway seven years ago, Jonathan had felt a love bordering at times on obsession for the man.

How could he not?

David was everything Jonathan's own father wasn't. Honorable. Loyal. Selfless. Plus he didn't stink of booze and piss, so there was that too.

The world was like this: There were trash people and there were quality people.

Jonathan's kin had been trash as many generations back as he knew of. His grandpa was a mean, mean drunk and there was family legend of how his great-grandpa used to steal money from old ladies by calling them on the phone and tricking them into revealing details so he could steal their identities and bank information.

But David's people? He was second in his family to go to West Point. All of them went to college. It wasn't just that—they were *good* too. His mom volunteered for charities before she died from Xtermi-nate. His *abuelita* had been studying to be a *nun* before she fell in love with his grandpa and dropped out of nun school to marry him instead.

Quality.

David was only ten years older than Jonathan but he did more than take him under his wing. He all but adopted him. Or maybe it was more accurate to say he took him on as a surrogate little brother. Because Jonathan knew he reminded David of his kid brother, Kevin, who'd died.

Sometimes Jonathan wondered if when David looked at him, he saw Jonathan at all. He'd get this real distant look, and Jonathan wondered if he was pretending it was Kevin he was teaching how to fire a gun, or how to shave, or how to follow all the millions of rules it took to be in the Army.

At first, they weren't very close at all. David just brought Jonathan back to the Army barracks at Fort Worth to live and train with all the other soldiers. But Jonathan studied for hours till his eyes hurt and spent day after day at target practice until he could outshoot every other cadet. He was smaller than a lot of other guys, but he ran farther, pushed harder, and stayed longer in the weight room, determined to be the best soldier that the General had ever seen.

He wasn't born quality, but maybe, if he tried very, *very* hard, he could rise above his trash heritage.

He didn't make many friends but he didn't care about that. Half the guys there slacked at everything they did because, hey, the world had ended, so they'd stopped giving a shit.

But General Cruz came by and watched the cadets at their drills. He'd fought a year beside General Goddard on the eastern front and everyone respected him. There were rumors that he was handpicking himself an elite force that would be able to make a real difference to stop the chaos that had become of the world after The Fall. More than anything in the world, Jonathan wanted to be a part of it.

And every time General Cruz came by, he'd stop to chat with Jonathan. How was he doing? he'd ask. Was he fitting in? Finding his footing? Did he need to talk to anyone about all the things he'd been through and seen? Because there were counselors on base.

Jonathan always got embarrassed at those questions. Did the General not think he was tough enough to handle his shit? He always reassured him that he was just fine.

Still, Jonathan worried he wasn't doing enough. The General seemed interested in his progress and occasionally he'd spend an afternoon one on one helping Jonathan perfect some skill or other. But just a couple afternoons twice a month? It wasn't enough—even though Jonathan knew how selfish it was to want to capitalize on the General's valuable time. He was trying to save a whole country and here Jonathan was wanting to bother him with just one dumb kid.

Jonathan had been on base for about two months when he passed by a room full of laptops. Like, *full*. They were stacked on the floor, on every counter space, in chairs.

At first he was confused. All electronics had been fried by the EMP blasts. But then he paused and tried the doorknob. Because what if some of them had survived it? Maybe if they were in a basement that was deep enough underground or in a building that for some reason had metal walls... okay, so it was a stretch, but somebody obviously thought it was a theory worth testing.

The door was locked but locked doors hadn't stopped Jonathan since seventh grade when he learned how to pick locks so he could sneak into the teacher's lounge to steal himself lunch. His dad certainly never packed him any or gave him money.

So Jonathan always kept a couple of big safety pins on him for that reason—a habit he still hadn't broken even though he knew the General would be pissed if he found out about it. General Cruz was fastidious about uniform—even more after the Fall when other commanders had let standards lax.

Jonathan slipped inside the room and saw a volt meter. And he sat down and started working thru the laptops. He was there for three hours before someone found him—the slacker who was *supposed* to be testing them.

So Jonathan made him a deal. If the soldier would let Jonathan have the task, Jonathan would give up an entire week's lunch rations. Getting out of what seemed like an endless, thankless task, plus extra rations? The soldier was gone with Jonathan's weekly ration tickets before he'd finished his next breath.

Jonathan spent every spare minute of the next three days in that windowless room. Cracking laptops open, testing the component parts, tossing the useless laptop into the growing mountain in the far corner.

He was starting to give up hope, sure he'd given up his lunches over nothing when finally, the little arm in the volt meter jumped, letting out a slight buzz. It was two in the morning and Jonathan was half delirious from being crouched over and repeating the same motion over and over and over and *over*.

At the positive result, he jumped so violently, the laptop almost slid off his lap and crashed to the floor.

He threw himself and caught it right before it did, eyes wide.

And then he clutched it to his chest and walked slowly, carefully, to the command barracks where he knocked on General Cruz's door.

The General was *not* happy to be woken in the middle of the night only to find a cadet at his doorstep.

But then he saw what Jonathan was cradling like precious treasure and his entire manner changed. He stood up straighter and his eyes focused.

"What do you have there, soldier?"

"I took over for Vernon in the laptop room, sir. I've been testing the machines for days. And tonight I found this one."

The General's eyes locked with Jonathan's and his voice was a whisper. "It works?"

Jonathan nodded.

"Show me."

They headed down to the General's office and Jonathan showed him. The office was powered by a generator and they plugged the laptop right into a wall socket. Right then and there, the screen lit up.

Jonathan could have wept—both for seeing the screen, and for the way the General hovered behind his chair, one hand on his shoulder.

Jonathan immediately started typing in commands, his curiosity taking over. Did some version of the internet still exist? It was possible. Satellites stored back up images of big portions of the internet If it did exist, was there anyone else out there using it?

It did. And there was.

"What are you doing there?" the General asked.

"Look," Jonathan said, shifting the screen so the General had a better view. "There's a whole SOS network. All over Texas. People with working laptops and computers who are talking to each other."

"Holy shit."

Jonathan looked up sharply. He'd never heard the General curse before but the General was too busy staring at the screen.

"How did you find this?"

Jonathan shrugged. "I've done stuff like this my whole life." In truth, he'd rather not get into his know-how of getting around the dark web—the internet *under* the internet.

Hacking was a hell of a lot easier than pick pocketing, and about a thousand times more lucrative if you were good at it. Which Jonathan was. While other people his age had wasted their high school years on social media, he'd been stealing people's identities and emptying their bank accounts. Unlike great-grandpa though, he didn't target sweet old ladies. Only rich corrupt corporate assholes. He'd had enough stowed away in offshore bank accounts to live comfortably by the time he'd graduated.

A lot of good it had done him when the EMPs wiped out all the bank balances.

And in the end, stealing was stealing. No matter how he justified it to himself, was he *really* that different from great-grandpa? Stealing was what trash did—taking a short-cut instead of earning a living the honest way.

"Jonathan, we've had three working computers and engineers trying to establish communication with the outside and have only had luck contacting a few people in Russia and China."

The astonished and proud smile the General shot Jonathan's direction made him feel warmer and more full than he ever had in his whole damn life.

This was what honest, good work felt like. It was work you didn't have to do in the dark. Work you didn't have to be ashamed of.

It was a feeling Jonathan had chased ever since. He'd chased it throughout all the years set up in the office beside the General's as the Chief Communications Specialist. The General stopped being just his commanding officer and instead became *David*, his friend.

But still, Jonathan lived for that proud smile from David, whether over a cold beer or on the battlefield as his right-hand man.

Smiles of any kind had been absent for a long time from David's face, though. Even before this latest catastrophe with the President's assassination.

No, David's face was always strained lately. He was prone to long silences and short monosyllabic responses. Jonathan knew it was because he was living in his head, trying to solve the multi-faceted problems facing all the people who relied on him. Jonathan *knew* that. But the small, petty part inside him couldn't help but take it personally.

If only he could cheer David up. If only David would *let* him.

Because no matter how close they became, David still held him at an arm's length. Even after all this time. After all they'd been through together. He still wouldn't let Jonathan *in*.

Take right now, for instance. They shared a cavern with three other officers, but they were out in the common caverns, so it was just the two of them.

And David stood, hands behind his back at parade rest, facing the wall. He'd been standing in the same position for fifteen minutes even though Jonathan was there, ready and willing to talk out all the things that were obviously on David's mind. When would he learn he didn't have to take the entire world on his shoulders?

Jonathan was his equal. Literally now, at least in practical terms.

The men had voted him their spokesperson on the Council, with a vote equal to David's.

"How do you think we should deal with the Valentine woman?" Jonathan asked, walking over to David and stepping between him and the wall. Maybe if he demanded attention, David would finally give him his due.

When David didn't respond, Jonathan continued pressing. "Do you think this plan of hers will have any merit?"

"Perhaps," was all David said, his eyes distant as he looked over Jonathan's shoulder.

"If she did what they said she did at the Black Skulls compound, then she's impressive."

David nodded absently.

Jonathan clenched his fists. "Jesus, I'm standing right here. Do you think you could spare me the briefest bit of your attention? At least five minutes of just listening and looking at me?"

David blinked and stood up straight, arms dropping to his sides as he looked at Jonathan. Really looked at him, eyebrows drawing together. "I am listening."

You never listen. Jonathan fought against huffing his breath out like a petulant teenager. As much as he admired and loved David, sometimes he worried he'd always feel like this—the boy that David had rescued. Never a true equal. No matter how many times he was voted Council spokesperson or that he had skills with a computer David could never dream of comprehending.

For once though, David was really looking at him. Now would he *hear* what Jonathan had to say, for fucking *once*?

"What?" David asked. "Jonathan, what is it?" He reached out and put hand on Jonathan's shoulder. "I'm listening. I'm here."

And just like that, Jonathan felt like the biggest jackass in the universe. How selfish and immature was he to be thinking so much about what *he* wanted at a time like this? The whole world had gone crazy and most of David's men were hiding out in the hills, not knowing where their next meal was coming from—much less if Travis or the Black Skulls would discover them. Of course David's mind was preoccupied with all the things Jonathan ought to be thinking about. Because David was honorable. Loyal. Selfless.

Quality.

Jonathan lifted his opposite arm to clap David on the shoulder. "Nothing. But it's getting close to dinnertime. We should go eat."

David frowned. "Are you sure? I know I've been distracted lately. I'm sorry. How have you been doing?"

Biggest. Jackass. Ever.

Jonathan attempted a smile. "Another time."

David looked like he was about to say something else when a female voice called, "Hello? Can I come in?"

The crease between David's frown grew deeper as he walked to the curtain closing off their small cavern they'd been given as a Command HQ and sleeping quarters and swept it back to reveal Drea Valentine.

What on earth could *she* want?

She strode into the room, right past David, not waiting for an invitation. "I'd like to talk with you. Both of you."

"Okay," David said, obviously just as confused about her sudden appearance as Jonathan was.

She walked to the middle of the room and stopped beside the lantern placed on a small shelf of stalagmites beside the far wall.

"Could this not have waited until the Council meeting?" David asked. Jonathan had been thinking the same thing. The Council meeting was scheduled for right after lunch, and lunch was only an hour away.

"No," Drea said. Then she was quiet another long moment like she was gathering her thoughts. Trying to think how to best butter them up so things would go more favorably for her at the Council? She obviously underestimated David if she thought a little feminine flattery was going to—

"The problem with any kind of attack on the Black Skulls in San Antonio is that they'll see us coming," Drea opened. She looked from David to Jonathan, making sure to lock gazes with each of them.

Jonathan swallowed and fought the urge to look away. Good Lord she was pretty. She was so hardened and usually scowling, it wasn't something you noticed right off the bat. But her features, those high cheekbones and bright, intelligent blue eyes—she really was uniquely beautiful.

"And that would be if we could mobilize my troops in the first place," David said. Jonathan was impressed at his ability to focus. "Which we can't—for the very same reason. They'll see the troop movements on satellite."

"Not necessarily."

"What do you mean?" David asked. "Of course they would." But he didn't sound impatient. More curious.

"All we have to do is blind them."

David looked disappointed in her answer. "Fort Worth might as well be Fort Knox at this point with all the military Travis has surrounded himself with. Even if we could get someone through to sneak in and destroy the computer they're using to track satellite imagery, they'll just find anoth—"

"Would you let me finish?" Drea cut him off, one eyebrow arched. She didn't sound impatient though, or angry or superior—completely unlike how she'd been earlier in front of the crowd. Which was when Jonathan realized that her persona earlier had been a show.

For who, though? Even as he asked it, he thought he knew the answer.

The women. She'd been showing them that this really was a safe place. A place where they could stand up to men and not be punished. A place they really could have a voice.

Jonathan took a step closer, fascinated. "So what is your plan?"

"The problem isn't Travis's computers." She looked Jonathan's way, keeping eye contact as she continued. "It's the satellites themselves."

Jonathan felt his forehead scrunch. Surely she didn't mean—

"We need to go to the NASA site in Houston and reprogram the satellites so they point away from Texas."

Holy shit, she *did* mean.

"You can't be serious," David scoffed. "NASA was in Houston. *Houston.* It'll have been destroyed along with the rest of the city on D-Day when it was nuked."

Drea was shaking her head and she pulled out a map from where it was rolled up and shoved in the back pocket of her jeans.

She unfurled it and pointed. "Johnson Space center was on the southernmost part of Houston. Barely in the city at all. And look. My colony was here by Galveston, just thirty miles south. I had women coming to me from all the surrounding areas. At least two came from right by where NASA was—one from League City and another from Friendswood. And they were both healthy as could be."

"At least that you could see," David murmured, studying the map.

Drea ignored him. "And it's common knowledge that the fallout cloud headed northwest after the bombs dropped. There's a very good chance that the NASA buildings are not only intact, but radiation free."

David was starting to look thoughtful so Jonathan spoke up. "It wouldn't just be blinding them without the satellites. It'd be blinding all of us." He looked to David. He couldn't really be considering this, could he?

"That's only if there's an *us* still standing when all of this is said and done," she shot back, moving her attention back to David. "And it wouldn't be forever. After we take San Antonio and deal with Travis once and for all, we can always retask the satellites and bring them back over Texas later. Just think about it," Drea said, lowering her voice. "They're depending on their eyes in the sky. Especially the nighttime IR satellite cameras. If we took those out and then took advantage of the element of surprise—"

"We could actually attack without them seeing us coming," David finished, eyes wide. Jonathan saw David's excitement in his eyes—this was the answer he'd been looking for. All his staring, his brooding silences, it was because he'd been killing himself trying to solve the problem that this woman just pranced in and offered the solution to on a platter.

But wait, they were all forgetting one very important sticking point.

"What about the EMPs?" Jonathan asked. "Even if it is still there and the site isn't poisoned by radiation, it doesn't matter. All the equipment will be fried." It would take months, years maybe even to try to figure out how to restablish connection to the satellites, even if he did have the broken equipment from the Space Center. He'd have to—

"It's not fried," Drea said. "Eric Wolford's father used to work there in Mission Control. He told me a story about his dad took him down there once. Down three stories into the underground bunker where the *real* Mission Control was built."

Holy shit. With every word she said, the ludicrous sounded more and more... plausible. Possible even. Jonathan exchanged a glance with David and could tell his friend was thinking something similar.

"Now," Drea went on. "I don't know computers. But there's a man in Clan Hale who's good with them, we'll have to see if he's willing to—"

"That won't be necessary." Jonathan took the last few steps until he stood right beside Drea. "I can do it."

"Jonathan," David said but Jonathan cut him off.

"No, David, you know I'm the best man for the job. You can't sideline me this time or try to keep me back where it's safe."

That was what David always did. Jonathan was his right-hand man... right up until the action hit, then it was always, stay back, stay back. *You need to watch over the coms, Jonathan, or, Stay back here with the valuable equipment, Jonathan.*

Jonathan hadn't been sure about Drea at all when she'd come barging in here but she'd made her case and made it well. They had to try. And he was only telling the truth—no one was better with computers or advanced systems than him.

But could David see past the role he'd pigeonholed for Jonathan? Jonathan looked at David, really looked at him, pleading with him to hear him. "Nowhere is safe. Not unless we make it that way." And then quieter, "I can do this. You need to let me do this."

It wasn't something he really needed to ask permission for, but out of respect for all that David was to him, he did anyway.

David let out a deep breath and then gave a single nod. "Okay. But I'm coming with you."

Jonathan was both happy and scared at the same time. It would be dangerous. But they'd be together. And maybe finally, *finally*, David would let Jonathan share some of that heavy burden he always carried around.

"I'm glad to hear it," Drea said. "But it's not all I came here to talk about."

Jonathan looked over at Drea, surprised. What else could she have to say?

"My clan and I have a proposal for you. The both of you," she clarified.

Neither Jonathan nor David said anything, waiting for her to go on.

"We'd like to invite you to join our clan. To marry me."

Wha—? Jonathan all but choked on his tongue as he started coughing.

Good Lord, don't be an idiot. She didn't say what you think you heard. She must have said *carry me*? Or *to bury weed*?

But then she started talking in the same cool tones as she'd discussed her plans for the proposed mission to NASA. About how such an alliance would be good for all of them. How they could present a strong, united front. How the intimacy would help shape them an unbreakable team.

Jonathan blinked on in astonishment.

Holy shit.

She actually *meant* it.

Jonathan had heard of the whole Marriage Raffle thing they were doing down in Central Texas South. A couple guys Jonathan knew had even gone down there to become Territory citizens so they could get their name in for the lottos. It was better than in Fort Worth, they figured, where the only way you got a wife was by being a rich SOB or saving up enough script to pay for a whore every now and then.

But a *wife*... Good Lord, Jonathan hadn't let himself think about anything like that in years. It just wasn't in the cards for a military man like him. He'd made his peace with it. His family was the military and he had David. It was enough. It was plenty.

Or is that just the line you've fed yourself for over half a decade now? Haven't you always wanted more?

Jonathan ran a hand down the back of his neck. Well, sure, watching families up close and personal since he'd come to the caves was, well... who wouldn't want that? Of course it looked great from the outside in. And well, Jonathan had never really had the whole loving Mom and Dad thing, so he was just sentimental about the idea of family. So he over-romanticised the whole thing. That was all.

He'd just been alone for so long.

Because when you couldn't sleep in the middle of the night, that's when you really knew it, down deep to the marrow in your bones—you were alone. So alone in the world no one would care much if you lived or if you died.

But a *family*...

Jonathan looked over to David, his chest clenching tight even as he did. Because there was no way David would go for it. Not in a million years.

When his eyes locked on David's though, it was only to find him already looking at Jonathan, a peculiar expression on his face.

"What?" Jonathan asked, only then realizing Drea had stopped talking.

"We could be a family for real," David said.

Drive a fucking ax through Jonathan's chest, would ya? Because of course David knew what Jonathan was thinking, probably before Jonathan had even had the thoughts himself. He only *thought* David had been distant lately. But David was always there. Connected to him closer than a brother, or a father, or any other human could possibly be.

Then David turned and walked closer to Drea. During the whole conversation so far, or maybe Jonathan would call it *negotiations* so far, David had been hard and straight-laced, every inch the General.

But as David approached Drea, Jonathan watched the softness come into his features he usually only displayed when it was him and Jonathan alone.

"You don't have to offer yourself up like this," David said, his voice gentle. "We've already agreed to come on the mission. We'll be with you a hundred percent."

Drea seemed taken aback by David's transformed demeanor. She blinked a few times and then her back stiffened, like David's softness made her want to throw up shields and become even harder.

"It's not just this mission. This is a war. One I intend to win. I will free my women from the Black Skulls and then I will give them a country where they can finally live without fear."

David's face tilted to the side, softening even more as he nodded. "That's something we both want." His brows drew together. "So you don't have to sell yourself in order to get our help."

Drea stepped toe to toe with David, her eyes glacial. Only at David's sharp inhale of breath did Jonathan see the hunting knife she held to David's crotch.

"Call me a whore again and see if you like the way I rearrange your family jewels."

"What?" Jonathan sputtered. "He wasn't—"

But Drea had already started talking again. "Arranged marriages have been the norm for most of human history. The only difference is that I'm doing the arranging myself instead of my father or some male relative. Do you have a problem with that?"

Her face was so close to David's she must be able to smell the orange-scented cornstarch they used in place of deodorant.

"No," David said, never breaking eye-contact with her. "No, I don't have a problem with it." And Jesus, the intensity burning between the two of them was enough to light the vapors from the oil lamp burning beside them on fire.

Jonathan had never seen David with a woman before but he could suddenly imagine him pushing Drea to the floor and dropping on top of her. He'd peel those jeans down her legs and then she'd spread her pale thighs wide open and—

"Excellent," Drea said, taking a step back from David and swallowing quickly before squaring her shoulders. "She gave a nod. "So we have an agreement?"

David's jaw tensed but he gave a hard nod. "We have an agreement."

Holy shit. Did that really just happen?

"We'll have a small private ceremony after the Council meeting," Drea said. "Then we'll consummate the marriage and spend tomorrow preparing for the mission. Tomorrow night we'll leave for Houston."

She turned and left the cave with a swirl of blonde dreadlocks but

Jonathan stood rooted in place, absolutely stiff—in every meaning of the word.

Because replaying on an endless loop in his head were the words she'd listed off so casually: *then we'll consummate the marriage.*

As in, tonight.

Tonight they'd consummate the marriage.

Holy. Shit.

CHAPTER TWENTY

DREA

Drea was shaking when she left David and Jonathan's cavern. David—that was how she'd decided to think of him. No more General Cruz this and General Cruz that.

General Cruz was an untouchable figure who commanded thousands.

David was a man.

No, he's neither of those. He's an asset. For as long as he remains useful.

She wouldn't be dumb enough to think that just because she was bringing him into her clan, into her *bed*, that she could trust him. Or that Lieutenant Colonel of his.

But this way, she'd be able to keep an eye on them. And when the time came, she'd be in the position to do whatever needed doing to take care of her women.

Keep your friends close, but keep your enemies closer.

As close as a lover.

Thomas had taught her that lesson and in a way that she'd never forget it. Back then she'd been Sophia's age and convinced it was love.

She could have written odes to true love—it's heights and depths and widths of being. She was pretty sure there was even some terrible half-scribbled poetry somewhere that attested to the fact.

But Thomas was slick, so slick, even back then at twenty-one, just three years older than her. *Keep your enemies close.* And when the time is right—*STRIKE!*

She remembered it like it was yesterday—lying in bed beside Thomas after having made love, swapping dreams of the future. Dreams that more and more centered around Thomas himself. Which only made sense to her, because at the time, he'd been her universe.

"We'll get married and then you'll take over for Daddy as Pres," she said happily as she played with Thomas's hand, intertwining her fingers lazily with his.

"And you'll immediately start knocking me up with as many babies as possible. Twin boys to kick-start things, so you'll have boys to pass the MC on to one day."

Thomas let out a bark of laughter.

Drea loved the sound of his laughter and she snuggled even closer against his side.

"Twins?" He shook his head, then grabbed her and rolled them, landing on top of her and pinning her underneath him on the bed, hands holding her wrists to the mattress.

"I think you're forgetting a few key details, Princess." He was smiling but his eyes were dark in that way that sent a shiver down her back sometimes.

She tried to lift up off the bed to kiss him but he held her wrists firmly in place.

She pretended to frown up at him and struggle. She knew he liked feeling in control and she was happy to play his little games. "And what, pray tell, am I forgetting?" she asked, finally giving up on struggling and flopping back to the pillow.

He smiled a wolf's smile and leaned down over her. She thought he was going to kiss her but he didn't. "Oh, I don't know. Maybe the fact that your dad only turned fifty last month and there's no way he's passing the Pres patch on any time soon. Let alone to the likes of me. He hates me, Belladonna."

Drea immediately started shaking her head. "No. Thomas, he just doesn't know you like I do. If you two could just—"

"Then there's *my* Dad, who sure as fuck wouldn't let me have Pres before claiming it for himself. Even if it meant gutting me with his bare hands to get to the throne. Though he'd make a fucking mess of the Skulls if he ever became Pres."

"Stop it," Drea said, frowning.

"Stop what?" Thomas laughed, and this was the laugh she didn't like—his *mean* laugh.

She wanted to pull her hands over her ears at the sound but he still had them pinned. "Saying what, Bella? Saying shit like it is?"

She tried to lift a hand to his face but of course he wouldn't let her. She rolled her eyes and huffed out in frustration at being forced to be immobile. Though secretly, she kind of liked it.

She was the daughter of the Black Skulls MC president. Thomas wasn't wrong when he called her *Princess*. No one else dared to treat her like Thomas did. Which she knew was part of why she was so wildly attracted to him.

He didn't obey her father's unspoken command of *do not touch* when it came to his daughter that everyone else in or related to the club understood all too well. Thomas didn't *handle with care*.

She had bruises on her shoulders and thighs from their lovemaking. She'd never felt more alive than when she was alone with Thomas.

But she hated when his moods went dark like this.

He climbed off her, still holding her wrists the whole time so she couldn't touch him.

"Thomas, don't."

"Don't what?"

She pulled the sheet up to cover her breasts after he finally let her go to reach for his pack of cigarettes. "Don't ruin it. We had such a nice night."

He laughed the dark, mean laugh.

"Princess Belladonna. Living up here in her beautiful house on the hill with all her designer clothes and trinkets." He picked up a pearl necklace draped on her little antique make-up bureau.

"Thomas, stop it. Put that down."

"Where did Daddy say he picked this up for you, again?"

"You know he got it at Tiffany's when he went to New York last year. You were with him on the run."

Thomas really started laughing now and she squared her shoulders, sitting up straighter.

"I'm not an idiot. I know my father does illegal things."

"Oh, you figured that one out all on your own, did you?"

"That's enough." Drea yanked the sheet with her as she stood up from the bed and pointed for her bedroom door. "Leave. You're being hateful and I've been nothing at all but gracious and kind to you. I don't want to talk to you again until you've apologized and learned what it means to have a civilized tongue in that barbaric head of yours."

Thomas just shook his head at her as he pulled on his jeans. "You're almost nineteen, Princess. Don't you think it's time to learn how Daddy makes his money?"

She glared at him, locking her jaw. "I know about the drugs, okay? And the guns."

Was it so bad if she just tried not to think about that part of her life? Dad was just Dad. Once when she was old enough to ask about it, he'd ruffled her hair and said, *Drea baby, don't worry your pretty little head about it.* He was the only one who called her by her first name and not Belladonna. *Sombody's going to be moving these products. And isn't it better if it's us rather than some violent Mexican gang like MS-13 raping and killing their way through our towns?*

She'd shaken her head and he'd kissed her hair. *Besides, it's our second amendment right to arm ourselves. Government shouldn't have a say in how we protect ourselves or what we put in our bodies when we want to have a little fun. You believe in freedom, don't you, Andrea?*

She'd nodded and he'd given her another kiss. *I'm glad we had this talk.*

But Thomas just laughed. "Guns and dr—" He shook his head. "Wow, Princess, you really are clueless."

She leaned over and picked his shirt up off the floor and threw it at him. "If I'm so clueless and naïve then why are you even here? Why bother with me at all?"

His face softened but only for an instant.

"Oh Princess," he sighed, running a hand down his face. He dropped his head for a moment and Drea frowned. In spite of the fight they were having, part of her wanted to go to him, to wrap her arms around his waist and bury her head against his familiar chest.

But then he whispered the words that would change everything. The words that were the catalyst for a chain reaction of events that ended with losing absolutely everything she ever cared about in the whole world:

"Princess, if you want to know how your father really makes his money, go look in the warehouse the MC owns, out by the docks."

CHAPTER TWENTY-ONE

DREA

Drea headed back through the section of tunnels the women used for sleeping when she spotted a familiar head of long, dark brown hair.

"Sophia," she called

Sophia's head turned from where she was standing with a group of women, eyes searching and then narrowing in suspicion when she saw Drea.

Drea let out a breath as she crossed the distance. Shit. Saying she'd started off on the wrong foot with the girl was an understatement. And now Sophia would be her... *stepdaughter?* Drea shook the thought off. She'd be family, anyway.

Because while Drea considered the arrangement with David and Jonathan business more than anything else, Eric was different. Eric was... well, *Eric.*

And if there was one thing she knew about him, it was that he loved his daughter. Drea owed it to him to try to make this right.

"Do you have a second?" Drea asked as soon as she got close to Sophia. "Could we maybe," Drea looked around at all the other people streaming past them heading for the dining cavern, "find some place to talk?"

Sophia crossed her arms over her chest. "I'm not sure I want to hear whatever you have to say, but go ahead. Talk."

Drea let out an annoyed breath. *Do not let her get under your skin. Do not let her get under your skin. Remember Eric.*

"At least come over by the wall?"

Not waiting for an answer, Drea headed for a small natural alcove off to the side of the main pathway. She didn't look over her shoulder but to her relief, a few moments later, she felt Sophia behind her.

Drea turned to her and held her hands out. "Look, I want to call a truce. I know we never got along the best—"

Sophia scoffed her assent.

"—but for your dad's sake, I was hoping we could change that."

Sophia's back stiffened. *Oh shit, here we go*, Drea thought.

"Because you and my dad have gotten so close all the sudden," Sophia said, eyes narrowed angrily. "The same man you couldn't stand just a few weeks ago. The same guy you had nothing but contempt for every time I tried to say he was a good man."

Okay. Drea deserved that.

"Look, I'm not saying that I'm an angel, okay? I fucked up. I get... prickly about certain subjects."

"Prickly?" Another scoff. "I could think of a few different choice adjectives."

So this was how it was going to be?

"Fine," Drea said, dropping all attempts at a conciliatory voice. "I was a bitch. Is that what you want me to say?"

Sophia's arms dropped. "For starters, yeah."

Drea shook her head. "Jesus, you really are such a—" *Princess.* She'd been about to say *you really are such a princess.*

Drea took a step back from Sophia, blinking. Holy shit. Was it really that basic? She'd disliked Sophia on sight because she...

She reminds you of you at her age.

"What?" Sophia frowned, obviously seeing the change in Drea's manner.

Drea held up a hand. "I— I—" she started but then she didn't know what to say, not for a long second. Sophia just watched on in bewildered silence.

Finally Drea took a deep breath. "Look, I think I've been really unfair to you."

Whatever Sophia had been expecting her to say, that had obviously not been it. She looked shocked and disarmed. And maybe any other time, Drea might have tried to use that to win points against her, but right now she was feeling too raw to do anything other than be honest.

"I was a lot like you when I was your age. I loved my dad more than anything in the world. He was my hero. I thought he'd always take care of me. Protect me." The last words came out on a choked whisper.

Because in the end, he had tried to protect her, hadn't he? In his own fucked up way?

Drea sucked in a breath, looking at the floor so she could get out what she had to say. "But my dad wasn't a good man like your dad. The person I'd idolized my whole life," Drea stopped, shaking her head, "he did terrible, terrible things."

Even as she said it, she was reliving that horrible night. After Thomas left, she'd gotten dressed and taken *Stella*, her Ducati motorcycle. She knew the warehouse by the docks. Her dad had taken her there only once, years and years before. He'd just gotten in a shipment of vintage muscle cars from overseas and he'd wanted her to see them fresh off the boat.

But when she cracked the chain with the bolt-cutters she'd brought and heaved open the door, it wasn't old cars she found inside.

It was women. Girls. Some as young as fourteen.

They were held in caged stalls like animals. It smelled terrible. They had no other choice but to shit and piss in the same cages where they slept. She'd learn later that the warehouse was merely a processing facility on their journey—the port at Houston was where they were trafficked in and out of the country.

That was how the Black Skulls *really* made its money—human trafficking.

And her father had been the President of the Black Skulls' charter chapter for almost fifteen years.

Drea's head bowed lower.

"When I learned the man he really was..." she let out a humorless laugh, fighting against the stupid tears threatening to choke her. "It all but broke me."

"What happened?" Sophia's soft question made Drea look up. Sophia's combative stance was gone and so was her petulant righteousness. She looked like she genuinely wanted to know. And the compassion in her eyes was too reminiscent of her father.

Drea looked away again. She didn't know if Sophia was asking what happened as far as her dad being a bad guy or how Drea responded. The first she wasn't about to get into. The second...

Drea shook her head. "I—" She breathed out, closing her eyes. "I confronted him when I found out who he really was. The things he'd done. The things he was continuing to do."

She'd wanted *so badly* for him to say he had no idea. That it was his VP, not him, doing it behind his back. That he'd go back down to the docks with her and help her free all those women.

Instead, "He threatened me. Told me if I knew what was good for me I'd stop asking questions I didn't want the answers too. That it was time for me to grow up and do what women in our world always did."

Drea opened her eyes and met Sophia's. "Look the other way. Get married. Have some babies. Spend the money he worked so hard for." Drea's mouth went hard. "The *blood money*."

Sophia's features twisted in sympathy and she looked like she wanted to reach out to comfort Drea. Luckily, she checked the impulse. Drea could only stand so fucking much.

"The thing was, before I found out what he did, that was all I wanted."

She needed Sophia to understand this. She didn't know why it was suddenly so important, but it was. "It was all I thought about, day in, day out. What kind of wedding dress I'd wear. What my boyfriend's and my children would look like. If they'd have my blonde hair or his brown eyes." Even thinking about it now sent a shudder of revulsion down her spine. God, how could she have been so stupid? So fucking *blind?*

"But of course he was in the same shit Dad was. Neck fucking deep." Drea's mouth twisted in disgust. "He set me up to find out about it all. I thought he was trying to help me. To show me the truth. But he was just manipulating me."

Sophia gasped. "No. Are you sure? Maybe he—"

But Drea shook her head in one violent motion. "Thomas knew me. He knew what I would do. Or at least suspected. I was Daddy's Princess. But I was also stubborn. So when my dad issued his proclamation that I needed to go be the good little daughter and stick my head in the sand about everything I'd learned, I went up to my bedroom. And then, in the middle of the night, I snuck out to a pay phone and called the cops telling them exactly where they could find Dad's..." she swallowed, unable to finish the sentence.

Even now, she couldn't admit what he'd done. One time over the phone to the cops, that was the only time she'd ever said out loud what she'd seen in the warehouse that day.

"So your dad got arrested?"

Drea let out a short, humorless laugh. "Of course not. Dad bankrolled the cops in that town. I was such a fucking idiot."

"So what happened?"

"Dad found out, of course. Someone had narc'd on the warehouse. Didn't take a genius to figure out who. Problem was, Dad didn't work alone and he wasn't the only one who found out about my call. The cops gave them the recording. All Dad's, well, his 'business partners' knew my voice. And with the kind of shit he was into, the absolute worst thing you can do is be a narc. They're also not the kind of people who give second chances."

Cueball, Thomas's dad, had dragged her out of bed by her hair. He was the MC's Sergeant at Arms, their enforcer, and he'd always enjoyed his job a little too much.

It was the only time she'd ever been in the room where they convened church.

They were all there, the men she'd grown up with her whole life, standing there in judgement of her.

Some she might have expected. Crow was VP and everyone knew he was gunning for Dad's spot. Handlebar was a big mean bastard who had always scared her, and she'd never much liked Tweeker.

But Tex-Mex? And Ragu, and Smokey? Those men had been as much fathers to her as her own dad. Yet there they all sat, some looking uncomfortable, but not a single one stood up in her defense.

Except Dad.

"Yes, she fucked up," Dad said. "But we kept her out of club business all this time. It's just cause her ma took off that she's been around the clubhouse so much the past few years. Now that's on me. I shoulda took better care to keep her separate."

"She still knows the code," Cueball said. "She betrayed us and traitors end up six feet under. That's the way it is."

Drea had been scared before, but it wasn't until that moment that it hit her. She was here because they were deciding whether to kill her or not. This was her tribunal. These men would be her judge, jury, and if they deemed that she deserved it, her executioners.

She scrambled to her feet and tried to make a run for it.

Stupid, considering the circumstances, where she was, and who surrounded her.

Cueball grabbed her by her hair—always the fucking hair with that one— and slammed her back to the ground.

As blood ran from her forehead down into her eyes, she looked around franti- cally for Thomas. He stood at the back of the crowd. As a prospect, it was unusual that he'd even been allowed in for church. But he was there.

She kept waiting for him to send some sort of secret signal—something letting her know that he'd get her out of there. That it would be all right.

More stupidity.

Even then she couldn't see.

This was the very moment he'd been hoping to orchestrate.

"They would have killed me. Then and there."

Sophia's eyebrows shot up. "So how'd you escape?"

"I didn't." Drea's voice was barely a whisper. "My dad, he—" Her voice broke and she took a long, deep breath. "He was a bad man but he still loved me." A truth she still didn't know how to reconcile. "He stood up to them for me. Said I was family and family came first." Before business. Before money. Before club.

"And when he saw nothing he said was going to change their minds, he did the only thing left."

"What?" Sophia asked, rapt.

"He offered himself in my place."

Drea looked up then, meeting Sophia's eyes for the first time since she'd begun her story. The tears that shone there made Drea's stomach hurt. Too soft. The girl was too soft for what this world would do to her.

"And they killed him?" Sophia cried, a tear spilling down her cheek.

Drea swallowed back her own emotion, embarrassed now to have revealed so much. "Of course they killed him. It was what all of it was for in the first place. Leaking the location to me. Knowing I'd do something stupid. Thomas and his father relied on me being a naïve, stupid, weak little girl, and I lived up to their every expectation. Dad was murdered in front of me and the—" Drea's jaw worked. "The evil fucking shit his partners were into continued on unchecked."

It still kept her up at night—those women in that warehouse. She'd been there. *Right there.* She already had the bolt-cutters. Why hadn't she just gone in and cut them out of those fucking cages?

But noooooo, instead she'd gone running to Daddy. And when that didn't work, she'd called the police.

Stupid. So fucking *stupid.*

"It wasn't your fault—"

"Don't." Drea held up a finger. "Just. Don't."

All those women spent the rest of their lives in sex slavery because she was— God, she couldn't even think of a word for what she'd been. Naïve and ignorant weren't strong enough words because she should have known better. She should have asked questions sooner. A better person would have.

A big part of her must not have *wanted* to know. How many women had come in and out of that warehouse during all the years she'd spent blissfully happy playing dolls and running track, performing in school plays and smiling out at her dad in the crowd. Daddy's little girl.

"I'll spend the rest of my life trying to make up for the sins of my father."

"Drea," Sophia shook her head. "You—"

"I said, *don't.*"

Sophia huffed out a breath but then nodded. "Fine. I won't. But I'm sorry about your dad. About all of it."

Drea shrugged her words off. "Anyway, all of that to say, I saw how blindly devoted to your father you were and it, I don't know, I guess it triggered some shit for me. So I'm sorry. I apologize. And it would really mean a lot to your dad if you were at the wedding later tonight."

Sophia's eyes widened and the sympathetic expression on her face evaporated. "Tonight?" she squeaked.

Oh shit, had Drea just stepped in it again?

"Look, I know it's fast—"

"Ya think?" Sophia crossed her arms over her chest again. "Just tell me one thing."

Drea held up her hands. "Anything. I'm an open book."

Sophia narrowed her eyes. "Do you love him?"

Fuck my life.

"Sophia, it's more complicated than that."

"No, it's really not. Do. You. Love. Him?"

"I respect him. I value his opinions. I'll always consider his feelings and will do everything I can to make him happy and comfortable, as much as it's in my power."

Sophia didn't even try to mask her disappointment. "But you don't love him."

"I— I—" Drea broke off, holding up her hands again, this time in a helpless gesture. "I don't know if I'm capable of the kind of love you're talking about. I could lie to you and give you the answer you want. But I just—" She shook her head. "I don't know." And as she said it, she realized it was true.

She genuinely didn't know if she was capable of loving anyone. She didn't know if Dad and Thomas's betrayal had broken her.

"That's not good enough," Sophia said, turning and walking away.

Drea wanted to stop her, but to say what?

She couldn't change the past. She couldn't change what it had all done to her.

After Dad said he'd take her place, everything moved fast. Cueball came and no matter how much she screamed, it didn't matter. Thomas came and joined the men holding her back while Cueball lifted the Colt 45 and put a bullet through her father's brain.

Then they yanked a black bag over her head and Drea was driven to the coast.

When the black bag came off, only Thomas was there.

Thomas, her Thomas. The boy she'd lost her virginity to. The boy she'd promised her forever. In her heart if not out loud.

He'd betrayed her.

She saw it then.

How he'd led her to the warehouse.

How he'd played her like she was a marionette on his string.

"*You fucking* bastard!"

She flew at him, half blind from her tears but determined to hurt him just as badly as he'd hurt her—to fucking kill *him. But he just caught both her wrists in one hand, easily subduing her. Because she was* weak. *Because she was a fucking* child.

He yanked her arms behind her back and then pulled her chest to his chest. She spit in his face and he slapped her.

She blinked, stunned.

Until that moment, she realized some part of her had been waiting for him to tell her that she had it all wrong, that he'd only been playing a part in front of the MC, that he hadn't been able to stop what happened to her dad but he'd saved her and now they'd run away together.

But he'd just hit her.

He must have seen the shock on her face because he laughed. It was the mean laugh and now she saw it for what it was—his true face. Cruel. The laugh of someone who inflicted pain and liked it.

She turned her head to the side and threw up.

"*Jesus Christ." Thomas let go of her and she stumbled backwards, landing hard on her ass and scraping her elbows. "You're a fucking mess." He wiped his hands on his shirt like she was something diseased.*

"*You're a monster," she whispered.*

He rolled his eyes. "You should be on your knees kissing my feet. It's only because of me that you aren't in a container ship on your way to South America as we speak. They pay big for blondes there."

Her mouth dropped open but she had no words except one. "Why?"

He shrugged. "Sometimes you were a good fuck."

Her whole body shuddered in revulsion. "No. Why are you doing this? Why did you—" Her voice broke. Images of her father's body falling to the floor flashed in her head and her hand went to her forehead. She felt faint with dizziness.

Thomas laughed. "Christ, you really don't know me at all, do you? I'm going to be President of the Black Skulls. And not twenty years from now when I'm a wrinkled old fuck. I'm on a two-year track, Princess."

Drea's mouth dropped open again though she didn't know how she still had the capacity for surprise at this point. Then she shook her head and laughed. "Crow will kill you the second you try to make a move on him. You're nothing but an arrogant little boy whose own dad couldn't give two shits about him."

Thomas sprang quick as lightning. One second he was standing over her, the next he was crouched, his hand at her throat, squeezing until she was gasping helplessly for breath.

He leaned over until she could smell the cigarettes on his breath. "The only reason I'm not going to kill you right here, right now, is because I want you to suffer knowing that you were fucking the man who got your father killed. In love with the man who got your father killed. The way you groaned when you sucked my dick, mmm baby, I never had it so good."

Drea screamed in rage but it barely made a noise with his hand cinched tight around her throat.

"You were boring as fuck in bed but you could suck cock like a pro, I'll give you that. And I'd just go fuck one of the club whores or better yet, one of the warehouse girls, when I really needed to get my rocks off." He squeezed even tighter. "See, nothing gets me off like a little pain with my pleasure."

He moved until he was whispering in her ear, pinning her in place no matter how much she struggled to get out from under him. "I like it when they scream. I've always wondered what you would sound like when you scream, Princess. Will you scream for me?"

Over the next twenty minutes, she did scream. He hurt her, violated her, and she screamed, begging for someone, anyone to hear and come rescue her.

But life was not a fairytale.

There were no white knights.

And when he left her there, broken on a dirty, abandoned beach in the middle of winter, she thought she would die. She wanted to die. But just like everything else that night, she didn't get what she wanted.

She woke to the sunrise, battered, bruised, and in so much pain she wasn't sure she'd be able to move.

But she did anyway. Because what did pain matter? She dragged herself across the beach to the brown waters of the Texas Gulf and gritted her teeth against the sting of the salt water on all her cuts and lacerations.

She fought the temptation to crawl further in and let the tide take her out to sea.

No, she'd never take the easy way out again.

She had penance to pay for her father's many sins.

And if it was the last thing she ever did on this earth, she would put every last Black Skull, and Thomas Tillerman in particular, in the ground.

CHAPTER TWENTY-TWO

ERIC

"I now pronounce you men and wife," Jonas said, holding his hands out and smiling widely. "You may kiss the bride."

All six of them, plus Jonas, stood in the tiny cavern their clan had claimed. The few witnesses spilled out into the hallway beyond—Audrey, Shay, Vanessa, a few others.

Not Sophia.

It hurt that she wasn't here but at the same time Eric knew the idea of him and Drea might take some time for her to get used to.

And as much as he worried over his daughter, there were more pressing matters on his mind as Jonas spoke the words to the familiar ceremony Eric had literally heard hundreds of times. But of course, none of those times had *he* been the one making the vows. And Drea had never before been the bride.

Eric couldn't take his eyes off her. And she couldn't take her eyes off of... the floor.

She moved quickly around the half circle, giving each of them the most perfunctory kiss her lips were just a brush of warmth against

Eric's before her mouth was gone again. Eric fought the urge to reach after her and draw her back to him as she moved on to Garrett.

Why was she doing this? *Really?* Why invite the two strangers in? Wasn't she the same woman who swore marriage was an outdated convention created by the patriarchy to oppress women? So why had she changed her tune all the sudden? Just because she thought it was the only way to sway General Cruz and his Lieutenant Colonel to their side?

Eric felt like he was going to crawl out of his fucking skin as the pastor thanked the guests and one by one, they filed out of the small cavern. Drea excused herself to slip behind the tiny curtained off corner in the back of the cave to change and Eric could only stare after, not caring if he was being a bad host.

If only she would have heard him out. They could have just left in the middle of the night and gone without the General's blessing. If they'd redirected the satellites, it wasn't like he'd say, no, I won't use the benefits of this thing you've done. Of course he would. They'd achieve their goal and their clan could stay as it was.

It was bad enough having to share her with two other men.

But *four?*

You're a hypocrite. You marry women off to five men like it's nothing all the time. But now that the shoe's on the other foot?

He squeezed his eyes shut. Goddammit. He was never supposed to be in this position. Hypothetically, he'd always assumed that, sure, of course he'd be fine with it if he ever got married again. But that was never going to be a reality for him. He'd decided that a long time ago, so it was a pretty damn easy assertion to make.

But now here he was. No matter how upset he'd been, the thought of backing out and not going through with the marriage... well he'd considered it for about point zero three seconds. But everything in him rebelled at the thought.

NO.

So now here he stood with his wedding night in front of him... and he'd be sharing the woman he'd just married with *four* other men...

His hands clenched into fists.

"Something the problem there, champ?" Garrett asked, staring pointedly down at Eric's fisted hands. "Cause if you cause any trouble for my *wife*, I'm gonna have to make trouble for you."

Eric narrowed his eyes. "Oh, so this is the part where you try to scare me with your strong-arm tactics? Because I don't intimidate easy."

Garrett smirked. "Oh you think I need to intimidate you? That's cute. How about I just bash your fucking face in? You can't screw shit up if you're unconscious, now can you?"

Eric had about a hundred comebacks to that. What redeeming qualities Drea saw in this dumb ape, Eric had no clue.

But he was currently struck speechless, because Drea had stepped out from the curtain.

And apparently the 'something comfortable' she'd been changing into was her birthday suit, because there she stood, naked as the day she was born and so fucking beautiful it was a battle for which hurt worse—Eric's heart or his ever-hardening cock.

"Holy shit," Jonathan swore. "You're the most beautiful thing I've ever seen." On this at least, Eric could agree with the newcomer.

Drea had the slightest little coy smile on her face. She certainly wasn't shy. Her shoulders were back, breasts boldly bared, and her gaze was direct as she looked from one man to the next. Eric couldn't help holding his breath as her eyes came to him.

But when they did, he frowned. Something was missing. Some spark. It was like she was operating on autopilot.

She didn't say a word as she walked forward, headed straight to Garrett, and went up on tiptoes to kiss him.

His arms wrapped around her clumsily as he kissed her back.

He only got several seconds though, because no sooner had he drawn Drea against him than she was pulling away again.

She turned to Jonathan next. First she reached for his hand and lifted it to her breast. Even from where he stood halfway across the room, Eric could see the man's hand shaking. He was young, maybe twenty-five. How much experience with women had he had before The Fall, if any? Unless he visited the capitol whores in Fort Worth, this could very likely be the first time he'd touched a woman this way.

Jonathan squeezed her breast and her hand dropped to the front of his pants. He groaned as he wrapped a hand around her naked back, devouring her lips.

Eric's fists clenched so hard he knew his nails were breaking skin. He was just supposed to stand here and watch while— while she—

That was it. Hypocrite or not, Eric couldn't stand to watch anymore of this. He turned, ready to leave.

"Not sure you want to do that, friend," said David by the exit, arms crossed like he was standing sentry.

Eric just glared at him.

He reached for the curtain, not able to bear the noises behind him for another goddamn second when the General spoke again.

"I think she might need you tonight."

Eric swung around, ready to give the bastard a piece of his mind when he caught sight of Drea again.

Jonathan was squeezing her breast experimentally, eyes wide with awe.

Jesus but Eric wanted to rip the man's hand away from her. He wanted to storm over there and sweep her into his arms. He wanted to yell that she was *his* and no one else's. He wanted to shove everyone out and yank the curtain shut in their faces. He wanted to look Drea in the eye and demand that she see him. Really *see* him. To stop whatever act she was putting on.

He blinked, looking closer. That's when he saw, or at least started paying attention to what might have had David pausing.

Her face was all wrong. That smile. The slight stiffness to her actions. He didn't think it was a game, precisely. Drea didn't play games. Not like this. She hadn't invited these men into her clan to hurt Eric or the others. At least not on purpose, he didn't think.

As he watched her move away from Jonathan and turn to Billy, that goddamned plastic smile still plastered on her face, he became even more convinced of it.

Jesus, here she was, completely naked, inviting them into her blankets—inviting them into her *body*—but it was all smoke and mirrors.

All of this was to push them away.

That moment earlier in the tunnels when he'd held her and she'd clung back. They'd been in a quiet bubble together for what felt like a lifetime even though it was only minutes. But they'd connected. Real connection. Eric had felt it and he *knew* she had too.

And how did she respond? By going and inviting more men into the clan—at least in part to drive Eric away. It had almost worked. Eric had almost let himself be alienated.

Jesus Christ, was she that terrified of intimacy?

How is that a fucking surprise, jackass?

He had no idea what her life had been like before he met her, but he sure as shit knew where Nix and the others said they'd found her. Locked in a closet beaten all to hell, abused and tortured for who knew how long.

Even the thought was like a spear through Eric's guts. It wasn't something he'd even let himself dwell on much before, it made him simultaneously sick and murderous feeling.

And before that? She'd obviously grown up in the Black Skulls MC. And the things she knew how to do? The person she was?

Eric shook his head. He'd bet a hundred to one odds her damage had started long before the Fall.

She'd dragged Garrett down to the floor where they'd piled their blankets, then she got on her hands and knees. She took Garrett's cock in her mouth while swinging her ass invitingly toward Billy. It was the opposite of how she'd taken them the first time, when she'd blown Billy while Garrett fucked her from behind.

Her mouth made a loud *pop* noise as she came off Garrett's cock and turned to Jonathan who was still standing, staring down with eyes wide and a hand stroking his cock through his fatigues.

"I like that," Drea said in a voice that sounded nothing like herself. "Take it out and touch yourself while you watch. It'll be your turn next."

Eric narrowed his eyes. This was what she was going to make of her wedding night? This fucking farce? Her playing at being some goddamned pre-Fall porn star?

No.

That wasn't happening. Eric wouldn't let it.

He marched across the small space of the cavern, right up beside where Drea had Garrett in her mouth, opposite where Jonathan stood.

Then he crouched down and Drea's eyes shot his direction, briefly clouding with confusion, no doubt at his close proximity.

He got down on his knees and leaned in to whisper in her ear, not missing her slight flinch. Fuck. He'd been an ass today. Getting jealous instead of focusing on what she needed. Did she think he was going to be nasty to her now, right when she was so vulnerable. God, didn't she know him better than that?

All he could do was make it up to her now. To show her the man he could be, if she'd just give him that chance. To show her he could be as brave as she was.

"Look up at Garrett, baby," Eric whispered in her ear, teasing just the tip of his tongue out to lick along the bottom of her lobe. "Look at what you're doing to him."

Eric pulled back just long enough to see her glance up Garrett's body. Garrett's worshipful gaze was locked on Drea, just as Eric knew it would be.

Eric leaned back in. "He loves you."

Drea's breath sucked in at his words and he pressed on. "Give him everything you have, baby. Not just a slice of you. Give him *everything*. Worship that cock in your mouth like it's the last thing you'll ever taste on this earth."

Drea's suction increased around Garrett's shaft. Eric could tell because every time she pulled off there was a loud *pop* noise.

"That's right, baby," Eric encouraged. "Now pump the bottom of his shaft with your hand and bob up and down right over the top ridge of his head. Lips over your teeth. Oh fuck, that's right. Don't be afraid to get messy with it. Goddamn you're so fucking hot, Drea baby."

Drea's eyes came back to his. The confusion had been replaced by lust. This was turning her on. Way the fuck on if her expression was any indication.

Eric leaned in and kissed down her shoulder, needing the contact. Because as much as he wanted this for her, Jesus, he needed it too. The connection. The intimacy. Not to mention his cock was hard as granite and if he didn't touch her he felt like he'd fucking die.

"You're so beautiful," he whispered, grasping one full breast in his hand before teasing the nipple between his forefinger and thumb.

She groaned around Garrett's cock and Garrett swore. Eric kissed down Drea's shoulder blade.

Even as he did, he saw Billy grasp her hips and knew he was finally about to penetrate her. Eric tweaked and released Drea's nipple, tweaked and released, helping to ensure she'd be turned on and fully lubricated for Billy.

Drea's pleasured moan when Billy entered her told Eric that they were all doing their job. Eric trailed his good hand underneath her body from her breast to her belly, and finally to her sex.

If he thought she'd moaned earlier when he was at her breast it was nothing to the ecstatic noise she let out when he finally made contact with her clit.

Eric felt Billy's cock moving in and out of her but he focused on that swollen bud at the top of her sex, at first circling gently, teasing, teasing. He wanted to drive her crazy. He wanted her out of her mind. Out of that constantly calculating head of hers. He wanted her to give herself over to them.

"Oh shit, honey," Garrett gasped, and Eric looked over at him. "I'm gonna—" He was trying to pull back from Drea's mouth but she lifted one hand to his ass, holding him in place, and sucked him even more fervently. Down her fucking throat. Jesus Christ. She was the sexiest thing Eric had ever witnessed or even imagined.

Garrett let out a strangled cry, one hand dropped loosely to the top of Drea's head as his hips thrust forward, all but flush with her pink lips.

Eric imagined the cum pumping down her throat and he couldn't help moving his hand to the front of his own jeans. Jesus fucking Christ. He wouldn't come without his cock inside her, but she was gonna make it damn hard, wasn't she? Hard being the operative word.

Garrett finally slipped out of her mouth and then all but crashed to his knees. He cupped Drea's face in his hands and kissed her.

Eric stopped teasing at her clit and rubbed her in earnest. He didn't want Drea pulling back now. She needed to give Garrett all of herself when her impulse would be to try to insert distance after the intimacy they'd just shared. Eric couldn't let that happen.

If she was crazy with lust then maybe her barriers would finally be down far enough to let them warm up the heart she'd let go cold for so many years out of self-preservation.

So Eric withdrew his hand from her drenched sex, but only for a moment so he could lay down on his back and wriggle sideways underneath her heaving body. His broken arm was jostled as he went but he didn't care.

Then he returned his hand to her clit and while lifting up to suck on her breasts, first one and then the other.

Jesus it was *heaven* to have her flesh in his mouth. Her nipples were beaded into hard little nubs and he grazed his teeth along them, which made her breath catch. He could tell because her chest moved suddenly with her gasps. Fuck but he loved being this close to her.

He could see himself could becoming addicted to her body. Drunk on her. Jesus, he already was and he'd only made love to her the one time.

Suddenly her chest began heaving more rapidly than ever and Eric heard her needy gasps rising in pitch as she kissed Garrett.

Oh shit, she was about to come. Eric didn't know if it was a clitoral orgasm or if Billy was hitting her G-spot or hell, maybe both, but he focused in on exactly what he was doing with his fingers. And yep, when he moved his fingers just the right way, circling and then pressing, circling and pressing, the little squeals she let out increased in pitch. Higher and higher.

Oh Jesus she was intoxicating. He sucked harder on her nipple, swirling and pressing, then just pressing and moving back and forth the tiniest bit until her scream was a howl muted only by Garrett's cock gagging her.

Eric had made her come. He'd made her come. Jesus he'd never felt like such a fucking god.

He wanted more. He wanted everything.

Which meant he had to prove to her all that this marriage could be. What it needed to be, had to be. Because Jesus he needed this, needed her.

He'd lived his whole adult life in service of others—first his country and then his daughter and Jacob's Well. And it was good, it was right that he had. But Sophia was grown now and maybe it was his turn.

Maybe it was finally time to live for himself. It felt blasphemous even as he thought it. But he also knew, deep down to his soul, it was what he wanted more than anything else in the world.

Because it was Drea. It meant having Drea. And that was worth everything.

Eric felt overwhelmed with emotion as he scooted out from under Drea. Part of him wanted to distance himself from such a powerful emotional response to her—but Jesus, that was hypocritical considering that was exactly what he was trying to keep *her* from doing. Would he be a coward when he was asking her to be strong and face the intimacy that scared her?

No. He'd faced down enemy insurgents. Survived his wife dying. Fought in the War for Independence. Created a stable Territory amid mobs and riots. He could face his own goddamned fears here.

So he pulled away from Drea, but only so he could reposition himself back at her ear. "Now give it to Billy, baby. Look over your shoulder at him. He's dying for you. Give him what you just gave Garrett."

Garrett obviously heard and, to his credit, he withdrew after one last, lingering kiss. And then Drea did what Eric said. She craned her neck over her shoulder to look at Billy.

Which Eric could tell Billy was over the moon about. Maybe he'd been feeling left out. Because as soon as Drea turned to look at him, his pace immediately picked up, his hands gripping her hips even more firmly.

"Kiss your wife," Eric ordered Billy and Billy was only too happy to comply.

Billy leaned over her back and kissed her, all the while pumping his hips back and forth, his cock sliding in and out.

He must have already been primed from all that had happened and Drea clenching on his cock when she'd come moments before. Because it didn't take long before Billy was grunting, one arm around her waist, body all but cemented to her back, coming as they kissed fervently.

They continued kissing for several moments afterwards before Billy slid off to the side, breathing hard like he'd just run for miles. He didn't close his eyes though or drop off to sleep. No, he kept them on

Drea, his expression similar to Garrett's. He worshipped Drea. Maybe already loved her even though he'd only known her a little over a week.

Eric understood the impulse—a realization that made him blink in surprise as soon as he had the thought.

But he pushed that away and beckoned Jonathan and David close, urging them down to the blanket pallet. All the while pulling Drea into his arms as finally, *finally*, he got to taste those berry lips of hers.

"So," *kiss*, "fucking," *kiss*, "beautiful." And then he kissed her so deep no more words were possible for several long minutes.

But finally, reluctantly, he pulled away. He had a plan and he wouldn't let it be derailed, even by the most luscious mouth on God's green earth.

"Jonathan," Eric turned to the other man. "Sit like this." He instructed Jonathan to sit with his legs crossed.

"Drea." He held out a hand for her.

Her eyes were wide, watchful. Her usual sarcastic, badass demeanor was MIA. She was stripped down and he didn't just mean on the outside. They were getting to see her at her most vulnerable and Jesus but Eric knew what a privilege it was. And what a responsibility.

She was actually giving Eric the reins and he could *not* fuck this up. Together, he and the other husbands were busting through her iron walls and Eric intended to imprint there so deep she'd never get him out. Never get any of them out.

Because as much as Eric had first hated the idea of more than just him and Drea in the marriage, the more he thought on it... the world they lived in now, there was no certainty any of them would live past tomorrow. And if something happened to him, wouldn't he want to know that Drea would have four other family members to still be there for her? The thought of her being alone again, Jesus, Eric couldn't stomach it.

So after Eric helped Drea climb on top of Jonathan's lap and then turned and beckoned David close, it was without any of the animosity Eric had felt earlier.

Because Eric was with Drea even here. She wasn't off in some dark room having relations without him. There were no lies, no secrets. He was here every step of the way.

"Sink down on him, baby," Eric coached Drea. "Reach down and guide his cock inside you."

The look on Jonathan's face was a sort of terrified wonder as Drea reached down between them.

"David," Eric said. "Sit down behind her. Keep her warm. Touch her."

David's eyes were watchful, cautious. But he did as Eric instructed. Something which probably went against the grain for a man used to being in charge. He still did it, though, without any balking.

Jonathan coughed out a pleasured cry, no doubt as he entered Drea's tight, slick little hole, and Eric's cock pulsed as he ran a hand down her spine, clenching her ass in his hands one last time before moving to make way for David.

CHAPTER TWENTY-THREE

DAVID

David swallowed hard as he crouched down behind Drea. She had her legs wrapped around Jonathan's back. Jonathan's legs were folded beneath her and he leaned back on his hands, face mesmerized as he watched her writhing on top of him.

Jonathan was many things to David—his second in command, his confidant, chief strategist, best friend, and yes, maybe a surrogate for the brother David had lost.

He knew Jonathan worried about it sometimes—that David only saw him as Kevin's shadow. Jonathan asked him straight out one night when he was extremely drunk. *Do you even see me? Or am I just Kevin to you?* David's only response was to grab the bottle out of his hand and help him back to his bunk. They both pretended it hadn't happened the next morning.

David didn't know if it was true or not.

All he knew was that what he wanted more than anything in the damn world was for Jonathan to be happy.

Maybe it did all come back to Kevin, dammit. Because the day

David had come back to the house to check on their sick mom and found her dead and Kevin upstairs in the bathtub, wrists slashed—what the fuck was the point to any of it after that?

No matter how big a part of him wanted to grab the razor blade Kevin had used to join his brother and mom, it just wasn't in him. So David was stuck living, and the Army was the only thing he'd ever known. Dad was military and they'd moved around every few years his whole life. It had been a given that David would attend West Point, just like Dad.

So David went back to soldiering. You could do it without thinking, mostly. It was a system that rewarded being more machine than man, especially after the world went FUBAR.

David rose quickly in the ranks that were barely hanging together in the chaos. Half the troop units were so undisciplined, the soldiers joined in the looting and mobbing instead of working to restore order. Not to mention the huge numbers of deserters just walking off base and going AWOL in the middle of the night.

David didn't put up with any of that shit.

There were rules. Order. Law.

The Army was the only damn thing that made any sense after The Fall, if you asked David. So maybe he clung a little harder than most to rules and regulations than might have been strictly healthy.

But David never stopped to worry about shit like that. If people accused him of being a robot, that was their damn problem. There was too much to get done in a day to bother sitting around wasting time on head-shrink BS.

He never put the barrel of his Sig Sauer in his mouth, so he figured he was doing just fine. So what if he slept for shit most nights? Who didn't after seeing all they had? He wasn't one for overthinking things.

Which was why he didn't stop to ponder the situation too long before leaning in behind Drea to sweep her hair off the back of her neck.

Her dreadlocks were unexpectedly soft. He wasn't sure what he *had* expected, but the soft, frizzy locks weren't it. They smelled good, too. Faintly of coconut.

David leaned in and skimmed his nose down the back of her neck. The barest touch and already his cock was swelling in his boxers.

His mouth went dry as he lifted his hand for his first real touch. First just the pad of his index finger, tracing the same path his nose had taken. Her shiver of response made his chest expand and the hairs on his arm stand on end.

More. He needed more. And he needed it now.

David massaged her neck, then ran his hand down the nubs of her spine.

She let out little pleasured noises as Jonathan fucked her and she arched her spine into David's hand. David watched in fascination, hand still on her warm skin.

She was so... *soft* was the only word he could think of. Her skin, and her body was soft in all the places where men were hard.

But it was more than that. She was nothing like he'd assumed when he talked to her over the sat phone that first time. Or even earlier today when they'd tangled in front of everyone in the central cavern.

Back then she'd been granite. All jagged, cutting edges.

But here she was now. Cotton candy soft as she wrapped herself around Jonathan and yawned backwards into David at the same time.

So fucking responsive.

Although, she hadn't been like that at first, had she? No, she'd tried to keep hold of that hard shell around herself in the beginning, but Eric hadn't let her. He'd drawn this vulnerability out in her.

And it was one of the most astonishing transformations David had ever witnessed.

He'd agreed to the marriage for Jonathan's sake. Jonathan needed this for so many reasons, David couldn't even count.

But as David leaned in and inhaled the clean, sweet aroma of Drea's scent, it came at him clear as if it was written on the cave wall.

David needed this too.

He hadn't been with a woman since before The Fall. And touching a woman like this? A hot-blooded, responsive woman—his *wife* no less, not some paid whore—his cock was so stiff he barely managed to shove the elastic of his boxers down.

His wandering hands gripped her hips and his forehead dipped to her back. He had to shift with her, back and forth as Jonathan fucked her.

Did she love it? Having Jonathan's cock so deep up inside her? Her noises said she loved it. So did the eager way she shifted her hips on Jonathan's lap with his every thrust.

The way she and Jonathan were positioned, her on his lap, neither of them could get long, deep strokes. Instead it was more of a shallow grinding, both of them moving their hips in sync to get the most friction possible.

David wanted to know what it felt like to be buried that deep inside her. To the hilt. The second Jonathan was done, he wanted to do exactly that.

It was all he could think about as he went up on his knees so he could rub his throbbing erection against her spine. Only after he'd ground himself against her for a good ten seconds did it register that —*shit*.

What the hell was he doing? They were still relative strangers and here he was, just rubbing his dick against her back for friction. What did he think was going to happen? That just because they'd gotten married tonight she was down with a train?

Talk about *FUBAR*.

David started to pull back, disgusted with himself. This wasn't him. When his men got stupid, thinking with their dicks, it was usually him slapping sense into them, so what the hell was he—

"Christ!" he all but shouted, looking down.

To where Drea's firm hand gripped his shaft, holding him in place.

Not for long and she didn't do much more than give it a brief squeeze but it was enough to get her point across. All the while kissing Jonathan like she was starving and he was her last goddamn meal.

Well shit. Looked like she did want him exactly where he was.

Sweat broke out across David's forehead even though the cave was cool.

Maybe this was all just par for the course for her. This was normal where she came from, right? Lottery brides and five husbands and all the rest of it?

So normal in fact, that when Eric nudged David's shoulder a

moment later and handed him a small bottle, he only had an encouraging look on his face.

"Baby," Eric said, running a hand down Drea's hair, "you want David to play with your ass?"

Drea broke from kissing Jonathan long enough to tip her head back on David's chest and nod.

David's heart felt like it was going to bust out of his chest at her nearness.

Or maybe it was the fact that at this angle, he could see down her front to her plump breasts—and even further below to the spot where Jonathan entered her.

David's hands immediately moved around to grasp her breasts. Shit but she was hot. And she gave definition to the word *supple*.

And then, finally, it fully registered what Eric had asked and she'd nodded so eagerly to.

Play.

With.

Her.

Ass.

Did that—

Eric handed him that bottle.

Were they—

David had dropped the little plastic bottle on the ground beside him when he went for her tits but now he eagerly picked it back up. He opened it and didn't waste any time.

He squeezed a little bit of the scented oil—was that lavender?—on his finger and then dropped his hand down to her back side again.

Play with her ass.

Play with her *ass*.

In the position she and Jonathan were in, her in his lap on the floor like that, the sex wasn't about fucking. It was too close for that. Too intimate.

She and Jonathan were making love.

And David loved that for Jonathan. No one deserved it more than him. And judging by the blissed out expression on Jonathan's face, he was loving it too.

But David was going to take it to the next level for Drea.

And for himself.

Because he was done pretending he could be a robot. He wasn't a machine. He'd had his years to mourn the loss of his brother. It was time to be a *man* again.

So he slipped just the very tip of his oil-drenched forefinger in Drea's anus, all the while studying her every inhale and twitch. He wasn't disappointed either. She definitely felt it even in spite of all the sensation Jonathan was giving her. There was a slight tightening of her muscles. Her biceps flexed as she drew Jonathan's head to her chest and she dug her fingers into his hair.

David wasn't in a hurry. Now that he had her beneath his hands, he wanted to linger in every moment of the experience. So he teased her. Ever. So. Slowly. He pushed in her tight, dark hole up to his first knuckle. He met resistance there so he stretched and teased at her entrance, bobbing in and out, swirling around constantly. Then, even when she'd loosened up so that he could push deeper, he kept his intrusion shallow until he could see her back heaving from short, quick gasps.

She was edging closer and closer to coming. But every time he withdrew now she let out a little disappointed whine.

David smiled and withdrew again, teasing at her rim.

That was when Drea turned to look over her shoulder at him, blue eyes flashing fire. "More. Deeper. Fucking *now*."

David grinned. Aha. So the sharp-tongued she-devil was still in there after all. David wasn't sure why, but the realization had his cock going even harder. Something he wouldn't have even thought possible, but goddamn, he was pretty sure his hard-on could punch through walls.

"Yes ma'am," he said, finally pushing his well-oiled finger all the way up her ass.

She cried out and gyrated even more energetically on Jonathan's lap.

"Another," she called, chest heaving. "Another finger. Stretch me. I need it. I need it now."

It was David whose breath caught this time. She wasn't going where he thought she was going with this... was she? David's cock throbbed almost painfully but he didn't reach down to touch it.

No, he just oiled up another finger, knowing he'd never be able to smell lavender again in his whole life without remembering this moment and getting a hard-on. And being completely fucking okay with that fact as he tried to squeeze a second finger in beside his first.

With no luck. Drea's little anus was just so damn tight.

"You're doing so good, baby," Eric said. "But you've got to let us in. Let us all the way in."

It didn't sound like Eric was just talking about her ass, either.

"Relax," Eric went on. "Let him in." He stroked her hair away from her face. "Take a breath. Jesus you're so hot. Ride that pleasure, baby. Fucking ride it. I can see how close you are to coming. I can fucking *smell* it. I can smell your honey, you're so turned on right now. So let David in. Let us fill you up completely.

Drea's whimpers escalated just like they had earlier when she'd come with the two other men. There was no doubt she was going to climax again.

David worked at her asshole even more insistently. How much more pleasure would she feel if he could fill her ass with two fingers instead of just one?

And even as he had the thought, finally, magically, his second finger slipped inside as she relaxed her sphincter. David didn't lose any time working his second finger up her ass right beside the first.

Which was apparently the last straw for her.

Eric had to put a hand over her mouth to muffle her screams of pleasure that echoed off the cave walls as she thrashed up and down on Jonathan like a wild woman.

But David, Christ, it was David who got to feel every response and shudder of her orgasm as she clenched down so hard on his fingers in her ass.

He felt it the moment Jonathan stopped thrusting, too, no doubt coming as well.

And it was one of the most powerful moments of David's life. Being included in this intimacy. Being wrapped up in Drea's flesh, being united not only to her but with Jonathan too, in the most real sense there was.

David never stopped moving his fingers, though.

Even when she was clamped like iron around him in the heights of her orgasm, he kept working his fingers, swirling them around, scissoring them when he could, moving them in and out—basically stretching her in every way he could think of apart from using a toy or other tool.

She liked it, too, if the way she shifted restlessly even as she kissed Jonathan sweetly was any indication. David loved that she was still giving Jonathan her full attention. Giving all of herself like Eric had demanded at the beginning.

When Eric first said it, David frankly thought it was too big of an ask. There were five of them and only one of her.

She had to be exhausted already. She'd come twice and—

Apparently Eric had been thinking along the same lines because he asked, "You want to rest, baby?"

Good. It was basic leadership skills 101. You pushed your troops to perform harder than they *thought* they could—but not past what they *actually* could. Their health and the well-being of the unit as a whole was always of primary importance.

After all, this fledgling little clan—that was what they called these families created by these multiple-partner marriages—their clan had the rest of their lives to explore this. However long or short a time that might be.

But, before David could even withdraw his fingers all the way, suddenly Drea's hand shot out and wrapped in a death grip around his wrist, holding him in place.

"It's my wedding night," was all she said at first, and then, several heavy moments later, "And I want all my husbands. Tonight."

CHAPTER TWENTY-FOUR

DREA

Even as the words came out of Drea's mouth, another part of her was shouting, *what the fuck are you doing???*

She'd had a plan coming into all this tonight. All right, so it hadn't so much been a well-thought out plan as... well, an *intention.*

Relationships were transactional by nature. This for that. Tit for tat. She wasn't the naïve girl she'd been so long ago.

Everybody wanted to fuck. Even her on occasion. More than that, though, she wanted a cohesive team she could rely on. Well, she'd never rely on anyone completely. Trust was something she was just incapable of. Not after Dad. And especially not after Thomas.

But marriage was the best solution given the situation. She'd have her team and they could all let off some steam. Most people needed sexual release of some kind or other and a marriage was a good, safe place for them to find that release. But it didn't have to be more than that.

Sex was just sex. It was the unevolved drive of the human animal that still required feeding. An appetite like any other.

So she'd approached her wedding night as more of a... team-building exercise than anything else.

But then there was Eric.

Eric fucking Wolford, who could never leave well enough alone.

He had to go poking and prodding at her. He just had to whisper in her ear, his breath stirring the hair at her temples which ridiculously sent her heart rate through the roof. Because of course *that* was the thing that turned her on, before he'd ever touched her. Even though she had Garrett's hard cock bobbing at her lips, no, it was Eric's whispered voice, Eric's breath on her ear that had her soaking her underwear.

God *damn* that man.

If he would have just let her do it her way, where she played the part of the seductress and they all reached climax at least once, then they could get a good night's sleep and wake well-rested and focused and—

David's fingers shoved in deeper and twisted and yet again, for the millionth time that night, all rational thought left Drea's head just like *that*.

More.

YES.

NOW.

They were supposed to be the ones lured in by her. She was supposed to be the one in control. But as she threw her arms around Eric's neck and pulled him in towards her, hiking her leg up to wrap around one of his hips even as she landed a punishing, devouring kiss on his lips, she felt anything but in control.

Which pissed her the hell *off*.

She took it out on Eric's mouth.

And David's fingers continued their torturous work in her ass. Stretching her. Preparing her. Because as she bit down on Eric's bottom lip, she knew where all the anal play was going to lead. Where she wanted it to lead.

Eric only jerked back slightly at her rough treatment of his lips. For a second she worried she hadn't been careful enough of his hurt arm. But the next second it was his teeth nipping at hers and she forgot the feel of everything but him at her front and David at her back. Her lips, Eric's tongue, Eric's teeth—biting and releasing, biting and releasing—always keeping her riding that knife's edge between pain and pleasure while David did the same to her ass.

Oh God, had she ever felt this fucking *alive* in her whole life? She'd never been this aware of her own body, that was for sure. Who knew the nerves on the inside of her elbow connected straight to her sex?

Drea knew. At least she knew *now*. Because when Eric kissed and nibbled down her arm, biting on the shallow, soft place, she gasped and arched like never before, not even when Billy was fucking her earlier.

Which was just totally insane. She'd already come *twice*. That was usually her limit, at least when she touched herself.

Eric fell back against a low shelf of rock, immediately widening his stance and grabbing his heavy cock with his good hand, ready to feed it into her aching cunt.

She didn't hesitate. Her pelvis drew toward his cock like it had a mind of its own. She hiked one leg up on the rock seat where Eric sat and kept the other on the floor.

And then she sank down on the most gorgeously fulfilling cock. It felt like everything tonight had been leading up to this moment. Eric's lengthy, fat cock filling her up felt different than Billy's long, thinner pole. Both felt delicious but in this moment, Eric's was perfect.

She sank down, inch by tortuous inch even though all she wanted to do was slam down and impale herself on him.

Even now she felt it—how close she was to losing all control, losing all of her damn sanity over this man. Over these men. Over all they were asking and all they were giving to her.

The alarm bells kept ringing in her mind, *too much, too much!*

While the louder voice kept screaming for *MORE*.

In the end, Eric made the choice for her. He must have gotten fed up with her slow slide because he grabbed her around the waist with his good arm and yanked her the last few inches down his shaft.

Oh God. Drea cried out and dug her nails into his scalp.

The orgasm was already there.

No warning.

No precipitation, it was hitting.

Oh—

Oh, *oh*—

She grabbed Eric's head and slammed it against her breast, not caring if her nails were cutting into his skin. This was what he'd wanted. For her to lose it. For her to become a sexual beast with him. She lifted up and then slammed back down, lodging his cock up against that spot so perfect deep inside her.

So deep and so perfect and oh— She did the hip twist and slam down again. Oh God, *right there*, the wave was hitting, pure fucking light—

It crashed—

A million needles of light prickled all down her hairline and exploded outward from her every nerve ending.

And through it, even through all of it, as she cried and shouted and as tears streamed down her cheeks from the pleasure, she felt the fullness at her ass change.

David's cock.

He'd removed his fingers and now had his cock there.

Right at her ass.

There was barely a let down in her orgasm before it went swooping up again.

Yes.

This was her darkest desire. The one thing she'd never asked for from any bedpartner before. But David knew. They all knew how much she wanted it.

No, how much she fucking *needed* it.

And she was an animal who didn't think. She was instinct. She was pleasure. She would be led where her masters were taking her. Just for now. Just for this one fucking second she wouldn't have to be the fucking responsible one. She could just *want* and then *take* what she wanted.

So with one hand still digging into the back of Eric's neck, she reached her other around to her backside, holding open her ass cheek as wide as possible. She didn't know if it would help David in accessing the hole any better but she wanted him to know that yes, yes she welcomed everything he wanted to give her.

She squeezed around Eric's cock in her pussy and continued rhythmically moving her hips on top of him even as she dropped her chest against his, forcing him to lean further back against the damp cave wall.

She kissed him then. Or maybe it'd be more appropriate to say she bit at him. Nipping and biting at his lips until he captured her in a devouring kiss that had her lips softening against his. But only until she remembered where she was and pulled back with another sharp love bite.

Maybe it would always be this way between them. It would always be a contest. And love-making would be their battleground.

If he thought he'd won because he had her in this position, right where he thought he'd wanted her, well she'd show him.

"Lean back more," she whispered low in Eric's ear. "I want to give David the best angle to fuck my ass. He'll be the first, did you know that? The first to have his big cock up my dark, private little asshole. You wanna feel my pussy clenching on you while he takes it for the first time?"

Eric growled into her mouth, reaching around and tugging on her dreadlocks so she was forced to bare her face up to his.

"I wanna feel fucking everything," he said, "just like I want you to feel everything." Then he crashed his lips onto hers again.

That was when the pressure at her back grew even more insistent. David was there, right at the edge. Pressing for entry. She only had to relax and let him in.

I want you to feel fucking everything.

Again the warning bells rang: *Too much. Too much.*

Eric was asking for everything.

Everything.

And if she let David in, they'd have it. Her everything. Her front and her back and her insides and her outsides.

But at this point, there was no choice. Or if there was, she'd already made it.

She relaxed her sphincter and gasped into Eric's mouth as the head of David's cock slipped past the ring of muscles in her ass. He swore and wrapped one arm like a handlebar around her waist, massaging her breasts with his other hand.

She squeezed her eyes shut even as she kept kissing Eric.

It's not real. It's just bodies. Her mind still rebelled even as her body gave in, went liquid. It's not *you.* You aren't here. *You* can't be here.

Sex is just for release. It can't *mean* anything.

"Jesus, Drea, do you feel that?" Eric barked at her like he could sense her trying to pull away. "You can't run from us here."

And dammit, he was right. Because every inch deeper David slid in her ass, she felt the wall she always kept between herself and everybody else around her slipping.

The further David drove in, it was like she could see it in her head —the reverse of continental drift. Continents she'd tried to keep separated by oceans were suddenly rescinding and colliding. Collapsing all artificial barriers. Becoming one land. Laid bare. Laid so absolutely fucking bare.

David thrust his hips forward the last inch and Drea was speechless except for a long, moaning hiss of air that she expelled through her teeth.

And together the three of them hovered there for what felt like an eternity, no one moving, connected more intimately than three humans could even normally conceive of being.

Then—and this was what took it over the edge, what washed away any last flimsy barrier Drea's mind might have been half-heartedly still holding up—Jonathan came on one side and Garrett and Billy on the other side of them. They touched her wherever they could. Like they were laying hands on her. Like it was a religious ceremony. And it that moment it felt that way—religious and holy.

Drea certainly had no other word for the unearthly pleasure and swamping absolute *joy* that rose up and swept over her like a tidal wave.

And every single one of her clan held her as she came and cried and came some more and cried some more.

All she knew was that when she spiraled back down to earth who knew how many minutes later, it was to Eric's voice.

Eric's hands cupping her face.

Eric's blue eyes piercing hers.

"This isn't a marriage where each of us get a sliver of you. No, baby, that's not how this is gonna work. You have to give every one of us *all* of you. Pour it all out. Every single fucking drop of yourself and trust that we'll fill you back up."

His grip on her cheeks tightened and the vein in his neck clenched as he searched her eyes with an intensity that, only half an hour before, would have terrified her and had her pulling away. But now she only looked back with all of her self.

"Because we will fill you back up. That's what we vowed today. We're your husbands. For richer or for poorer. In sickness and in health. Where one of us drops the ball another will pick it up. We will never leave you. Never forsake you. We are yours until the end of time. And baby, you are fucking *ours*."

CHAPTER TWENTY-FIVE

BILLY

Some part of Billy thought everything would be the same as it was when they all woke up the morning after the wedding night. Surely last night had been some sort of withdrawal-induced hallucination, right? Drea had been so... At the end there when Eric and David were... and the rest of them all came around and they were all together and—

Well fuck. That had really been somethin'. Something crazy he still wasn't sure he could wrap his head around. Cause the way Drea looked — Okay so he'd only known her for a total of what? Not even two weeks?

But she looked destroyed.

Like absolutely fucking destroyed in the most beautiful way Billy'd ever seen. Cause Billy had seen that look on people's faces before. Maybe it was a messed-up analogy, but it was the same face addicts who'd been without got once they *finally* got that sweet, sweet hit again. That moment of being totally blissed out and yeah, just destroyed. Problem was, it never lasted. Give it half an hour, hell, sometimes ten damn minutes, and it was gone and you were left chasing it like it was never there.

But Drea?

After they finished, cum spilling out her front and back, she let Garrett pull her into his arms beside him on his sleeping bag. When the rest of them crowded around, she flung her leg out over Jonathan and lifted her arms overhead to make contact with David and Billy. Eric spent a long time at her feet, massaging first one and then the other like he was her servant or something.

And her face just stayed like that. So open it was like you could see through to the very center of her. It was the first time he'd looked at her and realized, Christ, she must have been a girl once. Like a *girl* girl.

Before then he guessed he'd sort of seen her as this bionic woman who'd popped out full-grown. Like maybe she was a runaway from some pre-Fall secret government project because surely no one could be that badass in real life? An exaggeration but ya know, she was just so *on* all the time, so hard, so fearless.

But here she was, this beautiful girl. Bare in every way. She slept surrounded by the five of them, nestled alternately against Garrett or Jonathan or Eric. Christ, he even saw her cuddled against that massive, muscled automaton, the General.

Billy hadn't been able to sleep.

Because while Drea had laid herself bare, Billy had more to hide than ever.

The angelic creature on the cave floor beside him could never know.

She could *never* find out what he'd done.

Who he'd been.

So part of him had waited anxiously through the night hoping against hope that when Drea woke up, her armored shield would clang back down into place. That she'd be hard and aloof and yeah, just a little bit mean. It would mean the natural order had been restored to the world.

But he woke up to find her kissing Jonathan. Or really, being passed back and forth between Eric and Jonathan. While David and Garrett watched on, hands on their dicks.

Billy was only fucking human so of course he climbed over and joined the fray.

Shit got heated again after that.

When Billy entered Drea, she reached up and cupped his cheek. And that openness that had been in her eyes last night absolutely gutted him.

She gave a playful little smile and then rolled them over so that she was on top, riding Billy, her perfect plump little breasts swinging in his face. And God damn him—and fuck it, hell was a certainty at this point anyway so why not go with it?—Billy didn't push her away. He dug his fingers into her hips and dragged her up and down his cock.

The other guys were all around, too. Pulling her hair back and sucking on her neck. Tugging at her nipples. Pinching her clit.

And Billy might be bound for hell, but Christ if her body didn't clench around him like sweet, sweet heaven as she came and shuddered above him.

Okay, so she was soft in the bedroom. But surely once they got back into the main cave and started planning the mission, Ms. Hard Ass Give No Shits would return.

But she didn't.

All throughout the day, she was constantly reaching out to touch one or the other of them. Little things. Billy noticed her hand overlapping Eric's as they laid out a road map on the cave floor and Drea pointed out the best way to get around Houston on back roads, theoretically bypassing the nuclear fallout area to where it should be safe. Then she dropped a casual hand on Jonathan's thigh while David laid out the strategy they'd use once they got to NASA. Where the building they'd infiltrate was. What the strike team they'd be bringing with them would do if they ran into any trouble along the way or at the Space Center itself.

But while she might be a softer, gentler Drea, her iron determination hadn't wavered any.

"There's no reason for you to risk yourself by going," Gisela said, pulling Drea aside after lunch.

Instead of the ice-cold look Billy expected Drea to respond with, though, she just reached out and took Gisela's hands. "I'll be fine. I know the area."

Gisela just leveled her eyes at Drea. "Don't pull that crap on me. I grew up in Sugarland, right outside of Houston. I know that area the same as you. Better probably. I should be going. Let me—"

"No," Drea cut her off sharply.

Aha. There was the iron back in her voice Billy had been looking for all day.

"But—"

Drea's finger shot up between them, a warning clear in her look. "Gisela, leave it alone. The girls need you here. You were voted their leader and representative. So go lead."

Billy watched Gisela's jaw lock.

"I thought you rescued us so we could fight back." Gisela's words came through gritted teeth and any other day Billy would have said she reminded him of Drea herself. But Drea's eyes went soft as she reached out again and squeezed Gisela's upper arm.

"I didn't rescue you so you could join an army." Drea shook her head, obviously disconcerted. "I wasn't trying to get recruits. I did it so you could be *free*."

"And you think any of us will ever be free of that place without fighting back?"

Drea was clearly about to offer another rebuttal but this time Gisela cut *her* off.

"No. There are two transport vehicles going out on the mission and I'll be on the other one. If you get separated you'll need someone else who knows the area to get the second vehicle around safely. Maya here will be fine to lead the rest of the women until we're both back home."

But Drea wasn't having any of it. She stood up taller, gaze hardening. "You are *not* going and that's final."

Gisela's mouth dropped open in outrage. "I'm just as much a part of the counsel as you are. You can't just—"

"Oh yes I can," Drea said, eyes flashing. "I took you out of that prison and I can just as easily throw you into another one until we get back. And those trucks you're talking about? They belong to my husband. He's letting the counsel borrow them, but he has the final say who gets to ride on them. And believe me, you are not going *anywhere.*"

"But that— That's not—" Gisela let out a huff of exasperation and then threw her hands in the air. "That's not *fair.*"

Drea stood unmoved. "It's the apocalypse. Nobody said anything about fair."

Gisela stood, fuming but obviously having run out of things to say against logic like that. Then she spun and fled down the hall, people turning to stare as she went.

Drea immediately slumped and her hand went to her forehead as she watched Gisela go. "God, don't tell me that's what it will be like having a kid one day."

"You want kids?" Billy asked. He couldn't help it. It was that cognitive dissonance thing again. Drea plus pregnancy and kids? Even two days ago he woulda said, nope, you're crazy to anyone who brought up the idea.

But this Drea? The Drea after last night? Even the way she was looking after Gisela. Christ, the girl wasn't much more than six or seven years younger than Drea herself, but Billy couldn't think of any other word than maternal for the way Drea was looking after her.

Then again, Billy didn't know why it surprised him. It was sort of Drea's thing. She genuinely *cared* about helping people.

Billy wasn't stupid. He knew she used people to accomplish her goals and that she was probably even using *him*. It was handy to have a doctor around. She'd certainly been open to the same sort of logic when Billy suggested bringing the General into the clan for similar reasons.

But the thing was, even if she *was* using him and the others, she wasn't doing it for herself. Everything she did, she did for others.

The reason she was so hell bent and determined to redirect these satellites and get into San Antonio? It was all so she could free the women who'd been with her back in Nomansland. She was fucking unreal.

Which is why she'll hate you once she finds out the truth.

Billy squeezed his eyes shut, swallowing hard as he pulled Drea tight to his side and pressed a kiss against the side of her temple. "I'll see ya later, babe. Gotta go prep for the mission."

He started to pull away but she grabbed his hand before he could go.

"Hey." She linked their fingers and stepped closer. The intimacy of the small gesture made Billy's insides roil. He wanted to go find a knife and slice his own guts open for all he'd done. He wanted to grab her and thrust her against the nearest hard surface he could find and fuck her until she was walking bowlegged for days. He wanted to drop to her feet and beg her for forgiveness.

But they had a mission and Drea didn't need to get distracted by his bullshit right now.

"You want one of the guys to go down with you to get supplies? You've been doing amazing but there's no need to tempt yourself for no reason."

"I won't get in the stash," Billy promised. And he wouldn't.

Because the way she was looking at him right now? With those bright blue eyes so soft and full of concern?

He'd never give that up.

Never.

Not for pills. Not for smack. And certainly not out of some misguided moral principle that said he needed to come clean about his past.

Drea was his new drug.

And she was an addiction he'd take to the grave.

CHAPTER TWENTY-SIX

GARRETT

Garrett didn't love being crammed on the tiny benches that lined the sides of the van for the four and a half hours they'd already been on the road. Especially since they'd had to take bumpy back and side roads, had run into obstacles more than once that had to be hauled off the road, and had far fewer breaks than he would have liked to stop and stretch his legs.

But being by D's side was worth it. She had to be as uncomfortable as he was in the cramped space but you'd never know it.

She'd spent the first hour having the General run them through the op, over and over until Garrett thought he was gonna have to put his fist through the wall of the van if he heard the words "operational stealth" one more time.

Garrett was pretty sure they all got the fuckin' score. Sneak into the place. Smoke anyone who might already be there but don't be too loud about it. Don't draw attention to themselves. Duh, common fucking sense. Did the General think they were idiots?

But Drea just sat beside Garrett, eyes on the General, nodding along like she was running the job in her head, detail by detail. Shit, she probably was. She certainly asked enough questions—what they'd do in this scenario or that.

Point was, they couldn't be any more prepared, even if they'd had months to plan it. Cause maybe no one else in the van wanted to admit it, but a thing like this, you could run drills till you fell down dead and it wouldn't matter.

Garrett had been around long enough to know that plans didn't count for shit when you were in the middle of it. When bullets were flying and people were running around and you didn't know who was yours and who was theirs, when shit was blowing up? Fuck, you just tried to do your job and get you and yours back in one piece.

But hey, maybe this time would be different. Maybe this uptight Army fucker actually knew what he was talking about and it wouldn't be like the MC jobs Garrett had pulled his whole life.

At least there was Franco, one of the General's soldiers, to help pass the time with his terrible jokes. Garrett swore they got worse by the hour. Might have annoyed Garrett except it was too damn funny seeing Franco get on Eric's nerves.

That guy needed to loosen up and let go of the pole he had up his ass.

"So I'm in basic training, right?" Franco starts up, about five minutes after telling his last shitty joke. Franco was a little older than Garrett, maybe thirty or so? Still young but obviously one of the General's most trusted guys to be chosen for this mission. He had dark hair and tan skin and yeah, basically woulda been a lady-killer back in the old days.

Eric probably didn't like him cause he kept flashing that big ol' smile of his Drea's way but that was cause Eric was a jealous idiot. Did he not think Drea had her hands full with the five of them? Fuckin' dumbass.

In Garrett's book, anyone or anything that made Drea smile was a winner.

"And there's this guy, Benny," Franco went on. "Always getting in trouble with our Drill Sergeant. If we're going on a run, he's always dragging in last. If we're cleaning our barracks, his bed is always the one that's not done right."

Franco leaned over, elbows on his knees, face animated now that he saw he had the attention of everyone in the back of the van.

"So this one day, Sarge really lays into Benny. Just reams him *out*. And as he's walking away, he says, 'Guess one day you're really gonna enjoy walking on my grave, huh, cadet?'"

Franco sat up straight on his seat as he gets into character. "And Benny goes, 'No sir, Sarge!'

"'Oh yeah, and why's that, cadet?' the Sergeant asks."

"'Cause I promised myself after I get out of the Army I'm never standing in another line ever again, sir!'"

Drea busted up laughing and Garrett couldn't help smile too, cause he could feel Drea's body shaking beside him. He loved that about her. She didn't do anything in half measures. Laughing. Fucking. Going to war.

Garrett's hand tightened on the barrel of his rifle that he'd been polishing for the last half hour.

Garrett glanced over to Drea, so small beside him. Almost anyone was small compared to him, but D seemed especially so. Maybe just because he was rarely around women, but still. Just how pissed would she be if he tried to like, handcuff her to the steering wheel while they went down and made sure it was all clear in the building?

He knew the answer, though. She'd fucking castrate him if he ever tried anything like that.

Besides, who was to say staying in the van would be any safer than going in the building? No, the safest place for her was at Garrett's side where he knew he could kill any motherfucker who even looked at her sideways.

Because while D was here to save the world or some shit, Garrett was only here for one reason.

He was here for her.

So he'd protect her at all costs. With his life if it came down to it. He swore he would. He fucking *swore* it.

His whole damn life he'd taken the coward's way out. He still wasn't sure why Drea hadn't turned after capping his paps and put one right between *his* eyes.

But she hadn't.

So maybe he felt a little like he was living on borrowed time. He should have died that day with all of his so-called brothers.

Instead he'd been given the object of his wildest dreams. He'd gotten to fucking *marry* her. Life wasn't supposed to work like that. You were supposed to get what you deserved, like his dad finally did. Like the hellfire she'd bring down on Suicide once she found him.

But Jesus, a big part of him didn't care that he didn't deserve her. Now that he had her, all he wanted to do was grab her, throw her over his shoulder, point his rifle at the driver and demand they let him and D out.

Yeah he'd probably have to somehow slip her like ten of the Doc's old pills and then chain her to a tree when she woke up, but she'd be alive, so maybe it'd be worth it.

But damn it, part of loving D—and yeah, he fucking loved her, he had forever if he was being honest—part of loving her meant not caging her. It meant loving *all* of her.

That was the part her dad could never understand. He thought he could keep her separate from MC life. He thought she could be two people like he was—the loving dad by night at home, and the ruthless MC President slave trafficker by day.

But that was never D. She threw her whole being into what she believed. No compromises. Ever.

Everybody compromised. Their character. Their morals.

But not D.

And he loved her, for that and for so many other reasons.

"What month do soldiers hate?" Franco asked her?

"I don't know. What month?"

Franco grinned. "March."

D giggled. Fucking giggled, sitting there in combat boots, with guns and ammo and probably a few other weapons Garrett didn't even know about strapped to her body. Goddamn but he loved this woman and all her contradictions.

So for once in his sorry life, he wouldn't play the coward. He'd follow her to hell and back if that was what it took.

He'd be a man worthy of her.

Or die trying.

CHAPTER TWENTY-SEVEN

ERIC

David pushed aside the curtain separating the back of the van from the driver and passenger's seat where Drea sat. She'd moved up there as they got closer to Houston so she could direct them on the best roads to take. The Army driver maneuvered deftly around debris and abandoned cars and Drea held up a Geiger Counter.

They'd driven a wide circle around Houston, so they hadn't seen any part destroyed by the nuclear bomb, but they were still too close for Eric's comfort. Sure the fallout *supposedly* fell to the northeast... but what if they were wrong? What if they were driving straight into a toxic area?

Eric didn't think he was the only one holding his breath as everyone except the driver watched the little arm of the Geiger Counter bouncing around in the green zone, occasionally sparking up into the yellow along with a little crackle the machine let out.

If it went into the red and stayed there, this whole mission was fucked.

Well, they had *one* hazmat suit.

So theoretically Jonathan could suit up and Eric could *attempt* to direct him into the building where he *thought* they'd find what they need, if everything still was where it had been twenty-five years ago...

Eric clenched his jaw and looked out the window. Thank Christ the moon was bright tonight because they didn't dare use headlights. It meant they'd had to go slow, though, and even though they'd started out right after full dark, it would be sunrise soon.

If everything went as planned, though, that wouldn't matter, because Travis wouldn't have eyes in the sky for much longer. They could drive back to the caves during the day without worrying about him or anyone else being able to see them.

But if things took much longer than planned and he happened to be monitoring this area...

"Look," Drea said. "There." She pointed up ahead.

"Yes," Eric said. "That's it. Take that left up there. Turn in by the two planes."

He spared a glance at Drea and found her looking at him. They'd done it. Actually gotten here.

The Geiger Counter squawking jerked both of their attention to the machine.

The arm sat solidly in the yellow warning zone now.

Drea swallowed but straightened her back and looked forward out the windshield again. "Which building?"

Eric knew there was no stopping or going back. Not when they were this close. And as long as the meter didn't go red, the best he could do was try to get them in and out as quickly as possible.

Drea needed him. The whole team did. It was a position he wasn't completely comfortable filling. As was his uncertainty about whether he could ever live up to the job. But he'd learned early on as Commander of Jacob's Well that people didn't need a perfect leader, they just needed someone to look to and follow.

So he made his voice confident and sure when he said, "Take that road past the visitor center around the memorial trees to the outbuildings. The one we want is Building 30. I'll tell you when we get to it."

The driver nodded and they drove on. Eric glanced past Drea in the driver's seat to the side mirror and saw the second black van behind them following closely on their tail.

"I see a building but I don't know what number it is," Drea said when a building loomed up out of the darkness on their right. "It's too dark."

"Got another one over here," said the driver.

"No, it's further in," Eric said. "Keep following the road around. It's not much farther."

How many times had he and Mom driven this same road? In the summers, she liked to pick up Dad in the middle of the day so they could all go out for lunch at least once a week.

"Whoa," Drea said, shifting forward in her seat. "What the hell happened there?" She pointed to big chunks of metallic debris covering the road.

The driver pulled to a stop and David spoke into his walkie, ordering several troops out from the van behind them to investigate.

Eric slid over Drea's lap to push out the door, too.

"Where the hell do you think you're going?"

"I have a hunch," he said. "But I need to know if I'm right."

Drea grumbled something but then followed him down as the troops fanned out around the crumpled metallic lumps. But Eric wasn't looking at the metal in the road. He was looking at the building off to the left of them.

"Yep, it's what I thought." He pointed to a broken fence, overgrown with brambles and vines. "These are what's left of huge liquid nitrogen tanks that used to be right over there. They used them to simulate space conditions to test equipment. But liquid nitro has to be kept at minus 320°F. As soon as the power went out and the temperatures rose, they would've blown."

"And no one's been here or tried to drive down this road since? When it's such an important site?" Drea shook her head. "Not sure I buy it. And the way it's positioned here right in the middle of the road." She swung around, looking right and left. "No, I don't like it at all."

"Agreed," David snapped. "Back in the van. What are you doing out here without your damn vest on, anyway?"

Drea didn't even give him any backtalk. She just went back to the van. Damn, Eric thought. She must actually be worried.

They all got back in the van and the driver drove up onto the left curb and then onto the overgrown grass.

A second after they did, Eric wondered how smart it was. Because what if the metal in the road *had* been planted as an obstacle? And a landmine was planted here in the grass to blow if anyone tried to go around it?

But he must be just crazy paranoid because there was no *boom*. Nothing exploded. No gunfire erupted from anywhere.

The night stayed just as quiet as ever except for the growl of the van's engine as first one and then the other climbed up onto the grass and passed the debris in the road.

Jesus, he was freaking himself out with his over-active imagination. But maybe he wasn't the only one, because a second later, a smaller hand crept into his and he looked down to find Drea's hand squeezing his. She didn't look his way and that was the only point of contact she allowed between them. But it was enough. So much more than enough.

Today had been non-stop. They had to get everything ready and go over a detailed mission briefing. Twice. He'd had to say goodbye to Sophia again—she'd kept her face averted the whole time he explained as much as he could about why he had to go, her arms crossed firmly over her chest. Then they'd all snuck out of the caves and hiked the mile and a half to where the vans were stashed. And then there was the long, long drive. But that didn't stop the memories of last night and this morning from playing on endless repeat through his brain.

Jesus, the way Drea had eventually given herself over to them. With complete abandon. Complete vulnerability. It had been beyond his wildest fucking dreams. But then, she was always more than he expected. More than he'd known was *possible*.

And here they were. Risking it all right after they found it. The hair on his arms went up as he looked back and forth through the front windshield and then out both passenger windows. His eyes had long ago adjusted to the dark but still, he could only see clearly for maybe five to ten feet in front of the van. In the distance he could only just see the vague outline of buildings whose silhouettes rose here and there like gravestones out of the otherwise flat landscape.

"Here." Eric grabbed the bulletproof vest Drea had deposited beside her seat and helped her into it. Again, she didn't balk or bat his hands away or tell him she could do it herself.

His other clansmen and the soldiers in the back—especially that too flirtatious Franco guy who'd been flashing about a hundred too many smiles Drea's way—were all talkative on the drive, but everyone was dead silent now.

Eric guided the driver down the winding road past more and more buildings.

"That one," he said, pointing at the familiar shape of the Mission Control building. It was a little more distinctive than the others—there was an older portion of the building, and then a taller ten-story extension built on to the original.

Tour busses used to run non-stop on these roads, crowd after crowd pouring into Building Thirty and tromping up the stairs to the third floor where the historic Mission Control was located—the exact room where such famous communiques as *Houston, we have landed* and *Houston, we have a problem* were received.

Dad had tried to pressure Eric in high school to get a summer job as a tour guide but at the time, nothing sounded worse than being stuck outside in the Houston heat talking about ancient history to bored tourists and their snot-nosed kids. Much less doing anything his *dad* wanted him to do.

Eric winced just remembering what a little shit he'd been as a teenager. It still hurt, knowing how he'd wasted those last years of his father's life, fucking around trying to 'find himself' or some bullshit.

"I'm never gonna be you, Dad," he'd shouted in one of the last conversations they'd ever have on this earth. "I don't care about science or math or any of that shit. I don't want to help NASA continue to prepare for the eventual colonization of Mars. Don't you ever stop and look around you? There's enough that's broken right here on Earth. Maybe if you got your head out of your ass for long enough, you'd see that it's *people* who need help. I'm not gonna waste my life on some bullshit outer space *science*."

His dad hadn't said a word. But he had forced Eric downstairs and into the truck.

"What the fuck, Dad?"

His dad raised his hand sharply, his finger in Eric's face. "Don't curse like that anywhere near this property, you hear me? It'd break your mother's heart if she heard you using such filthy language."

And then his dad had driven him here.

As the van came to a stop and they all piled out, Eric couldn't help but compare the two experiences. With his dad it had been the middle of the night, like now, and the campus had been similarly abandoned.

Back then, though, the small courtyard in front of the Building 30, Mission Control, was swept with a row of nice, trimmed bushes lining it.

Now the courtyard was a mess. The grass and bushes were overgrown. Trashcans were overturned and trash scattered. One of the big front windows on the first floor had been shattered and vines had grown up around the opening, into the building.

"Careful," David said, taking the lead and stepping through the broken window. He had an automatic weapon out and another strapped to his back, along with a backpack that Eric could only imagine held more ammunition or weapons. His soldiers followed, guns raised, several staying behind to flank their clan.

"What the hell are you doing here?"

Eric had been watching David's guys and the building but at Drea's words he looked back. Only to find her squaring off with— Gisela? What the hell was she doing here?

Gisela squared her shoulders and jutted out her chin. "I'm just as good as any of these guys at standing watch. And I know how to work one of these." She held up a walkie, pushing the button on the side with her thumb. "All clear out here, over," she said into it, the walkie on David's waist crackling in response.

Eric could see Drea's head was literally about to explode, she was so furious.

David spun around, finger to his lips. He shook his head, obviously exasperated, before turning back to his men and gesturing them to fan out on the first floor.

Gisela looked guilty for a moment, realizing too late that right then might not have been the best time to show off her short-wave radio skills. For Christ's sake, if anyone *was* in the building, there was every chance that little stunt had just given them away.

It was a tense several minutes before David returned to the opening and waved them all through. "Clear in here."

Eric let out the breath he was holding but Drea didn't look any less relieved, nor did her glare for Gisela lessen. She pushed past her, their shoulders briefly knocking against each other.

Gisela rolled her eyes and jutted her chin out even further but it was clear to Eric how desperate for Drea's approval she was.

He should know. He'd displayed a similar kind of defiance when he'd walked this same ground with his father all those years ago.

Eric followed Drea through the window, only having a brief moment to look around before David asked, "Which way?"

The lobby was as much a mess as the courtyard. Worse, because the linoleum and drywall had never been meant for the outside elements.

The floor to ceiling mural on the wall depicting the moon landing with the words declaring *Historic Mission Control* was barely even visible.

Eric hadn't expected the pained nostalgia at seeing that. How many times had he walked past that wall growing up? He remembered how he'd gotten a little thrill when he'd finally gotten taller than the Neil Armstrong on the mural.

He swallowed and turned his back to the wall. "This way."

There was the well-traveled staircase leading up to mission control —both the historic one tourists got to see and the one on the second floor where active missions were run well into the mid-21st century.

They weren't interested in either of those, though. Well, they did need to take the stairs up to the second floor. But only so they could get across to the new building addition. Eric led and everyone followed. Up the stairs. Down the hallway that led past mission control.

He'd expected that they'd have to pull out the blow torch to get past the locked door at the end of that hallway, but—

"Looks like we aren't the first ones here after all," David murmured, his words barely audible.

He stepped in front of Eric and made hand signals. Two of his troops nodded and proceeded through the door, machine guns at the ready.

Eric stepped back, shielding Drea. David had been leaving guards stationed at each phase of entry. Two downstairs. Two more at the top of the stairs.

When he finally came back and gave the all clear, two more stayed at that door way. That meant there were only nine in the group that Eric led through the mazelike tunnel of hallways—the six of their clan plus Gisela, Franco, and another soldier, Wendall, who Eric had only met on the way here. Jonathan and David had brought a single pair of night vision goggles, but it was easier to switch on a couple of flashlights so everyone could see as they headed into the bowels of the building. He remembered how confused he'd felt the night his dad led him down this same path.

"Four rights, a left and a right," his dad muttered under his breath.

Eric whispered the same as he navigated the halls and brought them to a section of cream-colored painted brick hallway that looked... exactly like every other bit of hallway.

"What exactly are we looking for?" asked Franco. "Looks like somebody looted this place of anything that might have been valuable a long time ago." He gestured with his gun toward one of the many ransacked rooms they'd passed.

"They didn't know what they were looking for," Eric said. "Why do you think the internal walls of this building are made of brick? It was built well into the 21st century. Doesn't that seem odd to anybody?"

"Well it does now that you point it out," David said.

Eric nodded, feeling along the grooves of the bricks. It was somewhere in the middle here. Where had Dad touched? He closed his eyes and tried to remember. Dad had to bend over a little. Eric remembered wondering what the hell his dad was doing, squatting in a hallway to nowhere in the middle of the night.

Eric bent over slightly and continued running his fingers along the grooves of the bricks and—

Bingo.

He felt the button that his dad had pressed that night and he did the same. The reaction wasn't immediate and he worried that in the intervening years since his dad had died they'd made electronic what had once been mechanical.

But nope, when he looked toward the corner of the hallway several feet away, the panel of false brick about two feet wide had slid partially aside, revealing a long metal lever.

Eric hurried over to it. As he'd first thought, the panel had only slid part of the way open. "Here, help me get it all the way open."

He and David pushed the little two foot door open, fully exposing the lever. Good. It only made sense. This was the backup system. In case the electronics went completely down for whatever reason. Or in case of an EMP attack.

"You pull that and what?" Franco asked. "The curtain falls away and we find out we been in Oz this whole time?"

Eric rolled his eyes while David grabbed the lever with both hands, biceps bulging as he wrenched it downwards.

As he did, another panel of false bricks receded into the wall and then, the further he cranked, the panel slid to the side on a track and revealed a stairwell.

"There you go," Eric said, holding out a hand. "Emergency entrance to the *real* Mission Control. At least the mission control where all the things that truly mattered were done."

Eric could see some of the awe he himself had felt at first seeing the secret opening revealed reflected on the other's faces, especially Gisela.

"This is *awesome*," she whispered, eyes wide.

"You," Drea snapped at Gisela, "Stay up here." She looked to Eric. "You said in our briefings that there are two exits to the building from this point?"

Eric nodded. "The first is the way we came in. The second is to take this hallway, turn right, take a left, go down that hallway and you'll see a hallway branching off about halfway down on the right, with a door. That's the exit that goes down to the back parking lot. We parked the second van by the next building over to the east."

"You hear that?" Drea took Gisela's forearm. "Repeat back to me. Where are the exits?"

Gisela's jaw locked but she repeated what Eric had said. Drea only looked minimally appeased.

"The first *sign* of danger and you get the hell out of here, do you hear me?" Drea admonished.

"Aw what about me, darlin'?" Franco asked. "Where's my stern talking to?"

Drea ignored him, eyes only on Gisela.

"I got it," Gisela waved Drea off. "I can do this. Now go take care of what you came here for."

Drea didn't nod or look any happier about the situation, but she did pull her Glock out of her hip holster and hand it to Gisela. "Remember, safety off, feet a little more than shoulder-width apart, and you did better with the left foot forward stance so—"

"I got it," Gisela repeated, cheeks going pink as she looked around at the rest of them. Drea either didn't see or didn't care that she was embarrassing the girl. She just looked behind Eric. "Billy, Garrett, you two stay up here too."

"No way," Garrett said. "I go where you go."

"Me too," from Billy.

"All clear," came David's distant call from halfway down the stairs.

Eric expected Drea to snap at Garrett and Billy but instead she reached and took each of their hand. "Please. Guys. I need you here as my eyes and ears. If something happens, we'll be trapped down there. We'll need you to be able to clear the way for us."

Garrett's eyes flashed, no doubt at the idea of anything happening to Drea. Eric would swear that guy's DNA was half guard-dog. Which was fine by Eric. The more people looking after Drea, the better, as far as he was concerned. Especially with the lack of self-preservation she'd been displaying lately.

So Garrett accepted the walkie Jonathan handed him and Billy stayed put beside him as Drea headed down the stairs, flashlight in hand. Eric and Jonathan followed on her heels. Down one flight. Then another. A third. And a fourth.

When Eric finally got to the bottom, there was only a small

concrete landing and a door with— Holy crap, a little biometric scanner screen beside the door that was actually *lit up*.

Drea hurried forward to the scanner screen, placing her hand on the hand outline. It beeped and flashed with a red *Invalid Entry* sign on the little screen.

Drea's head swung to look at Eric. "It even works. You were right. The EMP couldn't penetrate this far underground. But what's been powering it for all this time?"

Eric tucked his own flashlight under his arm as he walked closer to look at the screen. "Dad told me there's a secondary generator for this place. Well, two generators. One that's solar-powered and a second that's powered by old-fashioned fossil-fuel. And it's motion activated, so we just turned it on when we came down here." Eric waved his hand around them.

"He's right. The screen lit up as soon as we came down the stairs," David confirmed. "All right, you two get back," he said, gesturing Eric and Drea away while Franco pulled on a mask and readied his blow torch.

It took over an hour to get through the door. No one spoke much but Eric clearly wasn't the only one feeling anxious. Drea's foot had been tapping non-stop for the past half hour, not even slowing when Jonathan started massaging her shoulders. David wasn't much better, jogging back up the stairs to walkie the others posted as sentries rather than doing it from downstairs.

They all knew it had to be far past sunrise by now and while they'd tried to park the vans under as much tree cover as they could—one right outside the front exit and the second a couple of buildings away, it was Texas. The trees were short and stubby and didn't give coverage for jack shit.

Anyone looking this direction and paying attention would see two very out of place black vans parked where none had been the day before.

A loud *CLANG* had Eric's attention swinging back to the landing and Drea popping to her feet. The door had fallen inwards with a great clatter.

"Watch where you step," David hopped up onto the middle of the fallen door and held out a hand to steady Drea as she stepped up to join him. "That slag will burn through your shoe in seconds."

Drea nodded and they made their way into the room. Eric followed, stepping as carefully as they had to avoid the metal where it was still sizzling orange. Jonathan came after him.

Eric swung his flashlight around the room, prepared for it to be as much of a mess as the rest of the building. For desks to be overturned and computers to be lying in pieces all over the floor.

But as he got inside and looked around, he saw everything was in pristine condition.

The room was filled with three rows of desks built in a large circle, stadium seating style. It looked much the same as it had the night his dad brought him here.

The only difference was that then, there had been the static hum of computers and in the center of the circle of desks, there'd been a lit-up 3D projection of the earth, about six feet in diameter, with hundreds of little satellites orbiting it.

Now though, the space was empty.

"All right. Let's hurry it up," David said, voice curt. "We've already been here too long."

Eric walked over to the console that had once been his father's. First row, second in from the aisle. Eric sat down and ran his hands over the crystalline screen and the little control orb resting in its cradle.

"Holy crap, look at this," Drea said.

Eric glanced over at where Drea came out of a storage closet, she and Franco carrying a heavy-looking crate that they dropped on the nearest desk.

"What?"

Drea reached into the crate and pulled out something Eric thought was a laptop at first but no, it was too big and clunky for that.

"Mini solar panel power bases," Drea said, excitement dripping from every word.

"Military grade," said Franco. "The kind that gets ninety-eight percent efficiency. Plug into this baby and you'll have power for hours."

"But plug what into it?" Drea asked dramatically, jogging back into the closet and then coming back out. "How about *these?*"

She smiled wide, holding up two slim laptops along with several crystalline tablets. The highest of high tech. Holy shit. If those actually *worked...*

"There are at least ten tablets in here. Five more laptops. And two crates of ten solar power bases."

"We might not have a city on a power grid, but we'll have as much tech as Travis himself," David said, a rare grin lighting his face. "More, maybe, and in better condition." Then his eyes went calculating. "Now we just need San Antonio."

Drea reached in her backpack and handed the satellite phone over to David. He took it, but looked to Jonathan who, during all of this, had been working at an open panel along the back wall.

"What's the word, Jon?"

"Just gimme another second."

And indeed, barely a second passed before the room lit up. Overhead lights. Console stations. Even the huge projection of the earth in the central circle between the desks came back to life, along with the hundreds of little differently colored orbiting satellites. Each color represented a different type of satellite. Blue for telecom satellites. Red for imagery and geospatial ones. Green for weather.

"All right, we're in business," Jonathan said, hurrying over to the closest console. Ever since the power had turned on, all the little navigation orbs had jumped to life, too, hovering about an inch off their bases. Jonathan touched the crystalline screen of the console tablet and then spun the orb, which had the globe in the center of the room turning on its axis as well.

Drea gasped and Eric had to admit, he felt short of breath at the show of technology, too. Sure once in a while they stored up enough energy to show a movie in the local theatre, but even that demanded so much coordination, planning, and energy resources, they only did it once a month if that. The casual display of energy usage before them was breath-taking.

If Jonathan was taken aback by it, though, he didn't show it. He just swiped through screen after screen, zooming in on the globe until North America was front and center, then Texas.

"Can you do it?" David asked. "Are you in?"

Jonathan didn't answer. His brows were lowered and his face was tense with concentration. He zoomed back out and the earth in the center of the desks grew smaller. Jonathan hit something on the tablet and all the red dots for the imagery satellites grew brighter. He twisted his wrist, rotating the ball and the earth zoomed out even further, instead providing a close up of one of the satellites itself.

Jonathan typed on a small keyboard that the tablet projected and then they all watched as the satellite twirled in position and began moving in the opposite direction it had initially been pointing.

"Holy shit," Eric whispered. He'd always been aware of just how much a long shot this mission had been, ever since Drea told him her idea. It seemed impossible that they'd actually get here, find everything intact, find the generators still working, that the area would be safe enough from radiation fallout in the first place, that—

"Alpha Hawk here. Napoleon is a go."

Eric looked up to find David barking orders into the sat phone.

"I repeat, Napoleon is a go." David nodded. "Black Hawk out." He hung up the phone then turned to the other soldier, Wendall. "Let's get all these supplies out to the vans."

Wendall gave a curt nod and Eric helped him get the first crate upstairs.

"I'll take it from here," Billy said, reaching for the crate. Eric raised an eyebrow but Billy just pushed him aside and took over.

When Eric got back downstairs, David was stowing a tablet, laptop, and solar charge base in the backpack he'd brought.

"Are we not taking up the second crate?" Eric asked.

"No, Wendall can take the second crate up when he gets back," David said. "I just like to be prepared."

"I thought that was the Boy Scouts' motto," Drea joked and David shot her a smile.

Eric just shook his head in astonishment. Could a woman really change overnight? It wasn't that the kinder, gentler Drea in front of him had nothing in common with the hard-ass, perpetually angry woman he'd come to know so well. Underneath, Drea was still Drea. She was too authentic to ever be anything but. Eric didn't even know how to describe the difference exactly. Except maybe to say that usually she held everyone at an arm's length and today, at least with their clan, she'd allowed them all into that inner circle she usually kept entirely private. She'd let them in. And it was so damn beautiful.

"Some day you're gonna grow up, son," his dad had said to him all those years ago, sitting in this very room. "And I want to make sure you're the kind of man who has his priorities straight."

"What the hell's that supposed to mean?"

"It means this smart-ass attitude is only gonna get you so far. Which far as I can see, isn't gonna be very far at all."

Silence. He was seething about how stupid and out of touch his dad was and how, as soon as he got home, he'd message his friends so they could go meet up at Trevor's house to get high and play Piper6, the newest FPS VR game to come out.

"Look here, son." His dad brought his console to life and the globe in the center of the room began turning as his dad spun the little orb off to the side.

"One of our satellites caught this earlier today."

His dad typed shit into his projected keyboard and then the crystalline screen above the globe came to life. It was an eagle's eye view of a city-street, but close up. Really close up. So much so that Eric could see the woman on screen was holding a lottery ticket after just coming out of a 7-11.

His dad tapped his tablet and the figures on the screen came to life as if it was a movie.

The woman shoved the lotto ticket in her pocket as soon as she saw a group of guys loitering on the street but it was too late.

She started down the street and the guys followed her. Eric doubted it was the lottery ticket they were interested in. They were stumbling and unsteady, drunk or high, he wouldn't doubt. But not so much that when she started running one of the group couldn't sprint and catch her, dragging her into an alley with a hand over her mouth.

"Jesus, Dad!" Eric jumped back from the desk, turning away from the screen. "What the fuck?"

"Keep watching."

"No. What the fuck is your point with all this?"

"Keep watching."

Eric refused, turned resolutely away. But when flashing light filled the room, from the screen behind him, he couldn't help but turn around to see what was happening.

Three police cruisers had pulled up to the alley. The attackers were being led away in handcuffs while a female officer helped the woman out of the alley with an arm around her shoulders.

Eric paused, frowning even as his nauseated stomach settled a little at knowing the woman was safe.

"Because our satellites are up there, we can stop this kind of thing from happening. Every day, we're making the streets safer. Not just inner-city streets, either. The whole world. We can keep an eye on Sudan, Afganistan, Russia. We can see dangers as they're developing and do something before people are hurt. This is what I've devoted my life too. I went to flight school but when I had the opportunity, I came to work here and be part of the team that maintains these satellites and maintains operations and information requests."

Eric shook his head, looking back at the screen. Back at the cops who were still shoving the bad guys into cop cruisers. Because of course this was the example his dad would choose to show him.

He looked back at his dad. "Jesus, Dad. Talk about a fucking nanny state. You work the fucking nanny cam. You think this is supposed to make me respect you? You invade people's privacy for a living."

His dad's mouth dropped open.

"The police were able to save that woman because of us!"

Eric scoffed. "That's the kind of logic dictators use to justify surveillance. We're protecting you. We'll put these cameras in your house to keep you safe from intruders. Who gets to decide who watches this? Who put you in charge and made you judge, jury and executioner? Because I know you use this same tech for drone strikes. Don't even bullshit me. You lock onto some poor bastard and then poof," Eric made a gesture with his hands, "they're gone in a quick explosion from a bomb that dropped out of nowhere!"

"But our government are the good guys." Dad took a step toward him but Eric only backed up even further.

"Sometimes you have to have faith, son. Faith that the people we elect to represent us in our government have our best interests at heart. That they are protecting us the best they can. The world today is a terrifying place. Believe me.

The things I see..." His voice trailed off and he looked into the distance, a slightly haunted look entering his eyes before they snapped back to Eric. "*All I ever wanted was to keep you and your mother safe. So I consider it an honor to serve my country. Haven't you ever had faith in something bigger than yourself?*"

Eric hadn't. Not in a way that mattered anyway. And he wouldn't, not until his dad died of a heart attack and he'd be forced to re-examine a lot of things.

His dad had been scared.

That was what he'd been admitting that night—but of course Eric had been too much of a self-involved ass to realize it. His dad was telling him the reason he worked sixty-hour weeks was because he was scared. It was the very same reason Eric would enlist eight years later. Endless wars. The terrorist attacks. The constant refugee crises all over the world. All the pundits arguing and no one offering real solutions.

Eric enlisted because he'd wanted to raise his daughter in a safer world than the one he saw looming ahead. Just like his dad had wanted for him. And maybe both of their beliefs that one man could ever make any difference in a world already so far down the path paved to hell had been ridiculous and naïve. No maybes about it. They'd definitely put their faith in the wrong institutions.

But if Eric and this team now could take down Travis and have a say in how the new government was built—if they could do even better than President Goddard. Not hard, considering what a disgusting, drunken slob the man had become...

They could push for more reforms. More law, more order. Maybe they could bring this country back from the brink and make it the nation it was always meant to be. The kind of nation America's Founding Fathers envisioned, but this time around, they'd be aware of all the mistakes and sins of the past and could God-willing avoid repeating them.

Eric looked over to Drea where she was still sorting through things in the closet, occasionally pulling items out and adding them to a growing mountain outside the door.

Her face was a mask of concentration as she sorted through another crate and Eric had a stray thought: *she'd make a good President.*

He blinked a little in surprise at the thought but then nodded, liking it the more he thought about it. Maybe what the country needed this time around was a Founding *Mother* instead of a Founding Father.

The sat phone rang then, interrupting his thoughts. David picked it up.

"Alpha here. Is there a problem with Napoleon?" David's head jerked toward Eric. "That's not what this line is for. Clear the line for official communiques only."

David's frown deepened into clear annoyance. Eric walked over to him. Why had he looked Eric's direction like that? Unless it was...

"Your father is busy—" David started but Eric yanked the phone away from him.

"Sophia? What's wrong?"

"Dad," came Sophia's voice. "Thank God."

"What's going on? Did Travis's men find the caves? Are you under attack?"

"No. God. No, Daddy. Nothing like that."

Eric scrubbed a hand down his face. This girl. He swore, she'd be the death of him one of these days. "Hon, the General's right. We really do need to keep this line—"

"I'm leaving," Sophia interrupted him. "I wanted to say goodbye because I won't be here by the time you get back."

"What?!"

"Daddy, don't yell."

"Then don't say ridiculous things."

"Dad, you can't pretend I'm a little girl forever. You were signing up for the Army when you were my age."

"I was twenty-one when I signed up for the army." Eric fought to keep his voice even. Sophia was impulsive sometimes and she had wild ideas. But Jesus, he was on a mission right now. He didn't have time for this. "You're not even nineteen."

"I'm nineteen in a week."

"Jesus, Soph, what are we even talking about? Stop this nonsense. You aren't going anywhere. I'll be back soon and then we can—"

"That. Right there. You just dismiss me like I'm a little kid. But we just got a call from the Governor of Santa Fe. They're rebuilding what's left of New Mexico but they need our help and they want to trade. They say they have plenty of men who'd be willing to fight on our side, Daddy. I'm going to go there as an emissary from Central Texas South to plead for their help."

"What the hell are you talking about?" Eric felt like the vein in his forehead was about to burst. This was the last thing he needed to be dealing with right now. "Some stranger talked to— You can't— You *will not*—" He could barely find the words for what a fucking idiotic idea everything his daughter had just said was. If she went out on her own — Jesus Christ, Travis's men were everywhere. If they got ahold of his baby girl, they'd—

"Look, Finn Knight's going with me. We're taking a sat phone so we can talk about this later. I can take care of myself, Daddy," she said, sounding annoyed and also like she wasn't listening to a single word he said.

"No you can't!" Eric exploded. "You really fucking *can't*! Your whole life I've made sacrifice after sacrifice so you'd never have to know exactly how fucking brutal and miserable and terrifying the world out there is. So no, you will not be going on some half-cocked idiotic—"

"General!" Jonathan shouted.

Eric looked over at the panic in Jonathan's voice and saw him pointing up at the screen above the central projection. It was the NASA compound. Jonathan had zoomed in on the very building they were all standing in.

And surrounding them were men climbing off of motorcycles, all fully armed.

CHAPTER TWENTY-EIGHT

JONATHAN

Jonathan rolled the orb to zoom in even closer.

The two men carrying the crate had obviously heard the roar of the motorcycles as they drove up. They'd dropped the crate and grabbed for their weapons.

But too late. There just weren't any defensive positions in that empty courtyard. One of the soldiers dived for a trashcan but it didn't matter, Wendall, it looked like.

Both were cut down before their eyes.

"Billy!" Drea shouted, hand out like she could stop what was happening.

"How much longer to get the rest of the satellites retasked?" David snapped.

"Too long," Jonathan said, flipping the orb back to zoom out. All the way out past the atmosphere and past seeing the globe until all the satellites were visible, not just the geostationary ones but the geosynchronous ones that created a band around the earth's equator like one of Saturn's rings.

There were hundreds. Thousands. It had always been ambitious to think they'd have enough time to come here and retask all the U.S.'s imaging satellites in a few hours but it had been a possibility.

Now that was gone.

"Go for *Black Dawn?*" Jonathan asked, voice shaking.

There was a moment of silence, but just a moment. Then David's sure voice ordering, "No. Go for *Hellen Keller.*"

And when Jonathan didn't respond immediately, David shouted, "Confirm, *Operation Helen Keller* is a go, soldier."

"Affirmative, *Helen Keller* is a go."

Frantic voices shouted in the background—Eric on the phone to his daughter, Drea shouting over the walkies to anyone that would listen, but Jonathan ground his teeth together and focused only on the projection in front of him.

He spun the orb handset and tapped through the tablet, selecting the grouping of satellites David had indicated.

All the satellites David indicated.

And then Jonathan went through the protocol to initiate the self-destruct sub-routines. They wouldn't just be redirected to point away from Texas. No, in eight minutes, all of the satellites he'd selected would aim themselves at the earth and burn up on reentry into the earth's atmosphere.

They'd all be destroyed.

No one would have eyes in the sky anymore—not Travis, not them, not anybody. At least no one relying on US satellites.

Ever again.

Well, that's what *Black Dawn* would have meant—no more eyes in the sky, destroying all the imaging satellites.

Operation Helen Keller though, took it one step further.

Jonathan's finger hovered over the tablet and the *Confirm Self-Destruct* command.

"Soldier, there's no time," David said, voice intractable. "You have your orders."

And so Jonathan did what he did best, at least ever since he'd met David Cruz. He followed orders. He pressed the button and the count-down began.

The countdown not just to take down the imaging satellites, but the communication ones. In eight minutes, no, in seven minutes and fifty-one seconds, sat phones would no longer work. The fledgling internet would probably go down.

David had just done what even the EMPs couldn't. He'd ordered them back to the dark ages for *real* this time.

No. David didn't do it.

Jonathan did.

He sat back in the chair and ran his hands through his hair. What the hell had he just done?

Neither Operation Black Dawn or Helen Keller was discussed with the Council. David wasn't sure they'd have the stomach for it.

If something goes wrong and we don't have time to retask the satellites, we have to assure the trip isn't in vain, David had said. *We have to take away Travis's eyes one way or another.*

This wasn't even your idea, Jonathan had argued back, *and suddenly you're its biggest proponent?*

I should have thought of it. It was shortsighted of me to assume NASA had been destroyed with Houston. It's brilliant. We blind Travis. And if it comes to it, we deafen them as well. We can't waste an opportunity like this. We have to take out the communication satellites while we have the chance.

Are you crazy? Jonathan had all but shouted, then quickly gotten ahold of himself so no one else in nearby tunnels overheard them. *We rely on the sat phones as much as Travis does. More maybe with our men scattered all over the Hill Country. You won't be able to communicate with them. At all!*

I'll prepare them so they know it's coming. Or at least that Operation Helen Keller is a possibility. Obviously the optimum choice is to be able to retask the satellites for a short time, and then bring them back online after Travis is dealt with. But Jonathan, you and I both live in the real world. You know what war is like. This plan is shoddy at best, thrown together in a day without knowing the landscape, blue prints, local threats, whether or not it's even still a viable—

I get it, Jonathan had cut him off. *But to take such a drastic measure—*

Have you looked around since we've been here? The vein strained in David's neck as he gestured at the cave around them. *This is a fight for survival. Not just for you and me, or even our men hiding in those hills. Haven't you seen the men and women in these caves? The families? You've seen the food stores. We've got enough to last* maybe *another week and a half with the seventeen hundred of us down here and then people will start to starve. Those women's children—the next generation that are the future of this* planet—*will start to starve or be driven out to Travis's mercy.*

A country is its people, Jonathan. We have the chance, and it's a very slim chance, to fight for this country, their country, before it's lost to a madman for who knows how long.

So yes, if I lose the convenience to pick up a phone and call someone a hundred or a thousand miles away, fine. Mankind survived without it before and we'll survive without it again. We'll figure out the fucking telegraph again if that's what it takes. But we'll have a country while we do it.

"We'll have a country," Jonathan whispered to himself as he pushed back from the console and stood up.

Six minutes, thirty-eight seconds.

"Hey!" Eric shouted.

Jonathan looked around, one hand still on his head. David was redialing on the sat phone, ignoring Eric. And Drea was darting for the stairs. Shit. With her savior complex who knew what she would do if they let her out of their sight. She didn't even have a gun—she'd handed it off to that stowaway, Gisela. Jonathan had the sudden urge to punch whatever soldier had let themselves be sweet-talked into letting that girl come along on the other transport. She'd be a distraction and Drea needed to be sharper than sharp if they were going to get out of this alive.

Eric was still arguing with David, who'd turned his back on him and was barking that *Operation Helen Keller* was a go to someone on the other line.

Jonathan grabbed Eric's arm. "Drea," he called and pointed toward where she was scampering over the fallen metal door.

It was all Eric needed. He immediately turned and ran. "Drea. Wait. Drea!"

Jonathan went after them both.

But she wasn't slowing down for anyone and damn she was fast. Even the small head start she'd gotten was enough so that she was a staircase ahead of them.

Jonathan passed Eric on the stairwell. Eric might be fit, but Jonathan trained under General David Cruz. Jonathan grabbed a hold of the handrail to steady himself as he ran in the darkness.

Still Drea got to the top ahead of him. Jonathan heard the shouting as he burst from the dark of the stairwell into the frantic dance of flashlights.

"Quiet," Jonathan called.

He looked around, doing a quick count of bodies in twos. There was Franco and Gisela, Billy and Garrett, plus the two soldiers they'd left guarding the entrance to the doorway where the mazelike hallways began—they must have run this direction when the attack began.

Drea was hugging Billy as he explained a soldier up front had taken the crate and sent him back here.

It was a short celebration though, because only moments later—

RAT TAT TAT TAT TAT TAT TAT.

Jonathan leapt for Drea, taking her to the floor as he looked around for the source of the live fire.

Franco had done the same with Gisela and she was screaming all right, but it was only into the walkie she clutched in her hand.

"Hello?" she cried. "Come in. Arthur? Art? Come in! Christian? Do you read me? Can anybody hear me?"

Jonathan definitely heard voices over the frequency, but it wasn't any of his and David's men. He crawled over and yanked the radio out of her hand.

"Quiet!" he ordered again.

"But the men!" Gisela said, half hysterical as she tried to crawl out from underneath Franco. "We have to go help them!"

Jonathan met Franco's gaze over her head.

"It's too late," Franco said gently, slowly easing off her. "They're gone."

Drea pushed Jonathan off her and went to her friend, taking Gisela in her arms. Jonathan shook his head. They didn't have time for any of this.

If the intruders were already in the building, then it was only a question of time before they found their way into the newer section. The hallways might be maze-like, but the building wasn't that big. The

MC fighters would stumble on them eventually. They needed to get out. Now.

Jonathan looked back toward the stairwell down to the basement Mission Control. Where the hell was David?

Gisela kept reaching for the radio. "You don't know they're dead! We need to know what's happening."

"Enough," Jonathan said with one last glance back toward the basement. "Franco, get her up. We go for the back exit. David will be right behind us."

Franco nodded and together, he and Drea got Gisela to her feet.

"Keep her quiet," Jonathan whispered harshly. "And turn off your flashlights. If we can stay quiet and stay dark, we'll have the tactical advantage. Now, form a line, hand on the back of the person in front of you."

They more or less did as Jonathan instructed, and one by one, clicked their flashlights off. Gisela's flashlight had to be pried from her hand and Jonathan was relieved to see Drea take her gun back as well.

Jonathan pulled on the night vision goggles he'd brought and reached for Drea.

"What are you waiting for?"

Jonathan looked over his shoulder to see David suddenly appear from the stairwell and had to bite back his furious frustration, especially when he saw the large backpack on his back and a second bag slung over his shoulder. Really? He'd been down there grabbing *supplies* and wasting precious minutes when his men were up here losing their *lives*?

Whatever, Jonathan couldn't afford to think about it now. He had a single mission—to get these people out of here *alive*.

Jonathan tugged on the strap of his machine gun, swinging it around to grab in his hands. He lifted it expertly to his shoulder and looked down the sight. He kept one finger on the trigger as he guided his team toward the back exit. He led the line down the hallway.

The silence after the arguing and gunfire over the walkie, along with the sudden and complete darkness of the inner hallways, all gave Jonathan the uneasy feeling of stepping into a different world. Or like waking only to find yourself in another dream. Or in this case, a nightmare.

Except Jonathan felt plenty awake with the adrenaline surging through his veins. They came to a T in the hallway.

Turn right. Jonathan remembered Eric's instructions, plus he'd looked at the blueprints for the building while he was downstairs.

He visualized them in his head. The path out was easy. Right, left, right.

They were far closer to the back exit than anyone coming through the door to the new building would be, especially since they'd be disoriented by the labyrinth of hallways. Unless of course whoever it was had been here before and knew there was a fairly clear path to the back exit if one took the third right and went all the way down the long hallway that ran the length of the building...

Jonathan quickened his steps as he turned the corner and kept his crouch low, always conscious to go slow enough so the person holding on to his back—Drea, he thought?—didn't lose their grip.

Okay, so far so good. Here came the next left. He slowed down, peeking his head around, heartbeat ratcheting up about five hundred times its normal rate.

But there was nothing. No footsteps, no voices, no light from flashlights. Just more green-tinged darkness through his goggles.

He hurried around the corner, pausing only long enough to make sure he hadn't lost the person he was leading. The slight tug on his tactical vest told him that yes, he was still being closely followed.

Jonathan didn't breathe any easier, though. If by some chance the intruders did know to take the other path, this was where they'd meet up, coming from the opposite end.

But halfway down this hallway was where the alcove to the back door branched off so there was no avoiding it.

They'd be fine. They were moving fast enough. They'd get there in—

"Where these fuckers at?"

In the distance, light flickered, illuminating the end of the hallway.

Fuck.

The bikers were coming—from down the long hallway just like he'd feared.

Jonathan gauged the distance to the alcove in the dim light. Thirty feet. They *might* be able to make it before the bikers rounded the corner and started shooting.

Drea. His wife. His family.

Might wasn't good enough.

"Run for it!" David whispered from the back of the group even as Jonathan turned and grabbed Drea roughly, pulling both her and consequently Gisela, who Drea was gripping, into one of the destroyed offices off the hallway.

Billy, Eric, and Garrett came too and finally, Franco and the other two soldiers. David was last and even though Jonathan couldn't see his face in the darkness, he could feel his General's fury. Not once in almost a decade had he ever defied a direct order.

But what the fuck was David thinking having them try to run for it? He could have gotten them all killed! And earlier, taking so goddamn long downstairs. They would've been out the back door already if he wouldn't have stopped to stock up on whatever the hell was in his precious bags.

All Jonathan knew was that he had new priorities now and until he knew David's heart was in the same place, he couldn't blindly follow him anymore. Not when the lives of his new-found family were at stake.

Less than ten seconds later, beams of light flashed down the hallway past the office where they were hidden. See? They never would have made it to the alcove.

Or... would they have? If Jonathan and David had opened fire as they'd gone, making the bikers back up long enough for their group to get to the alcove and out the back door? Dammit. Maybe David *was* right and Jonathan had just fucked them over majorly.

Jonathan's mouth twisted down. He hated this. Not trusting David. It was all wrong. But if David was making the wrong calls, someone had to question them.

There was no going back, though. In the dim light provided by the distant flashlights, Jonathan could see Drea shielding Gisela with her body and Eric trying to shield Drea. Billy and Garrett moved between them and the door. Jonathan joined David and the other soldiers standing in attack formation just inside the door.

David might be equally pissed at him, but they'd been in battle together too many times for him to address it now. David lifted a fist and then held up five fingers. Jonathan and the others nodded as they waited out the countdown.

The voices continued getting louder and the light brighter.

Five.

Four.

"Did you hear that girly scream over the radio? I call first dibs."

Three.

"Fine but don't wear her out. I want her tight when I tear into that little bitch's cunt."

Two.

"Well, I'm gonna—"

The fucker never got to finish his sentence because Jonathan and Franco leaned out of the office and fired their machine guns in the direction of the light.

CHAPTER TWENTY-NINE

DREA

Gisela let out a terrified squeal as the firefight began and Drea clamped a hand over her mouth. Drea hugged the girl to her, praying for the forgiveness she knew she didn't deserve.

People you love and trust will only let you down and hurt you—it was a truth Drea knew as deep down as the cigarette burn scar on her left forearm from that time Mom came after her during one of her meth rages.

But as Drea looked down into Gisela's terrified eyes, she realized this time it was her, Drea, letting down the people who trusted her.

Because she should have known exactly how stubborn Gisela would be. She'd seen it in the defiant look in Gisela's eyes last night. Of course the girl had found a way to stowaway and come on the mission after all. Probably in some foolish attempt to impress *Drea*. And it might get her fucking killed.

Then there was Billy. What the fuck had she been thinking letting him come? Someone back in the caves could have babysat him to make sure he stayed away from the medicine stash. It could have so easily been him she watched killed on that satellite feed.

Even Eric. He could have drawn out the directions to the secret room. He had a *broken arm* for Christ's sake. He had no business being on a mission. Okay, so whatever he'd done to get that last secret panel to open the lever to the stairwell had been somewhat specific—still, he could have walked them through it over the sat phone.

There was absolutely no need for all of them to come here. For all of them to *die*.

Drea's chest clenched and her hand tightened around the handle of her Glock. She consciously relaxed her finger on the trigger, though. God, the last thing they needed right now was her accidently shooting Jonathan or Garrett or one of the soldiers in the ass. They were in enough trouble without her adding friendly fire into the mix.

Drea kept her eyes locked on the door. She could barely make out who was who in the darkness—the men were just silhouettes against the flashlight lights in the hallway beyond. She watched tensely as one of the men shifted positions, leaning slightly further out to continue shooting as another pulled back to reload his cartridge.

Gisela's shrill scream pierced Drea's ear as one of the men at the door dropped to the floor like a stone.

Oh God, *no*. All the breath whooshed out of her chest. *Jonathan!* Was it Jonathan?

And just like that, Drea was back in that damp basement ten years ago.

Her father was being forced onto his knees in front of her.

His watery eyes searched for hers in that last moment as Thomas's father stepped up behind him and raised the gun to the back of his head and—

"Franco!" Gisela shouted, weeping and struggling to get out of Drea's arms. It was enough to pull Drea back to the moment and stem the tide of her own demons before they flooded her.

And for her to see that the body Garrett had tugged back into the office wasn't Jonathan after all. It was Franco, their driver, the man with the ten-thousand-watt smile and a thousand corny jokes. Billy was leaned over him, fingers to his neck. But he pulled back, shaking his head.

No. She wanted to deny it even as the evidence was so clear right in front of her. Franco couldn't be dead. Just a few hours ago he'd been laughing and telling dumb jokes and—

"Down," David shouted before throwing something into the hallway. Jonathan lunged toward her, shielding her and Gisela with his body as a huge *BOOM!* erupted in the hallway, shaking the walls.

"Go, go, go," David shouted, waving his arm toward the door.

Then Jonathan was grabbing Drea's elbow, and Garrett and Billy were helping Gisela to her feet and then they were all moving toward the door.

Drea could barely feel her legs. Everything was moving too fast. Too loud.

Get it together, Drea. Gisela needs you. Jonathan and David and Billy and Garrett and Eric need you.

She took a deep breath and pulled away from Jonathan, then reached for her Glock. David's grenade might have taken care of whatever immediate threat was outside the office but they were far from safe.

Jonathan looked her way, barely visible in the dim light. At least one flashlight must have survived. She gave him a sharp nod. She was fine. She wouldn't fall to pieces on him.

He and David took the first step into the hallway, machine guns to their shoulders. They didn't fire immediately though, so Drea guessed there weren't any bikers left standing.

She followed with the rest of her clan and Gisela, stepping far clear of Franco's body. She forced her eyes straight ahead so she wouldn't look down and see him. That didn't stop her boot from slipping in his blood though.

Drea swallowed against the rising bile and forced herself onward into the hallway. And holy shit. In the destruction of what was left of the hallway, visible by the light of one flashlight that had gotten thrown free of the rubble, it was clear no one had survived the blast. Bodies littered the floor, the walls were blown outward, and broken pipes hung from wrecked ceiling tiles.

Jonathan hurried through the rubble and bodies and Drea followed, letting Garrett move ahead so she and Billy could help Gisela keep moving, each of them taking one of her arms.

"Just ten more feet," Jonathan called back. "Turn right and there's the door."

But almost immediately after he spoke, more light appeared ahead.

Fuck. Drea felt her eyes widen even as she started running, all but dragging Gisela with her.

Drea swung Gisela in front of her at the last moment and shoved her the last few feet towards the alcove before taking a diving leap for it herself.

In the second before she cleared the hallway, pain exploded across Drea's shoulder like a spike had been shoved through it.

Hearing the gunfire came second.

Everything swam.

The darkness, the shouting, gunfire.

Hands pulling at her.

"Drea! Shit! She's been hit!"

"We've got to get the hell out of here. Now!"

"You know they'll be waiting out there for us. There's no way they aren't covering the second exit."

"Fuck. FUCK."

"Back. Go back!"

"We can't. They're right on our asses!"

And then blinding light as a door was opened to sunlight, but only for a moment. It was shut just as quickly.

Boom.

It was more distant this time than it had been in the hallway.

Every second that passed, Drea became more and more aware of what was going on again. She tried to sit up, blinking and wincing against the pain in her shoulder.

"No blood. There's no blood!" Billy's voice. "I think her jacket caught it."

"Great. So let's get her the fuck up and get the hell out of here."

Drea lifted a dazed hand to her head as Billy helped her to her feet. "Gisela," she said, looking around. "Where is Gis—"

"I'm here," Gisela said, weeping. "Oh thank God. Thank God you're all right. I'm sorry. I'm sorry I came when you said not to. I've slowed you down every step of the way. I'm sorry. Please, I'm sorry." Her words barely made any sense through her sobs. "All I ever wanted was to be like you. To be strong like you. I didn't want them to have broken me. They didn't break you. But I'm not strong. I'm weak. They *did* break me. I'm sorry. Oh God, I'm so sorry."

Drea shook her head, still blinking and trying to get her bearings as she reached for Gisela. "It's fine. Let's just get home safe. You are strong. You are."

Gisela shook her head, tears running down her face. Drea put her arm around her both to comfort and steady her even though Eric and Garrett were holding her up already.

David pushed the back door open again.

After being in darkness for so long, the light hit Drea like a knife straight to the brain, but she pushed forward anyway.

"I'm fine," Drea said, pushing off of Eric and Garrett. "I'm okay. I can walk." She heaved herself out the door with Gisela, lunging to grab hold of the railing beside the stairs. She kept her eyes down on her feet, half stumbling, half falling down the stairs, only managing to stay upright because of her iron grip on the railing. She and Gisela miraculously kept one another up somehow.

Even in the twenty seconds it had taken to get to the bottom of the stairs, her eyes had grown more and more used to the light.

Enough so that when she finally lifted her eyes up past her feet, she saw the man rise from where he'd been hiding behind his parked bike, rifle aimed right at her head.

"No!" Gisela screamed.

It was all over in a split second.

Drea once again found herself on the ground. But this time she wasn't alone. Gisela was laying on top of her.

Gisela, who had shoved Drea out of the way at the last moment.

"Gis—" Drea started, rolling both of them over.

And then she screamed.

Because half of Gisela's head was missing.

CHAPTER THIRTY

ERIC

"Drea!" Eric shouted, running down the last of the stairs even as machine gun fire exploded behind him in response to the shotgun blast.

No no no no no no. It couldn't be happening again. He couldn't be too late. He couldn't watch another woman he loved die right in front of him.

Eric skidded to his knees beside Drea. She was sitting up, cradling Gisela's limp form to her chest.

Drea was alive. Oh thank God. Thank *God*. But there was so much blood. Frantically, he ran his good hand over Drea's head, neck, arms, everywhere not covered by her flack jacket. His hand came away sticky with blood. But not hers.

That was when Eric really took a good look at Gisela. From the side he'd first approached, she'd looked bad, but as he moved around Drea— Oh Jesus! Eric swallowed down bile that rose at seeing what was left of Gisela's head.

It could have been Drea.

Drea's brains could be splattered all over the pavement, another woman he loved dead in his arms. Another he'd failed to save.

This whole fucking situation was out of control. They shouldn't have come until they'd been able to control more variables. Considered all the things that could have gone wrong. Brought a fucking battalion with them to protect—

"Get her up," David barked. "Garrett, get her up. We need to move out. There are more behind us."

Eric helped Garrett drag Drea to her feet. At first she fought them when they tried to get her to let go of Gisela's corpse.

"She's gone, D," Garrett said. "You gotta let her go."

Drea nodded mutely, finally stumbling to her feet.

"Eric. Eric Wolford."

Eric froze at that voice and he swung around, yanking his gun out of the back of his jeans.

Laughter then. A laugh he used to know as well as his own.

"Is that your girlfriend? Some MC bitch? Really, Eric? What would Connie say? And what sort of example is that for little Sophia?"

Eric swung around again.

The voice didn't sound right. It was like it was a recording, coming over a speaker... or a *phone*.

Eric looked down and there it was, a sat phone. It was on the ground, several feet away from one of the fallen bikers who'd been killed from the blast of the grenade David had thrown out the door.

Eric strode toward it and snatched it off the ground as David got everyone moving to where they'd stashed the second van.

"Aw, look at you all scurrying away like little mice," said the voice over the sat phone. Arnold Travis's voice. "Isn't that cute."

So Jonathan hadn't been able to turn the satellite away from viewing this area before they'd been forced to abort the mission after all. Wonderful.

"And any moment my men will be moving those satellites back into position and all of these people will have died for nothing. I look forward to seeing you face to face again. There's so much unresolved conflict between us. It's not healthy, you know. Isn't that what they say? Or what they used to say, back when people used to sit around on couches all day and talk about their feelings."

"Well you wouldn't know anything about that," Eric growled. "Feelings. Human emotion. Not your thing."

Arnold *tut tut tutted* at him. "You've got it backwards. You were always the robot. Work, work, work. I'd try to get you to lighten up and have some fun, but nooooo, the great Eric Wolford always had to take everything so damn seriously."

"I can't believe I never saw what a fucking sociopath you were."

"That hurts, *friend*. Does little Sophia know you'd say such a thing to the man you named her godfather?"

"Don't you fucking say her name again."

"Sophia?"

"I'm gonna—"

"Don't you want to hear about Jacob's Well? It really is a lovely little town. My first order as President was to secure that bastion of rebel sentiment. It's now the headquarters for all my Central Texas operations. It's quaint. I can see why it would appeal to your country sensibilities. You always did like to consider yourself one of the common folk, didn't you?"

Eric bit his tongue. Literally bit it. He might want to hurl the phone as far as he could throw it, but Arnold was giving up valuable information without even realizing it. Even if he was overexaggerating, this was the most information they'd had about what was going on in Jacob's Well since most of the men and women with families had evacuated.

"Of course," Arnold went on, "the public floggings in the town square do dampen the festive spirit a bit, but they'll learn to stay in line with the new laws soon enough. Some good citizens were even nice enough to offer up the location of several females their neighbors had attempted to hide from the authorities. That of course is an offense punishable by death, so we've had a few hangings as w—"

Travis cut off mid-sentence and Eric looked down at the phone. The light was still on but the connection had been lost.

"Let's go," David said, jerking the back doors of the van open and gesturing for everyone to get inside. Billy and another soldier helped Drea inside.

Eric hurried the last few feet, pausing only for a few moments. "Is this sat phone glitchy? It just cut out—"

"We killed all the communication satellites. Sat phones won't work now."

Eric felt his eyebrows shoot up as he went to climb into the van but David stopped him with an arm across his chest.

"How long have you and Arnold Travis been so chummy?"

Eric looked down. "Long story. I'll tell you later."

When he looked up, it was to David's fierce glare. "I'll hold you to that."

Eric nodded but only after giving the General a hard look of his own. "And you'll explain what the hell you mean about those satellites? The Council never talked about doing anything with the communications satellites."

David inclined his head and Eric climbed up into the back of the van.

David slammed the back door shut and went around to the driver's seat. The next minute they were lurching forward, before Eric had even gotten a chance to clip his seatbelt into place.

He looked to Drea, belted in between Billy and Jonathan, but her eyes were closed, head back like she was sleeping. By the rapid heartbeat thrumming in her neck and the way she kept swallowing rapidly, he knew there was no way she was, though.

But if she needed to shut them all out right now, that was fine. Everyone dealt with the aftermath of battle differently. Some people, if you tried to crowd them and get them to talk about shit right away, it just made it worse. And what she'd just been through was already fucking traumatic enough.

Jesus, that bastard with the rifle had been aiming right for Drea. It wasn't random. For them to target a woman like that instead of trying to capture her to sell, they'd had to know exactly who she was.

And it was clear from the phone call that it had been Arnold calling the shots on this live as it was happening.

The question was, did he target Drea because of how she'd taken over the Black Skulls compound in College Station or because of what she meant to Eric? No, Jesus, there was no way he could even know about his relationship with her.

You will see me again, brother. I promise you that.

Eric closed his eyes against the memories but they rushed in anyway.

Back on that terrible day, after Connie died, Arnie had dug a grave for Connie in the backyard while Eric stayed upstairs with Sophia. After a quick, unceremonial burial, Eric and Sophia had climbed into Arnie's truck and all three of them sped away from the house where Eric and his family had created so many memories. Eric covered Sophia's eyes as they went downstairs and they went out the back door so they wouldn't pass by the living room but she was ten. Not a little kid. She knew why her mother wasn't coming with them.

She cried the whole way down to the outer reaches of northern San Antonio where Arnie's militia buddies were shacked up.

Arnie found a safe place for Eric and Sophia, a cabin separate from the rest of the militia guys. But they were only there a few days when the lights went out and their computers and tablets died, even though they'd still had plenty of battery.

Cars wouldn't start.

Backup generators were dead.

Everyone had heard rumors of government trials of EMP weapons after the discovery of inert electromagnetic pulse technology, but that's all it had ever been. Rumor. Until it wasn't.

They didn't even hear about the nuclear attacks until a day later when refugees fleeing south Austin talked about seeing the mushroom cloud and running.

But by then, Eric and Arnie already had a plan.

Because the one group of people who take rumor and whispers of government conspiracy seriously?

Independent militia men in places like Texas. This was the exact sort of thing they'd been preparing decades for.

They'd stockpiled ancient antique vehicles that had entirely mechanical components and gotten them running again. There was barely an electric self-driving car in sight other than the one Eric and Arnie had arrived in.

And guns.

They had *a lot* of guns.

Plus men to shoot the guns.

Looking back, it was naïve of Eric not to see what Arnie had planned. But he was still so grief-stricken over Connie.

He did think it was odd that Arnie held so much sway over the militia men. He seemed to be their *leader* in fact. How exactly he'd managed that when he'd been stationed overseas just as often as Eric had, Eric didn't know. And didn't think to question.

After all, it was *Arnie*.

This was the same guy who'd been there for him when his dad died.

The same guy who he'd gotten drunk off his ass with and had a pizza-eating contest in college that saw them both eating so much they took turns hugging the dorm room toilet off and on all night.

And this was the same guy who'd risked everything to bust Eric out of going to military jail, for Christ's sake.

They were closer than best friends.

They were brothers.

So when Arnie talked about heading down to San Antonio to see if they could recruit more soldiers to their cause right after the EMP attack, Eric was immediately enthusiastic. They could *really* build a safe community. A place where Sophia could grow up protected.

"For sure, man," Arnie said. "And we could make the rules because we'd be the ones in charge."

Eric nodded. Yes. He'd seen firsthand overseas what happened after war and disasters created power vacuums. Someone always stepped in to take power and whoever that person was shaped the future of the country or region, for good or bad. Mostly for bad, because the people who were thinking about swooping in to take advantage of power vacuums were the rich and the corrupt.

But if he and Arnie could get control, well, they could use their power for *good*. To protect people. To keep people safe.

"Let's go," Eric said. "Now." The more he thought about it the more he was sure it was the right path. The only path, maybe, if he truly wanted to honor his promise to Connie and protect their daughter. How long could they really expect to stay safe in some flimsy cabin in the woods? Sophia would grow up and need more than just a house and four walls. He wanted her to have everything. Friends. School. Maybe even marriage some day.

But Jesus, even thinking such things after the world had just been destroyed, it seemed beyond impossible.

Unless he remade the world in his image.

So he climbed into the hundred year old trucks along with Arnie and his militia buddies, leaving Sophia with one of the few women at the militia encampment, kissing her and promising he'd make everything better soon.

And down they went to Lackland Airforce and Army Base.

Eric expected they'd meet some resistance at the gates. But the gates weren't down. There were no military police at the guard station either.

San Antonio hadn't been hit by any bombs but the usually bustling city was almost silent. Cars were stopped everywhere and occasionally they'd see people, usually darting here or there, but it was fucking creepy.

It hadn't really sunk in until then. That they were witnessing the end of the world.

Eric and Arnie just looked at each other as they drove the truck down W. Military Dr. At every military base Eric had ever been on, there was a constant hive of activity. Troops running exercises, drills, heading to the mess hall, vehicles going this way and that.

But this... quiet?

Had all the troops been called out to help deal with the disasters around the state? They only knew about Austin being bombed, but there could be more cities. Both Houston and Dallas had larger populations than Austin.

Arnie held up his fist and the lead van they were in stopped. He pushed open the door and jumped out. "Come on," he told Eric.

Eric followed him out.

"You," he pointed to the driver of the second van. "Drive him wherever he wants to go."

Then he turned to Eric and spoke more quietly. "You go one way and I'll go another. Let's see if we can find anyone left who wants to join us."

Eric nodded. He was intimidated at the thought of trying to convince anyone of anything apart from Arnie, but then he remembered Sophia back at camp waiting for him. Counting on him.

"Here, take this." Arnie pressed a gun into his hands and Eric looked up at him in shock.

"What? I'm not taking that!"

"Are you fucking kidding me? Did you or did you not see everything we passed on the way here? It's a new fucking world, man. You gotta stay safe. Plus, we're on a military base. These fuckers are gonna have guns."

"Exactly," Eric said, exasperated. "What would we do if someone walked into a base in Kandahar packing? We'd mow him down right where he stood. We're just here to talk to these guys. To give them options."

"Jesus Christ," Arnie swore. "For once in your life stop being such a fucking Boy Scout. I'm just trying to look out for you."

Eric took a deep breath. "I know." He put an arm on Arnie's shoulder. "I know, okay. Same back at ya. Having you end up full of holes wouldn't exactly be my idea of a good day, ya know? You're the only brother I've ever had."

For a second, Eric saw that comment hit. Arnie nodded and swallowed, but then he rolled his eyes and shrugged Eric's hand off his shoulder. "All right, enough with the mushy shit. Let's go get this done."

"You," Arnie snapped at a militia guy who'd been sitting in the passenger side of the second van, "move outta the way. My boy here's got shotgun."

The guy hurried to climb in the back to make room for Eric. If they objected to Arnie ordering them around or Eric suddenly being his right hand man, it didn't show on their faces. Then again, they seemed to follow Arnie with a sort of blind loyalty Eric didn't understand.

Arnie's van went left so Eric ordered his right. And it wasn't much further before he finally came upon some life.

In the Community Center, he saw a bunch of people milling around so he ordered the van to a stop.

Shit. He actually had to do something now. He had to say something. He wasn't good at speaking. He was good at repairing bridges and roads.

But it only took one blink of his eyes for the image of Connie's battered and broken body to flash through his head.

He shoved open the door of the van and jumped to the ground. Soldiers and

Airmen lounged on couches or at tables, some playing cards and Ping-Pong, others talking, some just sleeping. Alcohol was openly being chugged all around.

What the—

It was ten in the morning. Had the whole world gone fucking crazy?

*"A-ten-*hut*!" Eric called at the top of his voice.*

He might as well have shot a Taser into the ass of every man there, they all got to their feet so fast.

Even the ones on the floor sleeping. To a man. They were all on their feet, hands at their sides, staring straight forward. And they were all men. There were no female cadets in sight—they'd no doubt been taken by Xterminate or the frenzy that followed, or maybe, if they were lucky, they'd gone into hiding.

"Parade rest," Eric called, and all eyes came his way.

Which was when he realized that he was wearing fatigues. All the militia guys did. But he didn't want to pretend he was something he wasn't.

"I am First Lieutenant Eric Wolford. I served ten years overseas, one tour in Syria, another in Central Africa, and was most recently in Northern Pakistan. I've come back home to find the country I love in tatters, my wife..." He paused, swallowing back emotion before continuing on in a voice that nonetheless shook, "my wife dead, not of the virus, but of men's base and monstrous violence."

He took another step further into the community center. "This is not the America I fought and put my life on the line for. But it still can be."

"What the fuck you talkin' about?" one guy called out. "You take a look outside? Fuckin' apocalypse out there."

"Houston and Austin have been blown off the fucking map," *called another man.*

"Shit's like the rapture, 'cept Jesus forgot my ass."

Laughter at that.

"Enough," Eric said. "It's not the end of the world. I've got a ten-year-old little girl at home that proves it's not."

That got their attention.

"And I intend to make a life for her that's not about hiding in a hole moaning about the end of the world."

He took several more steps forward, walking back and forth now so he could get a better look at everyone in the room. So he could look each of them in the eye. Really take their measure and give them the opportunity to do the same with him.

"I'm going to be creating a community where it's safe for her to grow up. A community where the laws reflect the values that each of us signed up to the armed forces to protect. Maybe America's gone to hell. We'll remake her. We'll make a better country. One without corruption."

"Man, you're talkin' bullshit dreams."

But Eric just stubbornly shook his head. "I'm not. We'll start with a town. A small town in the Hill Country. One that has a good source of water. From what I've seen, I can't imagine any of these communities not welcoming a force that would come in and restore law and order. Obviously the government isn't doing shit for them. So we will."

The more he talked, the more heads around the room started nodding.

"Our CO just fucking flipped out," said one of the guys in the middle of the crowd. "When all the electrical shit cut out and Command stopped getting orders from the higher ups. They just started stealing shit and running."

"Especially when we heard 'bout the bombs. Everyone was sure San Antonio'd be next."

Nodding from all around the room.

"But you stayed," Eric said.

"Got nowhere else to go."

More nodding.

"My wife and sister died," said a nearby soldier. "I figured if I stayed on base, maybe I could do some good somewhere if they ever got their thumbs out of their asses. Fat fucking chance."

Eric jumped in. "I'm giving you that opportunity. Our government failed us. Where's the National Guard? The police? Who protected my wife from the mobs? No one."

He walked back to the other side of the room. "It has to start with someone. The rebuilding. Bringing order and sanity back in the midst of this madness. Let's start with us. It's not the end of the world. Or fuck, maybe it is. But it's also the beginning of a new one."

The nodding was becoming even more emphatic now and one man, a soldier, moved forward to stand beside Eric. "This bastard makes a lot of sense. And what else are we gonna do? Stay around here twiddling our dicks? Even if our CO comes back, any of you wanna take orders again from a dipshit coward like that?"

There was a loud chorus of nos in response.

An airman representative also stepped forward and soon, the entire room was with them.

Including a first sergeant who just happened to have the keys to two tanks on base that resided in an EMP proof hanger.

There was a positively jubilant mood as Eric led the men to the hanger. There weren't just the two tanks, either. There was also a fleet of army vehicles that still worked, all protected from the EMP. Eric ordered the men to load up as much rations and supplies into the vehicles as possible.

He already had a location in mind to create the community he'd pitched to the soldiers and airmen. It was a little town Connie had always loved taking Sophia to on the weekend for Market Days. It had a river that ran through it and once when he was home from deployment they'd spent a long Sunday afternoon splashing around in Jacob's Well, an amazing natural well from an underground spring.

He couldn't wait to tell Arnie. Several of the guys he talked to said that yes, there were other soldiers and airmen around, so maybe Arnie had found even more who would join them.

But it wasn't until he had the trucks all loaded up and the tanks began rolling out that he ran into his best friend.

And all Eric's joy popped upon seeing him.

Arnie was covered in blood.

"Jesus, what happened?" Eric ran forward, grabbing Arnie's arms and looking him up and down.

But Arnie was busy looking over Eric's shoulder. "Holy shit. You found us tanks. Right on, man."

"Arnie, for fuck's sake! You're covered in blood. What the fuck happened?"

Arnie blinked then and wiped at the specks of blood all over his face, which only had the effect of smearing it more.

Eric took a step back when Arnie just shrugged.

"Ran into a little trouble over at the Commissary. Nothing me and my men couldn't handle. And look, we got a helicopter. Supplies too. And a bunch of guys wanna join up. They're tired of this bullshit. They see that if they want shit in this life, they gotta take it. It's gonna be true now more than ever. We just gotta make sure we take it first."

Eric stumbled back a step but Arnie just kept nodding. "You should've seen me, man. I just started talking, and they were all totally with me from word one. The system's been rigged for years. But now's our chance. We can finally take what's rightfully ours. We can be kings."

"Jesus." Eric shook his head, then ran his hands through his hair. *"Jesus."* It was all he could say. *How many men had Arnie just killed? So he could be* king?

He realized then that he didn't know the man standing in front of him at all.

It wasn't just that they didn't see eye to eye on some things like Eric had thought. Or that they had different backgrounds growing up. Eric had always cut Arnie some slack if he was a little lax about rules Eric thought were important.

Arnie cheated on girls. Arnie occasionally did coke. Arnie fudged supply records and sold the excess when they were stationed in Syria together.

He'd never had good role models growing up, Eric had always reasoned. He'd been shuttled around from one foster home to another. He never knew his dad and refused to talk about his mom. Jesus Christ, Senior year, Eric found out that Arnie had been sleeping in the janitor's closet at school because his foster dad had kicked him out of the house, so Eric demanded Arnie come live at his house. They certainly had the space.

Arnie never said it, but Eric got the sense it was the most stable home situa-tion he'd had in a long time. Arnie was the one who got mad if Eric wasn't on time for what they started to call family dinner. *Eric's mom was a phenomenal cook, he couldn't deny that. But Arnie seemed to get a kick out of the whole thing. The dining room. The good china mom liked to eat off of because, as his mom always said,* well what good was it doing just sitting there in the cabinet?

"How many?" Eric choked out.

"What?" Arnie asked.

"How many men? Did you kill just now?"

Arnie looked at him like he was from a different planet. "Are you serious with this bullshit?"

"Bullshit?" Eric exploded. *"These are people's* lives *we're talking about!"*

"Yeah and it was either them or me," Arnie shouted right back, thumping his chest. *"Would you rather it was me back there dead?"*

"So it was self-defense?" Please. Please just say it was self-defense. *"Did they start firing first?"*

Arnie just shook his head. "I cannot believe this fucking bullshit. After all the years we've known each other? After all I've fucking done for you?" He ran *forward and shoved Eric hard in the chest. "You'd be rotting in a fucking prison right now if it wasn't for me!"*

Eric recovered from stumbling backwards right before he fell and stood back up again. His eyes were swollen from crying so much the past few days over Connie and he felt raw all over as he begged, "Just tell me who fired first."

"Your daughter would be dead *if it wasn't for me!"*

"Who shot fir—"

"I DID!" Arnie screamed right in Eric's face, spittle flying. "I fucking did! I went into that commissary and saw some fuckers with guns guarding the supplies and I ordered all my men to fire. And I pulled out this gun right fucking here," he whipped out his gun from the back of his pants and pointed it right at Eric's forehead, *"and when they were on the ground, begging for their fucking lives, I* ended *them. Just like I did to the fuckers who got in the way of my smuggling operations in Syria, and Lebanon, and Poland."*

"Why the fuck do you think I kept getting promoted so much quicker than you? Think." *He banged the barrel of the gun against Eric's forehead. "I knew how to play the fucking game. Something Eric the Boy Scout always refused to fucking do."*

Arnie finally pulled the gun back, waving it around them, to the soldiers who'd lined up behind him, along with the one's who'd grouped behind Eric.

Eric could feel it, the tension between the two groups.

Arnie seemed to revel in it.

"This is the real world, Eric. Wake the fuck up."

Eric just shook his head and took a step back. His voice was choked as he gave the only response he could. "I loved you like a brother." He swallowed and stood up straighter. "Let me and my men pass. I'll go collect my daughter, and then we never have to see each other ever again."

"Your m—" Arnie scoffed but all the men behind Eric shifted as if they too were standing up straighter, at attention, ready to fight.

Arnie laughed then. A fake, too bright laugh. It was the laugh Arnie gave when he cared too much. Eric hated that he knew that and he hated that he cared—it would be so much easier to hate Arnie if he didn't still love him so much.

Arnie shoved his gun in the back of his pants. "What the fuck do I care what you do?"

Eric didn't wait. Love the man as a brother or not, Eric had meant what he'd said. If he had his way, their paths would never cross again.

Like a shifting ocean tide, Eric and his men turned and headed back the way they'd come.

Arnie couldn't let him go without one last parting shot, though, apparently.

"You will see me again, brother. *I promise you that."*

CHAPTER THIRTY-ONE

DAVID

David pulled into the spacious parking lot of the abandoned outlet mall about ten miles south of Travisville, right off I35.

He breathed in deep at seeing his soldiers encamped all around the mall. So many had already mobilized in the short time since he'd made the last call from the sat phone before it went dead forever. They were a sight for sore eyes, especially after the shitstorm they'd just left behind.

But though they'd lost men—and women, David closed his eyes as he remembered the dead girl in Drea's arms, and Franco, and Wendall, and Benjamin and Keith and Vernon and Paolo—they'd accomplished their mission objectives.

Arnold Travis was blind to their activities. And so was Thomas 'Suicide' Tillerman, the Black Skulls leader and governor of San Antonio who'd be the defacto commander of the Army there now that Travis couldn't give orders remotely from Fort Worth.

Maybe the odds were still stacked against them, but it meant his plan had a chance. Whereas yesterday they'd faced sure defeat—and the sure capture and probable death of thousands of his men.

He waved to his men as he stepped out of the van and cheers erupted here and there as men recognized him.

He didn't have a lot of close friends. Or well, any, apart from Jonathan. But he had the respect of his troops, which was far more important.

So he waved and stood up straight and let nothing but confidence show on his features as he walked past his men. Tomorrow, they could mourn those they'd lost. Tomorrow, he could crack open the whisky he had stowed back at the cave and drink long and deep and chant the names of the dead. Seven more to add to the one hundred and eighty-two he already whispered aloud every night before he laid his head down to sleep. One hundred and eighty-nine now. Every night beginning with the name that was carved deepest of all: *Kevin*. His stupid, beautiful, idiot kid brother.

But in the meantime, he sucked in a deep breath and stood up taller, he'd stuff it all into a box and close the lid up tight. Vacuum seal that shit until the present crisis was done.

Eric and Garrett were helping Drea down from the back of the van as Sergeant Miles hurried up to David.

"General Cruz, we've got a staging area set up in this corner building here." He waved them toward a large structure in the corner of the mall.

They walked over the uneven asphalt, Jonathan shouldering the backpack and bag of supplies David had brought up from Mission Control.

The building Sergeant Miles led them to was a big, empty space. All the windows had been broken long ago but it had been swept out and it was clean enough, with a few chairs set out and enough sleeping pallets for all of them to be comfortable. Interesting. Just how many people knew about David's new... family situation?

Sergeant Miles showed them around. "There's a bathroom in the back there along with several gallons of water if you want to get washed up. And some rations up here if you're hungry."

David thanked and dismissed the sergeant.

Billy nodded and led a still dazed looking Drea through the large open space to the back, no doubt heading for the bathroom. Drea was still covered in blood. It was all over her clothes, her face—it had even stained the front part of her dreadlocks reddish brown. Garrett and Eric hurried to follow them.

Jonathan dropped the bag of supplies David had given him to carry and turned his back on David, pacing away from him. After all their years together, David knew him well enough to know he was upset. At the same time, David was fucking exhausted and didn't have the energy for Jonathan's passive aggressive bullshit today of all days.

"You have something to say, say it."

Jonathan spun back his direction, clearly pissed. "What the hell was that back there? You should have talked to the others before taking out the communication satellites."

David scoffed. "There wasn't exactly a lot of time if you recall."

"I mean yesterday. We never should have gone in like that without telling the others what we were planning."

"It wasn't our main objective. It was only if things went FUBAR, which they did."

Jonathan made a face and shook his head. "That mission was FUBAR from the moment it was conceived. And we went in with no idea what we were walking into, a shit exit strategy, and with extraneous personnel. That girl should never have made it onto that second transport."

"Agreed on the last point," David said, taking a step forward and getting in Jonathan's face. "But this is war. Or did those cushy years in the capitol make you forget what it's like on the front lines? We don't always have the luxury of complete intel. We have to act if we want to stay alive. Sacrifices have to be made—"

"Is that what Franco is to you? And Wendall? Just sacrifices that had to be made? For what? So you could take those extra minutes doing fuck knows what downstairs? Gathering a few extra batteries?"

"Watch yourself," David warned, his tone low and dangerous.

"No," Jonathan said, stepping toe to toe with David. "Fuck that. I'm tired of biting my tongue. I always looked up to you, so even when I was uncomfortable with your calls, I never said anything. He's the

General, I thought. He knows what he's doing. But you know what I realize now? You're just a man and you're making this shit up as you go."

"Of course I'm just a man," David exploded. "Only a little boy would try to make me into some sort of hero. I'm sorry if I didn't live up to whatever bullshit pedestal you put me up on. Except no, I'm not." Fuck that. Fuck walking on eggshells around Jonathan. He didn't want to be treated like a boy anymore? Fine. "That's not my fucking job. My job is to protect the men under my command and the country I swore an oath to serve."

David pointed a finger into Jonathan's chest. "Your fucking job is to obey my commands. But today you disobeyed a direct order. I told you to run. We could have made it around the corner to the landing and the exit before those fuckers rounded the corner. We could have been on our way out of the building but instead you thought you knew better and we ended up foxhole'd in that fucking office."

Jonathan's face went cherry red. "So you're trying to blame Franco's death on me?"

"I'm saying that when my men don't obey my orders, I can't control what happens."

"Fuck you." Jonathan shoved him hard in the chest and David locked his jaw as he took a step back.

"Walk away, soldier," David ground out through his teeth. "You'll want to walk away right this fucking second."

Jonathan let out a bitter laugh. "Oh sure. Anyone dares question the omnipotent General David Cruz and they're immediately dismissed. Disciplined within inch of their lives."

"I do what has to get done. What do you think would happen if those men out there didn't have someone to lead them? Do you think we'd be coordinating an attack tomorrow that would have any chance at succeeding?"

"Oh because we're all idiotic sheep who would be lost without you? That's what you've wanted me to believe my whole adult life, isn't it? So I'd never question anything you told me to do. So I'd just fall in line and step. Yes sir, General sir." He mocked saluting, going ramrod straight at attention. "Whatever you say, General, sir."

David shook his head. Jonathan was so far out of line he was off the fucking map. David had seen what the world looked like when no one stepped in and demanded order. It wasn't just chaos. It was hell on earth. "Maybe if you weren't such a—"

"Enough," Drea's voice rang out like a whip.

Both David and Jonathan swung their heads to look to the back of the room where Drea strode toward them. David felt his eyes widen in shock at her appearance.

She was in clean clothes and a tight-fitting green tank top and camo pants, but it was her hair he couldn't stop staring at. The dreadlocks that had hung down her back were gone. Lopped completely off. Instead, a halo of fuzzy blonde hair that just skimmed her shoulders surrounded her.

But nothing about the rest of her demeanor said soft. Far from it.

She stomped toward them, face hard with determination. And when she reached down to the hem of her shirt, there wasn't an ounce of hesitation as she ripped it up and off over her head. She threw it to the floor like it had personally offended her. She didn't stop there, either. She grabbed Eric's good hand and Billy's arm, yanking them along with her as she headed straight for Jonathan.

"Drea, don't you think you should—" Eric started but Drea ignored him. When she got to Jonathan, she let go of Billy and Eric and all but leapt on Jonathan. He caught her as she wrapped her arms and legs around him, crashing her lips onto his.

She kissed him hard, gyrating her hips in a way that made it clear where she wanted this to lead. And goddamn if David wasn't hard in seconds. He was exhausted, but he was hard and fuck if he didn't want everything she was offering.

Though it looked like she might be only offering it to Jonathan, the way she was so focused on him. David let out a deep breath. Fine. He'd go make himself scarce. Space from Jonathan was probably for the best right now anyway.

But right as he turned to go, Drea looked over her shoulder. Or glared, he should say. She glared at him over her shoulder. "Get your ass over here. How about you use all that energy you were wasting on fighting to fuck instead. Fuck out your problems."

She wiggled down out of Jonathan's hold only long enough to shove her pants down. She wasn't wearing underwear. Fuck. That ass of hers was so damn perfect. David was drawn toward it like a magnet.

Before he even realized he'd crossed the six feet between them, his hand was palming her ass. And her hands were on the button of his pants, roughly unbuttoning them, dragging the zipper down, and pulling out his already hard shaft.

"Fuuuuuuck," he growled. Especially when she dipped her fingers inside herself and then slicked his cock with her own wetness. She repeated the action until he was glistening with her.

Then she spun again, presenting him with her back.

Her ass. Which she wiggled, enticingly at him.

Oh Jesus. His cock pulsed with need.

"Drea," Eric started again, his tone wary and again Drea ignored him. Instead, she tugged Garrett closer by his beard, teasing his lips with her tongue until he growled and dragged her into a kiss. But David was too distracted by her ass to give it much attention.

He ran his glistening cock down the crack of her ass to the hidden spot, remembering just how fucking good it had felt the last time he'd ventured here. Jesus, the way her body gloved him so perfectly...

"Help them hold me, Garrett," she whispered when she finally pulled away from him and he nodded drunkenly.

Then she lifted one leg back around Jonathan's hip. He'd wisely shed his own pants. David sucked in a breath as Jonathan and Garrett helped hike her body up. Because with them lifting and spreading her legs like that, her anus was suddenly far more accessible.

"Jesus Christ," he whispered as he notched the head of his cock right at her opening. But then he blinked. What was he doing? Maybe Eric was right trying to bring some caution and sanity— Her friend had died only hours ago and—

"Put your fucking cocks inside me or you'll lose out because I'm sure Garrett and Billy will be happy to step in and take your turn. Isn't that right, boys?" She turned back to Garrett. "You haven't gotten to take my ass yet, have you, Garrett baby?"

"Drea," Eric snapped but this time it was Garrett shutting him down.

"Hey, shut the fuck up, man." Garrett moved between Eric and where Drea was sandwiched between David and Jonathan's bodies. "Drea's a big girl. She's a woman and she knows her own damn mind. Let her do what she needs to do."

And on that note, "*Yes,*" Drea cried out.

Jonathan must have answered her invitation. He'd entered her. *Fuck instead of fight.* David could certainly get on board with that.

He closed his eyes, wanting to savor every second as he breached her ass, pushing the fat head of his cock past the first ring of resistant muscle.

Oh Jesus Christ, it was heaven. It hurt so fucking good. He kept pushing and then *there*—he was through. He was inside her.

She clenched on him and for a second, he couldn't go any further. Did she want him to stop? Fuck, he'd die if she wanted him to pull out and stop. But he would. He'd do anything if she—

"Harder," she gasped. "Keep going. Fuck my ass harder. Shove it in. *Shove it.*"

He shoved. Another inch in. His dick was everything. All he was was centered down there, pushing further, boring in.

Oh fuck, yeah. Yes, more. He needed more.

Harder.

Deeper.

Fucking *deeper.*

He thrust the last inch and let out an animal groan of satisfaction when he was balls deep. He shifted his hips back and forth, loving the friction of her ass on his balls.

Jonathan already had a rhythm going as he fucked her from the front and Jesus but that felt good. Every in-thrust shook Drea's entire body and made her clench on David's cock. Best fucking thing in the whole entire world. Never had it so good. Never felt anything like— Never in the whole damn—

"Together," Drea said, voice a register lower than her normal speaking voice. "And hard. Fuck me *hard.*"

The morning suddenly came back, flashing in his mind's eye. The adrenaline. The gunfire. Franco's body dropping. Then Jonathan fucking accusing *him* of being responsible for it.

He dragged his cock out and then jammed it back in again. Drea cried out. If the sound had been anything other than one of pleasure, he would have stopped. But she cried out in ecstasy. Like him shoving his cock up her ass as hard as he could was flipping her switch like nothing else could.

So he pulled back out and then jackhammered back in again.

Drea shifted her hips restlessly even though it barely mattered. David and Jonathan were in control of this fuck. Jonathan had his hands under her thighs, dragging her into him every time he lunged forward, sandwiching her against David until they'd developed a natural rhythm, thrusting together and retreating together.

Which pissed David the hell off. Because they were always like this. Over the years, they'd developed such a natural working relationship. Jonathan was his right-hand man. But what, he'd been harboring these feelings for how long? Second-guessing everything David did? Secretly thinking that what? He could do it better? Ha. David would love to see that. Jonathan would crack within a fucking week.

David grunted as he shoved in harder than he had yet, glaring at Jonathan over Drea's shoulder.

Only to find Jonathan glaring right back. Together they rammed in again. Each time harder than the last.

Which was fucked up.

But then Drea wailed, "Use me. Fucking use me harder."

Fuck not fight.

Was this her plan all along? To have them fuck out their differences? And since they weren't gay, they had to use her as an intermediary? Or maybe that was overthinking shit too much and she'd just really wanted to get reamed out. He knew soldiers who reacted to action like that. They weren't right until they'd gotten tail and fucked out their demons hard. Just because Drea was a chick didn't mean she had to be any different.

"I had to get as many batteries as I could," David growled after they'd both thrust in, bottomed out in Drea. David reached around and gripped Jonathan's forearm, holding him there. "We had to have them for the anti-aircraft artillery. The ones we had weren't reliable and I didn't know if the units that even had those had gotten picked up by Travis's men.

The only way we'll have a chance in hell tonight is if we can take down any planes or copters they send up to try to count our manpower. I wasn't just fucking around down there for the fuck of it. It had to be done."

Jonathan jerked his arm free and they pulled out and stroked in several more times. Jonathan gritted his teeth and closed his eyes. Fine. He wanted to shut David out, whatever. David knew he'd done what was necessary.

But no, fuck that. More needed to be said.

"You don't trust me as your leader, you're useless as a soldier to me."

Jonathan's eyes shot open at that. "So that's it? After all these years you just write me off?" It was clear he was about to pull away from Drea, from both of them, so David gripped him again and told Drea, "Hold him."

She did. She wrapped her legs around Jonathan and enfolded her arms around his neck, burying her head in his chest. Apparently she was content to let their dispute continue without her... well, apart from the fact that she clenched her body on David's cock, and he'd bet on Jonathan's too like she was determined to hold onto both of them with every shred of strength she had.

"I said you're useless as a soldier if you've lost faith in me as your commander. But not as a friend. Not as my brother." He reached around Drea, holding both her and Jonathan to him. "We're family now more than ever. That's what this means. That's what Drea's giving us."

He leaned down and kissed down her neck, exposed now that her dreadlocks were gone. "We're family no matter if you want out of your post. You don't have to be—"

"I don't want out of my posting!" Jonathan exploded. "Jesus! But sometimes it would be nice to be treated like an equal. For you to explain *why* you're doing the shit you do instead of just barreling ahead and having you expect me to obey orders like I'm still a grunt on my first deployment. I'm the best at what I do and I'm a damn good tactician besides."

"I know you are!"

"So stop dictating to me."

"There can only be one commander on a battlefield. Is that what you want? To be number one?"

"*No*. I never fucking wanted that. I just want to be your equal *off* the battlefield. Not in the moment. I was fucking terrified today. I just need to know that you fucking see me."

"Well Jesus Christ, I see you! How much more could I fucking see you?" David sandwiched Drea between them, hugging her and reaching past her to grip Jonathan's arm. "We're all but fucking in tandem we're so in sync. You know me better than anybody on this fucking earth and we're fucking family now. We're making *love* together right now, for fuck's sake."

"Harder," Drea shouted, and Jonathan met David's eyes. For a moment they just looked at each other, gaze's locked, and then Jonathan nodded.

David knew exactly what he meant. That was the whole fucking point. They didn't need words.

They were square.

Now it was time to see to their wife and finish this thing. Instead of ending with a handshake to show everything was better between them again, they'd seal it with a fuck.

Jonathan curled his arms underneath Drea's, wrapping them around and holding onto her shoulders from behind, cementing their bodies together even tighter. David drew up just as close behind her until she couldn't take a breath without all three of them feeling it.

And they gave her exactly what she'd been begging for. They held her in place and Jonathan suckled at her throat while fucking her as hard and as fervently as they could.

It didn't take long, either.

The closeness, the intensity, the whole goddamned day and how absolutely insane Drea's ass felt around David's cock—he buried his face in the curve of her neck where it met her shoulder and shouted his muffled release as oh—

Oh—

OH JESUS FUCKING CHRIST—

David unloaded in her ass right as he heard Jonathan's cry of pleasure.

Oh fuck, oh fuck, oh fuck that was just— David stumbled back a little as he finally slipped out of her ass.

She spun and grabbed his neck down for a kiss, then she did the same to Jonathan.

David was both sorry when she let him go and glad, because that meant he could finally collapse to the floor and catch his goddamned breath. And maybe nap for a few minutes. Or years. Because Jesus Christ that was officially the best sex of his entire life.

He watched through drowsy eyelashes as Drea moved over to Eric. David had been prepared to pull her down with him, to make the effort to stay awake and cuddle her or whatever it was women liked after sex.

But somehow, after that earthshattering fucking sex, not only was she still on her feet, her hand was not only dropping to Eric's crotch, but slipping inside his jeans.

Oh damn.

Their wife was not done.

Not remotely by the look on her face.

CHAPTER THIRTY-TWO

ERIC

Eric was already stiff from watching her with the other guys, but her hand on his cock, even through the fabric of his jeans, had him going hard as stone.

Not that she was satisfied with that for long, the mood she was in. She immediately yanked his belt buckle open and started unbuttoning his jeans.

For a second, Eric closed his eyes and let her. Jesus, he wanted this. Wanted her. But was it what was best for her right now?

"Drea," he put his hand on hers right as she reached into his pants. Her blue eyes flicked up to his but they weren't full of her usual challenge. And it wasn't lust he saw there either.

Oh she was turned on all right, he didn't doubt that.

But what he saw in her eyes was a pain so deep it made his chest ache in response.

He remembered back when they'd escaped the MC compound and Maya had gotten hurt, how she'd blamed herself and how reckless she'd become. And now with Gisela *dying*...

"Baby," Eric crooned, reaching out to cup her face.

Drea knocked his hands away, a shutter falling over her expression like a door slamming shut. "I wanna fuck." She yanked his pants down and shoved him hard backwards so that he stumbled and sat down in the camping chair a couple feet away.

Which was apparently exactly what Drea had intended because she followed him, turning her back at the last second and sitting on his lap.

And he knew it wasn't by accident that she didn't want to face him for this fuck.

Because a fuck was exactly what it would be. Not making love. If Drea had her way, there'd be no connection at all. He'd just be a dildo with a body attached. And that was bullshit.

When she lifted up and grabbed his cock to put it inside herself, Eric put his hands on her hips to halt her so she couldn't sink down. Especially when he realized she put him at her back entrance and not her pussy.

His whole body tensed because *goddamn* did he want that ass. But this was wrong. Without the emotional connection, it was wrong. Not to mention they didn't have any fucking lube and not to be an ass, but he had a giant goddamn cock and he didn't want to hurt her. At least with David she'd lubed him with her own wetness first.

Drea swung her head around to look at him, surprise and fury on her face. "Stop it," she ordered.

Eric just shook his head, letting out an exasperated noise. "I'm not going to take your ass for the first time like this. You don't have lube and you aren't in the right state of mind—"

"Garrett," Drea snapped.

"Yes." Garrett came closer from where he'd been standing off to the side, hand palming his cock.

Drea grinned down at his shaft. She climbed off of Eric and dropped to her knees in front of Garrett, taking him deep into her mouth. Down her throat.

Eric's cock throbbed just watching it. Jesus she was getting good at that. But what the fuck? Was she playing games with them? Eric wouldn't do what she wanted so she was moving on to the next husband? Fuck it. Eric started to stand up but Drea suddenly pulled off Garrett's cock with a *pop* and glared at Eric.

"Who said you could move?"

Eric stared at her. Any other time, no way he'd put up with this bullshit, but maybe he was wrong. Maybe this *was* what she needed right now.

Maybe after all the shit they'd just been through, this could be exactly what she needed: To be in control. Surely if anyone could understand the need for control, it was him. After losing Gisela, after the shitstorm that the mission turned into, maybe she needed this little arena where she could have total power.

So he heaved out a huge breath and stayed put, though it cost him.

Drea immediately crawled over to him, tits and ass swaying and then—

Jesus! She sucked his cock into her mouth and started to swallow him just as deep as she had Garrett only moments before.

Except he was a little wider than Garrett so she gagged a couple of times. That only seemed to make her more determined. She dropped her jaw and relaxed her throat until his balls were tickling her chin.

Fuck— ohhhh *fuck.*

Eric's legs shook with how good it felt.

She blinked up at him, his huge cock down her throat and he saw it again—the stark, raw devastation so clear in her eyes.

Oh Drea.

He wanted to touch her. To comfort her. But goddammit, it would only make her pull away again. She'd slam that mask back in place faster than he could say, *Babe, let me make you feel better.*

The next second she averted her eyes anyway but Eric held onto it, that moment of her sharing her pain with him even though it was no doubt unintentional. She needed him even if she wouldn't admit it. She needed all of them.

She bobbed on his cock and then came up, releasing his shaft, but not all the way. She bobbed on the tip several times, driving him absolutely fucking crazy.

Finally he couldn't stand not touching her another second, so he gave her the only touch he thought she'd accept.

He grabbed the hair at the back of her head, holding her in place. She was still sucking on just the tip, not anywhere close to bottomed out, but apparently his move did the trick for her because she tugged violently against his hold, back and forth—at the same time dropping a hand between her legs.

Goddammit that was hot.

He gripped her hair tighter and she bobbed lower on his cock, letting out a low groan that vibrated up and down his shaft.

Jesus Christ.

But apparently she was done with that because the next moment she was lifting off him, spitting extra saliva to coat his dick.

And then, without a word or a look, she flipped back around and moved to sit on him again.

Shit. She'd lubricated him this time. And maybe he'd been wrong before. If she needed the control of this, then maybe it *was* okay. Maybe it was—

"Fuuuuuuuuuuuuuck," he groaned as she sank the tightest little ass on God's green earth down on his cock.

Hearing her little gasps only made him crazier. Were they gasps of surprise? Of pain? Of pained pleasure? No doubt she was feeling every huge inch of him.

He tried to reach around her to stroke her clit but she smacked him away again. "Garrett, hold his arms."

And Garrett, ever the trained gorilla, immediately snapped to attention. Eric glared at the man as he came close. "Don't you fucking dare."

Garrett just grinned, the silver cap on his incisor glinting in the sunlight that poured in through the broken windows. He'd put his dick back in his pants and he rubbed his hands together. "Not you I take orders from, brother."

Then he grabbed Eric's right wrist and jerked it behind the back of the camping chair with such force he might well have broken that damn one too.

And Drea seated herself fully all the way down on Eric's shaft with what was definitely a grunt of pain.

Goddammit—did she just want to hurt herself and use him to do it?

But then he remembered how she'd touched herself and genuinely seemed to be getting off when he'd yanked her hair. So maybe... as long as she didn't take it too far...

Fuck. He didn't like anything about this. Which was why he usually liked to be in fucking control. Not with one arm literally behind his back—and the other one broken.

But maybe that's exactly what she needs. Absolute control.

Could he be man enough to let her take the reins completely? Even if just for this once?

Yes. Yes, goddammit, he could.

But did he appreciate having his arm held behind his back like he was a naughty goddamn child?

He still glared over his shoulder at Garrett. "I've got it, thanks. I think I can control myself."

Garrett was still just grinning, getting way too much of a kick out of the whole damn thing, the bastard.

"Billy," Drea snapped. "You're up."

Billy didn't need to be told twice, that was for damn sure. David was stretched out on the sleeping bag on the floor and Jonathan was on a chair beside him. Even though they'd both gotten off earlier, they were watching the show, lazily stroking their cocks as they watched.

Billy apparently had none of the hesitations Eric did because he was already buck naked, walking toward Drea with worshipful eyes.

"How do you want me, gorgeous?"

"Do exactly what I say," she growled, leaning up and grabbing his hips as soon as he got close.

"Exactly as you say," Billy breathed out.

Eric couldn't see much, but he saw the way she wrapped her legs around Billy and knew by seeing the blissed out expression on Billy's face over her shoulder he was entering her.

Soon he felt her tightening impossibly around his cock and knew Billy was inside her, too.

Does that feel good, baby? he wanted to ask. *Feeling so full of both of us at the same time?*

He knew she loved it, the way she'd sought it out with David and Jonathan. Though he didn't miss that she hadn't come when they were fucking, though she'd been close. Why hadn't she gone over the edge? More like, why hadn't she *let* herself go over the edge?

Eric shifted his hips, the little he could, trying to give her some friction. She immediately moaned.

Oh yeah, she loved it. Maybe she needed it right now, even. Maybe she wouldn't let herself have pleasure without pain's biting edge.

He pumped his hips again, jerking back in the chair and then thrusting up. Her hiss of breath was his reward.

Apparently Billy did something wrong, though, because Eric heard the telltale slap of her hand against skin.

"Did I tell you to reach for my clit?"

"Um," Billy said in the tone of a chastised kid. "No?"

"No, I didn't. Now pull your cock out of me."

Billy must have complied because pressure on Eric's shaft lessened slightly.

"Now fuck my ass."

"I am," Eric said.

Drea whipped around and glared at him. "Did I look like I was talking to you?"

The next second her head was turned back around and she was repeating the command. "I said to fuck my ass."

Wha— Eric tried to sit up in the chair but Garrett only held his arm tighter.

"Bu— But—" Billy stuttered.

"Are you a fucking liar? You said you'd do exactly as I say. Step closer and give me your cock. I'll fuck myself with it if you won't."

So they were dildos attached to bodies after all.

Eric breathed out, trying to fight his building fury. This was Drea. Of course she'd push it to the edge of going too far. And really, wasn't this better than her driving a goddamned death-cycle recklessly during a car chase when there was gunfire and bad guys trying to drive her off the road?

"But I won't fit!" Billy was still arguing. "Not with him in there."

"You'll fit if I fucking say you will. If you don't get your dick inside me in the next three seconds, you're done. I'll call Garrett and he'll do it."

Eric looked over his shoulder, though, and Garrett looked just as wigged out as Eric was. He was opening his mouth like he was going to say something, actually but Eric shook his head. Garrett frowned down at him.

"I'll always give you what you want, gorgeous," Billy said, finally stepping closer again. "I just don't want to hurt you."

Billy let out a sharp gasp and stumbled a step closer. No doubt Drea had grabbed his cock just like she'd threatened to.

"Sometimes it needs to hurt," she whispered, and then Eric felt it, pressure of a different sort as Drea crammed Billy's cock right beside his at her ass.

Maybe it won't fit, Eric thought hopefully. Because Billy wasn't small. It was hard not to catch an eyeful when they all had their dicks out around Drea all the time.

There were no two ways about it. If she actually managed to get Billy past that first ring of muscles, it *would* hurt her.

But she was Drea and she was determined and Billy was equally as determined to please her.

So they managed it.

Drea let out a guttural, anguished cry when Billy's cock finally made it in.

"Now fuck me. Jackhammer me with that fucking cock."

And Billy did what she asked, ramming all the way in.

Fuck!

Every nerve ending up and down Eric's spine lit up.

Never so tight—never had tighter in his whole fucking life. Never dreamed of so tight.

"Harder," Drea demanded through clenched teeth. "Goddammit, Billy. Fuck me like a goddamned *man*."

Eric opened his eyes to see her grabbing Billy's hips and dragging him closer. Every time she did, the friction and the pressure against Eric's own shaft was fucking insane, almost unbearable.

And at the same time she was tearing him apart on the inside —*why? Why, baby? Why?*

Every command for harder came through gritted teeth. She was in pain. And it wasn't like with the hair pulling. She wasn't finding any pleasure in this.

This was only punishment.

He saw it clearly now. This wasn't for catharsis like he'd hoped. She just wanted to punish herself.

Suddenly the grip on his right arm disappeared. Eric looked behind him surprise to see Garrett stepping back, expression disturbed as he watched Drea.

"Fuck me like you fucking hate me," Drea cried, and he meant *cried* because there were tears in her voice now.

She was breaking Eric's fucking heart. Maybe she always would. Maybe she could never accept the love he wanted to give her. Because goddamn it, he did. He fucking *loved* her. And she was broken. Shattering to pieces right in front of him—right on top of him. And he refused to let it happen for another goddamned second.

"Garrett," Eric growled, "bring our wife to climax."

And then he wrapped his good arm around her, pinning both of her arms to her chest.

"What?" Drea's head snapped back around and immediately she started fighting against his grasp.

Billy moved back and Garrett stepped into his place, dropping to his knees.

"What are you—?"

Drea continued thrashing but Eric held her firm to his chest, occasionally thrusting his cock still buried up her ass as Garrett ate her out.

"You can't—" she screamed, furious as she turned her head Eric's direction. "You fucking bastard. Why do you always ruin everything? You're such a conniving, controlling, fucking sanctimonious—" She seemed to lose her train of thought as her eyelashes fluttered, Garrett's ministrations obviously getting the better of her.

Her chest heaved and her mouth slackened as pleasure overtook her. She clenched around Eric's cock up her ass probably unconsciously but Jesus, *yes*.

Finally.

This was what sex was supposed to be about. They could angry fuck to Drea's heart's content.

But he needed there to be *some* sort of connection. He needed her here with him.

And now that she was, he fucking let go. She wanted hard? He could give her hard. She wanted to ride the edge? He'd fucking give her the edge.

He pulled out and thrust back in with as much force as he could. Without the second dick in her ass, he knew it should be just enough but not too much.

From her escalating cries of pleasure, he knew he was getting her just where he wanted her. So he kept at it. With his arm around her, he could really maneuver her, too. So he dragged her down, reaming her the fuck *out*. Then he lifted her while he pulled his hips back. Then down again, with all his might. It jarred his broken arm. He didn't fucking care. Garrett followed their movements. Eric could hear him with how fucking sloppily the man was eating.

And always, Drea's pleased noises like she was just infuckingcapable of keeping quiet. That was exactly where Eric wanted her. Out of her mind. In touch with the very bottom of her emotional well. Pouring it all fucking out. All her hurt. All her pain. All that anguish that would fester for days, fucking years if she didn't deal with it one way or another.

"Give it to us, baby," he growled, ramming in up to his balls again.

And he felt it in a way he never had before because he'd never been so in tune with her body as right now when she was so raw and vulnerable. He felt her every twitch, every inhale, every gasp and breath.

Her ass tightened on his cock and her breathy whines notched just *that* much higher. She was coming. She was about to blow.

"Fucking *give it to me*," he shouted. And she did. She threw her head back against his chest, screamed through clenched teeth, and he pumped his cum into her as she came all over Garret's face. She came and came and fucking came, squirting, until her legs were shaking, fuck, her entire body was shaking and tears poured down her cheek.

Even after she was done, all three of them just sat there like that, Garrett with his head resting on her inner thigh, her with her head dropped against Eric's chest, his cock still hard up her ass, heart thumping like a runaway train.

It was only when David and Jonathan came over and helped them to their feet that they made their way over to where they'd unrolled several sleeping bags.

On the way over, Drea reached for Billy's hand. "I'm sorry," she whispered and he immediately pulled her into his arms.

They fell asleep, all cocooned around her.

But when Eric woke several hours later as the sun was beginning to set, Drea was gone.

CHAPTER THIRTY-THREE

DREA

Drea walked outside and held her hand over her eyes, looking up. It was still hot as fuck but there were big gray clouds billowing in from the north and in the far distance she heard the rumble of thunder.

The sound sent a chill down her spine. She'd always hated thunderstorms, ever since she was a kid. She didn't have many memories of before she went to live with Dad, but one of them was crouching under her bed, holding some dumb stuffed animal that was missing one of its button eyes, and wishing her mama was home.

Naturally Mom thought nothing of leaving her fucking six-year-old at home alone during a storm when she needed to go get her next fix.

Drea stomped her boot in the dirt. Then she looked over and saw a group of soldiers smoking. Fuck but she could do with a smoke. She walked over to them and plucked the hand-rolled cigarette out of the closest one's mouth right before he could light up. He held out a lighter and she gave him a wink. He'd probably soil his damn fatigues these boys were so hard up for a woman. But they were David's men, so she felt safe enough.

She lit the cigarette, took a long, satisfying drag, then tossed the lighter to the guy that had handed it to her.

Then she turned and walked away, back to her lonely outpost outside the store where her husbands were sleeping.

She cringed even thinking the word. *Husbands.*

Fuck but that was a mistake.

What the hell right did she think she'd had getting married?

Poison.

She sucked in another long drag and then flicked the ash onto the cracked concrete underfoot.

She'd had the dream about Mom again. She'd been having it more and more lately. Well, if it was a memory, could you really call it a dream? More like it was just her subconscious fucking with her.

Although, this time it was two memories morphed together. She was back at NASA. David had just thrown the grenade and they were running down the stairs. About to escape.

In the distance, Drea saw the man with the rifle.

Except the dream fucked with time, so she saw him cock the rifle. Saw the bullet explode from the barrel. Watched it flying toward her.

It would have hit her right between the eyes.

That bullet had her goddamned fucking name on it.

But Gisela. That stupid fucking cunt just had to— She just had to—

Drea tried to suck in another draw on the cigarette but she couldn't. Because she was fucking crying too hard.

She spit the cigarette to the ground and stomped on it. Then she swiped furiously at her eyes. Oh, cry for her. *Yeah, cry for her, Drea.* Like that will do her any damn good, laying with her head half blown off back in Houston

Drea slapped her own face. Once, then again, harder. Then harder still until the tears stopped.

At the end of the dream, she'd been sitting there, holding Gisela uselessly in her arms, weeping like a useless little bitch, and Gisela had twisted and turned her face toward Drea.

Except it wasn't Gisela anymore.

It was Mama.

She wrapped her hands around Drea's throat. *"You're the devil's child. Satan came and raped me one night. You little demon hell bitch! You're poison! POISON!"*

Thunder cracked in the distance and Drea jumped, hand flying to her chest.

The chest with her still beating heart.

Because she was alive and Gisela was dead.

"Hey."

Drea jumped again in surprise at the voice coming from right behind her, swinging around to see Eric looking adorably rumpled from sleep.

"You disappeared." He reached out for her hand but she turned away from him, facing back toward the storm clouds as they rolled in.

"Couldn't sleep."

What she wanted to say, no, what she wanted to *scream* was, *RUN. Run the fuck away from me!*

But Eric, Eric fucking Wolford, of course he just stepped up right beside her. The man had no fucking instincts for self-preservation.

She turned her face away from him.

"Drea. You know I'm here if you ever want to talk."

She huffed out a harsh laugh, finally turning toward him.

"Since when have I *ever* wanted to talk to you? But you're good to keep around for a fuck, I'll give you that."

It both hurt and pleased her when his jaw tensed at her remark.

Poison.

"Don't do that." He moved in front of her so that mere inches separated their chests. "Don't push me away. You know I care about you."

She shoved his chest and took a step back. "Well maybe that's your mistake. Sorry I'm not the person you want me to be. But hey," she shrugged, "that's not my job. Don't put your shit on me, man."

He stalked after her. "Don't fucking do that."

"What?"

"You know what."

She shrugged again, looking down at the ground and really fucking wishing she hadn't stomped out the rest of that cigarette. It would look desperate if she got down on her hands and knees and tried to scrape the little bit of tobacco into another paper so she could smoke the last little bit, huh?

"I saw you," Eric said, getting in her face again and taking her shoulders in his hands. She tried to shrug him off but he just held her tighter. "Drea. Drea! Stop it. Stop pushing us away. I saw you when we were having sex. I *saw* you. Your friend died. You're allowed to be upset about it. To grieve her."

If he kept talking, she'd scream. She'd scream and scream and never stop screaming until she was fucking dead her throat would be so raw.

So she jerked back from him and shoved him in the chest again with all her goddamned might.

"Gisela wasn't my fucking friend. She was a pathetic, fucked up girl who died for *nothing*. The only reason she got on that fucking van in the first place was because I thought I could be something I'm not. I gave all those girls fucking delusions about how they could leave their pasts behind. Become fighters. Fucking bullshit. They'll all be broken till the day they *die*."

"Just like you? Is that it? You think you're broken?"

Drea took another step back and started to clap her hands. Slowly.

"Bravo Dr. Wolford. You've got me all figured out now. Give yourself a pat on the back."

"Goddammit, you are the most exasperating fucking woman I have ever fucking met—"

"So *leave*!" Drea said with an exasperated shout. God, just please *go*. Run. Fucking *run*.

"Drea—" he started again, breathing hard but with a conciliatory tone.

"Jesus Christ!" she swore. What would it take with this guy? "I'm tired of people seeing in me what they want to see. I'm not the savior Gisela saw. And I'm not whatever damsel in distress or whatever the fuck you want me to be."

"That's not what—"

"I don't give a shit," Drea cut him off. "I'm done with all of it."

"So, what? After this mission, you're just going to go off into the woods and live alone?"

She nodded. "Sounds like a plan to me." Then she walked off.

"Drea." He grabbed her arm to stop her but she yanked it away and spun on him.

"Don't," she spat the word. "Don't fucking touch me."

She glared at him. *Run, goddammit!* Everything inside her screamed it.

At the same time, she wanted to reach out and claw at his clothes with her fingernails, clinging to him. To fall at his feet and beg, *stay. STAY. Be my home forever. Please God be my home and save me from the nightmares.*

But she'd already killed one person she loved today. And it was with Gisela's face in her mind that she uttered her next words:

"This kind of shit is exactly why I told Sophia she had to go off on her own to discover who she *really* is, away from you." As out of it as she'd been on the ride back from Houston, Drea had heard Eric telling Jonathan about his phone call with Sophia. Nothing would drive him away quicker than making him think she was the reason for Sophia fleeing, even if she'd never said any such thing to Sophia. But it didn't stop Drea from pressing on. "You fucking suffocate people and call it love. You're a fucking *leach*. I told Sophia to get away from you the earliest chance she had and for once she fucking listened."

Finally, fucking *finally*, Eric stepped back, eyes wide like he was looking at a stranger. "You told her wha—" He trailed off, blinking in confusion and betrayal. "You know how dangerous it is out there. How could you?"

Drea's insides were being shredded through a cheese grater but she forced herself to shrug noncommittally. "She's stronger than you give her credit for. She'll be fine. Plus, if you were so worried about the well-being of women outside of your precious little communal bubble, I guess you could have lent me some help to go rescue my girls a helluva lot earlier, huh?"

His mouth dropped open and he took several more stumbling steps back from her. "Jesus Christ." He gave the bitterest laugh she'd ever heard. "All this time, I thought, if you're just patient enough, Eric, eventually she'll let you in. She's been hurt before. She's worth the wait, worth the effort."

He shook his head, the hurt in his eyes so clear it was like a knife slicing straight down the center of her chest. She'd have thought nothing could hurt worse. But then he opened his mouth. "But I guess you're just too fucking broken after all."

Don't. Fucking *don't* let him see. He's almost gone. You've almost done it.

Drea made her jaw into iron and lifted a single eyebrow. "Are you done?"

He huffed out a short breath and shook his head again. "I'm going to go find Sophia and protect her like I have my entire life." He came close, so close Drea thought he was going to either kiss her or scream in her face or spit on her or something. Something, fucking anything. But he just stood there and all she could do was breathe him in and try desperately to memorize his scent because she knew, she *knew*, this was the last time she'd ever see him, ever smell him, ever know this most amazing man who'd captured her heart.

"Because that's what family does," he whispered into her ear. "We're stronger together. But you enjoy being alone your entire life."

And then he turned on his heel and left her.

CHAPTER THIRTY-FOUR

DREA

Drea waited until he was halfway across the parking lot and then it was like her lungs stopped working right. Her hand flew to her chest and she gasped for air.

She blinked and gulped and could barely breathe and soon had her head between her knees, half hyperventilating as she gasped for breath, only managing a hiccupping wheeze every few seconds.

He was gone.

He was *gone*.

She'd gotten her wish. *He's safe. He's safe from you. It's a good thing. So get ahold of your fucking self.*

"Get your fucking hands *off me!* When Suicide hears about this, you're fucking dead. You're all fucking *dead!*"

Drea looked up to see two soldiers dragging a man in a Black Skulls cut across the old parking lot straight toward where Drea stood.

What was—

The soldiers' faces were impassive as he continued to hurtle curses at them but Drea noticed they didn't bother being gentle when he stumbled. They just continued yanking him forward even though his legs now dragged along the ground.

"You sons of whores! I'm an important member of the Skulls. They call me Suicide's right-hand man—"

Drea got her first full breath in minutes as the soldiers dragged the man past her and into the building where David and the others were. It'd be a cold day in hell before Thomas had a right-hand man.

Drea followed them in, if only for the distraction. Anything not to think about Eric walking farther away and the distance that grew between them every moment that passed.

"What the fuck'r you doing here, Pee Wee?" The biker sneered Garrett's direction. "You sure are lookin' awful fuckin' cozy. You turn snitch, that it?"

Garrett just shook his head and laughed. "No shocker you got picked up, Bucket. You always were one sloppy sonofabitch."

Bucket reared back and then spit in Garrett's direction and Garrett just laughed harder.

Bucket looked around at everyone else, still jerking so hard in the soldiers' grips Drea was sure he was about to dislocate one or both arms. He must've joined the Skulls after she'd left because she didn't recognize him.

David stood looking on passively. He was still every inch the General even though he was only in his boxers and a gray T-shirt.

But turned out Garrett wasn't the only one he knew in the room.

"Doc? That you?"

Drea swung her head to look in Billy's direction, and it was like she could feel the blood drain from her face because she immediately felt light-headed. She'd still just barely gotten her breath back and now—

How. The. Fuck. Did. Bucket. Know. Billy?

"Wait, you're her, aren't you? Suicide's bitch? The one who's daddy used to be Pres for the Skulls?"

"What do you know about this man?" David asked, pointing at Billy.

"Well shit," Bucket grinned Drea's way, but her eyes were zeroed in on Billy's pale face. "He done runned away a couple months back. But up till then he used to fix up Suicide's girls after we used 'em too rough. Still gotta have good product to sell the customer's ya see. But don't mean we can't still have our fun before we move 'em out. Suicide's got his *appetites* after all."

Drea was going to be sick.

It was like with Daddy all over again. Discovering how he *really* made his money. That the food she'd eaten her whole life had been paid for by sexual slavery. The clothes on her back. The roof over her head. The stupid fucking pink Chevrolet she'd been so excited about on her 16th birthday her dad had surprised her with. How many girls had been sold to pay for that?

Poison.

It was a curse that went both ways. Everyone she ever loved would betray her. The same as she would betray and hurt anyone she ever loved.

"Drea, wait, let me explain. I swear I didn't know when I took the job, I thought I was—" Billy started to plead but Drea cut him a look as cold as ice and offered him more than he fucking deserved, a moment more of her time, a single word: "*Don't.*"

Then she turned to David and Garrett but Garrett was already ahead of her, cracking his knuckles, eyes on Bucket. "Let me at him. I'll get him to fucking talk. He'll spill his guts about exactly where Suicide is—"

"*Thomas,*" Drea all but shouted. "His name is Thomas Tillerman."

"About where Thomas Tillerman," Garrett amended, "is holed up."

David gave a short, hard nod.

When Drea looked back at Bucket, she had at least the smallest consolation of seeing that he looked scared as Garrett approached.

Which meant that Garrett had a reputation. As an enforcer? Who exactly had he become in the years since she'd last known him?

No one was who they fucking seemed. God, how had she not learned that by now? She saw exactly what Billy had been. She didn't doubt he hadn't liked the job Suicide had forced him to do.

But Billy had still done it.

Because of the consistent access to his next fix.

Suicide knew exactly what pressure points to push to get people to do just what he wanted.

And when Billy finally saw one too many fucked up girls brutalized and broken, did he try to free them? To save anyone?

No.

He took as many drugs as he could and then fled.

Just himself.

Just with all the drugs he could carry.

Until one day he heard that Suicide's best pal and ally, Arnold Travis, had just invaded Fort Worth, and he crawled out of whatever little weasel hole he'd been hiding in.

And ran straight into her and Eric who'd just had their unfortunate introduction to those fucking road spikes.

She shook her head, fucking furious at herself for letting him in even the tiniest little bit. What, did she think by saving him she was somehow saving her mom? How pathetic was she?

Every time she'd tried to *save* someone lately, it had only blown up in her face, so fine, she was fucking done.

She obviously wasn't cut out for the role of hero. She'd leave it to people like Eric and David. Cowboys and Generals.

"Take him somewhere out of the way," David said to the soldiers, nodding toward Bucket. "Preferably out of the hearing of the troops."

Garrett grinned and rubbed his hands together and Drea didn't miss the way that Bucket's brash talk and curses had dried up on his tongue.

Maybe Garrett had changed, but he'd never tried to hide who he was. She remembered the first night she'd found him as he stood waiting for her in the dark.

Waiting for his judgement and execution.

If ever there was a kindred soul, it was him. A boy born and raised into the same heritage of blood and violence as her.

If she had her way, by the end of the day, they'd both atone for their sins one way or another.

CHAPTER THIRTY-FIVE

GARRETT

Hours later, Garrett closed the door on the weeping man tied to the chair. Garrett's hands were slick with blood and he wiped them on a spare shirt he'd brought for just that purpose.

Usually he was bothered by how easy it was for him to break men's bones and pull their fingernails off one by one, but today it had been almost a pleasure.

He still remembered the day Dad first stuck him in a room with a man tied to a chair just like Bucket was in the room behind him. He was a prospect at the time, of course Dad made him prospect same as any other dipshit who wanted in the club no matter that he'd all but grown up in the damn clubhouse. Dad laid out his cut by the door and said it was his if he could get the information they needed out of the man in the chair.

Drea was gone by then. Three months gone. No clue where she went or if she was okay. The whole club had changed, too. After he learned about what the club did—what they *really* did—selling women?

He wished every day of his life that he'd taken Drea up on her offer back when she'd been trying to convince him to leave the club.

He shoulda strapped her down on the back of his Harley and took her across country. Up north maybe. Somewhere they had seasons other than hot, hotter, and dead dry. He'd build her snow men and every year they'd go cut down their Christmas tree from the yard and he'd make her fat with his babies and—

But that was all just piss in the wind.

Gone like it was never there.

And there Garrett still fucking was. Stuck with his dad and the MC.

So he'd picked up that goddamned bat and he'd beaten the man within an inch of his life.

He didn't get his cut that day, though, because he never asked the guy a single question.

What he did get was a reputation. Last few years, he barely had to lift his fist if he didn't feel like it.

Most days, though, he wouldn't lie... he did feel like it.

Cause it turned out, once you got a taste for violence like that, it was hard to quench. Especially cause he was so *angry*. All the time.

Turned out he'd been angry for a full decade and didn't even know it.

Not till *she* came back and life unfurled its wings again like one of those butterflies coming outta a cocoon.

Garrett used to like watching nature shows after Mama left and he spent so many hours alone. Bugs and insects and shit like that. Eventually he even started using them in his work. Spiders especially. He liked the big, fuzzy ones. Turned out some people'd shit their pants if you put a couple tarantulas on their faces. Literally. Shit their pants.

Garrett didn't get it. He kept the things as pets. Ozzy and Sharon. They were docile as could be as long as you didn't go screeching and smacking at them.

Sort of like him.

He could be Mr. Nice Guy, no matter what people assumed about him because of his size or aloof demeanor.

But fuck with his family? Fuck with his woman?

Well the gloves were coming *off*.

As Bucket, aka Leslie Smith, back there, had just learned. Yup. *Leslie*. Wonder why he grew up to be an asshole.

But Garrett was done thinking about Leslie's shitty little life. He stalked back down the still mostly intact covered walkway of the outlet mall to where he'd left Drea and the rest of them.

When he walked in it was to see David at the front of the room talking to a large gathering—well, large as in there were about twenty people in the room. As well as a door that had been overturned and set up on some sawhorses like a table.

On it a big map was spread out.

"—told you, it's an old battle tactic called *defeat in detail*. Today all three battalions have been making their presence known in these three strategic locations—New Braunfels in the center. Canyon Lake to the North. Seguin to the South."

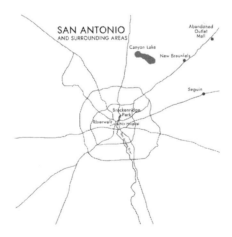

Garrett didn't see Eric or that little shitstick Billy. Then again, maybe Eric was out somewhere dealing with Billy. Drea was standing near the back of the group. She jumped a little when she noticed him and her eyes immediately went to the bloody cloth in his hands, then they shot up to his face.

For a second, his stomach clenched. Would she be disgusted by him and pull away?

But all she asked was, "Did you get what we need? Do you know where Suicide is?"

He breathed out and nodded. "He's in a hospital on the Riverwalk." Then he nodded toward the front of the room. "What's going on here?"

Drea rolled her eyes. "Men playing with their armies."

Garrett shook his head. Drea was nothing if not single-minded, he'd give her that. He focused in on what David was saying.

"All three battalions have retreated but it will almost certainly have gotten reported before comms were shut down earlier. Which was exactly what we wanted. When confident of great numbers, protocol is to meet any attack with a show of force. They'll divide their army up and send troops to each of the three locations because they have larger numbers.

He started drawing on the wall with a black marker. "I estimate they'll send up to 5,000 troops to defend each location."

A murmur went through the crowd. People were obviously not happy to hear that number.

"But sir, even with the new volunteers, we only got at most 8,000."

David shook his head. "Defeat in detail," he repeated the earlier phrase. "It's how Napoleon defeated the Italians during the French Revolution. In the Civil War, General Stonewall Jackson took down a force of 60,000 men with only 17,000."

Damn. Even Drea stopped rolling her eyes and looked interested hearing that.

"Any more modern examples of this working?" asked someone else.

David shook his head. "The way it works is you split up your smaller force into three or four locations. Let the enemy know you're there with a big force, like we did today at Canyon Lake, New Braunfels, and Seguin. But they don't know exactly how many it was. All the people will say is it was thousands. Which it was. A little over 2,500 to be exact. But they don't know how many we've got. So they send their 5,000. Here, here, and here."

"Shit, General, aren't they gonna wipe the floor with our asses? They got twice as many men as us!"

"Well see," David started smiling, "this is why this little trick didn't work past about 1914. Airplanes. If you can just fly over and see how big the enemies force is, you can't trick them. Satellite imagery made it even worse."

"Enough congratulating yourself," Drea called out. "Get to the point."

The soldiers laughed and David waved them down. "Okay, okay. So we've got anti-aircraft artillery stationed outside all three locations. Anyone tries to do a flyby overhead, *BAM*, they're going down."

"And in the meantime, we leave just 500 men at Canyon Lake and Seguin and have the rest meet up with the central force in New Braunfels," he drew arrows on the wall, "and then we attack those motherfuckers, except now we've got over 6,500 to their measly 5,000."

"Holy shit," Garrett whispered.

"Then that force moves on, up to Canyon Lake, again with superior numbers."

"We've got more volunteers coming in all the time, too," Jonathan said, stepping up beside David. "After the Black Skulls killed the governor of this Territory and took it for themselves two weeks ago, they've terrorized the people and they're ready to fight back. Tonight we give them their chance."

A cheer went up from the crowd.

"Damn, they're sure good at givin' speeches," Garrett said.

"And they know their military history, which is all well and good for them." Drea turned his way, giving him her full attention. "But I don't give a shit about saving the world. All I care about is getting in that damn city, getting the women I made promises to out of that hellhole, and putting a bullet in Thomas Tillerman's brain. You hearing me?"

"Loud and clear. Loud. And. Clear."

Drea nodded. The soldiers were dispersing as David moved from group to group giving what sounded like personalized instructions for tonight's attack. They'd move out after sundown. Drea supposed these were squad leaders or whatever the hell you called people in the military who led smaller groups of men.

She moved past them and straight to the map on the makeshift table. Garrett came up right beside her.

It was a large map of San Antonio with a cutout to the side with an enlargened view of the Riverwalk.

"So where is he?" she whispered.

Garrett made sure his hand was dry so he wouldn't smudge it, then traced his big finger over tiny lines that indicated the San Antonio river.

"There," he said. "Nix Hospital. It's old as fuck even though it's been renovated a buncha times But it's been there forever. Built hundreds of years ago or some shit. Bucket said that Suici— I mean, *Thomas*, likes it cause apparently the old exam rooms make for good holding cells."

Garrett could see Drea bristle at his words but he pushed on. "It opens right up onto the river, though."

Drea's mind was already moving a million miles an hour and her hand came to the map, tracing the river upstream. He'd had the same thought and shook his head.

"Thought the same thing, but the river sprouts up in the middle of San Antonio. It's not a way in."

Drea frowned as she looked down at the map. "Where *exactly* does it start?"

"Shit if I know." Garrett shrugged.

Drea dropped down, her face inches from the map. Garrett shook his head. "It's not a way in, I'm telling ya. I don't think it goes any farther up than that park where the zoo is."

Drea's head came up so fast she almost busted him in the chin. He jerked back right in time.

"What zoo? What park?"

"Uh, the San Antonio Zoo. I don't know what the park's called."

"Show me."

Garrett blew out a breath, but then he bent over the map. It was just visible in the little cutout part of the Riverwalk. "There," he pointed. "See the zoo? And that park there." He squinted. "Bracken-ridge Park."

Drea smiled.

Uh oh. Garrett didn't like that smile.

"Cheer up, darling husband." She lifted up on her tiptoes and kissed him on his cheek, right above his beard. "Tonight we cut the head off of the Black Skulls for good."

CHAPTER THIRTY-SIX

JONATHAN

Well damn but Jonathan was glad he'd seen Drea and Garrett scheming over by the map earlier. He still shook his head at the thought of them driving straight into San Antonio all on their own without even *telling* anyone or thinking it through more.

Good Lord, it was like they were *trying* to get themselves killed. He paused at the thought, head moving sharply to look at the two as they slid on Black Skulls biker vests that they both insisted on calling *cuts*.

He narrowed his eyes at Drea. She hadn't been in the best head-space lately. He'd tried to convince her that there was no need to go in and do it like this. Why not just let David do his thing—they were attacking for night for God's sake. Wwithin days they'd be taking San Antonio... at least if everything went according to plan.

But she insisted that the man most called Suicide would bug out if he heard there was an invasion. That he'd take the women she was so desperate to save, or worse, kill them all to save himself the trouble.

And considering Garrett's reports about Suicide—something he'd asked about when Drea was *not* around—it didn't sound out of character.

So Jonathan had agreed they could go. On one condition.

He was going with them.

And they'd do it *smart*, or not at all.

David had been less than thrilled with the idea. He'd turned away as soon as Jonathan told him what he wanted to do.

"You're going to abandon me on the eve of one of the most important battles of the New Republic?" The words were spoken to the wall. "Is this about earlier? Because I didn't include you in my planning for the NASA mission?"

Jonathan shook his head and grabbed David's shoulder.

"No," he said firmly once David was looking at him again. Then he frowned. "Ok, I don't know. Maybe that's part of it. Sometimes I have to go my own way. But it's not just that—you know every female life is crucial to the future of the Republic. From the intel Garrett gathered from the biker, Thomas Tillerman has more than eighty women held in Nix Hospital. If we can secure their safety until you arrive with the army, it could make a real difference."

Jonathan gripped David's shoulder harder. "Please, David. I don't need your blessing for this mission. But I'd still like to have it."

David glared stonily for several more moments before finally breaking and nodding, drawing him into a tight hug. "For Christ's sake be careful, brother. Who else around here's going to call me on my bullshit?"

Jonathan laughed and clapped him on the back.

"Good, so now that you're on board, there's also the little issue of some equipment I wouldn't mind borrowing. We still have that diving gear, right...?"

"Oh now I see why you wanted my so-called *blessing*," David laughed, grabbing him in a headlock.

But David was a good sport and gave him everything he asked for.

"Biker looks good on you," Drea said but then laughed as Jonathan stared in bewilderment at the folds and flaps of leather she'd referred to as *chaps*.

Weren't chaps for, um, strippers?

"Here." She came over and tugged him close by his belt loops. And shit, her closeness reminded him of earlier when she was riding him, those firm legs of hers wrapped around him while he was buried so d—

"Hey," Drea snapped in his face. "Soldier boy. Focus."

He blinked and looked down at what she was doing. Shit. His stiffy was tenting his fatigues but Drea ignored it, efficiently looping the belt of the chaps through his belt loops and then buckling it with a sharp tug.

She went up on her tip toes and whispered in his ear, "There you go, big boy." Before she turned away, she gave his cock a squeeze.

Good Lord, was she *trying* to kill him?

He could only stare at her as she walked over to one of the three motorcycles and bent over to check something in the saddle bags on the back of the bike.

His head tilted sideways as he took in all the fineness that was Drea Valentine.

His *wife*.

Who he had to protect on the mission, no matter what. Lord knew she didn't look out for herself. Garrett would do anything for her, Jonathan believed that. But Garrett was just as crazy as Drea, most times.

No, it fell to Jonathan to be the level-headed one. He was the military man. The one who knew how to follow protocol. He might not have gone to West Point, but he'd spent the last seven years steeped in the rules and regulations of the military.

He might have been born trash, but he was worth more than that now. He'd prove himself. To David. To his wife.

To himself.

"You think you're gonna pass as a dude if you keep bending over like that flashing that sweet ass at everyone, D? Cause all any guy in three counties lookin' at you right now would be able to think about is—"

Drea spun around and flipped Garrett the bird. "Don't finish that sentence if you want to keep your balls intact."

Garrett held up his hands. "All right, all right, I'm just sayin'."

Drea rolled her eyes and pulled on the Black Skulls cut that was laying over the seat of the motorcycle. When she was standing up straight and her pants hung loose, with the black shirt and biker vest, she could *almost* pass for a guy.

If you didn't look at her face.

She'd cut a little more of her hair and had it slicked back, but her face was just too pretty to really be confused for masculine, even with the short hair.

But when she put the motorcycle helmet on, it helped to complete the illusion.

She slung her leg over the Harley and revved the old rebuilt gas engine. It sputtered to life and sitting there, she could be any Black Skulls thug—if a tad on the small side.

But with Garrett and Jonathan on each side of her, she shouldn't look too out of place. At least that was what they were banking everything on.

Because they were going to drive down I35 straight into San Antonio, right into the heart of Black Skulls territory.

———

So far so good. The ride had been uneventful for the fifteen miles to New Braunfels but Jonathan started slowing down as they came up on the first Army blockade.

Garrett took the lead as they slowed down and came to a stop right in front of the Army trucks that were stopped sideways, blocking the highway. Sometimes the best leadership was knowing when to let someone else take the lead, and in this case, Garrett was the best person for the job. Out of the three of them, Garrett was naturally the most convincing Black Skull considering he *was* one up until a little more than a week ago.

Several soldiers stepped up, automatic weapons drawn.

Garrett took off his helmet. "What the fuck?" he shouted. "It's fuckin' us. Let us through. Suicide's expecting us. We been scouting out those fuckers up in the hill country and we gotta make our report."

The lead soldier lowered his weapon. "Oh yeah? How many did you see?"

"There were fucking thousands of them out by Canyon Lake. That's where we started this morning. Then we came out this way and we saw more of the fuckers just about thirty miles up the highway."

The soldiers all exchanged glances. They didn't look worried, per se, but they were definitely interested in the embellished information.

"So you gonna let us through? We gotta get this info to Suicide in person since coms got fucked."

Jonathan felt his heart speed up and he had to work hard to keep his breathing calm and easy so he didn't draw any attention to himself.

The lead soldier nodded and held up a hand, palm flat. Behind him, one of the trucks growled to life and then rolled back, opening just enough space for them to squeeze their bikes through.

Jonathan and Drea never said a word or took their helmets off and soon they were back on the open road again.

This portion of I35 had been cleared. Old electric cars and trucks littered the sides of the roads but there was a nice, clear corridor down the center.

Jonathan had only driven on a motorcycle a handful of times before and the bike underneath him was far from the military issued motor- bikes he was used to. He was pretty sure he'd be feeling these vibra- tions into next week. It was a wonder bikers ever had any kids. His balls were sore and he'd only been on the damn thing for half an hour.

The next stretch was longer than the first. Thirty miles of silence— well, except for the incomprehensible roar of the bike in his ears. But after a while, it became a sort of white noise in the background—a very, very loud white noise, but still. It was *almost* calming.

Was Drea calm or was she wound as tightly as he was?

Jonathan spent the next thirty minutes running over the plan in his head... and imagining all the things that could go wrong. Just like with the NASA plan, this had been designed hastily and it too was built on information that was flimsy to say the least. They were walking right into enemy territory.

"Exactly," Drea said when she'd explained the plan to him. "They'll never expect such a bold approach. Not while the Army's amassing outside the city. They might be looking for spies trying to infiltrate the city in the usual ways because Suicide and Travis share the same weakness—they think they're smarter than everyone else in the room. So they don't think anyone could *possibly* outsmart them. They won't expect this sort of approach."

So she said anyway. Jonathan preferred to never underestimate his opponent.

But when they pulled up at the second blockade at the highway that made the outer ring of San Antonio and Garrett pulled up in the front, it was a similar experience to that at the first gate.

As they drove away, Jonathan kept an eye on his bike's side mirror. But the soldiers didn't make a move to follow them or even look after them.

Holy shit. He couldn't believe that had gone off so smoothly. They were really doing this. The soldiers hadn't even looked twice at Drea.

He spent the next several miles down the road sure that any moment he'd hear the roar of a truck behind them. But nope, no one was coming after them. And the road ahead of them was all clear. They hadn't aroused anyone's suspicions.

He needed to calm the hell down. Good Lord. They were due a bit of luck considering how sideways the last mission had gone.

He just needed to stay focused. Now they'd make their way to the park beside the zoo and—

Up ahead of him Garrett swerved slightly and then moved to the side, decelerating so that he fell behind Jonathan.

What was he—

Then Jonathan saw it—up ahead, another blockade.

And this time, it wasn't an Army blockade. There were trucks across the highway again, but they weren't military. And the cross of beefed up motorcycles parked by the trucks made it clear who was in charge at this barricade.

Jonathan took a deep breath and revved the throttle to accelerate until he took the lead Garrett had acceded to him.

They'd planned for this. Okay, so not exactly for this. There were only supposed to be *two* blockades, both of them military. But they'd prepared for Jonathan to be their spokesperson in case there were any Black Skulls members visible at the other blockades who might know Garrett. And know that Garrett had taken Drea's side back in College

Station if any of the few bikers who'd managed to escape that night had made their way to home base here in San Antonio.

So it was Jonathan who pulled to a stop at the lead of their little pack and pulled off his helmet. He might have only heard about MC life second hand, but he'd spent two years of his life on the street. A thug was a thug was a thug, any way you sliced it.

Jonathan propped his helmet on his thigh near his hip—or rather, near the gun holstered at his hip—as he clocked the situation. There were four men all together. Three who'd been sitting in camping chairs playing cards with an overturned box for a table. The fourth was in one of the trucks.

"Who the fuck are you?" growled a man with a height and girth that rivaled Garrett's, stomping forward and getting in Jonathan's face. With his gun in hand. "I ain't never seen you before. What chapter you with?"

"I don't gotta explain myself to some little shit stuck on guard duty." Jonathan glared down his nose at the huge man, difficult to do since he was still on his bike and the other man towering over him. "Suicide's waitin' on what we know about the troops back there. So you wanna get the fuck outta our way or you want me to tell him that the dumb fucks at the border slowed us down?"

Jonathan saw the slightest bit of uncertainty enter the big man's eyes. But the next second he glanced behind him at his other comrades and then jutted his chin when he looked back Jonathan's way. Except he didn't stop with Jonathan.

"What about the rest of you. Take off your fucking helmets. You can't all be from the fucking Beaumont chapter and that's the only one I don't know."

Jonathan didn't miss the way the bastard's hand tightened on the gun in his hand.

Shit.

They might have to—

But he never even finished the thought before there was a dull *thud* of a gun with a silencer being fired and a bullet hole appeared in the man's forehead in front of him.

Fuck! Jonathan didn't know if it was Drea or Garrett who'd shot the guy, but they could have just seriously fucked them all over.

The biker slumped to the ground in front of them and Jonathan raised his gun right as the bikers in the distance scrambled to their feet.

Jonathan fired at one of the truck's tires but it glanced off. *Shit.* It was a sloppy shot. The truck's engine roared and then it launched forward. If it got away, they were screwed. Their plan only worked if no one knew they were in the city.

"Cover me while I get the truck," Jonathan called out.

Then he ran forward, right out into the open and got a good shooting stance—legs slightly wider than shoulder width apart, knees slightly bent, both arms extended.

Gunfire went off all around him. Part of Jonathan's brain knew he was a wide-open target but he couldn't focus on it. He trusted that his team could cover him, and he *had* to stop that truck. Stopping the truck was all that mattered.

The truck that was getting further and further and *further* away.

But Jonathan took a breath in and lined the shot up in his sights. He wasn't going for the wheels anymore. No, he was aiming for the back of the driver's head.

As he breathed out, he pulled the trigger. He absorbed the kick back and was about to fire off several more rounds when the truck veered sharply to the right and crashed into the vehicles piled up on the shoulder of the highway.

Jonathan immediately dropped to the ground. Then, ten seconds and two more gunshots later, a whoop from Garrett. "I finally got the fucker!"

Jonathan sat up just in time to see Drea running swiftly over to the two men laid out by the motorcycles. She leaned over each and put another bullet into their heads.

"She always was a stickler for detail," Garrett said fondly as he stared after her like he'd never been more in love.

Jonathan shook his head at the both of them and got back to his feet. "I take it was her who took the first shot?"

Garrett shrugged. "We all knew shit was about to go sideways. She took initiative." He grinned wide at Drea as she walked back to them.

She paused and then came right up to Jonathan, sliding the visor to her helmet open at the last second.

He wasn't sure what he expected, but it wasn't the shaking fury he saw on her face.

"Don't you *ever* risk your life like that ever a-fucking-agin. I should never have let you come." Her voice was icy and she slammed her visor back down and turned away before he could say anything back. He could only watch as she walked back to her bike, swung her leg over, and kicked it into gear.

That was when Jonathan realized several things—first of all, he saw who was *really* in charge of this mission, no matter how he'd been trying to delude himself otherwise.

Drea slipped so naturally into the role.

And Garrett certainly saw her as invincible. Watching her in badass mode like this, it was easy to. Easy to think she could walk through fire and not get burned. Scale a mountain and not get winded. Walk through a desert and never thirst.

She worked so hard to project the façade of a woman who had no vulnerabilities.

But Jonathan had spent the last seven years of his life around a man people called robotic when they were feeling charitable. And Jonathan knew better.

Drea was as much flesh and blood as David was. So did that mean... had David been holding Jonathan back all these years out for the same reason underlying Drea's harsh words? Because... because David was afraid Jonathan would get *hurt*? Not because he didn't think Jonathan couldn't do the job?

Jonathan blinked hard.

Drea flipped her visor again, but only so she could bark, "Let's *go*," in much the same tone as David usually shouted, "Move out!"

Jonathan jogged quickly back to his bike, reloading his gun as he went. As he kicked his own bike into gear he was more determined than ever to have Drea's back.

Because whether she knew it or not, she, like David, needed him.

CHAPTER THIRTY-SEVEN

DREA

The rain held off until they got to Brackenridge Park, but once it rained, it poured. Story of Drea's life, right?

In this case it was good, though. It meant no one was around as they hid the bikes in the bushes and changed into their scuba gear.

The San Antonio River was only a narrow stream by the park, but as they slipped into it one by one and made their way downstream, it widened and deepened. The only tricky part was jumping over the dam the five feet down into the part of the river that went downtown to the Riverwalk. Not terribly dangerous but a little nerve-wracking all the same.

And the river itself—God, it was *filthy*. They all had goggles but they were effectively useless. Upstream they realized the best way to navigate without losing one another was to literally hold on to each other. There were only a few places where that was impractical because of debris or the river getting too narrow with overgrowth.

But they'd made it. They were in the Riverwalk itself and they'd swum along with the current down the streets they'd memorized.

In front of her, Drea felt Jonathan stop, holding onto the rocks and other debris piled at the bottom of the Riverwalk to halt his forward momentum. Drea did the same, and Garrett beside her.

She only popped her head above the surface when she got the signal from Jonathan, two taps on her shoulder. He was more familiar with the scuba gear so in this, she'd let him take the lead.

As she lifted her head the smallest bit out of the water, though, it was hard to tell what she was looking at, the rain was still coming down so hard. Garrett lifted his whole head out of the water beside her, not smoothly either. He made a big splash and God, he looked like a crazy walrus or something dressed in the scuba suit with that huge beard of his poking out.

She shook her head, about to grab his shoulder and shove him back under but Jonathan was emerging from the water too, grabbing the stone ledge of the sidewalk that edged the river. Drea guessed that meant it was all clear?

She grabbed hold of Garrett's arm and hauled him toward the sidewalk. She handed him over to Jonathan and together they pushed/pulled him up onto the ledge.

Then Drea herself slipped onto the sidewalk and was up on her feet while Jonathan was still helping Garrett struggle up.

Garrett was many things but graceful in a scuba suit was not one of them. Drea pulled her face rebreather off and glanced around. Shit. They were so exposed. She helped Jonathan haul Garrett to his feet and together they scrambled into the shadows underneath a wide bridge over the river.

She took her first real deep breath once they were hidden deep back in the recesses under the bridge. There were many footbridges over the river, but this one was for an actual road so it was wider.

Still, they all stayed silent as they peeled off their scuba gear. Jonathan pulled off the waterproof backpack he'd been wearing in addition to his small oxygen tank and set it on the ground, pulling out all of their clothing. Drea was happy to pull her jeans and shirt on and even happier to slide her gun holster into place at her hip.

She secured her switchblade in her boot and then stood up, the first ready. She snuck to peer out the other side of the bridge.

Jonathan hissed at her but she just held up a finger to quiet him.

There it was. Nix Hospital. It towered above the Riverwalk, a twenty-four story triangular building.

"What sort of house of horrors have you set up for yourself here, Thomas?" Drea whispered under her breath.

She shut her eyes and images of what Thomas had made of her beloved Nomansland flashed like the reel of a horror movie.

Women screamed at all hours of the day. One after another, Thomas tortured the women who were Drea's roomates. They'd return after hours of rape and torture. More bloody. More bruised. More broken. Their eyes more and more bereft of life until one day they stopped coming back at all.

The whole while Thomas never laid a single finger on Drea herself.

The sadistic fuck knew he was delivering a torture far worse than if he broke her body.

He'd been trying to break her mind.

Her spirit.

Her soul.

Some nights, she couldn't deny, he'd gotten close.

But in the end, she hadn't let him. And now she was here. Ready to mete out vengeance and take him fucking *down*. To take back the lives he'd stolen. To be the bringer of life instead of death. For once. For fucking *once*.

When Jonathan tapped her on the shoulder, she all but jumped out of her skin she'd been so lost in her memories.

"Hey," he whispered, voice gentle. "Are you okay? Because if you need to sit this one out, Garrett and I can—"

"Don't be fucking ridiculous," she cut him off, voice cold.

She felt bad immediately afterwards for her curt tone but then she breathed out and shut her eyes briefly. No. Like Eric, it was best if Jonathan didn't become too attached.

She opened her eyes, her gaze cutting back up to the hospital, to the top floor. The man Garrett had 'interrogated' said that was where Thomas stayed and it made sense. He always was particular about having the best, though he could rarely afford it back when she'd known him. Oh but how he'd moved up in the world. And how hard he would fall.

She was about to motion them forward when voices stopped her. The rain had lightened a slightly, otherwise she wouldn't have heard them at all and would have blundered forward right into the path of two men lumbering down a set of stairs from the road above the bridge.

"—you believe this shit? Fuckin' both of us still havin' to make these fuckin' rounds even in the middle of a goddamned flood? Shit's bullshit, that's what I'm sayin'."

"Shut the fuck up about it already. You think your whining makes it any better? Fuck, the bitches upstairs ain't as whiny as you when they're on the fuckin' rag and got half their faces broke up."

"You wanna say that to my fuckin' fist?"

"Jesus Christ, this sorta shit's why you're always on guard duty. Ever hear of takin' it down a fuckin' notch? Now let's get outta this fuckin' rain for a fuckin' second."

Drea's eyes widened as she and the guys backed up as fast as they could.

Right in time, too, because the next second, the two so-called guards stepped under the bridge, umbrellas dripping. The bigger one dropped his to the ground and reached in his pocket, pulling out some matches.

Drea didn't give him the opportunity to reach for the cigarettes. She already had her gun out and a bullet in his head.

Meanwhile Jonathan was braining the other with his oxygen tank. It was smart not to waste bullets.

But when he moaned and tried to stumble to his feet, Drea figured fuck it about the bullets and emptied a round into the back of his head.

Jonathan just barely jumped out of the way in time to avoid a face full of brains. He was a smart boy like that.

"Good Lord, was that really necessary?" he asked, still stumbling back and looking down at the guy she'd just dropped. "I had him. One more good conk to the head and it would've been lights out for the guy."

Drea shrugged, reloading her Glock. Fifteen bullets. She shoved the magazine home and cocked the gun.

Garrett had been rifling through the pants of the two dead bikers at their feet and came up with two keycards.

Bingo. Time to party.

Drea took them and after Garrett and Jonathan dragged the two bodies into the darkest recess of the shadows under the bridge, she led the way, jogging swiftly toward the back entry door to the hospital along the Riverwalk.

She held the keycard to the door and a second later, after a little beep, she pushed it open. There were lights on inside, no surprise. Of course Thomas's building would have electricity. They'd been banking on that.

She nodded at Jonathan and Garrett and they hurried into the building ahead of her. Thunder cracked and lightning flashed as the storm picked back up again. Drea spared one last quick glance outside to make sure no one had seen them, then closed the door quickly behind them, cutting off the noise of the driving rain.

After the surprise of the third blockade, they didn't know how reliable the information Garrett had gotten from the biker back at the outlet malls had been. He said that people didn't go down to the basement often but then again, he hadn't mentioned the guards outside, either. It was possible both had been new additional security measures taken in the last day because of the reports of their own Army approaching San Antonio. Or it was possible that Garrett had been in a rush and not done as thorough a job as he thought.

Still, as they crept through the basement—what looked like it once might have been a restaurant back when the Riverwalk was still a tourist attraction?—they didn't run into anyone. And the stairwell that led both down to the sub-basement and up to the rest of the building was exactly where their unwilling informant had said they'd be.

They'd just started down the stairs to cut power to the building when suddenly—

The lights went out.

Drea froze, one hand shooting out to the rail and the other going to Jonathan, who'd been closer to her. She didn't say a word but she heard and felt Jonathan fumbling. No doubt to put on his night vision goggles.

They only had one pair among them because David had needed the rest to equip his troops for the battle tonight. And it made sense for Jonathan to have them because he was the best shot. They'd planned for him to wear them after they cut the power.

But why the hell had the lights gone out before they'd even gotten to the fucking power line?

A moment later, Jonathan's strong hand was on her arm, tugging her against the wall of the stairwell.

"It's probably the storm," Jonathan murmured in a voice so quiet it barely counted as a whisper.

"Probably?" Garrett whispered harshly. "And what if it's not?"

"Shh," Drea said, holding her breath for a long moment, just listening. She counted a full sixty seconds and she didn't hear a thing. No boots on the stairs. No other voices. Not even the rain outside.

She let out her breath and reached out for Garrett, grasping when she felt his larger forearm. "It's just the storm. You heard what it was like out there. Which means the power won't be going back on anytime soon. No one will be out fixing anything in that storm."

Quiet for a long moment. Then, "Okay, D. Whatever you think's best."

Any other time she'd be disturbed at how blindly Garrett trusted her, but they were too close. They just needed to get this done and over with. She needed to end Thomas once and for all. She was close she could *taste* it.

She wouldn't let her women down. For once in her fucking life, she wouldn't let down the people depending on her the most.

She pulled out her gun and switched off the safety, holding it low to the ground. Jonathan shifted in front of her, taking the lead.

"All clear," he whispered. Good. The stairs must be as empty as they sounded.

They started up the stairs behind her and she was suddenly very aware of the fact that she wasn't wearing a tactical vest this time. It would have weighted her down too much to be able to swim effectively in the scuba suits. Something she was acutely aware of every flight of stairs they climbed.

Her hand tightened on her gun, finger hovering over the trigger the further up the stairs they went. Every moment she expected one of the doors to open. It was twenty-two stories for God's sake.

And *they* knew they hadn't screwed with the breaker box in the basement but no one else did. Did they all just assume it was the storm? That was a pretty dumb assumption to make considering everything that was happening with the armies amassing.

Although earlier when they were planning, Garrett had mentioned that he thought that Thomas would send most of the Black Skulls out to guard the city, believing himself invulnerable to the attack here deep in the heart of the city.

Thomas's ego was big enough for him to assume nothing could touch him... but on the other hand, he was also smart and conniving. Hadn't she learned one too many times that things were rarely what they seemed when it came to him?

So the higher they climbed, the tighter her chest wound. What if the informant gave Garrett all bad info? What if they were in the completely wrong building? Garrett had seemed convinced the man was telling the truth but—

A door crashed open two stories above them, light spilling into the darkness. Jonathan's arm immediately came across Drea's chest as he pulled her back against the wall and out of the line of sight of the middle of the stairwell.

He pushed the goggles up to his forehead and Garrett moved back, too. Drea could make out their dim outlines from the light of the flashlights above. Of the three of them, Garrett was the only one who was breathing hard from all the stairs, but he was good about doing it as quietly as possible.

"You hear that storm out there? Man, I hate tall buildings. Don't see why we gotta stay locked up here twenty stories off the ground never able to fuckin' breathe just cause the boss has a hard on for—"

"Shut the fuck up," said a second man.

"What?"

"Did you hear that?"

"Hear what?"

"Maybe if you'd stop fucking jabbering, you'd hear it."

Drea looked over at Garrett who had a hand over his nose and mouth. Did he just sneeze? It looked like he was fighting back another one. Shit.

Drea glared at him and he shoved his second hand to cover the first. Then his whole body shook as he sneezed again. This time, only the barest noise came out.

Drea swung her head back in the direction of the voices.

"Man, you're fucking paranoid. Let's just go get this done and then get back upstairs. That Monica chick is getting *trained* on giving BJs this week and I don't wanna deprive her of her chance to practice, if ya know what I mean."

"Aw man, she's a goddamned hoover. Boss'll be able to sell her for a thousand, easy."

The noise of feet on the stairs sounded right above them and light bounced off the walls.

Jonathan kept trying to tug her back tighter against the wall.

But Drea couldn't take in any of it. She heard only three words echoing until they were a scream in her head.

Monica.

Trained.

BJs.

Monica. She'd known a Monica. Monica had been a shy, modest girl, barely sixteen when Drea had first taken her in and given her shelter at Nomansland. So shy she'd barely spoken to any of the other women for nearly three months. And here these men were...

And finally, right as the footsteps and flashlights rounded the bend right above them, another thought intruded, clear as a bell.

Kill them.

So even though she felt Jonathan's urgent tug, she tightened her grip on the handle of her Glock and stepped out into the landing, right in the men's path.

"Hello boys," she said, smiling because she knew it would be the last thing they ever saw on this earth.

And then she lifted her gun and shot them between the eyes, one and then the other, *bang, bang*, before they could even pull their weapons.

Well, more like *thud, thud* because of the silencer, but Drea had to admit she took more than a little satisfaction from the crash of their bodies as they tumbled down the last half staircase to land at her feet.

Jonathan swore a few times behind her but Garrett just grabbed one body, hefted it up, and slid it over the railing of the center hole between the stairwells. Then he dropped it and repeated the action with the second body. Drea ignored the dull *thud* of the bodies hitting the concrete floor at the bottom, instead continuing her way up the stairs. Those guys were no loss to humanity.

She was even more on edge now, but they didn't encounter another person the rest of the way up.

Don't look a gift horse in the mouth, Drea.

Before they switched off the men's flashlights, Garrett's eyes brightened and he grinned so wide he flashed all his teeth when he noticing an old fireman's ax that was miraculously still in its glass case on the wall.

A situation he quickly remedied, using the back end of the flashlight to break the glass and grab the ax.

Jonathan rolled his eyes but Drea was all for out of the box thinking when it came to taking down murderous, rapist motherfuckers. They switched off the men's flashlights—they didn't want to give anything away in case anyone else showed up in the stairwell too—and then up they continued upwards, bound for the top floor.

Even Drea was winded after taking the last ten stories at a jog. She and Jonathan paused at the top for a couple of minutes to give Garrett a chance to catch up. He'd fallen behind a few stories ago.

She wanted to ask Jonathan what he saw now that they were at the top floor. Was it just like the blank white door she'd briefly seen in the light of the biker's flashlights before they'd turned them off? Or was it something grander? She waited, her gun at the ready, and then waited some more after Garrett finally got there and caught his breath.

"Shit," he whispered, but Drea clamped her hand over his mouth.

They needed to be silent as the grave until the very last moment.

Thomas could be on the other side of that door. At least *if* the intel Garrett had gotten out of their prisoner had been right—something she was beginning to doubt very much.

She couldn't put her finger on it, but something felt off.

Way off.

"Stay back, guns up," Jonathan whispered under his breath. "I'm trying the door knob."

Drea held her breath.

"It's locked," Jonathan breathed out. "Okay, taking it out."

Yeah. Duh, what did he expect? Doorway to evil bastard's secret layer? Pretty sure it was supposed to be locked.

"In three," Jonathan started the countdown. "Two."

It was still pitch black as Jonathan blew the lock off the door. Screams erupted as soon as Jonathan shoved through the door. Female screams.

Drea tried to get through the entrance but Garrett blocked her way. She still couldn't see a damn thing. "Garrett, move!"

But he stood there like a damn redwood in her way. Goddamn him.

"Jonathan," she called. "What do you see?"

"Jesus," was all he said, swearing under his breath. "Garrett, turn the flashlight on. Help me get them down."

Drea's blood went cold at his ominous words. What the fuck did that mean?

She didn't have to wait long to find out because the next second Garrett had his flashlight on and—

"Oh God!" Drea cried, shoving Garrett to the side. Or trying to. He still wouldn't let her past him—he moved out an arm to block her when she tried to squeeze between him and the door.

But she couldn't take her eyes off of the horror she was seeing. All around the room, women hung limp, naked and chained to the painted cinderblock walls by their wrists and ankles. There had to be eight or more of them and—

"Elena!" Elena was *alive*. Oh God. Oh God, *oh God*. Drea pushed at Garrett. "Let me through, dammit!"

Garrett finally moved forward into the room, but he kept his arm out, still trying to hold Drea back. "Stay back until we know it's safe. We'll get them down."

Son of a bitch. As soon as this was over she was going to be having a serious fucking talk with him. But for now, she ducked underneath his arm and finally got into the room. It looked like it had once been a lobby though it was now stripped of all furniture. There was still a glassed-off little room inside the larger one where a receptionist might have sat.

Drea took this all in with a quick glance before running straight to Elena.

"Drea," Garrett shouted, following her with a hoarse, "fuck."

She didn't care. She'd left Elena behind all those months ago when Nix had saved *her* from Nomansland. *Her*. When it was the women like Elena who'd been tortured for almost a year at that point. Raped over and over. God, Drea had only gotten glimpses of them except when Thomas wanted her to see, to know what was happening to the women she'd only ever wanted to protect—

"Elena," she shouted again as she got close to her once friend, and then she said her name again, except this time, it was full of anguish. "*Elena*."

Elena had been among the most beautiful of all the women who'd sought refuge at Nomansland.

And now— Oh *God*.

It was dark but for Garrett's single flashlight but when Elena turned her face toward Drea, into the light, Drea saw that scars covered the once perfect skin of her face. Like it had been slashed repeatedly with a razor. Some of the scars were old, red and raised, but healed over, while another was so fresh, dried blood was still crusted at the edges and smudged down her cheek.

"Drea," Elena croaked, reaching out feebly with one of her cuffed hands.

"Oh honey, I'm here. I'll get you free. Once and for all. I swear I won't fail you this time." Drea turned desperately to Garrett. "Help me get her down."

He nodded though he kept looking around the room anxiously. Drea got it. She did. Where was Thomas? Why were these girls here laid out like sacrificial lambs? It all stank of a trap. But Drea refused, she fucking *refused* to leave Elena behind a second time.

Drea didn't care if it was a trap. Death had been knocking at her door for ten fucking years now, ever since the night her father stupidly volunteered to take her place. Well come and fucking take her.

But let Elena go free. Let all these girls go free first. Please God. Just that.

Drea held on to Elena while Garrett lifted the ax he'd grabbed downstairs and smashed the chain where it was attached to the wall. One of Elena's wrist shackles came free and her arm fell around Drea.

"Get the other one, the other one," Drea said, pulling Elena further away from the wall. Garrett hurried around and smashed the other. It took a few blows to get her ankles free, but in less than a minute, she was detached. They'd have to worry about getting the actual cuffs off her wrists later, but it was enough to have her free of the wall for now.

"The other girls," Drea nodded to the girl hanging beside where Elena had just been. Across the room, Jonathan was using well aimed gunfire to get girls free of the wall. He had one down and was onto his second.

Drea turned back to Elena. She was probably dehydrated. Drea would have to find somewhere to stow the girls until the army got through and it was safe to show themselves. Maybe an abandoned store along the Riverwalk? Somewhere just deserted enough so they could escape notice until—

"Drea, look out!" Garrett shouted and Drea spun his direction just in time to see the woman he'd just freed from the wall lifting a knife behind him.

"Garrett!" she shouted, lunging toward them both.

But she was too late.

The waifish girl sank the blade deep into his back. He dropped where he stood.

"No!" Drea screamed, rushing forward. But before she got two steps, she tripped and landed hard on her knees.

She looked down and behind her, realizing in the same moment that she'd tripped on Elena's chains and that Elena was the one who'd thrown them in her path.

On purpose.

"Wha—"

"Shoot her!" Jonathan shouted from across the room. "*Shoot her. Now!*"

Right then the lights turned on—completely blinding after the near total darkness.

Drea scrambled to sit up but was knocked back down almost immediately.

By Elena.

Elena who'd jumped on top of her and was grabbing for her gun she'd tucked back in her waistband.

"What the hell? Elena. Elena!"

Elena didn't say a word, she just bit her lip, the vein in her neck pulsing with strain as she grappled for Drea's gun.

What the fuck was going on? Had everyone gone crazy?

Drea grabbed Elena's wrist right as Elena's fingers wrapped around the grip of the Glock. Elena grinned as she jerked it upwards.

Oh fuck.

Drea jerked Elena's wrist to the left only milliseconds before Elena pulled the trigger. The bullet fired harmlessly into the floor. But if Elena'd had her way, that would have landed in Drea's belly.

And the other girl had stabbed Garrett.

They were trying to *kill* them.

Little Elena. Sweet Elena. *Why?*

Elena growled and twisted, trying with all her might to wrestle the gun so it aimed at Drea.

"Stop it," Drea barked, even as she rolled them so that Elena was on the bottom and Drea on top. "Elena. It's me. Drea."

"I know who you are," Elena spat. "You're the bitch who abandoned me. Who abandoned us *all*. You promised us we'd be safe on your little make-believe island. When all you were really doing was making us a *target*. Then the first chance you had to get free, you fucking left us there to rot!"

"No. That's not how it was! I tried to get them to go back for you. I swear. I tried. Elena, if we could just—"

"No!" Elena screamed. "I don't have to listen to your lies anymore.

I know what real love is now. And I'd do anything for him. Everything. I'll give him *everything*."

Then, with a burst of strength Drea wouldn't have thought her capable of, she tore her wrist free and aimed the gun at Drea's head.

"Elen—"

Drea grabbed her arm and jerked the gun down again but Elena just jumped on her, tackling her back to the ground, both of them rolling several times.

Drea didn't even know when the gun went off. Her finger wasn't on the trigger, she knew that much.

But it didn't matter. Because when she scrambled backwards...

"Noooooo!" Drea screamed. "No! Elena!"

Elena was naked so there was no hiding the bullethole that sliced through her chest or the blood that pumped out with every last pulse of her heartbeat.

Drea scrambled to put her hand over the wound. If she just put enough pressure, she could stop the bleeding long enough for— And Billy could— Or one of the other doctors. This was a hospital, they had to have—

"He'll love me forever now," Elena whispered, bloody spittle spilling out the corner of her mouth.

And then her eyes rolled back in her head and her body went completely still.

"No. No," Drea shook her head. "No, no, no. Elena. Elena!" she shrieked, hand still over the gunshot wound.

She looked around desperately. There had to be something she could do. Someone. Something. "Help! Please!"

But all she saw was the two girls Jonathan had freed holding him at gunpoint, his hands raised in the air.

What was—

But as she watched on in befuddled confusion, the other girls who'd been chained up all freed themselves with keys they'd had in their mouths the whole time.

Drea recognized only a couple of their faces as girls who'd been with her at Nomansland. The others must just be women Thomas had picked up along the way. Women he was trafficking but had decided to keep for himself?

What was going on? What sort of trap had they walked right into —had she *led* them into?

Drea glanced over again at Jonathan. Oh God. He would die, too. Just like Garrett. Oh God. All because of her and her crusade that in the end was for nothing.

But surely not all of these women were under Thomas's control.

Then, as she watched, all but the two not holding Jonathan at gunpoint raised knives.

In unison, they said, "You did this to us, Drea Valentine."

And then they slit their own throats.

Drea screamed and tears blinded her vision. Blood. So much blood. Drea looked down at her own hands, covered with Elena's blood.

And all around the room. All the blood.

"Why?" she screamed, sobbing. "*Why?*"

She was crying so hard, she didn't see him come into the room. Jonathan must have, though, because distantly she heard his shouts but it was like through water. Everything was muted, moving slightly slower than it ought to be.

She was only jerked out of it when firm hands wrapped around her neck and a body landed on top of her.

She sucked in one last breath before all her air was cut off.

And then she looked up into his face, his dark features twisted into cruel and mocking delight.

Her own personal demon.

Thomas Tillerman.

She twisted and fought to get him off of her but he sat on her chest, pinning her arms down by her sides with his legs.

Her gun. Where was her fucking gun? Her eyes searched frantically, finding it on the ground—all the way across the room. Thomas must have kicked it there before he'd jumped on her.

"How many people have to die for you, little Belladonna?" Thomas's dark brows narrowed as his hands tightened around her throat even tighter. "First Daddy. And then all the women on that little island? Was that you trying to make up for the women in the warehouse you failed to save that night? It was, wasn't it?`"

He lifted her head up slightly only so he could slam it back down against the tile. She blinked as the world slid and tilted sideways.

"But that's become a pattern with you, hasn't it?" he continued. "Failing people? Getting them killed? These two men you brought with you today. Elena. If you'd tried harder, you could have saved her. She was half starved, for Christ's sake. But you took the easy way out and just killed her."

He tutted. "And growing up all I ever heard was how strong the Valentine stock was. Valentines this, Valentines that. How the Valentines had led the Black Skulls to prosperity for generations."

He shook his head. "But all it took was a few months tickling your titties and one whispered rumor in your ear, and you took down your own dynasty, didn't you?"

Drea wept, the little breath she had left escaping with her sobs. She tried to suck in air but only a trickle made it in through Thomas's death grip around her throat.

She hated him.

Hated *him*.

Needed more air.

Hated— Hated—

Herself.

She was the daughter of a slave trader and a crack addict. Every time she'd tried to prove she was more, to do good and help people to make up for all the bad they'd done, all she did was end up getting more people hurt.

Her father wasn't the devil but he might as well have been. Yet still, she'd loved him. He was a monster and she loved him, even after learning what he was. Her whole life she'd paid penance for that original sin.

And now the reaper was calling, wearing the face of her greatest tormentor.

This was how it was always meant to end.

Her poison could only be stamped out by an even more vile poison.

"That's right," Thomas cooed as he smiled above her. "Let go. Give in and let go."

Drea let her eyes fall closed. He wouldn't be the last thing she saw in this world. She thought of her father. The familiar contours of his face beneath the skull tattoo. The way his eyes would crinkle when he smiled at her.

Sure do love you, Lil' Bit. Always have, always will.

I love you too, Daddy.

Always have...

... always... will.

"Drea, no!"

Eric?

Drea's eyes flew open and she twisted in Thomas's grip. No! Two bikers dragged Eric into the room from the open elevator, two more following with a struggling Billy. How had they—? They couldn't be here!

"Drea. What are you doing? Fight him!"

"Muzzle him," Thomas growled above Drea, pressing down harder on her throat. Spots immediately began dancing in her eyes. He hadn't been pushing with his full force before—he'd been allowing in just the tiniest bit of air to draw it out. He enjoyed her struggle. Her torment. But he was done with that now.

Because Eric had come. Eric had come in spite of those terrible things she'd said to him.

"I love you, Drea," Eric shouted, struggling against the bikers who were trying to gag him. "Fight for us. Fucking *fight*."

Eric was fighting for her.

He was here.

Eric *loved* her.

"He'll be just one more who dies because of you," Thomas growled, eyes flashing as he squeezed even harder.

No!

Eric couldn't die. Not Eric or Jonathan or anyone else.

Thomas was the fucking poison.

Drea felt herself growing weaker with every moment that passed.

But Eric was here. *Stronger together.* They were stronger together. She didn't have to fight alone anymore. Ever again.

But as much as she needed him, he needed her right now too. They all did.

She was still pinned as firmly as ever by Thomas sitting on her chest. But while she'd thought about her gun earlier, she'd forgotten about her secondary weapon. She bent her knee. Fuck, it was an awkward angle with Thomas still on top of her.

She reached frantically for her boot with her right hand.

Almost there. *Almost—*

"Well, this has been fun, cunt," Thomas said, "but now it's time to—"

Got it!

Drea grasped the hilt of the knife, flipped it, and then buried it to the hilt in Thomas's lower back, in and upwards with all her might.

Thomas screamed and the pressure on her neck immediately released but Drea tried to keep her focus even as she gasped in a deep breath.

"Kill her!" Thomas shrieked.

Drea ripped the knife out and then stabbed again even as Thomas twisted off of her, crawling away.

She yanked the knife out again and launched herself at him, throwing her arms around him from behind like she was giving him a bear hug.

Except for the fact that this hug was lethal, because she didn't wait to hear his last words or to hear him beg.

No, she just slashed the knife she held in her ruthless grip across his neck, ear to fucking ear. He collapsed to the floor and she fell on top of him, still gasping for air.

Any moment now, she thought. One of his thugs would come and kill her. Or one of the brainwashed women.

No, goddammit. She couldn't just lay here and give into death. She owed Eric and Jonathan more than that.

So she rolled off of Thomas, ignoring the pool of blood spreading outwards from his body and holding her knife feebly in front of her as she struggled to a sitting position.

Only to see Billy shakily holding his gun on the two women who'd previously had Jonathan at gunpoint while Jonathan and Eric kicked ass.

Of the four bikers who'd brought Eric and Billy in, three were already on the floor unconscious or dead, and Eric and Jonathan were closing in on a fourth.

He lunged at Eric. Right in time to get a bullet in the head from Jonathan.

"Watch them," Drea cried out, pointing to the women. "They've got knives."

Eric turned toward the women Billy was guarding right as they pulled the knives. They didn't advance on Billy or the other guys, though.

"Stop them!" Drea shouted as they lifted the knives to their own throats like the other women had earlier.

"You did this to us, Dr—" they started to say in unison, but Jonathan jumped in front of Billy and knocked the knives out of their hands before they could cut their own throats.

They tried to fight him to get back to the knives, but Billy helped in holding them back. In the end, they had to tie their arms behind their backs to keep them from harming themselves.

Eric stumbled over to Drea and collapsed down beside her, dragging her into his arms.

But she immediately struggled away. "Garrett," she cried, but Billy was already at Garrett's side.

"He's alive!"

Billy pulled the knife out and Drea crawled over to him as Garrett sat up. She didn't even try to hold in the tears anymore.

"*Garrett.*"

He blinked and winced as he experimented moving his arm. "Shit, I think she hit the metal disk replacement in my shoulder."

"Oh my God." Drea buried her face against his thigh and cried and cried and cried, Eric rubbing her back as Jonathan and Billy hovered nearby.

It was minutes later before, hiccupping, she finally lifted her head and turned to Eric. "How? How are you here?"

He dropped his forehead to hers.

"I didn't get very far before I realized that it doesn't matter."

"What?" Drea coughed out incredulously, tears still running down her cheeks.

"It doesn't matter how mean you try to be. I know you in here." He pressed his palm to her chest, right above her heart. "And I promised you forever. You're my family as much as my daughter is. And while she *might* be heading into danger, I *knew* you were. And I knew you needed me."

Which just made the tears start up all over again.

"I'm sorry," she sobbed into his chest. "I'm sorry for the things I said to you earlier. I didn't mean any of it. I was just so afraid. And I never said those things to Sophia. She and I talked but not about that. I never told her she should go out on her own. I told her what a wonderful father you are. What a good man. I told her I'd been wrong about you all along."

Eric's arms came around her and he squeezed her tight, kissing her hair.

"Jesus, I love you, you stubborn woman."

She smiled through her tears. "I love you, too."

She pulled back and looked into his blue eyes and repeated it. "I love you."

And it was like something inside her chipped loose of the concrete it had been encased in and was finally set free.

She looked around at Jonathan and Garrett and Billy. "I love you," she said to them. "All of you. I love you."

Now that she'd said it, it felt like she couldn't say it enough. "I love you," she repeated, laughing and crying all at the same time.

They all crowded around her—at least Eric, Garrett, and Jonathan did. Billy stood back and she looked up at him through her tears and waved him down.

She'd finally forgiven herself, at least, she thought that was what this felt like. How could she not do the same for him?

He fell to his knees and dropped his forehead to the floor at her feet, his shoulders shaking. "I'm sorry. I'm so sorry."

Drea put her hand on his head and it felt like she was giving him absolution, though maybe she was giving it to herself, too.

But their pasts didn't have to define them.

It could be their futures that did.

"Come on," she said quietly, tugging on Billy's shoulder so that he sat up. His cheeks were streaked with tear tracks and his eyes were red.

"Let's go see what shape the rest of the girls are in."

CHAPTER THIRTY-EIGHT

BILLY

"I'm just going to clean this out and then get you stitched up, okay?" Billy asked the skinny, wan girl on the exam table. He fought to keep his voice steady as he dabbed antiseptic against the gash in her forehead. He'd already cleaned away the crusted blood that had been there for who knew how long.

"You're doing great, honey," Drea said, squeezing the girl's hand. "Jenny, right? You said your name was Jenny?"

The girl nodded, eyes shooting back and forth from Billy to Drea.

"It's okay, Jenny. You're safe now. Billy will take good care of you. I promise."

Billy swallowed hard at Drea's words. How could she say that? How could she even *look* at him now, knowing what she did? That while he might not have been in these exact exam rooms with these exact girls, he'd been in ones very similar, working for the same evil bastards, *helping* them—

But he couldn't think about that right now. His patient deserved all his focus. So he gave it to her as he began suturing the gash on her forehead shut with a practiced, careful hand.

After he was done, Drea went to bring in the next girl.

She'd been tireless all night long as they cleared and secured the hospital floor by floor. Garrett's initial assumption had been right— most of the Skulls had been sent out to secure the city and only a skeleton crew had been left behind.

After realizing that Suicide was dead and most of the other Skulls in the building were dead, one finally got smart and started talking. Apparently Suicide had always been certain that Drea would come to him, especially after the attack at College Station. Hence the little scene he'd had prepared on the penthouse floor. When the two guards circling the perimeter didn't check in, Suicide had ordered the building's generator shut off, to be turned back on at his command.

He ignored the suggestions of his VP and others to just kill Drea on sight or to at least have more men up in the penthouse with him. Suicide ordered them to go with the men he was sending out to defend the city.

So Drea and the guys got to the fifteenth through twenty-fourth floors that were filled with women locked inside exam rooms, there were only two guards stationed on every floor.

Jonathan made Drea stand back when they unlocked the first room of women, not sure if they'd run into more who were brainwashed like those upstairs.

But they weren't. They were just terrified, abused girls who couldn't believe they were finally free.

Drea sent the ones who didn't need medical attention down to the fifteenth floor lobby to be all together and the ones who needed medical attention she was seeing to personally. They'd obviously not had a proper doctor on staff because while some had problems that just a matter of popping joints back into place, others had far more serious conditions. Broken bones. Infected wounds. A couple he suspected had internal injuries that he was going to x-ray as Jonathan got a make-shift machine Suicide's crew had on hand working again.

None of the girls who'd walked through the door were ones that Billy had seen before.

Because they were all sold to the four corners of who the fuck knew where by now.

And you did nothing. Instead of helping them, you ran. You saved yourself.

God, the look on Drea's face as she realized what he'd done. Not just about what he'd done while he was there as the doctor, but the running, too. And then his stupid fucking bumbling excuses cut off by her icy: *Don't.*

The horror and disappointment on her face said everything he'd been trying so desperately to silence with pills for the past two years. A year and a half he'd worked for Suicide at his South Texas 'processing facility.' In conditions that were bad enough to haunt any sane man.

But he'd stayed. And swallowed more and more pills until he felt only numb while he patched up girl after girl that Suicide and his men broke during so-called 'training' and then sent back down to him to be repaired again.

If it wasn't him, it'd just be someone else, he told himself. He'd give them more care and consideration than any other doctor, he told himself. He wouldn't further abuse them, he told himself. Such paltry fucking excuses.

More than one girl had begged him to kill them.

Being here in this place, with these girls, fuck, all of it had him wanting to run right back to the place he'd been yesterday—the bag of medical supplies back at the outlet mall, the bottle of pain pills in his hand.

After Drea stormed out, bound and determined to go on her mission to save the world, all the rest of the men who were worthy of her trailing after, Billy had run straight for the pills like the weak, pathetic fuck that he was.

He'd picked it up in shaking hands and heard the voice roaring in his head.

Yes.

Please.

Take this pain away!

Forever.

How many pills would that take? He popped the top of the pill bottle and looked inside.

It was full. Still, if he wanted to be sure the job was done, he should swallow all of them.

And then he'd laughed bitterly. So he'd be selfish even in this, huh? Depriving them of so much precious pain medication because he was a coward to the last?

One last great disappointment.

On one hand, it'd be fitting, he thought, sliding to the floor with his back against the wall. He could die as he'd lived. A *coward*.

But on the other hand, what would Drea feel when she came back and found out what he'd done?

Eric was always going on about how Drea took the whole weight of the world on her shoulders. How she blamed herself for Maya getting hurt and for what had happened to Gisela.

God, the whole reason Billy had gone on that mission was to try to prove to everyone and himself that he wasn't a fucking coward. But when it came to it, had it been him shoving Drea aside to take a bullet for her? No, yet again he let a woman pay the ultimate price while he stayed safe in the background.

Fuck, Drea had to know this was all on him. He just wasn't strong enough. Some people were too weak to handle the shit life threw at them, and he was one of them. Weak.

He'd write a letter, he decided. That way Drea and everyone else would *know* it was no one else's fault except his own.

So he went hunting for something to write on. Turned out people in a war zone weren't big on carrying around writing utensils.

Finally he settled on a cardboard box and picking up the marker David had been using to draw on the wall earlier.

He sat down on the floor and tried to start the letter. He tried explaining about how he used to think that everyone did whatever they had to to survive. That *everyone* compromised their morals. How he'd thought morality itself and right and wrong were pre-Fall luxuries. And that was how he'd justified...

But then he'd stopped and looked at what he'd written. It was such *bullshit*. Such whiny, self-justifying *bullshit*. Excuses. They were the excuses of a fucking coward.

So he started manically scribbling COWARD all over the cardboard, on every surface he could find, all over the other shit he'd written until he was scratching so hard with the marker that he was tearing the box apart.

That was where Eric found him, prostrate on the floor, Billy didn't know how much later.

Billy didn't even know he was there until Eric said, "Enough. Get up. We've got to go back up our wife and keep our family safe."

That was all. He said it so coolly, so matter of factly that Billy would swear he was channeling Drea herself.

So Billy got up. Eric had found another motorcycle for them. Billy thought Eric was terrified of the things, but Eric just climbed on behind Billy without so much as a word of protest.

Was it weird riding a motorcycle, something Billy had done maybe only five times in his whole life, with a dude's arm around his waist— only one arm at that since Eric's other arm was broken—and trying to balance for both of them? Well, yeah, sure it was.

But everything since running into Drea and Eric on the road that day had felt more than a tad surreal.

There was a part of Billy that wasn't sure he hadn't gotten into some bad mushrooms or some shit and this was just a really wicked, really intense trip.

Either way, riding through two Army checkpoints and letting Eric bullshit about them being the last of their crew to make it out of Seguin before the Army there supposedly crushed their defenses seemed about par for the course. As did driving through the third checkpoint and finding nothing but dead bodies.

No doubt the work of their illustrious wife. The woman who was afraid of nothing.

Except that when they'd finally been dragged up to that room, Billy had finally seen it, what Eric had been talking about all along—Drea's demons on parade.

She'd been about to give into that snake-tongued bastard.

Billy hadn't had many run-ins with Thomas 'Suicide' Tillerman but every one of them had left him feeling unsettled, like the man had seen straight through him. Like he'd seen his cowardice and reveled in it.

But like every other obstacle Drea had ever faced in her life, she overcame that bastard and whatever he'd stirred up for her. She put him and his lies *down*. Slashed his motherfucking *throat* like the Amazon warrior that she was.

And then she'd fallen into their arms—including Billy in the embrace. Because while perfection wasn't supposed to be possible on earth, she was as close to it as humanly possible, he was pretty damn sure.

Where he was weak, she was strong. He was cowardice. She was courage. She was all he'd never be.

So how could she—? With him—?

He shook his head as Drea brought the next woman in.

Drea had her hand behind the woman's back. She was dark-skinned and walked with her arm cradled against her body.

Billy winced. It was broken. He could tell from across the room. But he had only one thing to offer Drea, and that was his doctoring. So he'd care for these women until his hands cramped and his feet bled.

He'd donate pints of blood and as much plasma as possible before he keeled over. He'd—

"This is Billy."

The woman immediately started backing up when she saw Billy but Drea put a hand to her back. "It's okay. He's like the men outside. He's safe. We just need to have him take a look at your arm. He won't hurt you."

Five minutes later, Billy was really wishing she hadn't promised the woman, Denise, that. Because it turned out, her arm had been injured about a week ago, and he had to rebreak the bone to set it.

Even with the shot of morphine the woman still screamed and sobbed into Drea as Billy did what needed doing. Drea had tears in her eyes as she stroked the woman's hair and whispered that it was okay, it was over, it would all be okay now.

Billy knew her words were for Denise. He *knew* it. But was it so bad if he took comfort in them too, and her nearness as he wrapped Denise's arm in a proper cast?

Fuck but you're a selfish, self-obsessed bastard, he castigated himself. God if he could only get a break from himself for two damn seconds. He'd like to live in Drea's head. He imagined himself there.

Caring about other people. Loving them. Sitting in a quiet corner just absorbing her strength and endless determination.

"Something's happening," Garrett burst into the room, causing Denise to flinch as Billy finished wrapping the last bit of her cast.

"Oh shit. Sorry." Then Garrett looked to Drea. "D. You gotta come. It's the Army. They're in the streets."

Drea immediately headed for the door. "Which Army?"

"That's the thing. It looks like both of them."

Drea stopped sharply. "What do you mean, *both?*"

Billy whispered quick after-care instructions to Denise and then hurried to follow Drea and Garrett.

"I mean *both*. All mixed up together. Come look."

They were still high up in the building, on the nineteenth floor and the sun had risen about an hour ago.

So there was plenty of light to see the soldiers marching down the streets wearing the distinctive black of Travis's army interspersed with the normal green fatigues of David's army.

"What the hell does it mean?" Drea whispered.

"I'd say we're about to find out," Eric said, "because it looks like they're coming right this way."

"Shit, you're right," Garrett said.

"It could be a trap," Eric said. "If they defeated David's army, they could have easily captured enough soldiers and taken their uniforms. If they weren't fooled by his *defeat in detail* tactic, they could have sent their full forces against David's troops at New Braunfels. David would have had no choice but to surrender or get all his men killed."

"If there was no other choice," Jonathan spoke up, "if it was hopeless, he'd surrender."

"And they could have had them strip out of their uniforms like Eric said—" Drea moved down the window like she was trying to get a better look. "—to trick us after they couldn't get ahold of Thomas on the shortwave."

There had been incoming transmissions attempted all afternoon but they hadn't picked up. If they pretended to be Suicide and were found out, then his lieutenants would definitely know he'd been taken down, but not answering at least left the possibility of interrupted coms.

Drea continued looking out the window for another long moment, brows furrowed. Then she pulled back and said decisively, "I'll go down."

"What?!" Garrett exploded.

"No way, you could be walking straight into a trap," Jonathan said, sounding no less exasperated.

"We have to know one way or another," Drea said, "and I'm the best representative—"

"I thought we were past all your self-destructive bullsh—"

"It's not that, Eric," Drea cut him off. "I promise. But there's an *army* down there. And if they did capture David's men, then we have to—"

"I'm going," Billy called loudly from where he stood, already in the elevator. He'd snuck over while the rest of them were arguing.

"Billy," Drea called out in alarm, hurrying over like she meant to stop him.

But his finger was already on the *Door Close* button.

"I love you," he said to her right as the doors were closing.

As the elevator descended, Billy expected to feel the normal terror he did when heading into dangerous situations—his usual instinct for survival and self-preservation that usually overrode every other thought.

But instead, he felt... calm.

No matter what he faced when those elevator doors opened and he stepped out, for the first time in so, so long, he was doing the right thing.

And he was at peace.

CHAPTER THIRTY-NINE

ERIC

"I can't tell what's going on, can you?" Drea asked, face pressed anxiously to the glass of the window.

Eric was down at the opposite end of the room with his forehead to the window. "I can't see anything either. Just a bunch of soldiers all bunched in a group in the street."

Goddammit. To have made it this far only to be trapped up in this building. It was infuriating. They should have had a better exit strategy than to just wait for the army. They should have had contingency plans in case David—

Behind him, the elevator dinged.

"Get back," Garrett growled, running over and standing in front of Drea, cocking his rifle and aiming it at the elevator. Eric was right behind him, Jonathan by his side.

"No," Drea said, pushing to get through them. "Put your weapons down. They'll shoot you. Stop it!"

But before any of them lowered their weapons, the elevator doors opened.

Revealing Billy and David.

Drea let out a cry and pushed past Eric and the others. She flung herself first at Billy, hugging him and then pulling back and shoving him hard. "Don't you *ever* do that to me again, do you hear me?" she shouted. Then she hugged him again before turning to David and yanking him into the embrace too.

"David," Jonathan said hurrying over to them. "What's going on? How—?"

David just laughed, pulling away from Drea, though Eric noticed he did grab her hand, unwilling to completely let go of her.

"We went in and the battle began exactly as planned. We had the greater numbers and we were winning."

Drea beamed at David. "Of course you did. You're brilliant."

But David shook his head. "Well I didn't count on one big contingency."

Drea's eyes popped open wide. "What? What happened?"

"A couple hours in, we were making headway, cutting down Travis's army, not taking too many losses, when suddenly, we saw them in the distance. Just this huge wave of soldiers coming in as reinforcements."

"Oh my God," Drea whispered, panicked eyes going outside again. "So did they—?"

"No, no, it's okay," David immediately reassured her. "But yeah, I was all but shitting my fatigues at the time. I thought it was all over."

"So what happened?" Eric bit out. Enough with the storytelling dramatics. Military men and their war stories, he fucking swore.

"Well it turns out, the army who'd already been stationed here in San Antonio didn't much like the change in leadership when Travis killed President Goddard. Travis tried to pin it on you guys," he nodded Eric's way, "but no one believes that. They know it was Travis. Some of these guys had fought with Goddard way back in the day. Even if they hadn't, patriotism still means something to them."

"So when they saw we had a force that actually had a fighting chance of taking San Antonio and leadership capable of holding it," David grinned at Drea, "they joined our side. They turned on the soldiers loyal to Travis and helped us round them all up. Now you have an army of twenty-five thousand at your disposal."

He looked at Drea as he said it and she was obviously as confused as Eric was.

She glanced behind her but obviously no one was there. "What do you mean?" she asked. "I don't get it."

But then Jonathan started laughing, obviously picking up on something that Drea and Eric still weren't.

"They wanted a strong leader," Jonathan said.

David nodded. "And they'd heard about you, Drea. What you did in College Station has become legend."

Drea scoffed. "But that was just—"

"And then taking out the satellites? That just cinched it." David either missed or ignored Drea's flinch as he waved around him. "And then this. You've freed so many women. They call you The Liberator, Drea."

Drea's eyes narrowed. "That's ridiculous."

But Eric was already shaking his head. "No, it's not."

Drea shot annoyed eyes his way but he kept going, "No, hear me out, Drea. Think of what you could do as President."

"*President!?*" she sputtered, half coughing the word, but Eric was on a roll now.

"Yes. President. You've always said women should have their own voice. This is their chance. Are you really going to let some man step in again who will make God knows what arbitrary rules concerning women? You didn't like the laws I made and you *like* me." He waved a hand. "Most the time anyway."

She sputtered again. "But, I— I—"

Then she turned away from all of them, hands running through her newly bobbed hair.

"What?" David asked. "I think it's a great idea. I was going to suggest you as governor of San Antonio Territory but this makes more sense. We declare you as the alternate President. There's no scenario in which we don't have to unseat Arnold Travis."

That was when Drea spun on them and Eric witnessed the stark terror on her face. "It can't be me, don't you get it?" she cried. "I let down anyone who depends on me. Haven't you looked around you at the women in this hospital? This is what happens to the people I try to lead! And what happened to Gisel—"

"No," Eric crossed the room until he was standing in front of her. "That's bullshit and I thought you'd finally understood that earlier. You didn't do this. Evil bastards did this. *Not you.* The fact that you've stood up again and again to these fuckers is why people keep wanting to follow you."

Billy joined his side. "God, Drea, if only you could see yourself the way we see you. You're so much stronger than you even know."

She shook her head, looking from each one of them to the next. "But I'm *not*."

Eric only reached out and took her hand, and then, one by one, so did all the rest of her husbands.

"You *are* strong enough," Eric said. "Because our strength is your strength. If you fall down, we'll pick you up."

"If you stumble," David said, and Jonathan picked up, "We'll catch you."

"We'll always be there for you," Garrett said.

"We'll always love you." Billy said.

"Always have and always will?" Drea asked, looking around at them with a vulnerability that gutted Eric. He would be this woman's strength until the day he died if she'd let him.

"Always," Eric swore, and pulled her into a kiss.

EPILOGUE

SOPHIA

Sophia held her purse up on her lap and let out an irritated huff at Finn who'd pulled their truck over to check his compass for the ten *millionth* time.

"Oh my God, Finnigan, we're going west. The sun just came up, so guess what? If we go in the opposite direction, we're heading the right way!"

"Oh wow, please do edjumacate me some more, Miss Sophia. Me big dumb boy. Don't know my ups from my downs," Finn quipped as he snapped the compass shut and pulled the truck back on to the road to head—you guessed it—exactly where Sophia had pointed out they should go five minutes ago. "It's not like I'm the one with all the tracking experience who's been out on about a hundred Scrapper runs. How many have you been on again? How many trips have you taken out of Jacob's Well, in point of fact?"

Oh, how she wanted to smack her purse in his superior face. Instead, she smiled sweetly. "You mean the *diplomatic missions* I've been on? Seven. Compared to your... how many was that again?" She held a hand to her ear. "Oh, zero? Hmm. How about that?"

"And to think, we're only a day into this little adventure. I thought it'd take at least five before you turned into a harpy fishwife."

"Harpy f—" Sophia cut off in a huff, turning her face furiously away from Finn. Finnigan Knight was absolutely, positively *the* most annoying boy on the entire planet.

She wished she could go back in time and uninvite him from her little diplomatic trek over to New Mexico.

Except... well, she most likely did need the big, dumb oaf.

When they'd received the call from the governor of Santa Fe in New Mexico, she couldn't have been more excited.

New Mexico! No one had heard anything from them in years other than the occasional trader who claimed to have passed through on treks from farther lands. They claimed it was all but abandoned apart from roving herds of bandits.

There'd been rumors that there was some sort of war between the southwestern states like New Mexico and Arizona around the same time as Texas's war with the Southern Alliance States. No one had any real concrete information, though. Which was in itself odd and not a little spooky. An entire states' citizens didn't just *disappear*.

Well, the person who'd called Jacob's Well's sat phone had answers.

There *had* been a war, which they'd lost to Colorado. Apparently Colorado was the state they'd all been fighting, just like the Southern States had all been ganging up on Texas. And like Texas, Colorado also won—and when they did, they apparently took *all* the women from the losing states.

Sophia hadn't been able to stop herself from gasping at that. No women? At all?

None, said the Governor. At least none that hadn't been hidden extremely well. But that was difficult to manage for long since New Mexico wasn't the most forgiving land.

New Mexico was finally starting to rebuild, though. At least in Santa Fe. They'd gotten Jacob's Well's number from President Goddard's trade secretary, the man said. And not only was Santa Fe a thriving community that had restored a portion of the power grid, but they were eager to establish trade relations with The New Republic of Texas.

Anything Texas wanted—in exchange for brides.

Brides.

That was the term they'd used. If they'd said *women*, like they were trying to sell women or barter them like cattle, Sophia might have hung up right there.

But no, apparently they'd heard of Jacob's Well's lottery system. They wanted in. And they'd pay big for the privilege.

"It's the future of our nation-state at stake, you understand, Miss Wolford?" the man on the phone had pleaded. "Without you, we'll disappear in a generation."

How could she say no to that?

But she wasn't going to just rush in. She had to make sure they were who they said and that they could offer what they promised.

And she wanted to show them good faith that they could deliver the goods as well.

So she was going.

To offer herself as the first bride.

It was ingenious, really. Dad needed men. Troops to fight Travis and take back the Republic. New Mexico had men. Plenty, it sounded like. And Texas had women. There were all the ones Drea had just freed and even more once they liberated San Antonio.

Plus, Sophia was sure Daddy wouldn't let some other jerk take the Presidency. Not another President Goddard. Maybe Daddy himself would be President. He'd done such a good job with Jacob's Well. Imagine what he could do with the whole New Republic! He'd definitely honor whatever agreement she made.

Then Sophia frowned. He hadn't exactly been thrilled with her the last time they'd talked. And they'd gotten cut off so abruptly and then the battery on her sat phone had run out and she hadn't wanted to go back to the caves to get another. Nope, she didn't want to run into Dad again until her mission was a success.

Besides, she could use the sat phone they had in New Mexico. Or better yet, just show back up with her new army behind her, like a modern day Joan of Arc.

Sophia sighed happily.

"Do I even want to know what it is you're plotting over there?"

Sophia glared Finn's way, her good mood immediately souring again. Right. Finn. The unfortunate tag-along she'd been forced to ask to help her.

Because while she might like to pretend she was a warrior-diplomat, yeah... the warrior part might be a stretch. She felt confident of her diplomatic abilities—hadn't she watched her dad at work for years and welcomed every new girl to Jacob's Well since she'd turned seventeen—if some bandit or smuggler came after her while she was traveling, she'd have no idea what to do.

She'd thought carefully about all the people she might approach to help her. Maybe Nix or one of Shay's husbands. Or maybe Vanessa would lend her those big, burly twins of hers...?

But talking to Dad had put the kabosh on that. Any of those people would only side with her dad. They'd tell her she should wait. That she should take more people. Or more likely, that *she* shouldn't go at all. That was *definitely* what Dad would say.

So she had to go before he got back. And take someone with her who was totally reckless with little appreciation for authority or doing things the proper way: Finnigan Knight, *ding ding ding ding!*

Because no matter what Drea or anyone else thought, she was more than just Daddy's little girl. She cared about the future of the Republic as much as anyone else. She loved her country. She'd fight for it. She'd... she'd *die* for it, if it ever came to that.

A shudder ran down her spine at the thought, but she only stiffened it and sat taller. But it was true. Those courageous boys out with the General fighting in San Antonio weren't the only ones who could be brave.

Maybe most people wouldn't think much of a couple of days travel and then throwing an elaborate wedding... well, there was still something to be said for a feminine form of warfare.

Sophia had dreamed of her wedding for as long as she could remember.

And obsessed about her lottery so many times she'd about crawled out of her skin waiting for the day to finally come.

Well, here it was. She turned nineteen next week. And maybe the wedding wouldn't be exactly as she'd always imagined, in the old Catholic church in Jacob's Well, with the big bell that rang out over the town and echoed in the hills. And maybe her dad wouldn't be there standing beside her to give her away. And maybe she wouldn't be surrounded by the faces she'd known since she was a little girl.

But she'd be married and finally get a start on her lifetime of loving someone, several someones, and learning what it felt like to be loved back.

And that was all she'd ever wanted.

She let out another happy sigh, imagining her future husbands. Would they be big men with lots of muscles? Or sleek and refined? Maybe one of each? Would another be musical and sing her to sleep at night? Ooo, or a poet! She'd love to be married to a poet.

Sophia, how I do love thee, let me count the ways...

She couldn't help the happy sigh that escaped.

"Are you like, constipated over there?"

"*What?*" Sophia jumped in her seat and glared again at Finn even as she felt her face heat. "No I am not— Why would you even say—"

"I don't know," he said, one hand casually on the wheel as he glanced her way before looking forward again. "You just keep making these little noises. *Hmmmm. Ooooohhh*," he mimicked.

She crossed her arms over her chest and huffed, turning her back to Finn and looking firmly out the window.

"Oh come on, Soph," Finn laughed. "I'm just joshin'. You're just so pretty when your cheeks get all pink like that."

So— *Pretty?* Did he just—

She swung her head back around to look at him but he was watching the road again. He did glance her way, though, and caught her looking at him. He shot her a quick wink, then went back to looking at the road like nothing was out of the ordinary.

Sophia let out an infuriated huff and swore to herself that as soon as she was married, she would have *nothing* to do with Finnigan Knight ever again so long as she *lived*.

Continue reading to enjoy an extended preview of Sophia's book, *Theirs to Ransom*.

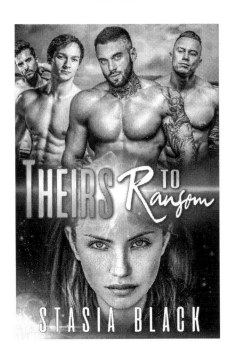

CHAPTER ONE

(Was the epilogue of *Theirs to Defy*)

CHAPTER TWO

FINNIGAN

"Finn, I need to go," Sophia said, that little breathy whine in her voice that drove Finn crazy. "I need to go. *Bad*."

Finn clenched his hands on the steering wheel and repeated what he had the last million times. "It's not safe to stop around here."

They were close to the border with New Mexico and this whole area was notoriously dangerous. There was a reason there wasn't open trade with Texas and whatever the hell was left of New Mexico.

And a reason people considered everything past the Texas border to be wildlands where only fools or the insane dared tread.

So naturally Sophia had come into his cavern two days ago declaring she was going not just over the border, but deep into the wildlands. All the way to fucking Santa Fe.

She wasn't normally a fool but when it came to the real world outside Jacob's Well, the girl didn't have the good sense God gave her. Or shoulda gave her.

So if she was gonna survive the trip, he was going to have to go with her. Get the girl to Santa Fe. Come hell or high water, he'd get her there. And get her there in one piece.

"You said it wasn't safe to stop around Fort Stockton." Sophia threw her hands up. "And then it wasn't safe to stop around Pecos. But we passed Pecos twenty minutes ago. I'm seriously gonna pee my pants if we don't stop soon!"

Finn glanced her way. By the way she was twisting on her seat, it looked like she wasn't just being dramatic.

He looked back at the road. "I told you not to drink that whole bottle." Any Scrapper worth his salt knew you rationed your water intake so you weren't forced to stop somewhere you didn't want to. Either that or you got real familiar with pissing into a bottle.

Sophia let out a little exasperated huff and Finn shook his head. After thirty hours in a car together, he was becoming more than familiar with all her little noises. For the most part, they were damn cute.

Not that he'd ever tell her that.

"Look, Soph, it's just another three hours till we get there—"

"Three *hours!* No way. Finnigan Knight, you will pull this truck over right this instant."

He glanced her way again. "It's cute that you think you're the one in control here."

Her mouth dropped open for just a moment before she clapped it shut and ground her teeth together. "This is *my* mission. You just happen to be along for the ride."

"Oh is that so?" Finn laughed. "How do you figure it? This is my truck. And you're depending on navigational expertise. Seems to me like if it's anyone's, it's *my* mission. So we'll go by *my* rules. Which means no stopping on the most dangerous stretch of road we seen yet. Here, if it's that bad..."

He rustled around the seat behind him and then held out an old plastic Big Gulp cup toward her.

"Don't be crude." She yanked the cup out of his hand and threw it back behind the truck seat.

"I was being serious."

She made another huffing noise. "Why are you being so stubborn? There's nothing to be afraid of. It's flat." She flung an arm out toward the front windshield. "We can see for miles in both directions and There. Is. No. One. We're perfectly safe stopping for five minutes so I can relieve myself. Now stop the damn truck!"

Oh shit. The perfect Sophia Wolford had just cursed. Sure it was just *damn* which was like the most Mary Sue of all curse words but still. She was really upset. Looking at her, he could see she did look almost panicky.

This time it was him huffing out a loud breath. He spent all his time around guys. It was hard to remember that chicks might work different. Sure whipping out your dick and peeing in a bottle was nothing for dudes but Sophia? Prim and proper Sophia? The idea of losing her composure like that? Or worse, actually pissing her pants?

Goddammit. A guy would just laugh it off and Finn would make a joke about having to scrub down his seats but fuck, this truck had seen a lot worse. Johnson almost died on that seat, guts half falling out, blood everywhere. The seats were that fake leather so it mostly came off. Johnson survived too, so wins all around.

But a girl like Sophia? She had a working *shower* in her house for Christ's sake. She cared about, like, dignity and shit. Something most folks he knew had given up on long ago.

Finn checked the rearview mirror for about the tenth time in as many minutes. Like she said, it was clear. Road ahead, too.

"Fine," he said. "But you get *two* minutes, not five."

"Thank you, Finn. Thank you."

Well damn, she really must be desperate if she was actually *thanking* him.

He pulled the truck off to the side of the small country highway and jammed it into park. "Go," he said, reaching under his seat for his rifle.

"Don't look," she said as she pushed open her door and he rolled his eyes and did the same

"Oh yeah, I can't wait to get a view of your backside as you squat and—"

"Don't you dare finish that sentence!"

Finn lined the butt of the shotgun up against his shoulder and looked down the sights back the way they'd come. There was a little bit of dust kicked up from their truck, but other than that, nothing. He swung around to the road ahead and it was clear there, too.

Okay, good.

He listened and didn't hear anything but the sounds of late summer.

"You done?" he called.

"Just give me a second."

"Jesus Christ, I thought you said your bladder was about to burst."

"I'm used to a toilet. You pressuring me isn't helping."

"Jesus Christ," he muttered again, swiveling back to look behind them.

He'd swear he could feel the seconds ticking by. He turned around he didn't know how many times checking to see if anyone was coming.

And still nothing from the other side of the truck. But so help him God, if she didn't start to piss soon, he'd—

Fuck!

Someone was coming from behind. Multiple someones, on motorcycles.

"Done," Sophia called.

"Get in the truck," Finn shouted as he tore his door open.

"What is it?" Sophia asked, door open with one hand over her eyes as she looked behind them.

"Get in the fucking truck, Soph!

She must have finally seen the bikes because her eyes widened and she scrambled up into the seat, pulling her door shut behind her.

"What do we do?" she asked frantically as she put her seatbelt on.

"We drive." Finn yanked the gearshift into drive and jammed the pedal to the floor. The wheels spun on gravel and then finally got purchase. The truck jerked forward as Finn pulled back onto the road.

The ancient engine whined at being pushed so hard. The truck was close to ninety years old, one of the reasons it had taken them so long to get here. He rarely pushed her above fifteen to twenty miles an hour. Using old vehicles like this meant you spent half the time with them up on blocks in repairs. Most of the Jacob's Well fleet was held together with duct tape and prayers.

The bikes behind them weren't sparing on speed though. Finn glanced in the rearview and counted. One, two, three, four, five, *six*. Shit. Who the hell had that many working bikes, this far out in the middle of nowhere?

He hadn't been stupid enough to take them straight through Pecos, they'd gone in a wide circle around it on back roads, but surely the town that was barely a smear on the map couldn't be that well supplied.

But they were near the border. He'd had a bad feeling in his gut all morning as they got closer. Place might as well be the Bermuda Triangle for as many people came back who ventured over the border.

He should have tried harder to dissuade Sophia from leaving for this damn fool mission. He knew exactly how dangerous the world was. But he'd known the only way to stop her would have been to tie her up, something that had seemed too extreme to him at the time.

Now he was kicking his own ass for not doing it, no matter if she hated him the rest of her life. At least she would have *had* the rest of her life to hate him.

"Finn, they're getting closer!"

He looked in his rearview and goddammit, she was right. They were almost on their tail. And the one in the lead was lifting a machine gun.

"Get down!" Finn shouted only seconds before the back windshield shattered as the truck was peppered with gunfire.

Sophia screamed but bent over and Finn ducked down as much as he could. He hadn't gone another ten feet, though before the inevitable happened.

He'd just clicked his seatbelt into place as the back tire blew out.

Shit.

Sophia.

He threw out an arm to try to hold her in place as the truck spun out off the road and then—

They were rolling. Sophia screamed. Glass shattered. Everything was ass over end—

Fuck!

...

...

Finally the truck settled.

Finn blinked and groaned, trying to get his bearings.

Upside down. They were upside down.

"Soph?" Finn looked frantically in her direction. "Soph, are you okay?"

She groaned in response and put a hand to her head. Fuck, her hand came away bloody.

"I'm fine," she said. "Where are they?"

Oh shit. The bikers. How had he forgotten, even for a second? Some protector he was turning out to be. He reached around for the rifle. Couldn't feel it. Godfuckingdammit. Where was the rifle? He looked this way and that.

And finally spotted it. Out the shattered front windshield. Lying in the grass about five feet away.

He reached for his seatbelt and undid the catch. And promptly fell on his head.

"Shit!" He tried to right himself and climb through the shattered front window at the same time. He could hear the bikes. They were almost on top of them. Then he heard the roar of an engine cut off. Fuck. They were here.

He shoved his body through the windshield and army crawled to the shotgun. "Don't move," he hissed in a whisper to Sophia.

Did she listen?

Of course not. She released the catch on her seatbelt and tumbled down but he couldn't watch her. He moved along the back side of the truck, hidden by the long bed.

He cocked the rifle and then peeked out past the tailgate.

Two motherfuckers approaching, machine guns at their shoulder. Again, what the fuck? The waste of bullets was incomprehensible.

He closed his eyes. One, two...

On three, he swung the rifle around the back of the truck, lined up the shot. *CRACK*. He recocked. *CRACK*.

Two motherfuckers down. Four to go.

He cocked the rifle again. He only had six shots.

That meant he couldn't waste a single one.

No pressure.

He glanced around the back of the truck. He'd given away his position with the fire but that was part of his intention. To draw them away from Sophia back in the cab.

He glanced around the corner of the truck again, yanking back only milliseconds before gunfire erupted. He hunched down against the ground. Thank Christ these old trucks were made so solid.

The gunfire pinged like rocks against the metal but didn't penetrate.

Finn crawled back to the front of the truck. With so many of them, no doubt they'd try circling around from behind—which meant they'd find Sophia. Right as he came back around the front, more gun fire sounded.

It was Sophia. Shooting blindly behind her as she crawled out the front of the truck, looking terrified.

Finn grabbed her arm and pulled her around the side of the truck right as more machine gun fire came.

"Where the hell did you get a gun?"

"Dad gave it to me."

"Do you know how to shoot?"

She nodded shakily.

"Then don't waste any more bullets."

"Here. I have this too."

Finn had his rifle at his shoulder, swinging back and forth trying to prepare for either direction they'd attack from.

"Finn," Sophia said insistently.

He was about to tell her to stop distracting him when he spared a glance her way and grinned. She was holding out a grenade.

He grabbed it and dared to pop up over the back of the truck to gauge their position. He couldn't waste their one advantage.

He ducked right back down, to the predictable gunfire.

They were split up as he'd thought. Two up front, two coming around back.

"Okay," he whispered to Sophia. "Follow me. I take one, you get the other. Got it?"

She nodded. Then he pulled the pin and lobbed the grenade toward the men at the back of the truck. Then he jumped to a crouch and ran toward the front.

There was shouting a moment before the *BOOM*.

Finn didn't waste a second. He ran around the front of the truck and shot a guy still reeling in surprise from the explosion.

The last man standing wasn't so slow. He had his gun up, also a rifle. Sophia had her gun up... but she didn't shoot. Why the fuck wasn't she shooting?

Finn cocked his rifle again so he could take the bastard out himself.

Except it didn't cock right. The pump action was caught on something and didn't eject the last casing.

There was no time to think or try to fix it. The man with the rifle was lifting it to his shoulder. He'd kill Finn and then go for Sophia.

Finn shouted at the top of his lungs and then rushed the guy. Finn grabbed the end of the man's rifle and jerked it upwards right as the guy got his finger on the trigger. The shot went off into the air and Finn jerked the gun out of his grasp, then, grabbing both ends, he smashed it into the man's face.

Finn didn't stop there, either.

He smashed the stock into his face, again and again until the guy's face was bloody and unrecognizable.

Only when he was sure the guy was down did he pull back and look around.

Sophia was crouched against the side of the truck, hands covering her head, her gun on the ground beside her.

What the fuck was she thinking?

He looked to the back of the truck. At least the grenade looked like it had done its work. The two bodies back there weren't moving. Still, if Finn had learned one thing in the years since The Fall, it was to make sure an enemy couldn't come back to bite you in the ass.

Or put a bullet in your head.

He walked over to Sophia, snatched her gun off the ground, and went around, putting a bullet right between the eyes of every man there.

"Sophia. Keep watch behind us while I clean up here."

She jerked at the sound of his voice and he breathed out hard.

"Look, Soph, you can fall apart later. But we're exposed. You gotta keep your shit together right now. You hear me?"

Her head lifted at this, tear tracks staining her pretty cheeks. "I'm sorry if I can't help feeling human emotions when my life was just in danger," her voice cracked, "and human people just *died* in front of me."

Finn shook his head. "Look, Princess. You were the one who thought you could just waltz out here into the big, bad world. Well this is what it's like," he threw his hands up gesturing around them. "Kill or be killed. I learned that lesson when I was thirteen. So just be happy you got to be a kid as long as you did."

Her chest heaved and she opened her mouth like she had a hundred retorts but then she closed her mouth again, into a tight line. She stood up, her back rigid, and swiped angrily at her eyes.

"Fine," she said coldly. "I'll keep watch."

Finn shook his head and grabbed the hunting knife from his belt as he jogged over to the bikes. What the fuck did she think it would be like out here? What did she think her dad created Jacob's Well for? Everything Eric Wolford did to create that little paradise in the center of chaos was to protect his daughter.

But did she appreciate it?

No.

Just like she didn't appreciate Finn.

He'd just risked his life for her.

Jesus Christ did she realize how close they'd both come to dying?

He jammed his knife into the tire of the bike with the lowest gas in the tank and slashed backwards with all his might.

In only helped release a little of his fury. Ten tires later and he was feeling mildly calmer.

He went back to Sophia and she'd gathered the weapons along with a giant hiker's backpack she'd brought along stuffed to the gills with who the hell knew what.

"No way," Finn said, gesturing at the backpack. "We aren't taking that thing. The weapons, yes. But not that."

She set her jaw. "I'm not leaving it. This is a diplomatic mission. You don't show up for a diplomatic mission without gifts."

"You do if you almost die on the way getting attacked by road bandits." He threw an arm out in the general direction of their upended truck.

She ignored him, hiking the backpack up higher on her shoulders and flouncing past him toward the last bike standing.

"I take it this is our transportation?"

"Women," Finn muttered under his breath, picking up the guns and slinging them across his chest. He grabbed a few belongings from the wreckage and then joined Sophia on the road. At least she'd had the good sense to pull a long-sleeved linen shirt out of her backpack so she wouldn't burn under the punishing Texas sun while they drove. But she looked ridiculous with the pack on her back. It dwarfed her small frame.

Whatever. He wouldn't waste his breath arguing with Her Highness.

He climbed on the bike and took a deep breath.

Something he needed, especially when she climbed on behind him and her slim arms slid around his waist, her thighs contouring to his.

Jesus Christ.

He swore he couldn't make up his mind about Sophia. One minute he wanted to strangle her and the next, all he could think about was—

He swallowed hard and gritted his teeth, trying to ignore the tightening in his jeans. Especially since he knew it was about way more than lust when it came to Sophia Wolford.

He'd been a damn goner for her ever since he stumbled into Jacob's Well at fifteen years old and the brown-haired beauty had served him soup and smiled shyly at him his first day in town.

After years scrambling just to keep body and soul together, she was the symbol of everything he'd ever wanted his whole life but never had —she was good, clean, sane. *Innocent.*

She was perfection and he was the shit people tried to scrape off their boots. And now he was dragging her down into his world.

What the hell was he doing?

"Soph." He turned his head to the side, not quite looking her in the eye. "Let's go home. We can turn around right now. This bike could probably get us as far as Central Texas North. I know that land like the back of my hand. I could get us back to San An—"

"No!" Sophia exclaimed. "Finn, no. I'm not giving up just because of this... setback. Look, I'm sorry if I—" He felt her shift behind him which really wasn't helping distract him from the warmth of her against his back. "I'm sorry I didn't shoot when I was supposed to. I had my finger on the trigger and I was standing just like Dad taught me but I just—"

Finn shook his head and put his hand over Sophia's that she still had on his waist. "Don't. It's not a bad thing you don't want to kill a man, Soph. I shoulda never asked it of you."

"What does that mean? Just because I'm a woman?"

Finn rolled his eyes. "Jesus, Soph. You know what I mean. You're you. You should be planning weddings. Long as I've known you all you could talk about was raising babies. There's some things once you do them, you can't ever scrub 'em from your head. Your dad didn't want this kinda life for you and neither do I."

She didn't say anything for several long moments.

"So we turning around?"

Her arms tightened around his waist and he couldn't help the small catch of his breath.

"No. I can do more than have babies. We're at war. Colonel Travis is threatening everything we hold dear. He's enslaving women just like me, Finn. We have to keep going. We have to."

See? It was stuff like this that made Sophia Wolford get under a man's skin. She was more than a pretty face. So much more.

"Hold on," Finn muttered gruffly, then kicked the bike into gear and took off down the road.

CHAPTER THREE

SOPHIA

Sophia had decided while holding on to Finn for dear life as they sped down the deserted highway, weaving in and out of stalled out cars left on the road from a decade ago, that she should be nicer to him.

Because back there? With those bikers?

She would have died. Without Finnigan, she would have died.

When she'd gotten the call from Santa Fe, it had all sounded like such an adventure. She'd charge in. Save the day. Bring home an army to Dad.

Like something she read in one of her novels.

But watching that man's face explode as Finn's rifle shot hit its target?

There was nothing romantic or heroic about that.

She'd been supposed to shoot the other man. She'd felt confident she could. He was the bad guy. He was trying to kill them. She knew how to shoot. Dad practiced with her twice a month ever since they'd gotten to Jacob's Well. It should have been simple.

But after witnessing the gore of Finn's shot, she froze. Even watching the man lift his gun and aim it right at Finn. Even seeing the panic in Finn's eyes when his own rifle got stuck.

Finn didn't freeze, though.

No, he just charged the man about to blow his brains out.

Sophia thought she understood what courage was but she hadn't.

Courage was running straight toward a loaded gun even when you were afraid.

But Sophia? Fear paralyzed her. It always had. Because she was a coward.

Cowards froze. Cowards dropped their guns and put their hands over their heads and waited for all the shooting to be over.

Cowards stayed upstairs hiding in a closet, doing nothing while their mothers were downstairs being brutalized and murdered.

Sophia clenched her eyes shut and pressed her forehead into Finn's back. No. She didn't remember that. She never let herself remember that.

Anyway, none of that mattered. What mattered was keeping positive now. So they didn't have the truck. This bike would get them there faster anyway. If anyone could look at lemons and see lemonade, it was her, dad blam it.

Only seconds after she had the thought, though, there was a loud *POP* noise, followed by sputtering. The bike swerved violently.

Sophia squeaked in terror and clung even tighter to Finn. She felt the flex of all his muscles as he fought to keep the bike upright.

The bike wobbled back and forth and Sophia squeezed her eyes shut. She forced them back open the next second. She would *not* be a coward. Finn couldn't afford for her to be.

They were slowing down but not as quickly as they should. What-ever had happened, it was clear the something had happened to the engine. Were the breaks shot, too?

Oh God, please don't let her come all this way only to die before she'd ever even done anything with her life.

———

"Are you okay?"

"Fine, I'm fine," she said shakily. In fact she felt like running over to the side of the road and barfing her guts up, but it wouldn't do to be telling Finn that.

He'd managed to bring them to a stop. It had all happened so fast, she could barely even recollect how he'd done it. He put his boots down to the asphalt, all his muscles tense, but he'd kept them steady as they slowed down and finally, finally came to a stop.

"Come on," she said, pushing her hair out of her face. It was a mess, having been whipped all over the place by the wind. She pulled out her ponytail and redid it as best as she could without a comb.

"We should get off the road, shouldn't we?"

Finn stood there watching her another long moment before nodding and gesturing toward the other side of the road.

"We can follow the Pecos River up. Safer than staying on the road and we'll have water."

Sophia nodded, hiking her backpack up on her shoulders. Finn must have noticed because he held out a hand.

"Give me the pack."

"Oh it's fine. I've got it—"

"Sophia, don't be a brat. Give me the backpack. You look like you're about to tip over backwards any second."

She shot him a glare. She was really making an effort to be nice to him but did he have to make it so dang difficult?

She slung the backpack down off her shoulders. "I totally could have handled it. It's not very heavy." She threw it towards him.

He caught it and staggered back a step. "Damn, girl. You're stronger than you look."

She rolled her eyes. "All right, jackass. Which way to the river?"

"I wasn't kidding. This thing is heavy. What the hell you got in here? A few bricks you just couldn't bear to leave behind?"

She frowned, looking over at him as he readjusted the straps and slung it over his shoulders. She couldn't tell if he was joking or not about the weight and her being strong. Sometimes she thought she was strong from constantly carrying huge cornmeal bags and soup pots here and there between the kitchens and the serving window in the soup kitchen but it wasn't like she had many people to compare herself to.

"How far is the river?" she asked, lifting a hand over her eyes in the direction Finn had pointed.

Even though it was late autumn, the day was sweltering. She'd already sweat through her linen shirt but knew she couldn't take it off no matter how hot she got. Finn must have been thinking along similar lines because he came over and pulled a baseball cap from his back pocket. He settled it on her head.

"River's probably about twelve miles."

"Twelve..." Sophia's mouth went dry even at the thought. "How much water do we have left?"

"Two bottles were all we could carry. But I also grabbed a pot so we can boil the river water and drink all we want once we get there." He turned slightly and she saw both the bottles and the pot tied on to his belt. With that and the pack on his back, he looked ridiculous. But efficient.

Still. Only *two bottles*?

"Here, have a swallow now and then not again for a while, all right?"

He untied one of the bottles and held it out to her.

She took a swallow, feeling panicky at the thought of how tightly they'd have to ration the water. As soon as she handed the water back, she realized just how much she'd drank and felt embarrassed and guilty.

"We'll be okay, Soph. I been in worse situations, believe me."

She nodded and smiled brightly in spite of her anxiety. "I'm not worried. Get to the river, follow the river up to Santa Fe. No problem."

Finn just stood there looking at her.

"What?"

"Soph, you gotta know that's not realistic. You think we're just going to walk across New Mexico? Santa Fe's clear on the other side of the state. We don't know what's going on in this territory. It was one thing when we had a vehicle. Gas was gonna be an issue but we maybe could have figured our way around it. But without something to drive—"

"We'll make it," Sophia said determinately. "We have to."

"I'm sure your dad and Drea and General Cruz have it under contr—"

"But they don't," she said, unable to help her exasperation showing through. "Don't you get it? Dad never expected Jacob's Well to get attacked. I overheard General Cruz talking about how outnumbered his men were. It's two to one against Travis's forces. No one saw this coming. No one prepared for the President getting assassinated or Travis making his power grab, and—"

"Soph, don't you think taking on the world's problems all on your own shoulders is a little much, though?"

"Drea never did. She saw something that needed doing so she did it. She never waited around for someone else to do it."

"Why are you bringing her into this? I thought you hated her."

"What? I don't hate her! Sometimes I may have thought she lacked a certain... grace. But I admire her. She went into that MC compound and singlehandedly freed all those women." Sophia shook her head.

She couldn't even fathom the courage something like that would take. And she was finally mature enough to say that all her attitude toward Drea over the months might have been partially driven out of envy.

Drea was everything Sophia wasn't. Cool, calm, collected, and a total badass. When Drea stepped into a room, people took a step back, either in reverence, fear, or dislike. Some people didn't like so much confidence and drive in a woman.

When Sophia stepped into a room, there were smiles all around. For a long time, she'd thought that meant she was doing everything right. But maybe that just meant people thought of her like they did pretty pictures on the wall. Nice enough to look at but basically useless when it came to anything else.

"Come on." Finn looked around. "I don't like being on the road."

"Not that it will make much difference." In spite of how hot it was, Sophia shivered when she looked out. And out. And out and out and out.

There was nothing.

Not even trees.

It was just flat. With the barest of scrub brush.

She knew in theory that east Texas was basically a desert but seeing it up close like this. Being *stranded* here...

Finn didn't seem bothered though. He'd just started walking and several paces later turned back around, frowning.

"You coming?"

Sophia nodded because all the sudden, her throat felt incredibly dry and she wasn't quite sure she'd be able to get any words out.

They continued on like that for half an hour, Sophia just focusing on putting one foot in front of another on the dry, cracked earth, avoiding the occasional shrubs. She'd never seen earth so scorched. She'd just taken water for granted, living in the hill country like she had all her life. Before The Fall water came out the tap and afterwards, she'd thought she'd suffered learning to adapt to walking two houses down to the well to get water most of the time.

She knew in a sort of esoteric way that she was privileged. Good Lord, twice a month Daddy even let her use the solar panels on the roof to run a bath or shower and have hot water in the house.

But God... What did people out *here* do?

Then again, she didn't see any people.

She knew there were people. Finn had driven wide circles around towns so she hadn't seen any close up but there *were* towns. She supposed they had wells too. Aquifers ran underneath all of Texas, even out here if she wasn't wrong.

But what did they do for food? This ground couldn't be good for farming. Maybe ranching, but how fat could cows get, eating this scrub?

"Whatcha thinking about so quiet over there, Sophia pizzeria?"

She shot Finn a look. "Pizzaria?"

"It was either that or tortilla. Not that many words that rhyme with Sophia. I've been thinking on it the past, like, fifteen minutes. I got pizzeria, tortilla, and diarrh—"

"I get the idea," she cut him off.

He smiled. "I figured I like pizza better than tortillas."

"Tortilla rhymes better."

"But I like Pizza."

She shook her head. "I think you just like being contrary."

His smile turned to a grin. "I wouldn't say that."

"Only proving my point."

They were quiet for awhile after that. Finn tried engaging her in conversation a few more times but Sophia couldn't give him much in return.

She was too busy trying to ignore the growing pain in her feet.

The hiking boots she was wearing?

Well, she hadn't exactly had much time to break them in. And they were chafing something awful.

She hadn't expected she'd have to *walk* so much in them. She thought they'd be driving the whole way.

She'd just grin and bear it, then give her feet a nice long soak in the cool river tonight.

At least that had been her plan, but after walking a couple hours, it was too much. She stumbled and fell.

And landed on a cactus. Because oh yeah, in addition to the scrub brush, the only other thing that grew in abundance? Friggin' prickly pear cacti.

"Son of a *witch*!" she shouted, not daring to move and get even more cactus spines in her butt. She'd at least twisted as she fell so she had a butt full of cactus spines rather than a face full. Something that was little comfort at the moment.

"Shit, Soph!"

Finn hurried over to her, took her hands, and helped her up off the cactus. But standing just hurt worse, her feet were in so much pain.

"Turn around, hon. I gotta pull the spines out."

If there was anything more humiliating than bending over in the middle of nowhere so Finnigan Knight could pull cactus spines out of her behind, Sophia didn't know what it was.

He was at it a good twenty minutes. Sophia finally had to get on the ground on hands and knees because she just couldn't handle standing another second.

"All right, I got all the ones I can see. If you got another pair of jeans in the backpack, I think you should put them on cause if I didn't, you don't want to accidently sit down and get an unpleasant surprise later."

Sophia nodded as she turned around and crawled toward the pack.

"Hey, Soph. You crying?"

Sophia shook her head back and forth rapidly, turning her head away from him. God. Of course she was crying. She'd been crying ever since she fell into the damn patch of cactus. But crying silently was a skill she'd perfected a long time ago.

"I'm fine," she said and her voice didn't even break.

She unzipped the backpack and her cheeks colored. She hadn't anticipated having to open it in front of Finn.

"Can you turn around? While I change."

"Sophia. You're hurt. Let me help."

"I said turn around," she spat.

"Jesus. Fine."

She swallowed but her throat felt as dry as the desert around them even though Finn had insisted she take a long drink of water right after she'd fallen.

She unzipped the backpack and pulled out the bag that took up the largest portion of the big camping pack.

She reverently touched the plastic as she set the huge bag on the dirt beside her.

Her mother's wedding dress.

The fact that she still had it after all these years was something of a miracle.

She'd insisted they take it that horrific night so long ago. She and mom had talked about it so many times.

Some day you'll find your Prince Charming who sweeps you off your feet.

Just like Daddy did you?

Just like Daddy did me.

And I'll wear your dress, Mama.

And your daddy will walk you down the aisle. I'll be in the front row bawling my eyes out at seeing my baby all grown up.

Not much would be like her mother envisioned all those years ago. Mama died. Daddy was off fighting a war.

But she still had Mama's dress and by God, she'd be married in it. No matter if she had to carry it all the way across New Mexico.

Except... she wasn't sure she could walk ten more steps, let alone across an entire state.

More tears slipped down her cheeks and she sniffled and swallowed again.

She'd figure it out. Somehow. She had to. Daddy needed—

"What the hell is that?"

Sophia swung around, mortified. And then furious.

Finn was walking toward her, eyes locked on the wedding dress in the plastic bag beside her. She grabbed it before he could grab for it, clutching it to her chest.

"Nothing that concerns you."

Finn had tied a handkerchief over his nose and mouth to protect his face from the sun but she could still see his eyes and he looked furious.

"Sophia Wolford, tell me that is not a fucking wedding dress."

Sophia pursed her lips. She was having the worst day of her life and he was going to yell at her? Screw him.

"I told you this was a diplomatic mission. They want to start instituting the Marriage Raffle. I'm going to offer myself as a sign of good faith."

"That's the stupidest fucking thing I've ever heard." He tried to snatch the dress away from her but she just held on tighter.

"Don't you dare! Let go, Finn! I'm not kidding. Let go!"

"What the fuck are you thinking?" he shouted, finally letting go and standing up, running his hands through his hair and turning away from her, but only for a second.

"Jesus Christ, Sophia! Your dad spent his whole life making the Raffle safe for *you*." He threw his hands toward her. "Why do you think there's such a careful vetting process that men who want to enter as potential husbands have to go through? You have to live in town for two years and have regular meetings with an elder before you're even qualified for the outer tier of eligibility. And now you're just going to go throw yourself like a sheep among wolves. They'll tear you afucking part! No. I won't let you. We're going back home."

"You do *not* get to say what I do and don't do," she cried, painfully getting to her feet. She could ignore it. She was so furious, she could ignore anything. "You're not my father. And even if you were, I'm nineteen. I'm a grown woman. I can make my own choices. I can do my part!"

She shoved Finn hard in the chest but he didn't even stumble backwards. She shoved him again.

She shouted in fury and when she went to shove him again, he pulled her into his arms.

She fought him at first. She was furious at him. She hated him. Stupid Finn. Stupid men. Stupid feet.

Why was everything going wrong?

If only those bikers hadn't come after them and wrecked the truck.

If only the bike hadn't malfunctioned.

If only she'd packed better shoes.

If only she weren't so goddamned weak.

She buried her face in Finn's chest and wept. He pulled her close and then his strong arms wrapped around her.

She didn't know how long he held her like that. She was the one who finally pulled back, feeling stupid and panicky at the thought of how much water she was wasting by crying. And because her feet still hurt like all hell.

"My feet," she said, feeling her face crumple.

Finn's features were awash with concern but he cupped her face and forced her to look at him when she tried to avert her eyes.

"You are going to let me help you. Without giving me any lip. We'll figure this shit out. But we'll do it together, okay? No more secrets."

Sophia hiccupped but nodded. And staring into Finn's eyes... How had she never noticed the fact that he had green eyes before? Green with little flecks of gold.

God, maybe she was getting loopy with dehydration in all this heat. Because she let Finn help her. With everything.

Her legs felt shaky as he tugged her jeans down. He unbuttoned the long-sleeved denim shirt he was wearing and laid it out on the dirt for her to sit down while he took a look at her feet.

And she couldn't help looking at *him*. It was so ridiculous to even be looking or thinking anything like *that*.

But his back was broad and his shoulders were muscled. Since when had Finnigan Knight gone and grown into a man?

She quickly averted her eyes when he turned back toward her, pulling off her first boot.

"Jesus, Soph, why didn't you say something earlier?"

She winced with pain as he tugged down her sock. The back of her heel was bleeding and the outer side of her foot looked worn raw, too.

"I thought if we could just get to the river..."

She thought he'd yell at her again but he just looked pained as he gently lifted her ankle and looked at her foot from all sides.

He was so gentle with her it just made her want to cry again.

"How are we going to get to the river now?" she whispered, more stupid tears seeping down her cheeks.

Finn gave her calf a squeeze and looked her in the eye. "We'll make it there, Soph. I promise, I'll take care of you. Okay? I swear."

His voice and gaze were so intense as he said it, it made Sophia's insides quiver. She bit her lip and nodded, just barely stopping herself from asking, *why?*

Why, Finn? Why did you agree to come in the first place? Why are you looking at me like that?

But she just bit her lip harder as Finn pulled off the other boot, giving that foot just as thorough an examination.

"You got a first aid kit in the bag?"

She nodded and he rooted around for it. But even while he did, he kept one hand on her leg. It was presumptuous but she liked the contact. Maybe he felt like he needed to stay tethered to her as much as she suddenly needed to be to him.

She could have told him that she could put on the ointment and bandages herself. She should have.

But she didn't.

She let him do it. Marveling the whole time at how gentle his big, clumsy fingers were at the task.

All she'd ever seen Finn do was haul around Scrapper junk and do construction. Oh and she'd seen him going in to visit Ana Martinez, one of the few single women in Jacob's Well who shared her favors widely, about six months after he turned 18. One of the many men who did.

That was when she'd seen Finn for what he really was. Just another man. Not special or romantic or any of the other hundreds of stupid little fantasies she'd woven around him since he'd first strutted into town like a prize peacock the handful of years before like he was God's gift.

But now here he was, bending over in the dirt to patch up her *feet*.

"It's okay, I think they're good now," she said, putting out a hand on Finn's as he looked over his work, again examining her right foot from all sides.

She withdrew her feet away from him, bending her legs as modestly as she could. "Can you get me another pair of socks?"

Those hazel eyes of his flicked back up to hers again. She felt snagged by his gaze. Like suddenly her lungs felt too big in her chest.

"Sure," Finn said, suddenly looking away like he was embarrassed to have been caught staring. Didn't he realize she'd been staring too?

She put a hand up to her cheeks. They didn't feel any warmer than they had all day but she'd swear they were flaming.

He rummaged through the backpack and pulled several items. He handed her socks and another pair of jeans.

She gingerly pulled on the socks first and he turned his back as she leaned on her elbows and lifted her bum to wiggle into the jeans.

She was sweating more than ever when she sat back up with the jeans on. Putting stifling denim back on made her feel like she was suffocating but the only other things she brought were skirts and dresses.

Still, looking around and then back at her boots, she had no idea how she'd be able to keep going.

"Here," Finn said, "put these on."

"Those are house slippers."

He kept holding out the fuzzy slippers. He flipped them over. "They've got soles. And there's no way your feet are getting stuffed back in those boots. I think these are our best option."

Sophia looked doubtfully at the thin soles that were little better than cardboard. But she took them because really, they were her *only* option if she didn't want to walk through the desert in her socks.

And she'd decided that maybe Finn *did* know what he was talking about when it came to surviving in this outside world. All she'd ever known of it was life before The Fall and then that one last horrific day—

She put it out of her head and pulled the slippers on, wincing even at the slight pressure they put on her sore feet.

Finn stood up and held down his hands to her. The sight of him standing above her, shirtless, his silhouette surrounded by golden sunlight... well, it was sure a sight to behold.

Sophia swallowed again before grabbing hold of his hands and letting him pull her to her feet. He shook out his shirt and then pulled it back on. He fastened the buttons quickly and then without a word, put all their supplies back into the backpack.

Including the wedding dress. Though Sophia didn't miss his sharp, jerky motions as he shoved the wedding bag to fit into the backpack. Or the hard line of his mouth as he slung it across his shoulders.

Still, when he next looked her direction, his features softened again. "How does standing feel?"

"It's— It's okay," she stuttered.

He frowned. "Here, take another drink of water."

He reached around to the side pocket of the backpack and pulled out a water bottle. It was almost empty and he'd barely drunk any.

Sophia took a small sip and then held out the rest to him. He just shook his head and went to put the bottle away when she stopped him.

"Don't be stubborn, Finnigan. You're no use to me passed out in the desert because you wouldn't take care of yourself."

He arched an eyebrow but finally nodded and took the last swallow of water from the bottle. Then they headed out.

Sophia's feet did feel much better but she'd already done so much damage to them that it was still rough going. Not to mention that she was much more cautious about where she stepped now. She was also aware the whole time about how much she was slowing Finn down.

She tried suggesting he go on ahead of her but he shut her down every time she brought it up.

"Jesus, stop talking like that. I'm never gonna leave you alone out here in the middle of nowhere. Not in a million years so just stop saying it, okay?"

She bit her lip and they went on in silence for another long while. Maybe even an hour. The sun was punishing and it took more concentration than Sophia would have thought to stay upright and trudging ahead.

Finn paused every once in and awhile for them to take sips from the water bottle and Sophia was far more careful about how much she drank. Still, with as much as the both of them were sweating, she couldn't imagine the little they were drinking was enough to keep them hydrated.

"What we *should* talk about is what I'm carrying around in this backpack," he said sometime later, as if picking up their conversation right where they'd left it.

"I don't want to get in another argument," she sighed. She was already *so* tired. She couldn't handle arguing with Finn on top of everything else. Her feet felt battered and her legs like jelly. How long had they been walking? Hours. But how far had they come and how many more miles was it to the river?

"I don't want to argue. Hey." Finn reached out and touched her shoulder. "No arguing. Okay?"

The earnestness in his eyes made her pause. She didn't know what to do with earnest Finn. It was kind of freaking her out. She shrugged and then started forward again.

It didn't stop him talking though, as he easily kept up beside her with his long legs. "I worry about you. You look at people and see the best in them. But the world out here isn't like that. You can't just trust people. Everyone out here is only looking out for themselves. They'd betray you as soon as look at you."

Sophia shook her head. "Just because you're a pessimist doesn't mean I have to be. Some people see the glass half full."

"It's not—Jesus, Soph."

"Look, I'm not trying to argue," she said, reaching out and putting a hand on his arm. She pulled it back almost immediately because touching Finn was... weird. It made her feel weird. *Anyway*. "I know the world's a bad place, okay? Dad drummed it into my head. *It's dangerous out there, honey*," she lowered her voice in an imitation of her dad's. "But regardless of if it's dangerous or not, we still have to live in it. The hard stuff still has to get done. Somebody has to do it. So I don't see the harm in trying to stay positive."

"The harm is that you aren't prepared for when the awful things happen."

He said it so vehemently that Sophia couldn't help turning to look at him again. His jaw was clenched and there were two bright spots of pink high up on his cheekbones. She didn't think they were because of the heat, either.

"What happened to you?" she asked. The question came out almost as a whisper but his head jerked her way violently, but almost as quickly, he looked away again.

"I'll tell you," he said. "And then maybe you'll get what I mean. You can't trust people. Anyone."

Sophia frowned but then he started speaking.

"I was eleven when D-day hit. My mom had split years before, she was a real winner like that, so I still don't know what happened to her, but I guess she probably died. Anyway, Dad was in prison doing a nickel for trying to rob a 7-11—and I was living with my Uncle Murphy."

He shook his head, like he was getting off track. "I was a little shit. Always in trouble at school. I got in fights and stole stuff all the time. So then there's the Fall and the Death Riots and to Uncle Murphy it was like Christmas had come early."

Sophia's mouth dropped open but he just kept going.

"There was so much to loot, you see. And I was small enough to slip in between all the other looters in the riots. So he'd use me and we'd work in pairs, me running into stores and snatching what I could off the shelves and bringing it out to my uncle."

"But you were just a child!"

Finn held up his hands and wiggled his fingers. "Light fingers, heavy pockets. And the other looters were still less likely to beat up a kid to get to the loot. Most of the time."

"They hurt you?" Sophia felt breathless as she asked it, and not just from the exertion from walking for hours under the boiling heat.

Fin shrugged. "It got worse the more time went on when there was less and less to find in the stores."

"And your uncle just kept sending you in there all alone?"

"Oh, that and much worse than that. I was like you once. Well, maybe I always thought the glass was just about empty going on gone. But I still thought, I don't know. No matter how desperate things got, some things still mattered more. Like family. But I was wrong. Really, really wrong."

Sophia felt her stomach go sour. "What's that mean?" She asked it even though she wasn't sure she wanted to know the answer.

"It was a couple years after The Fall and supplies were running low. Uncle Murphy said he'd heard of a trading post where we'd get good trades for the little we did have left. We had some gold and jewelry stashed and I thought that's what he was gonna sell. Instead, after we got to Hell's Hollow, Murphy sold me."

"Finn!" Oh God. Finn just kept on walking though, so she hurried to keep up with him.

"I don't even know how much he got for me. He left me in the outer room while he went in and made the deal. Then he wouldn't look at me while two men dragged me away."

Finn shook his head. "Big fat fuck he sold me to tried to bugger me that night. But I'd got strong in the two years since The Fall. And I'd always been a fighter. So even though I was small..." He shook his head again, like he was trying to shake off the memory. "Anyway, I killed him that night."

Sophia's mouth, already dropped open, fell open even wider. "How?"

"Shard from a vase I broke."

Sophia blinked. She wanted to ask a million more questions but had the sense not to from the look on his face.

He'd said he'd killed a man when he was thirteen. This had to be what he'd meant. God. She couldn't even—

"And you got away?"

Finn nodded, jaw flexing. "I ran."

"But you were fifteen when you came to Jacob's Well, right?" She knew he'd been fifteen but she still asked it as a question. For a short period of her life, she'd made it her business to know everything about Finnigan Knight. But she never wanted him to know that.

"Yeah."

"So what happened in the two years in between."

"I kept running. Went east. Did any work I could. Stole when I couldn't. Fought on the front. They were so short on soldiers they didn't care I was just fourteen. I could hold a gun."

"God, Finn!"

He shrugged and rolled his eyes. "It's okay. I'm okay. I didn't tell you all this so's you'd feel sorry for me. I'm just tryin' to make you see. It's not a nice place out here, Soph. People will use you, abuse you, sell you. Everyone's got an angle. You can't trust anyone."

I trust you, was her immediate thought.

He finally stopped and put a hand on her arm. "And control is just an illusion. You don't have any control out here. There's no steady ground underneath you. The second you think you've got some, it'll shift. Even Jacob's Well. Look what happened. Your dad worked for years to make it a safe place for you. And even he couldn't keep control for long and he's one of the strongest men I've ever met."

"Finn." Sophia wanted to reach up and hold his face. Pull him into a hug. "I'm so sorry for all you've been through. I can see why you see the world the way you do. I might too, having been through all you have."

She searched his green eyes. "But it doesn't have to be that way anymore. That's what Dad's trying to do. What all of us are trying to do. We're going to build a better world. One where you don't have to be afraid all the time. One where you can feel safe."

But Finn only looked frustrated at her response. "Soph, you aren't hearing me. The world's not changing. It caught up with Jacob's Well, that's all. No place is safe."

"Then why are you here?" she asked, exasperated. Her voice was a croak, her throat was so dry.

He just looked at her like she was missing the obvious. "You, Soph. I'm here for *you*."

What?

Sophia's breath caught. Had he just— What did he—

Those damn blue eyes of his were more intense than ever as he moved closer. His head dropped and hers rose like they were magnets attracted to one another.

Sophia's heart was thumping so hard she was sure it was about to beat right out of her chest.

Did Finn— Did he like her? Like her like *that*?

His head dropped and she felt dizzy. Was he about to— Was this her first kiss? Where was she supposed to look? It felt weird looking at his face, he was so close. She'd be cross-eyed. That wasn't sexy. And she suddenly very desperately wanted to look sexy. So should she close her eyes?

But what if he thought that meant she didn't want to?

So she opened her eyes again and looked away from his face which was closer than ever.

And saw a glint in the distance.

"The river!" she exclaimed, pulling back from Finn. She realized a second too late that she'd ruined her own first kiss.

Finn jerked back and looked over his shoulder.

No, she wanted to say. *I mean, yes. The river. After we kiss, we'll go to the river.*

But Finn was hiking the pack higher on his shoulders, clearly focused on the river now. He did hold his hand back for hers, though, so maybe she hadn't ruined everything.

She took his hand.

It was so strong and steady and it made her stomach swoop to hold it.

It was only after she'd held it for several steps, furtively stealing glances at Finn that she asked herself what the hell she was doing.

You're about to get married!

To strangers.

From a strange land.

She clutched Finn's hand even tighter, his warnings swirling in her head. Could she really do it?

She'd been so sure of her path for so long. Did what just happened really change anything? The closer they came to the river, though, she couldn't think about anything else but taking a long, cool drink of water.

She couldn't. She knew they had to boil it first but still. Water. She could soak her feet. Take off all her clothes and soak her whole body.

She couldn't help her eyes inadvertently flicking to Finn at the thought. Her tongue flicked out to wet her dry lips. It didn't help much considering how dry her tongue was, too.

Finn turned to her and grinned. He pulled out the water bottle and handed it to her. "Here, have the last bit. I'll get to boiling some more."

He was always thinking of her needs first. Taking care of her. He was a good man.

You, Soph. I'm here for you.

She took the bottle and drank the water but left some for him. And she didn't take her eyes off his as she held out the bottle.

"You can have it all, Soph."

She shook her head and pressed the bottle into his hands.

He took it and drank, doing the same as her, looking at her the whole time. No, not just looking at her.

She'd never been *looked at* like that before.

She felt like a meal he wanted to devour.

She was about to get that first kiss after all. She stepped close, breathless after he finished the water and tossed the bottle to the ground. He threw the backpack and the guns he had slung over his shoulder to the ground the next second.

He reached for her, eyes full of that devouring hunger and she wanted it just as badly—

When the bank of the river was suddenly full of the sound of stomping hooves.

Finn's eyes jerked up, over Sophia's shoulder. In a single moment, desire was exchanged for terror.

He shoved Sophia behind him, arms out to protect her, but it was too late.

Men on horseback had them surrounded.

———

Sophia's book, Theirs to Ransom, is AVAILABLE NOW

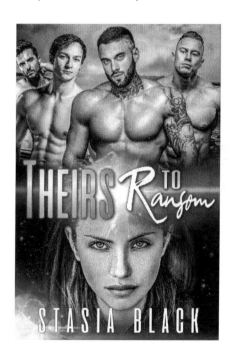

Want to read an EXCLUSIVE, FREE 45 page novelette, Their Honeymoon, about Audrey and her Clan's honeymoon that is available only to my newsletter subscribers, along with news about upcoming releases, sales, exclusive giveaways, and more?

Get *Their Honeymoon* by visiting
BookHip.com/QHCQDM

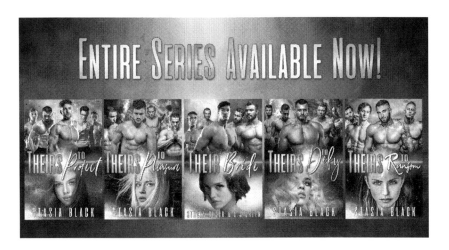

ALSO BY STASIA BLACK

ACKNOWLEDGMENTS

Oh my gosh but this book was a doozy. I can't think of a book in recent memory that has wrung me so absolutely dry, emptied me out, and then demanded more when I felt like I had nothing left to give. But I was able to keep going because of some very special people who were an INSANELY AMAZING support system.

First of all, hubby, babe, I can't even. Without you, fuck, what would I do? I'd be like a jellyfish flopping around on the beach. There's a reason I keep writing about marriages where only together are partners able to be strong and make it through lief. I love your fucking face.

To my assistants, oh my gosh, each of you provides such an amazing and unique support that makes it possible for the wheels on this insane bus to keep going round and round. I would literally not be able to keep writing books at the pace that I do without you gorgeous ladies.

Melissa Lee, I would literally explode from stress without you helping to keep my schedule together and patiently nudging to keep me focused. Thank you SOOOOOO much. And for switching things around not just once, but like 3 times with this book as the date kept getting moved... and moved... and moved!!!!

Melissa Pascoe, zomg, you also free up so much time for me so that I can pop onto FB and just have fun with my groupies without feeling stressed that I'm always letting people down. That means SO much to me, you have no idea. And then the ARC madness and answering my freaked out emergency SOS for a read, I cannot thank you ENOUGH TIMES!!!!

Christine Jalili, you have stepped in and also made being online so much fun instead of stressful. You have no idea how amazing it is to know that I can pop on and always be able to rely on you to answer a question or take care of something or help me when I'm in a crazy time crunch. Worth your weight in GOLD, babe!!

Jenn, omg, this last month has been so much fun as you learn the ins and outs!!! I have loved teaching you how the sausage gets made, lmaoooooooo. You too have freed up so much time for me to be able to work my BUTT off. I'm just sitting here feeling SO insanely grateful for you all.

Aimee Bowyer, thank you as always for being my beta reader extraordinaire!!! You worked your butt off to get notes to me under the wire when I gave you zero time turnaround on this one and saved me from some suuuuuuuuper awkward mistakes. <3 always hon.

Last but not least, thank you to my lawyer, Margarita Coale. When I was under attack, you stepped up and were my badass defender. I didn't have to be scared or confused anymore because you were friendly, cool-headed, logical, and wicked smart. I am so grateful to have you in my corner!

ABOUT THE AUTHOR

STASIA BLACK grew up in Texas, recently spent a freezing five-year stint in Minnesota, and now is happily planted in sunny California, which she will never, ever leave.

She loves writing, reading, listening to podcasts, and has recently taken up biking after a twenty-year sabbatical (and has the bumps and bruises to prove it). She lives with her own personal cheerleader, aka, her handsome husband, and their teenage son. Wow. Typing that makes her feel old. And writing about herself in the third person makes her feel a little like a nutjob, but ahem! Where were we?

Stasia's drawn to romantic stories that don't take the easy way out. She wants to see beneath people's veneer and poke into their dark places, their twisted motives, and their deepest desires. Basically, she wants to create characters that make readers alternately laugh, cry ugly tears, want to toss their kindles across the room, and then declare they have a new FBB (forever book boyfriend).

Join Stasia's Facebook Group for Readers for access to deleted scenes, to chat with me and other fans and also get access to exclusive giveaways:
https://www.facebook.com/groups/StasiasBabes/

Printed in Poland
by Amazon Fulfillment
Poland Sp. z o.o., Wrocław

25474855R00237